Disney · PIXAR

FINDING NEMO

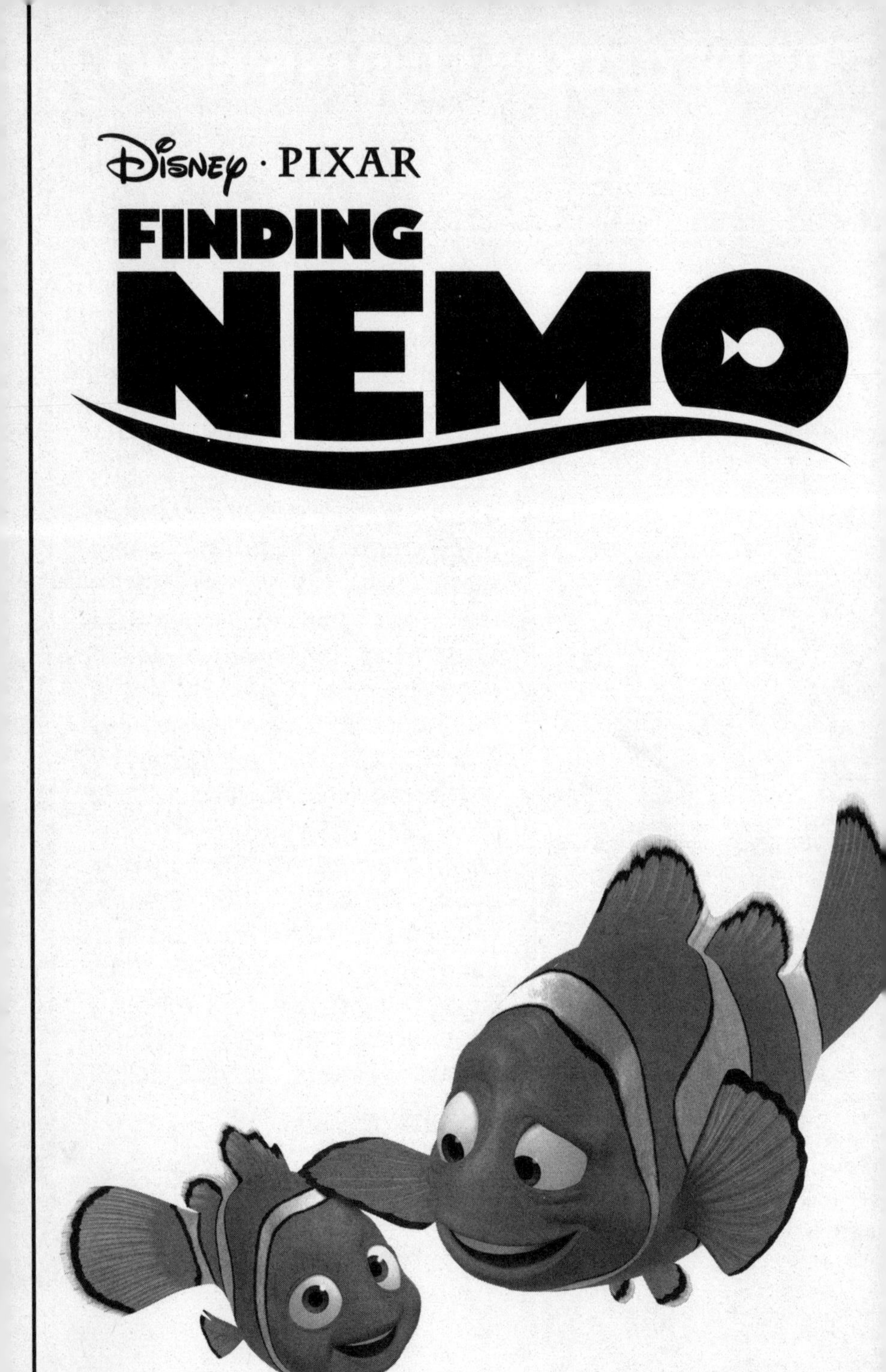

DISNEY·PIXAR FINDING NEMO
MANGA COLLECTION

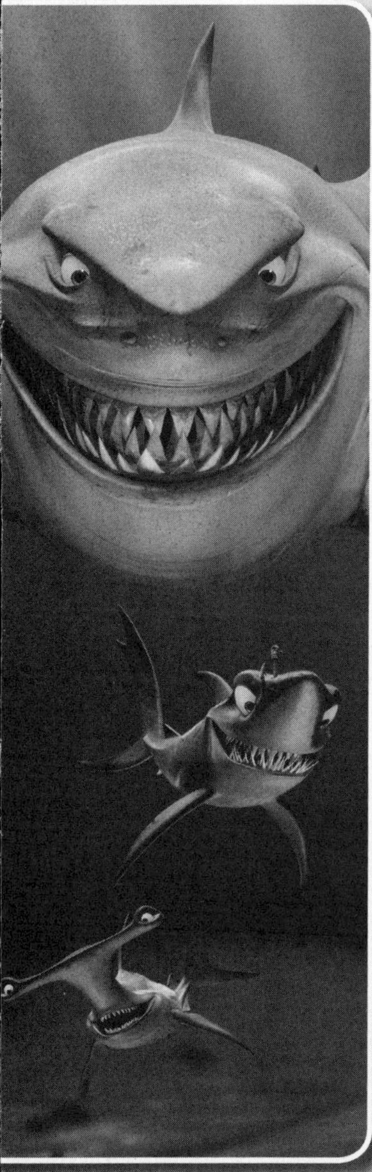

Welcome to the TOKYOPOP® presentation of Disney·Pixar's legendary animated film *Finding Nemo!* This manga version of Disney·Pixar's adorable aquatic adventure originated in Japan, where Nemo and his father Marlin are quite popular clownfish! Illustrated by manga artist (and professor) Ryuichi Hoshino, this collectible edition includes an original cover illustration by Japanese artist duo UrumaDelvi (and an interview with the duo); a series of Disney·Pixar book concept illustrations; and fun introductions to our fishy friends from the film! Enjoy this extra special reading experience as the wonder of Pixar meets the magic of manga!

--Team TOKYOPOP®

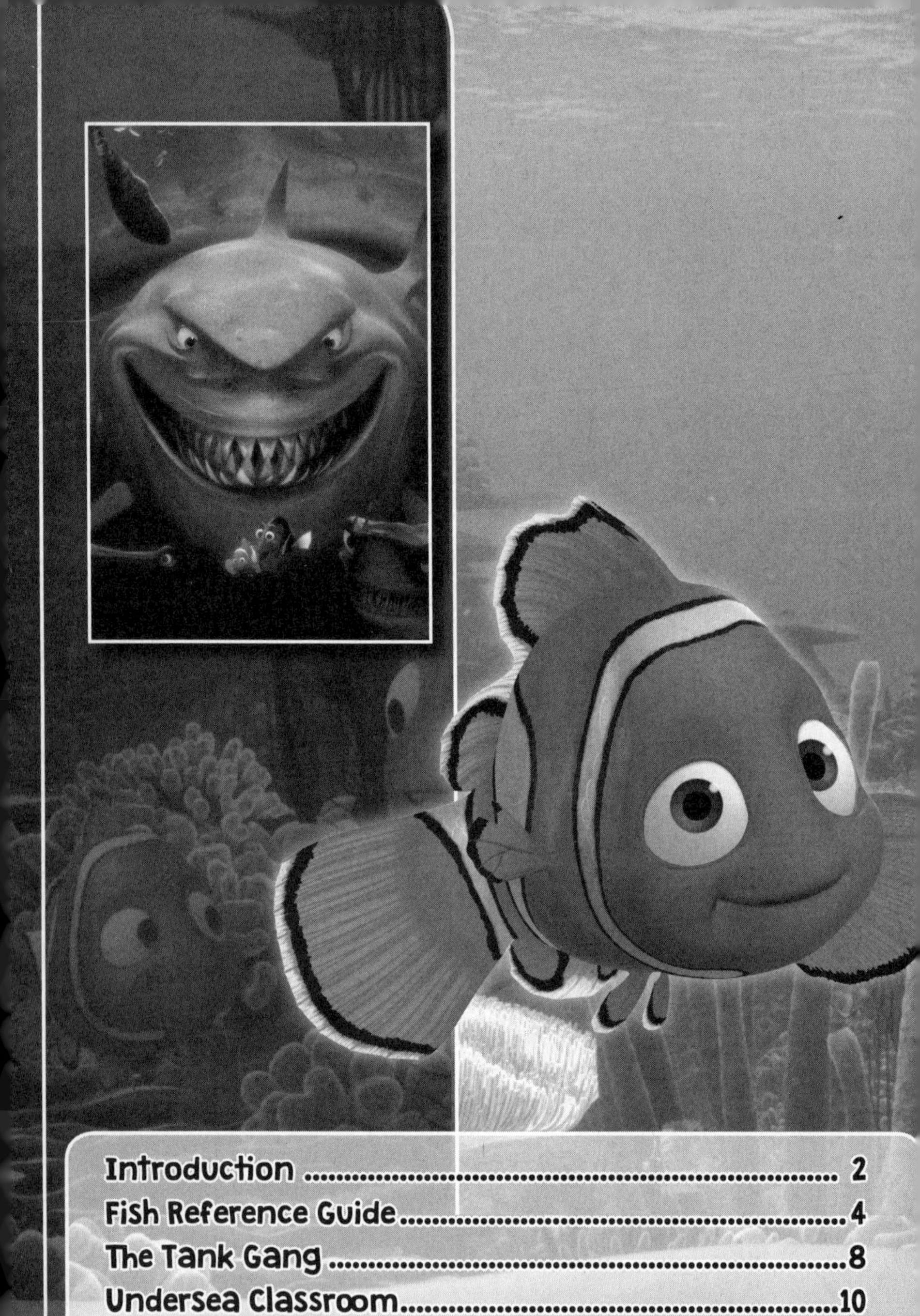

FISH REFERENCE GUIDE

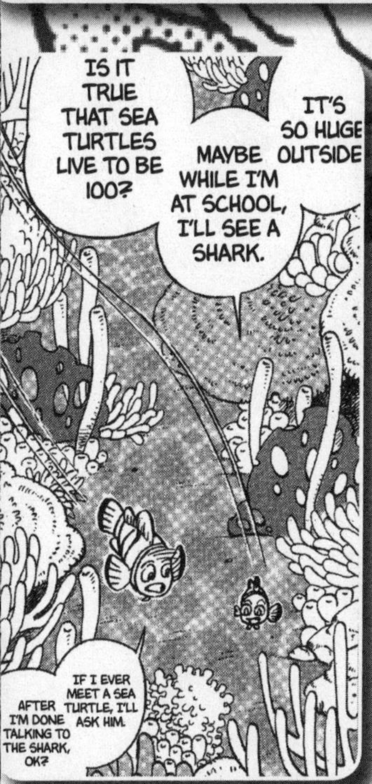
IT'S SO HUGE OUTSIDE
MAYBE WHILE I'M AT SCHOOL, I'LL SEE A SHARK.
IS IT TRUE THAT SEA TURTLES LIVE TO BE 100?
IF I EVER MEET A SEA TURTLE, I'LL ASK HIM.
AFTER I'M DONE TALKING TO THE SHARK, OK?

Nemo
(Clownfish)

A six-year-old fish ready for an adventure. He's had a small right fin from birth, which Nemo and Marlin call his "lucky fin." One day, Nemo gets picked up by a human diver.

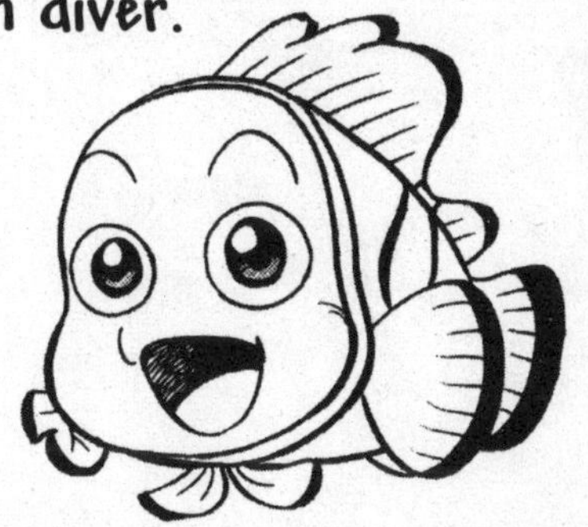

This is the beautiful ocean coral reef where Nemo grew up. Nemo and Marlin find shelter in their anemone home.

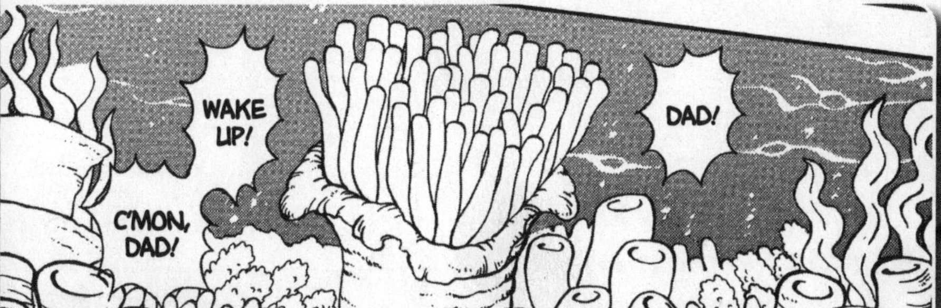
DAD!
WAKE UP!
C'MON, DAD!

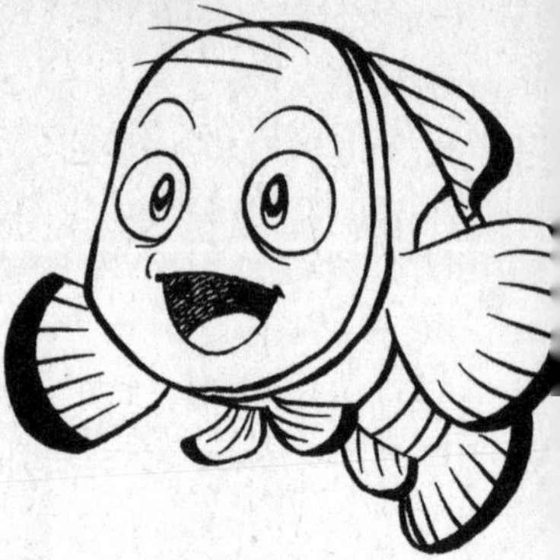

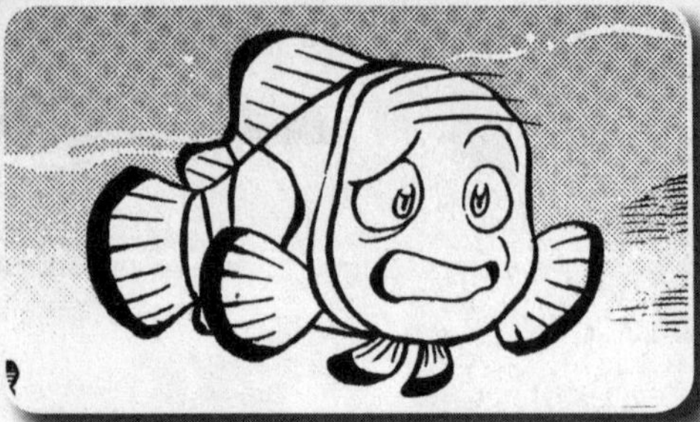

Marlin
(Clownfish)

Nemo's doting father. Ever since Nemo's mother was attacked and lost to a barracuda, he fears and worries about everything.

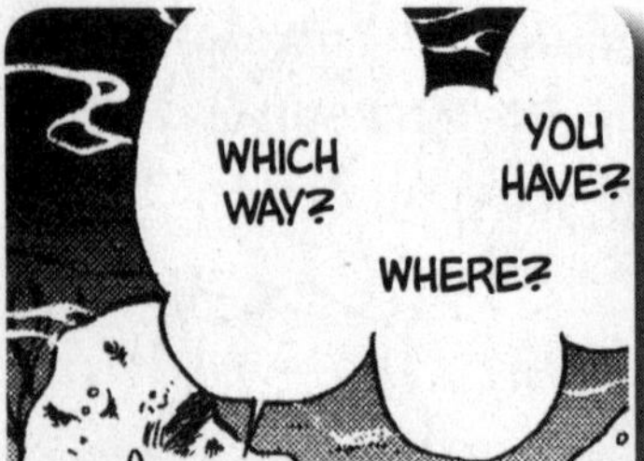
YOU HAVE?
WHICH WAY?
WHERE?

Dory
(Regal Blue Tang)

A cheerful and friendly fish wh joins Marlin on his journey to find Nemo. She may be smart enough to read, but she suffer from extreme amnesia and forgets things easily.

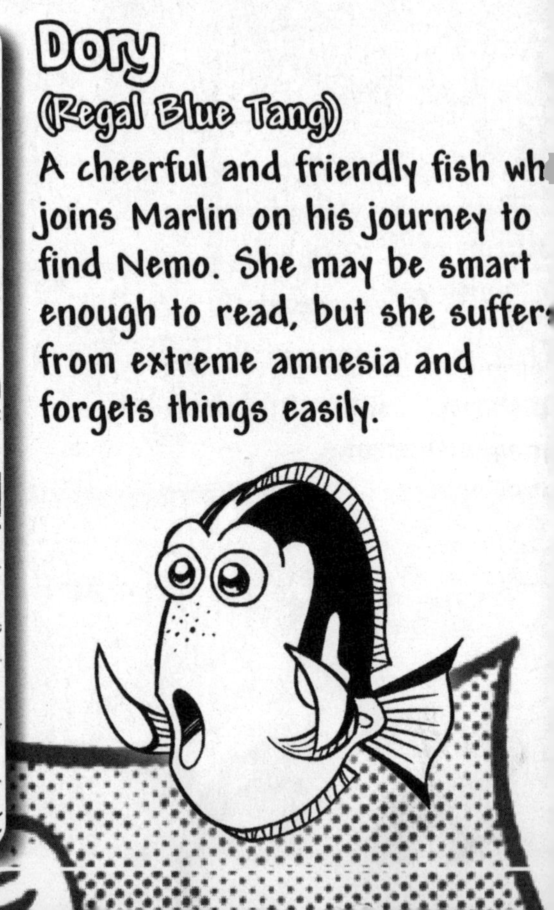

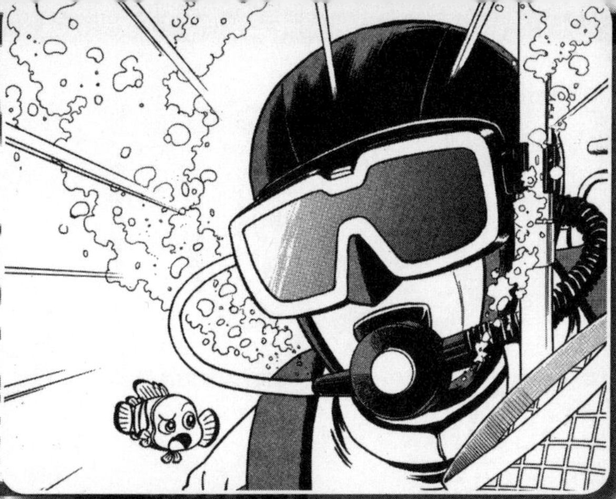

lownfish are very
opular fish, thanks to
eir bright colors and
eautiful appearance.
or this reason, they're
ften snatched up by
umans if found.

Be careful not to touch a jellyfish's tentacles - they have stingers! You don't want to be surrounded by a huge jellyfish swarm.

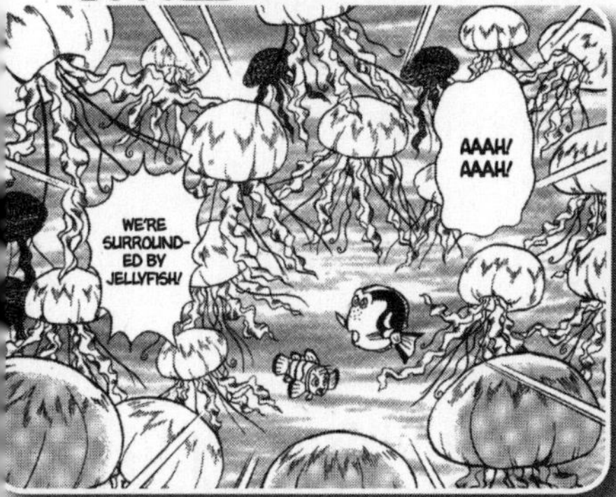
AAAH! AAAH!
WE'RE SURROUND-ED BY JELLYFISH!

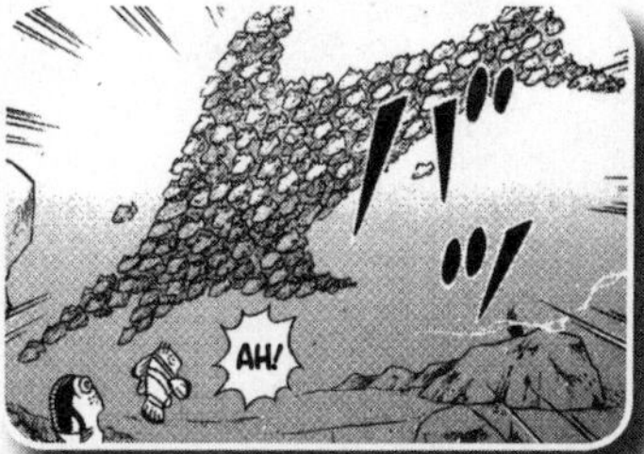
AH!

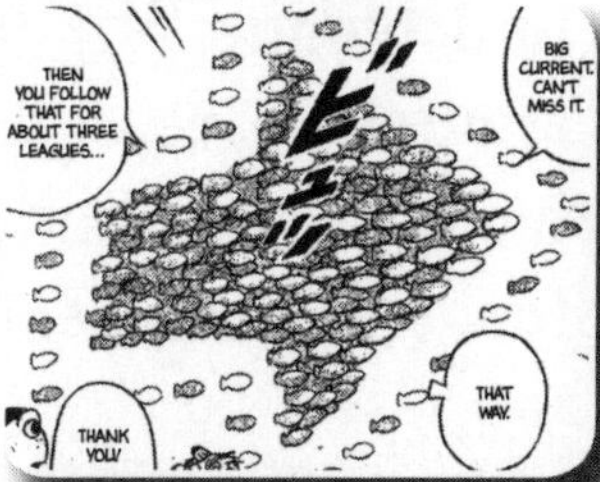
BIG CURRENT. CAN'T MISS IT.
THEN YOU FOLLOW THAT FOR ABOUT THREE LEAGUES...
THAT WAY.
THANK YOU!

chools of
noonfish are
uite good at
opying all sorts
f shapes - any-
hing from ships
o octopuses.

The turtle families ride the current and travel quickly throughout the ocean.

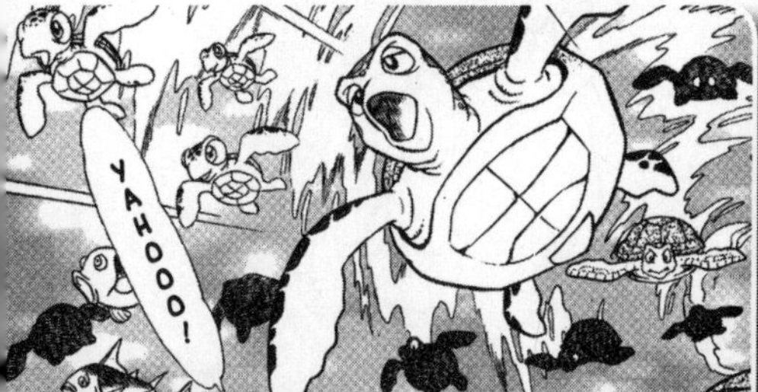
YAHOOOO!

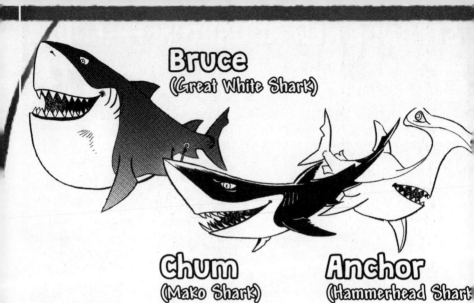

Bruce
(Great White Shark)

Chum
(Mako Shark)

Anchor
(Hammerhead Shark)

These three sharks are working to improve their image and trying to befriend - not eat! - fish. Can these fish-eating sharks stay on the path of vegetarianism...?

Crush
(Green Sea Turtle)

Leader of the green sea turtles. He may be 150 years old, but among turtles that's just a typical adult. When it comes to being a current-riding surfer, even young turtles can't keep up with Crush. Compared to the worrywart Marlin, Crush takes a relaxed approach to raising his son.

Squirt
(Green Sea Turtle)

Crush's son. He may just be a kid, but he's a very talented surfer. He's super impressed with Marlin, and looks up to him like a great adventurer.

STRANGE NEW AQUARIUM FRIENDS
THE TANK GANG

Sydney – a huge city full of humans. Nemo is somewhere out there.

Peach
(Starfish)

He's the lookout for the tank and is always giving reports to his friends on what's happening in the dentist's office. This has given him a pretty good understanding of dentistry.

Gill
(Moorish Idol)

Leader of the group living in the dentist's fish tank. He has tried to escape countless times in order to return to the ocean, but he always fails. As a result, he's covered in scars and his fins are all torn up. He masterminds a plan to get Nemo back to the ocean.

Bubbles
(Yellow Tang)

Loves bubbles and is fixated on those coming from the treasure chest at the bottom of the tank.

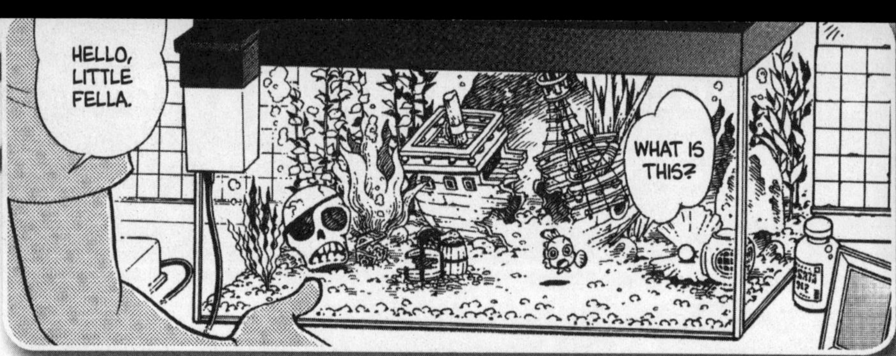
HELLO, LITTLE FELLA.
WHAT IS THIS?

When Nemo was put into the tank in the dentist's office, he met a strange group of friends called the Tank Gang.

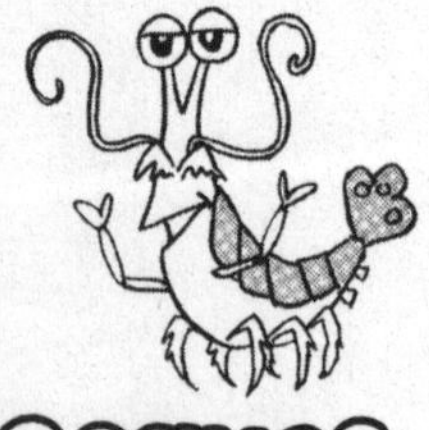

Jacques
(Scarlet Cleaner Shrimp)
In charge of cleaning the tank and believes he is the marine researcher Jacques Cousteau.

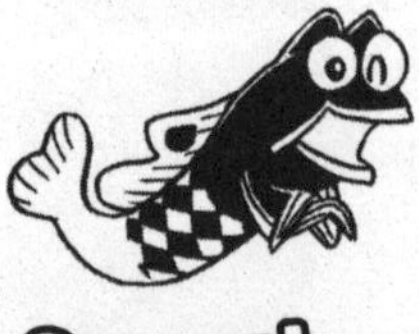

Gurgle
(Royal Gramma)
Incredibly germophobic fish who won't touch anything dirty.

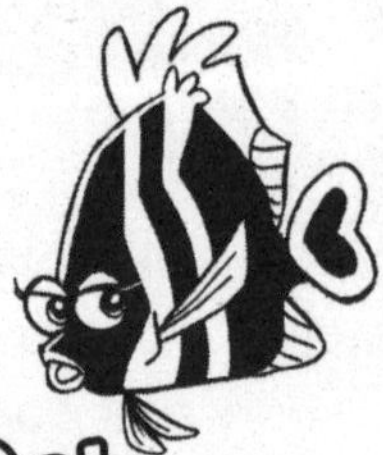

Deb
(Damselfish)
Believes that the image she sees reflected in the fi tank glass is her twin sister, Flo.

Nigel (Pelican)
Enjoys watching over the dentist's office and is a friend to the gang. He tries to reunite Marlin and Nemo.

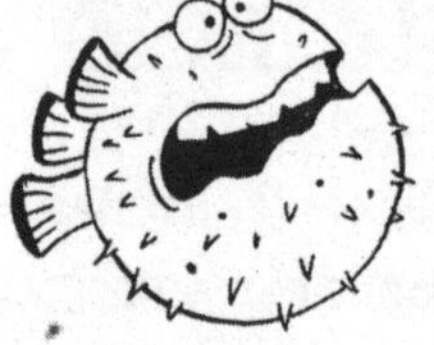

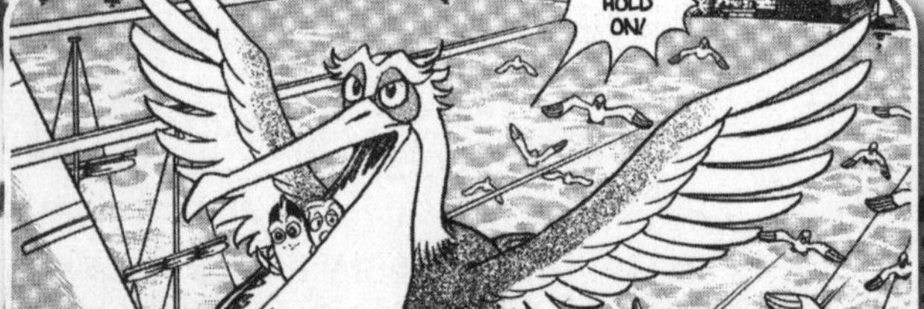
HOLD ON!

Bloat
(Porcupine Pufferfish)
Quick to anger. When he's upset his body puffs out.

THE AMAZING MOBILE UNDERSEA CLASSROOM

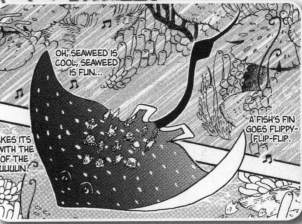

OH, SEAWEED IS COOL, SEAWEED IS FUN...
A FISH'S FIN GOES FLIPPY-FLIP-FLIP.
AKES ITS WITH THE OF THE UUUUUN.

Nemo's school is mobile classroom n Mr. Ray's back. It an travel anywhere!

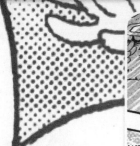

Sheldon
(Seahorse)

An H_2O-intolerant seahorse who befriends Nemo on his first day of school.

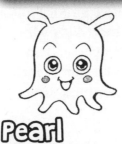

Pearl
(Flapjack Octopus)

Loves to make the hem of her skirt flutter about. She shoots ink when surprised.

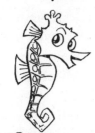

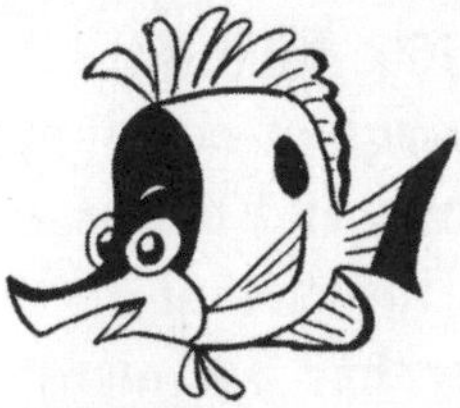

Tad
(Butterfly Fish)

A rambunctious young boy who makes fun of how small Nemo's right fin is and gets told off by Sheldon.

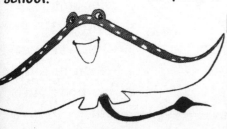

Mr. Ray (Spotted Eagle Ray)

Nemo's school teacher. He puts all the students on his back and takes them exploring so he can teach them about the ocean.

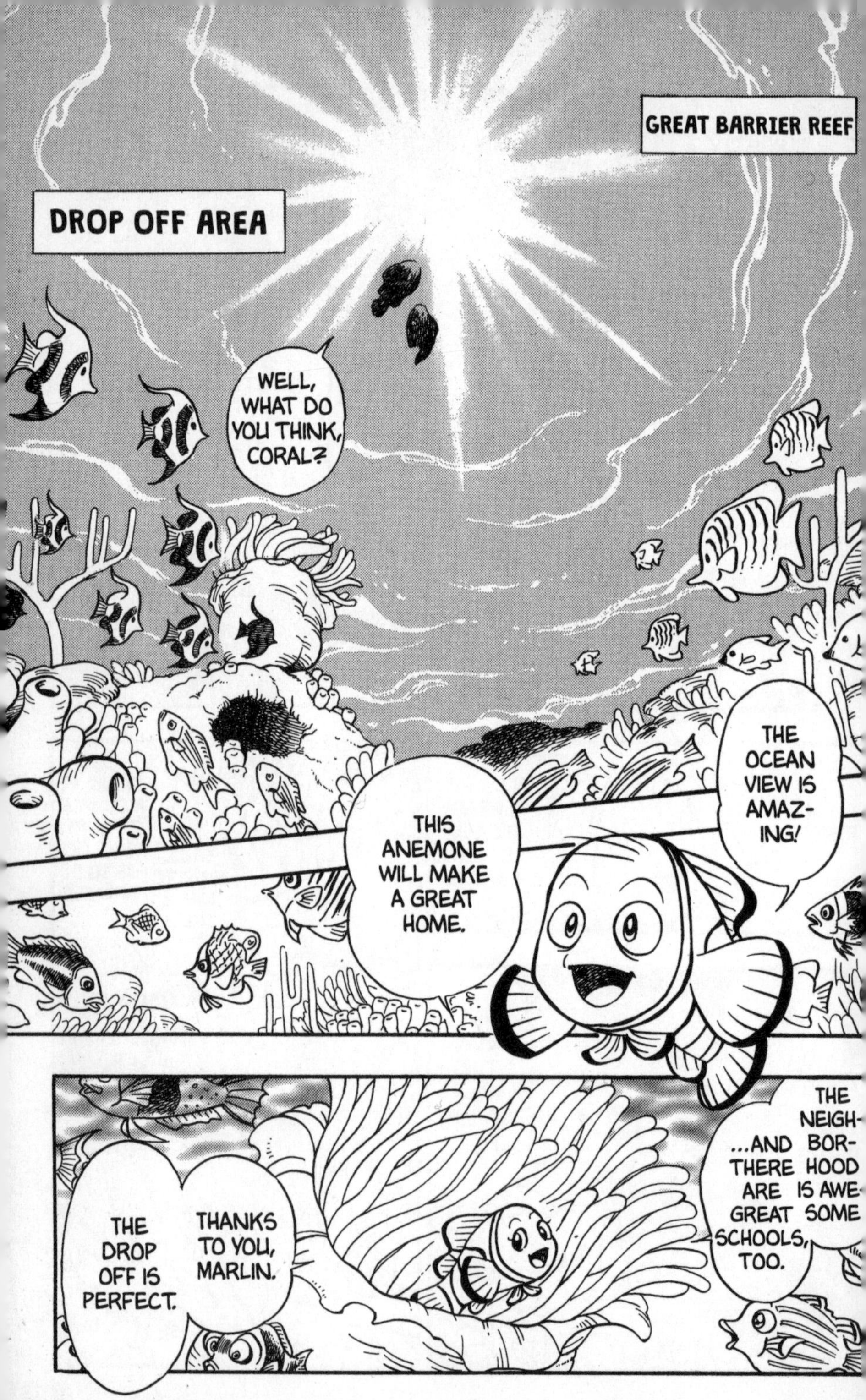
GREAT BARRIER REEF
DROP OFF AREA
WELL, WHAT DO YOU THINK, CORAL?
THE OCEAN VIEW IS AMAZING!
THIS ANEMONE WILL MAKE A GREAT HOME.
THE NEIGHBORHOOD IS AWESOME
...AND THERE ARE GREAT SCHOOLS, TOO.
THANKS TO YOU, MARLIN.
THE DROP OFF IS PERFECT.

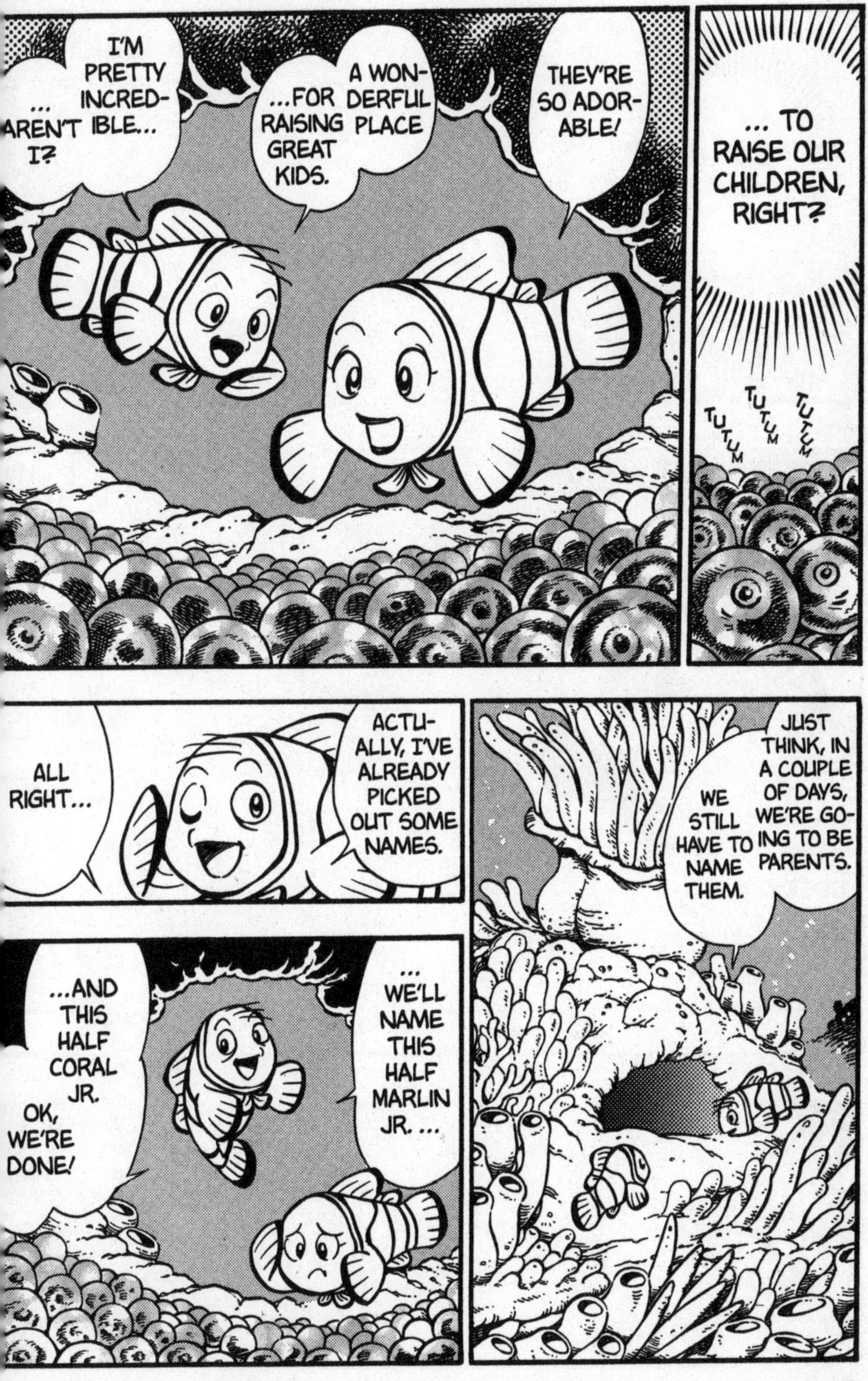
... TO RAISE OUR CHILDREN, RIGHT?
TUTUM TUTUM TUTUM
THEY'RE SO ADORABLE!
A WONDERFUL PLACE
...FOR RAISING GREAT KIDS.
I'M PRETTY INCREDIBLE...
... AREN'T I?
JUST THINK, IN A COUPLE OF DAYS, WE'RE GOING TO BE PARENTS.
WE STILL HAVE TO NAME THEM.
ACTUALLY, I'VE ALREADY PICKED OUT SOME NAMES.
ALL RIGHT...
... WE'LL NAME THIS HALF MARLIN JR. ...
...AND THIS HALF CORAL JR.
OK, WE'RE DONE!

READ THIS WAY

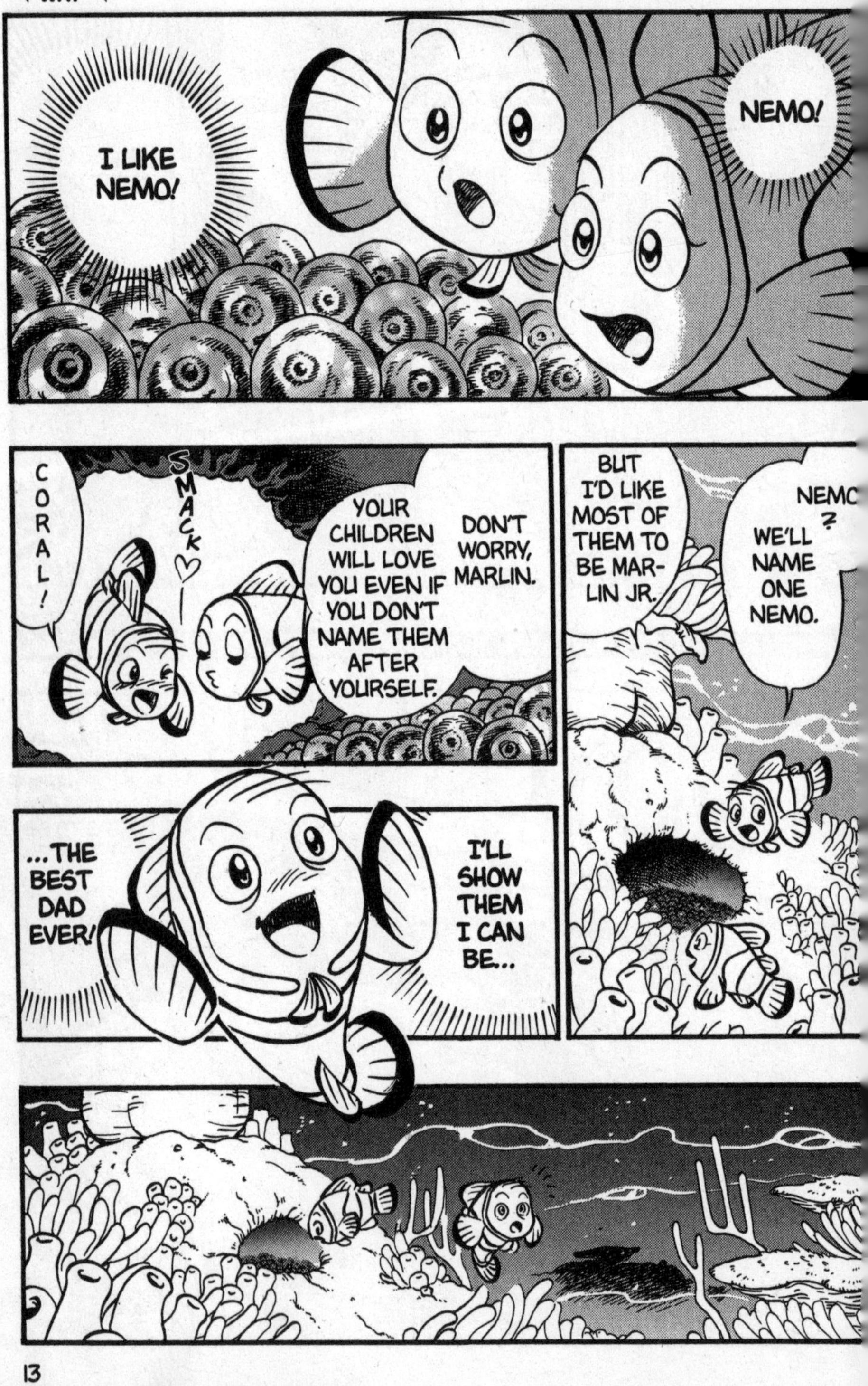
NEMO!
I LIKE NEMO!
NEMO?
WE'LL NAME ONE NEMO.
BUT I'D LIKE MOST OF THEM TO BE MAR-LIN JR.
DON'T WORRY, MARLIN.
YOUR CHILDREN WILL LOVE YOU EVEN IF YOU DON'T NAME THEM AFTER YOURSELF.
SMACK ♡
CORAL!
I'LL SHOW THEM I CAN BE...
...THE BEST DAD EVER!

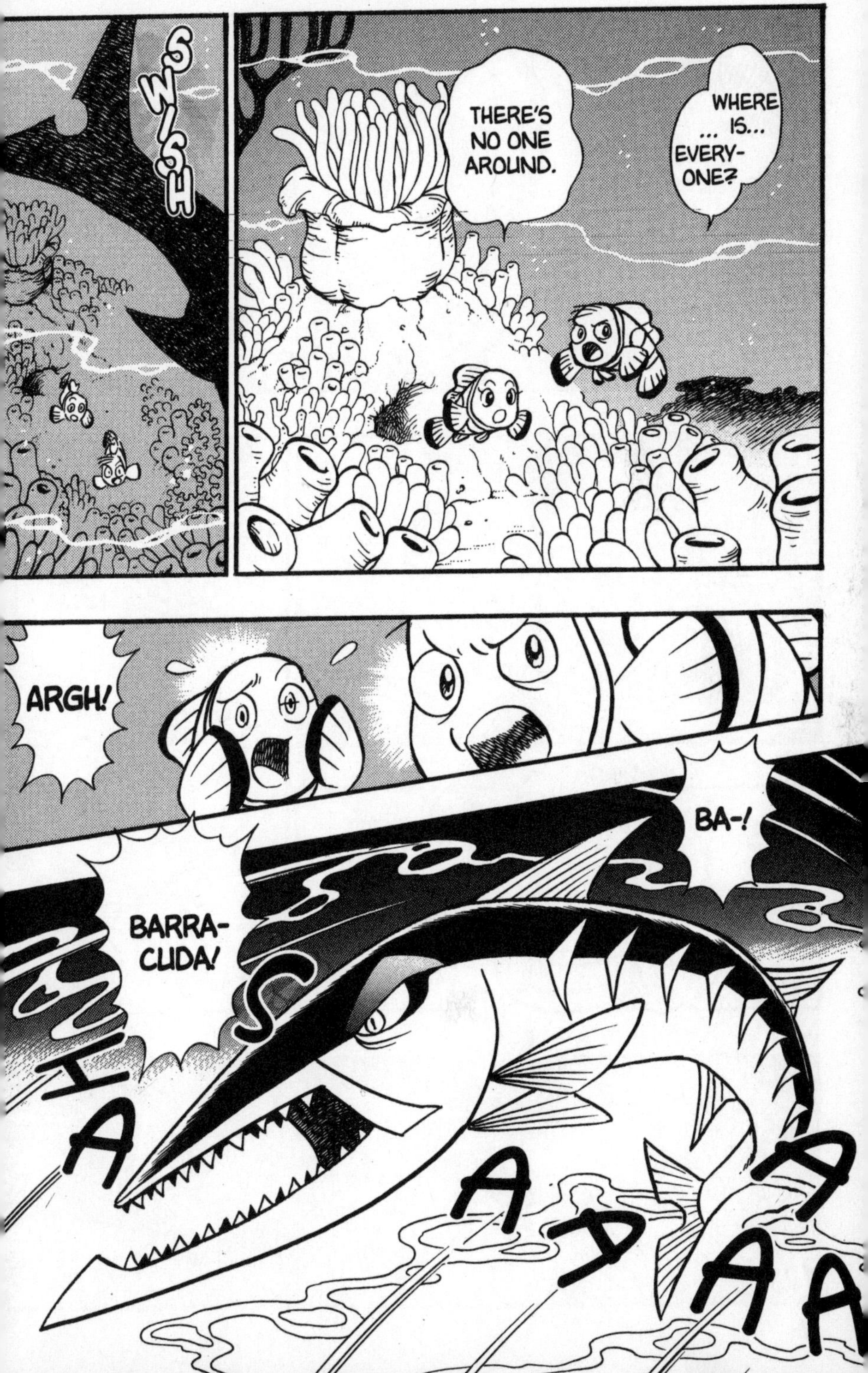
... WHERE IS... EVERYONE?
THERE'S NO ONE AROUND.
SWISH
ARGH!
BA-!
BARRACUDA!
SHAAAAAA

READ THIS WAY

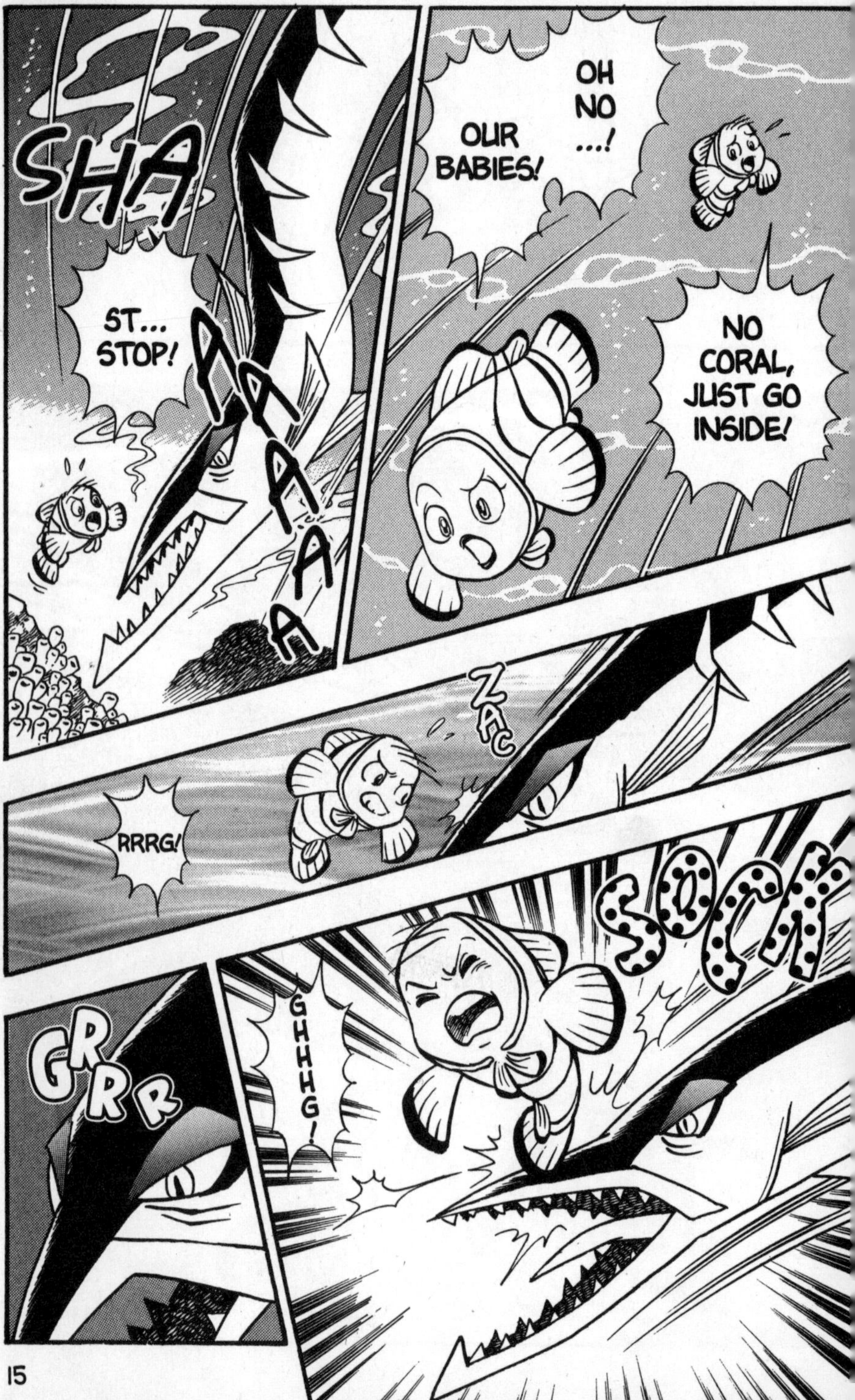

OH NO ...!
OUR BABIES!
NO CORAL, JUST GO INSIDE!
SHA
ST... STOP!
AAAAA
ZAC
RRRG!
SOCK
GHHHG!
GRRR

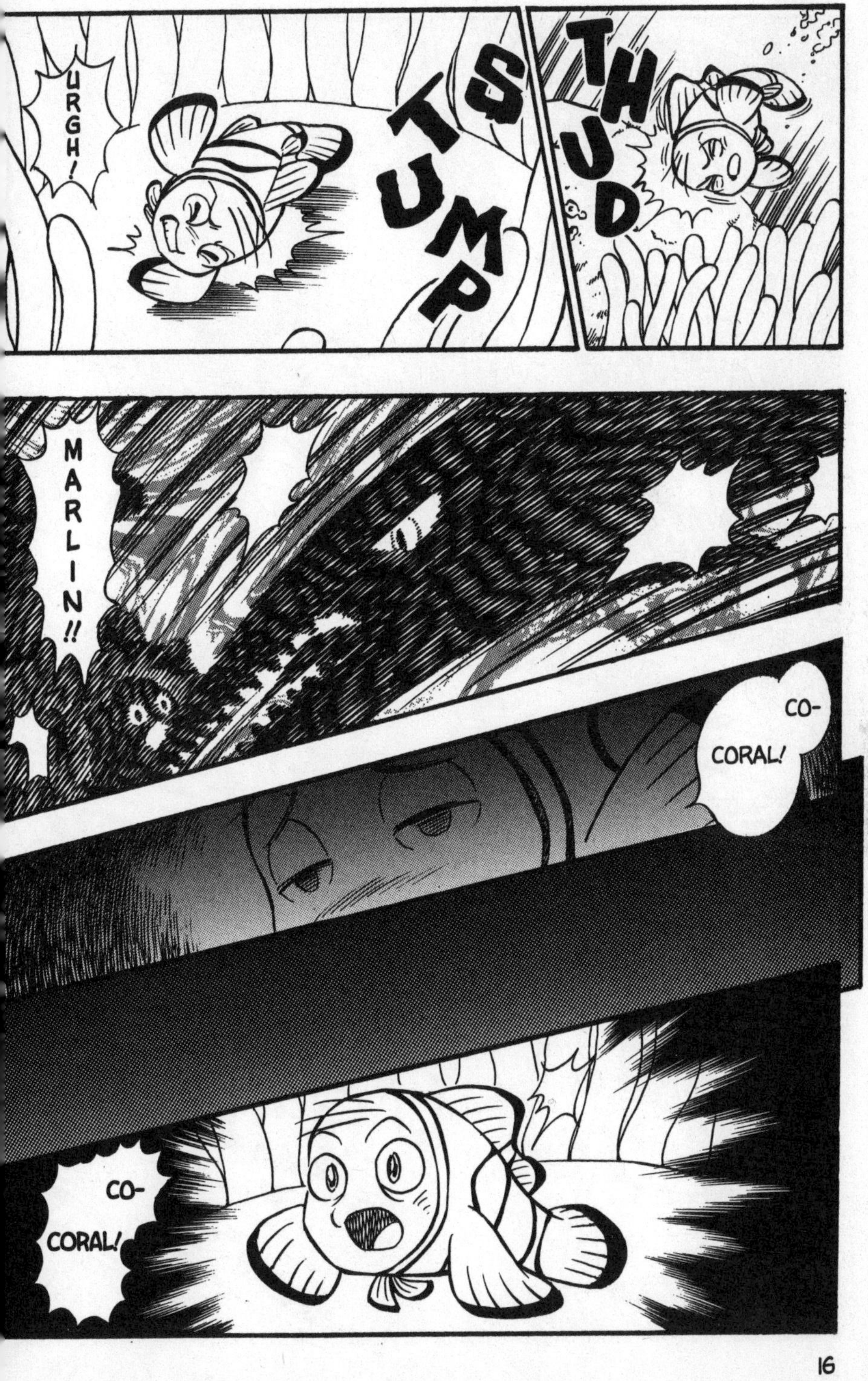
THUD
STUMP
URGH!
MARLIN!!
CO- CORAL!
CO- CORAL!

READ THIS WAY

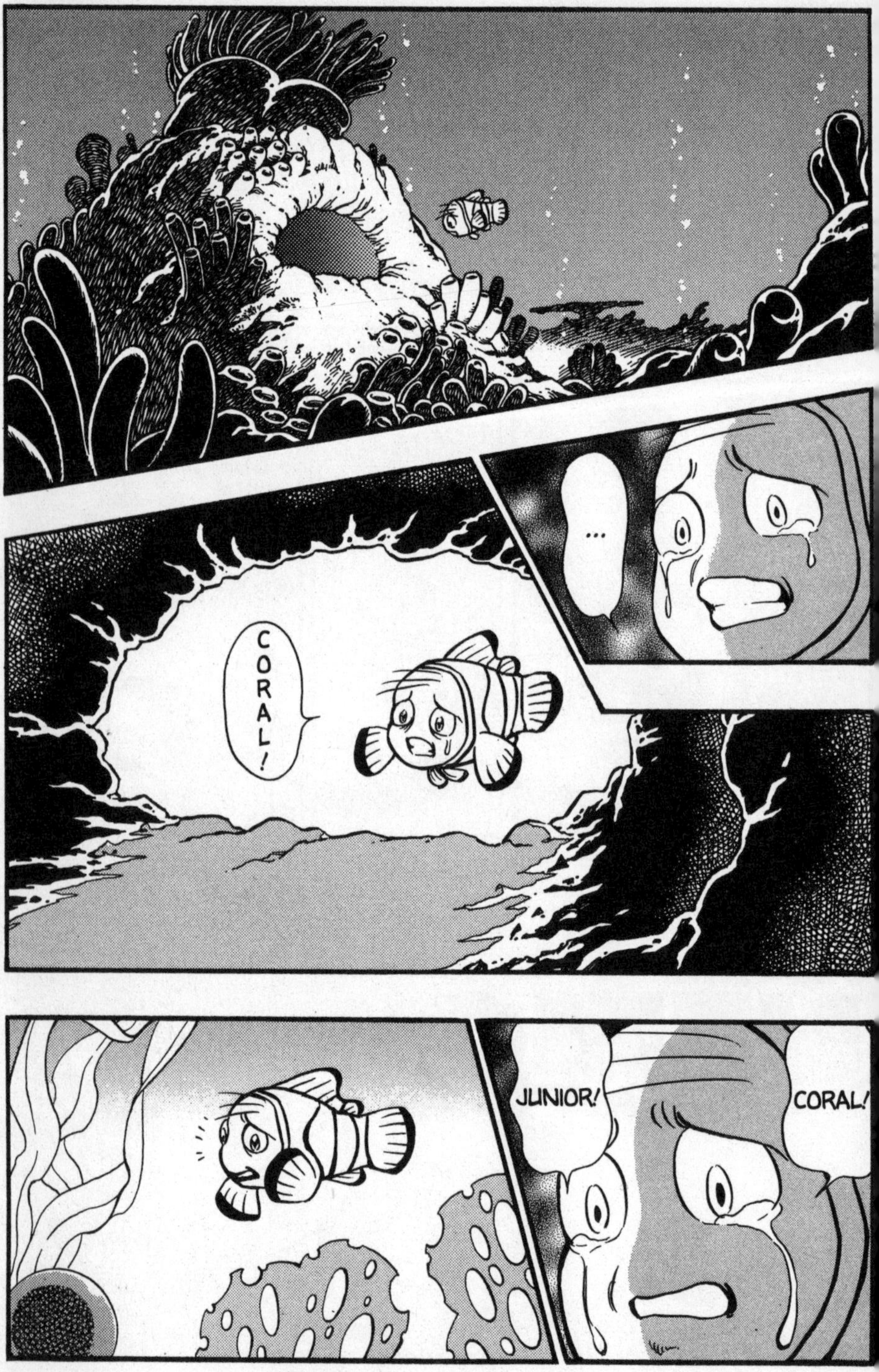
...
CORAL!
CORAL!
JUNIOR!

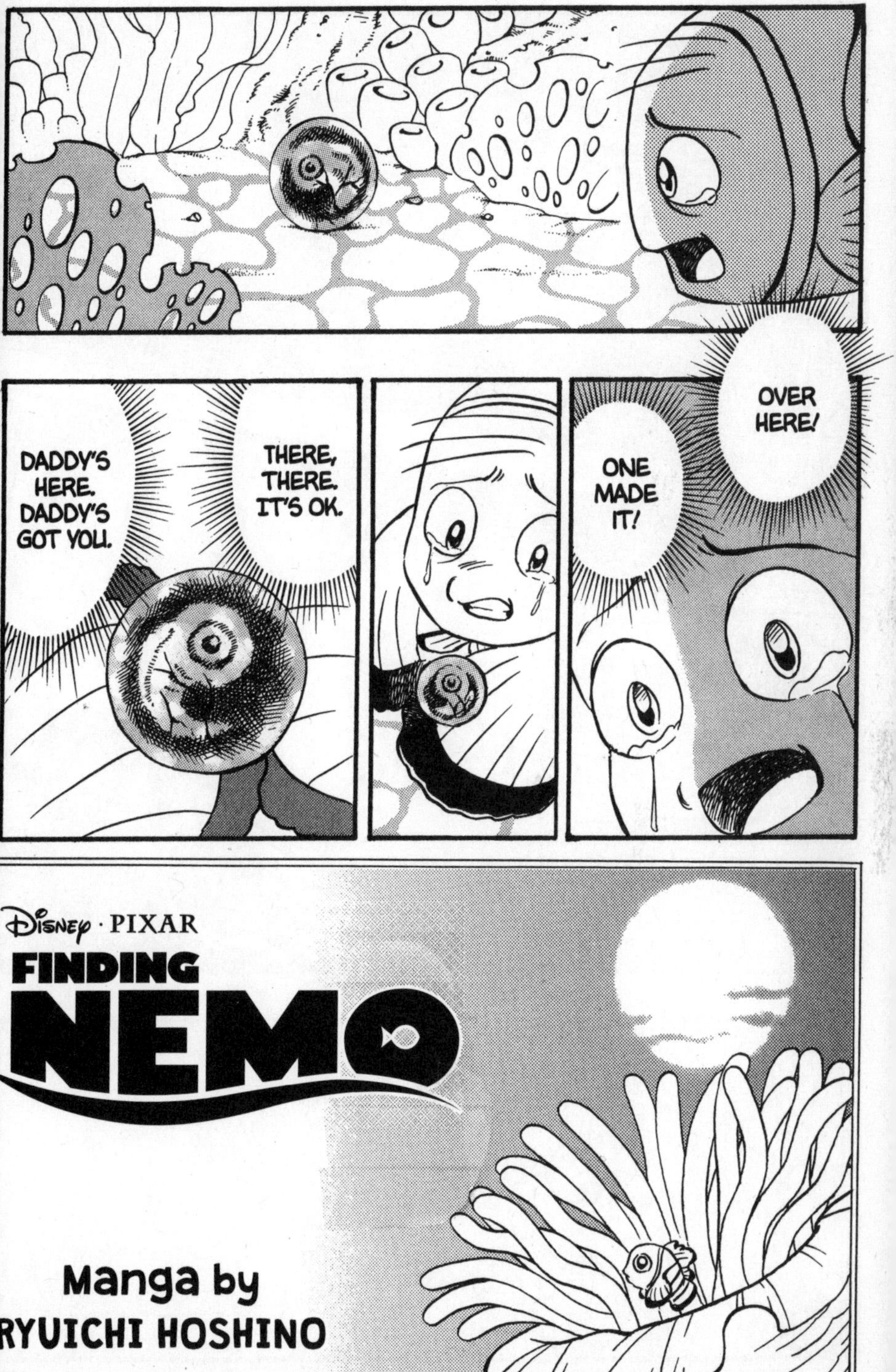
OVER HERE!
ONE MADE IT!
THERE, THERE. IT'S OK.
DADDY'S HERE. DADDY'S GOT YOU.
Disney · PIXAR
FINDING NEMO
Manga by
RYUICHI HOSHINO

READ THIS WAY

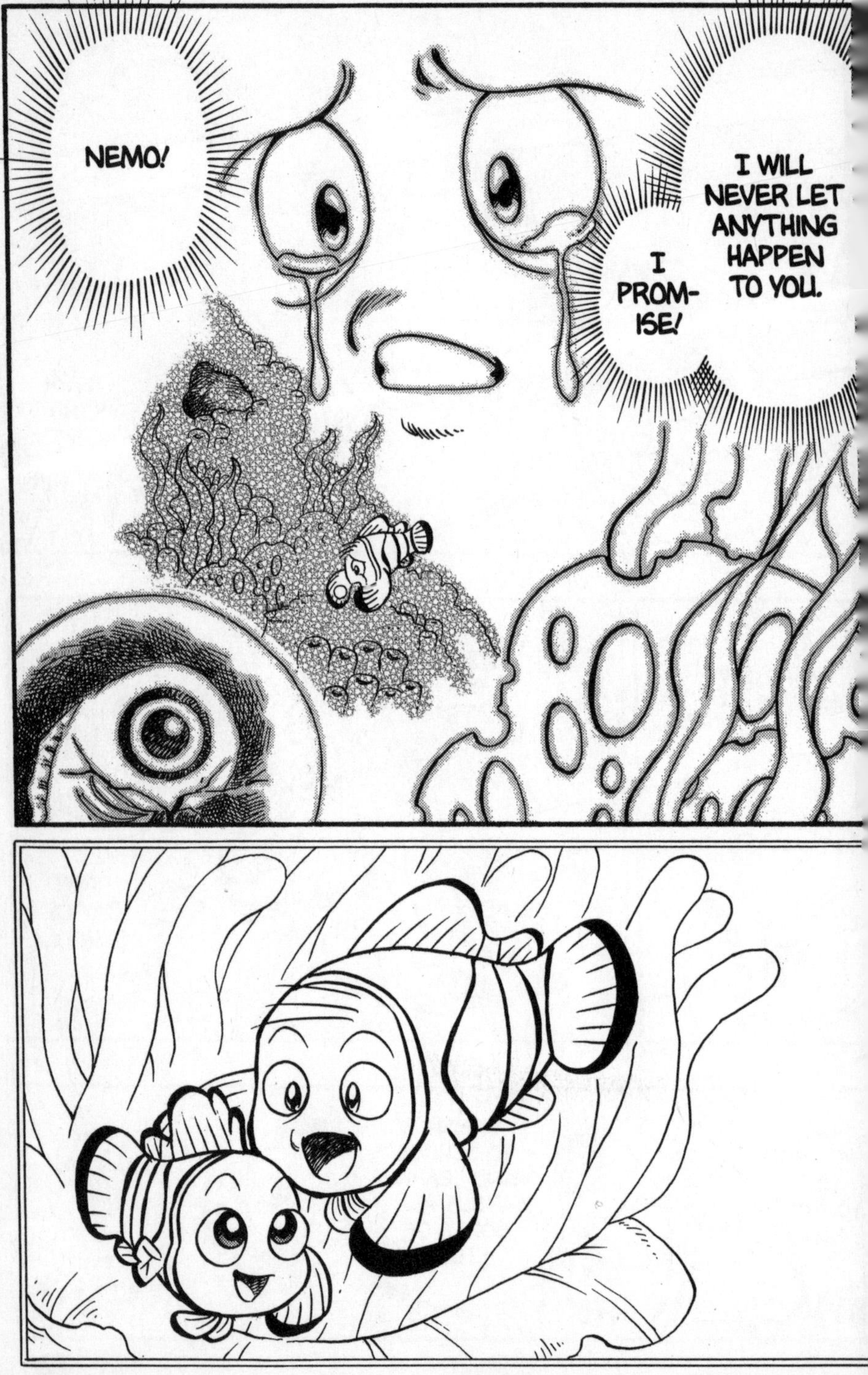

I WILL NEVER LET ANYTHING HAPPEN TO YOU.
I PROMISE!
NEMO!

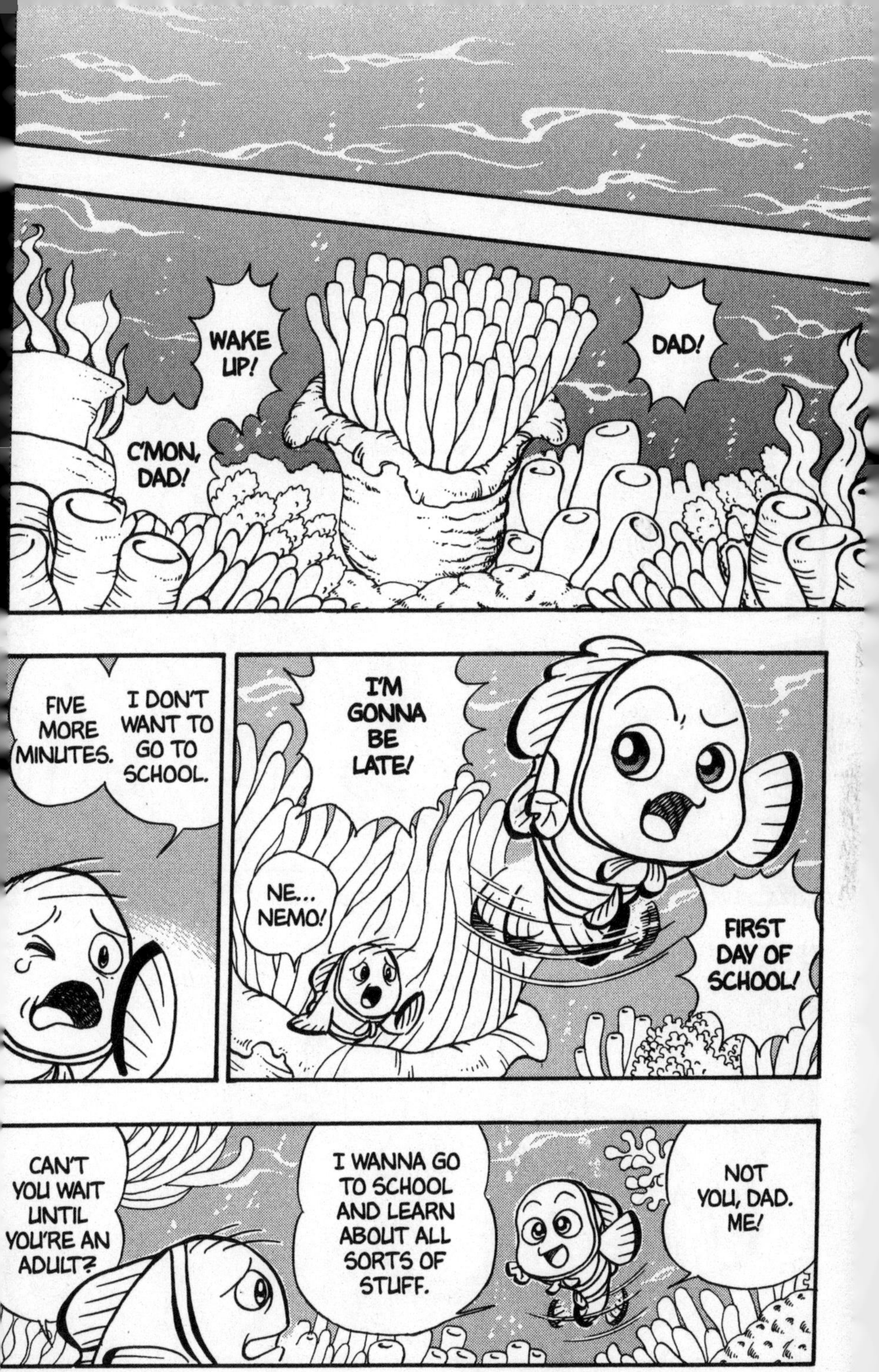
DAD!
WAKE UP!
C'MON, DAD!
I'M GONNA BE LATE!
FIRST DAY OF SCHOOL!
NE... NEMO!
I DON'T WANT TO GO TO SCHOOL.
FIVE MORE MINUTES.
NOT YOU, DAD. ME!
I WANNA GO TO SCHOOL AND LEARN ABOUT ALL SORTS OF STUFF.
CAN'T YOU WAIT UNTIL YOU'RE AN ADULT?

READ THIS WAY

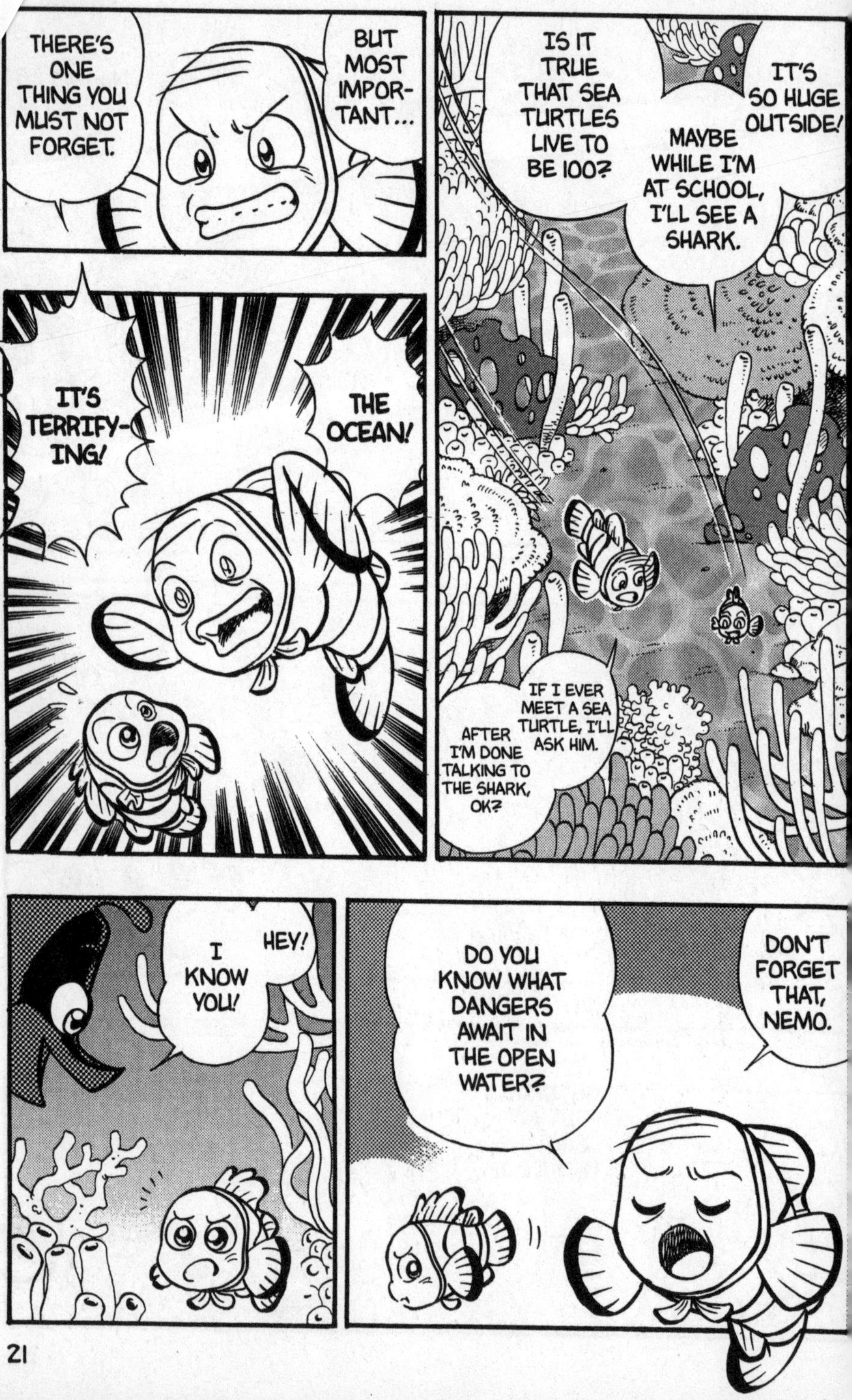
IT'S SO HUGE OUTSIDE!
MAYBE WHILE I'M AT SCHOOL, I'LL SEE A SHARK.
IS IT TRUE THAT SEA TURTLES LIVE TO BE 100?
IF I EVER MEET A SEA TURTLE, I'LL ASK HIM.
AFTER I'M DONE TALKING TO THE SHARK, OK?
BUT MOST IMPOR-TANT...
THERE'S ONE THING YOU MUST NOT FORGET.
THE OCEAN!
IT'S TERRIFY-ING!
DON'T FORGET THAT, NEMO.
DO YOU KNOW WHAT DANGERS AWAIT IN THE OPEN WATER?
HEY!
I KNOW YOU!

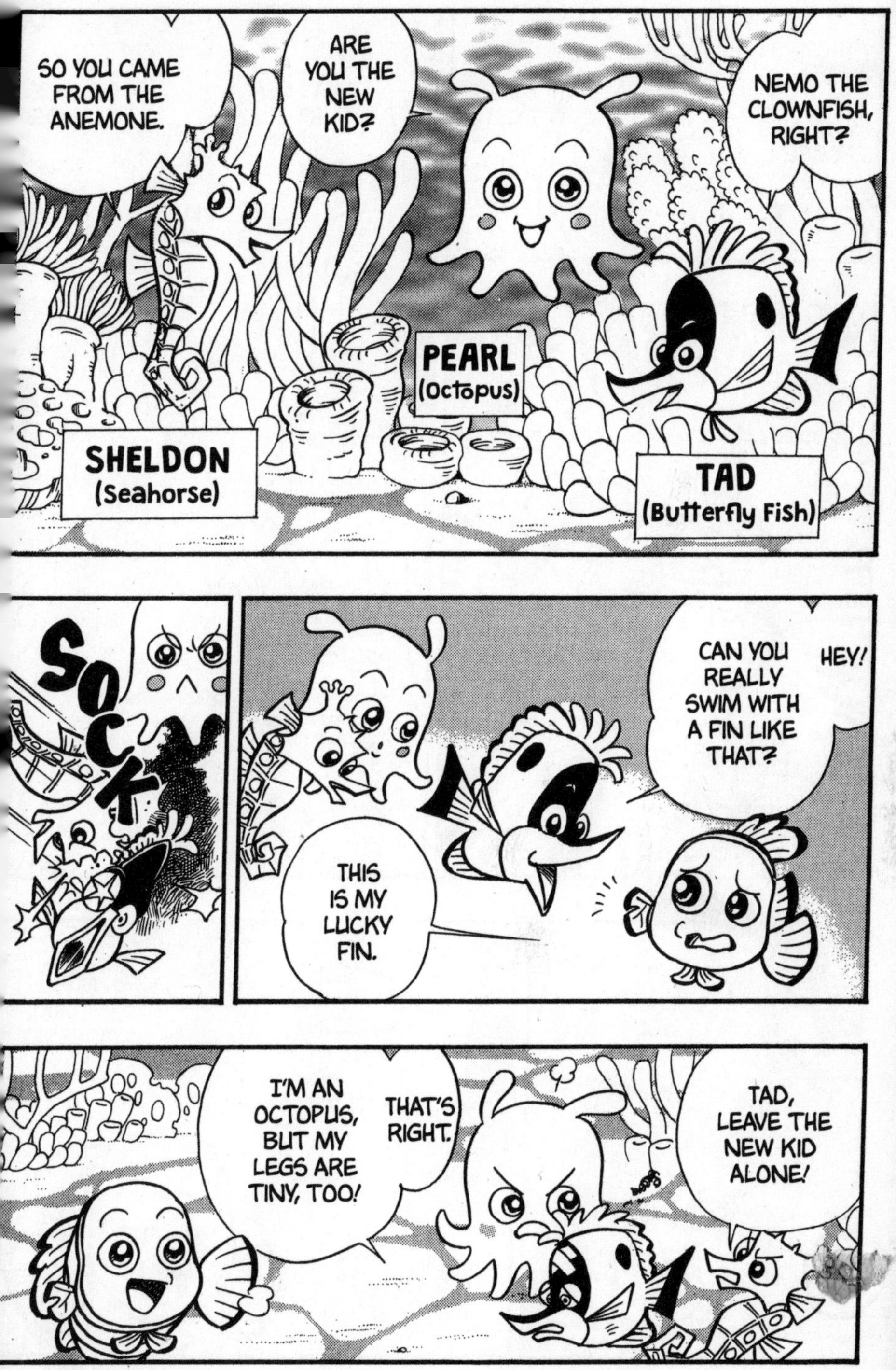
NEMO THE CLOWNFISH, RIGHT?
ARE YOU THE NEW KID?
SO YOU CAME FROM THE ANEMONE.
TAD (Butterfly Fish)
PEARL (Octopus)
SHELDON (Seahorse)
HEY!
CAN YOU REALLY SWIM WITH A FIN LIKE THAT?
THIS IS MY LUCKY FIN.
SOCK
TAD, LEAVE THE NEW KID ALONE!
THAT'S RIGHT.
I'M AN OCTOPUS, BUT MY LEGS ARE TINY, TOO!

READ THIS WAY

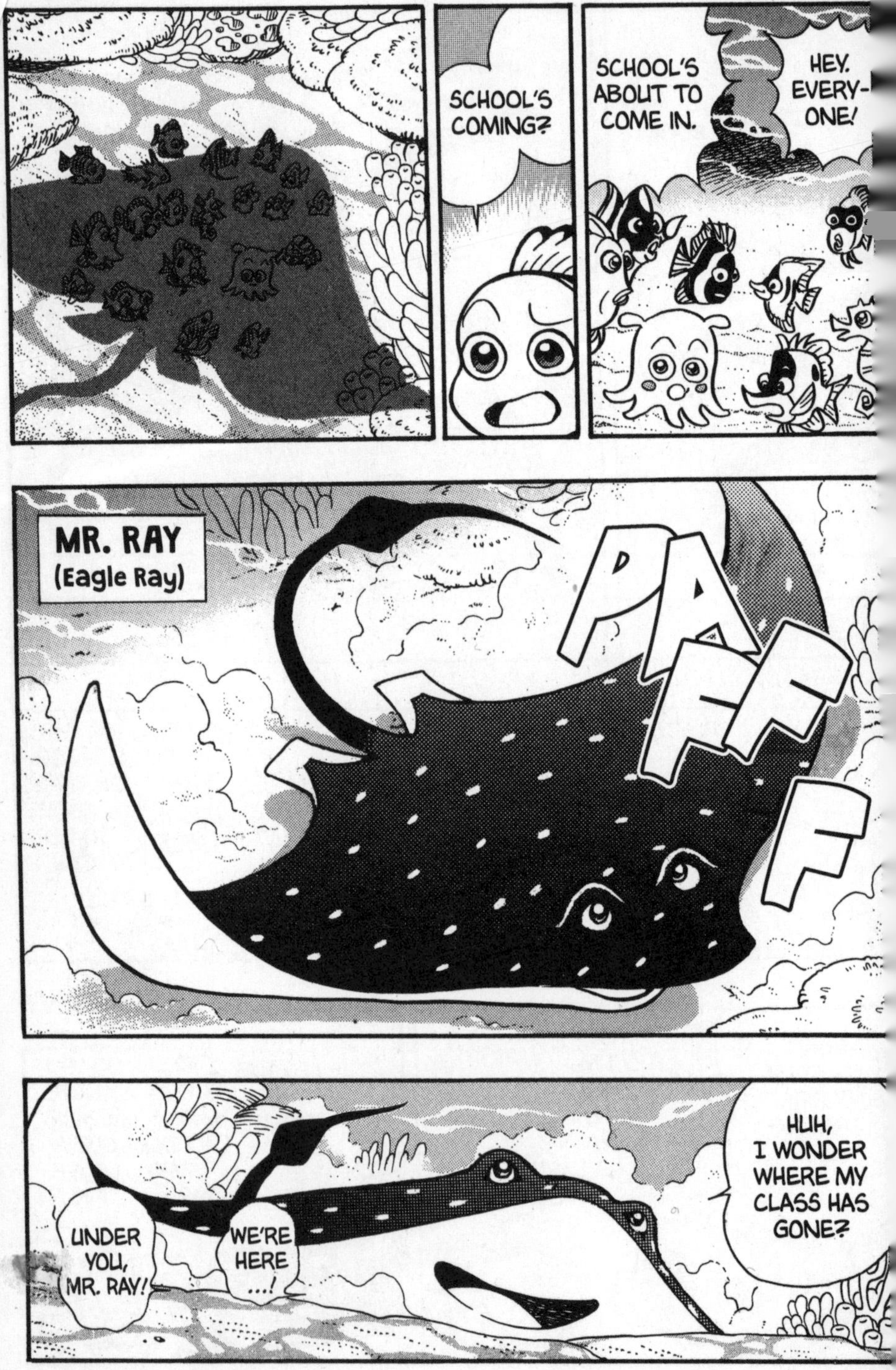
HEY. EVERY-ONE!
SCHOOL'S ABOUT TO COME IN.
SCHOOL'S COMING?
MR. RAY (Eagle Ray)
PAFFFF
HUH, I WONDER WHERE MY CLASS HAS GONE?
WE'RE HERE ...!
UNDER YOU, MR. RAY!

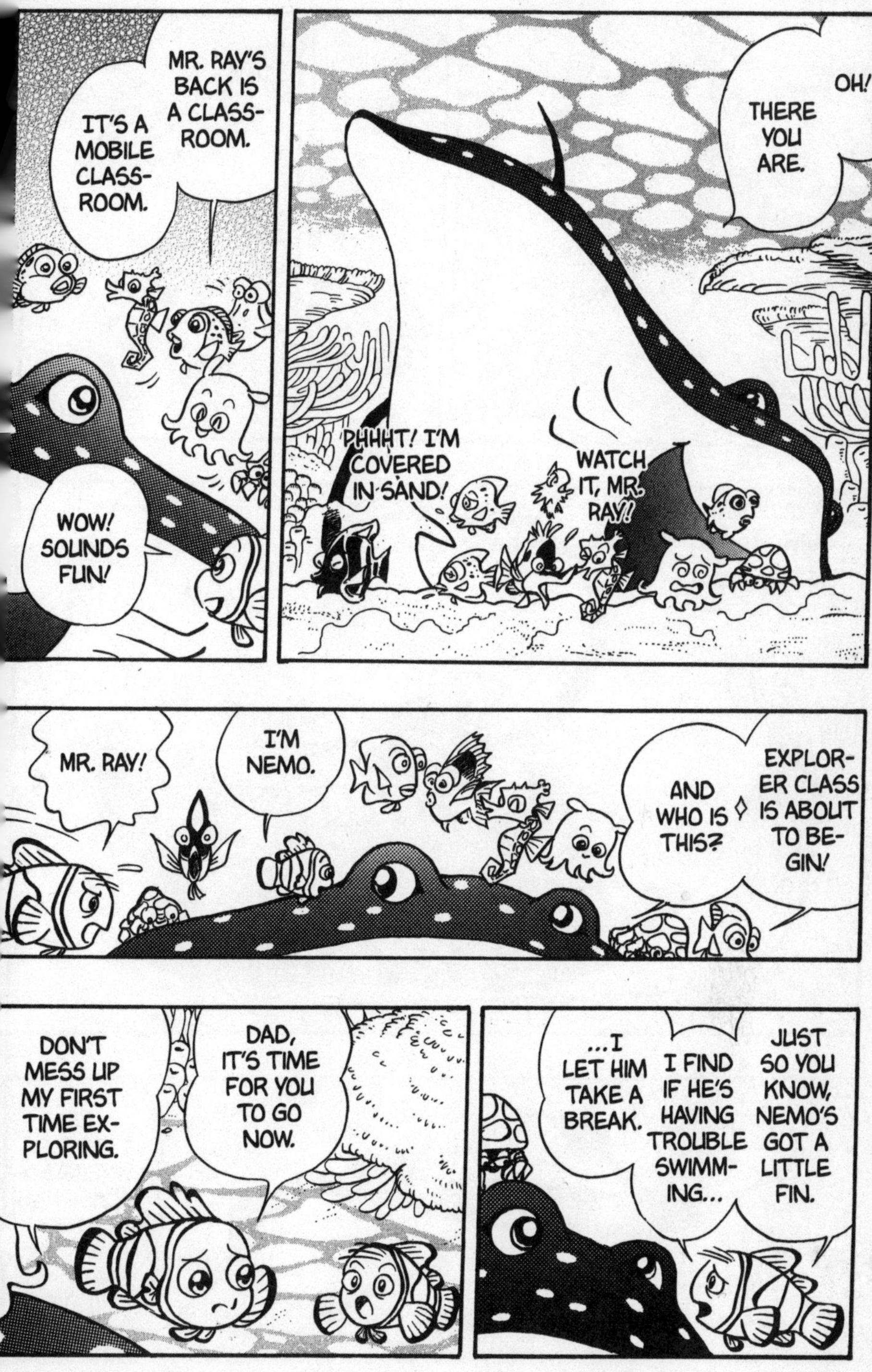
OH! THERE YOU ARE.
WATCH IT, MR. RAY!
PHHHT! I'M COVERED IN SAND!
MR. RAY'S BACK IS A CLASSROOM.
IT'S A MOBILE CLASSROOM.
WOW! SOUNDS FUN!
EXPLORER CLASS IS ABOUT TO BEGIN!
AND WHO IS THIS?
I'M NEMO.
MR. RAY!
JUST SO YOU KNOW, NEMO'S GOT A LITTLE FIN.
I FIND IF HE'S HAVING TROUBLE SWIMMING...
...I LET HIM TAKE A BREAK.
DAD, IT'S TIME FOR YOU TO GO NOW.
DON'T MESS UP MY FIRST TIME EXPLORING.

READ THIS WAY

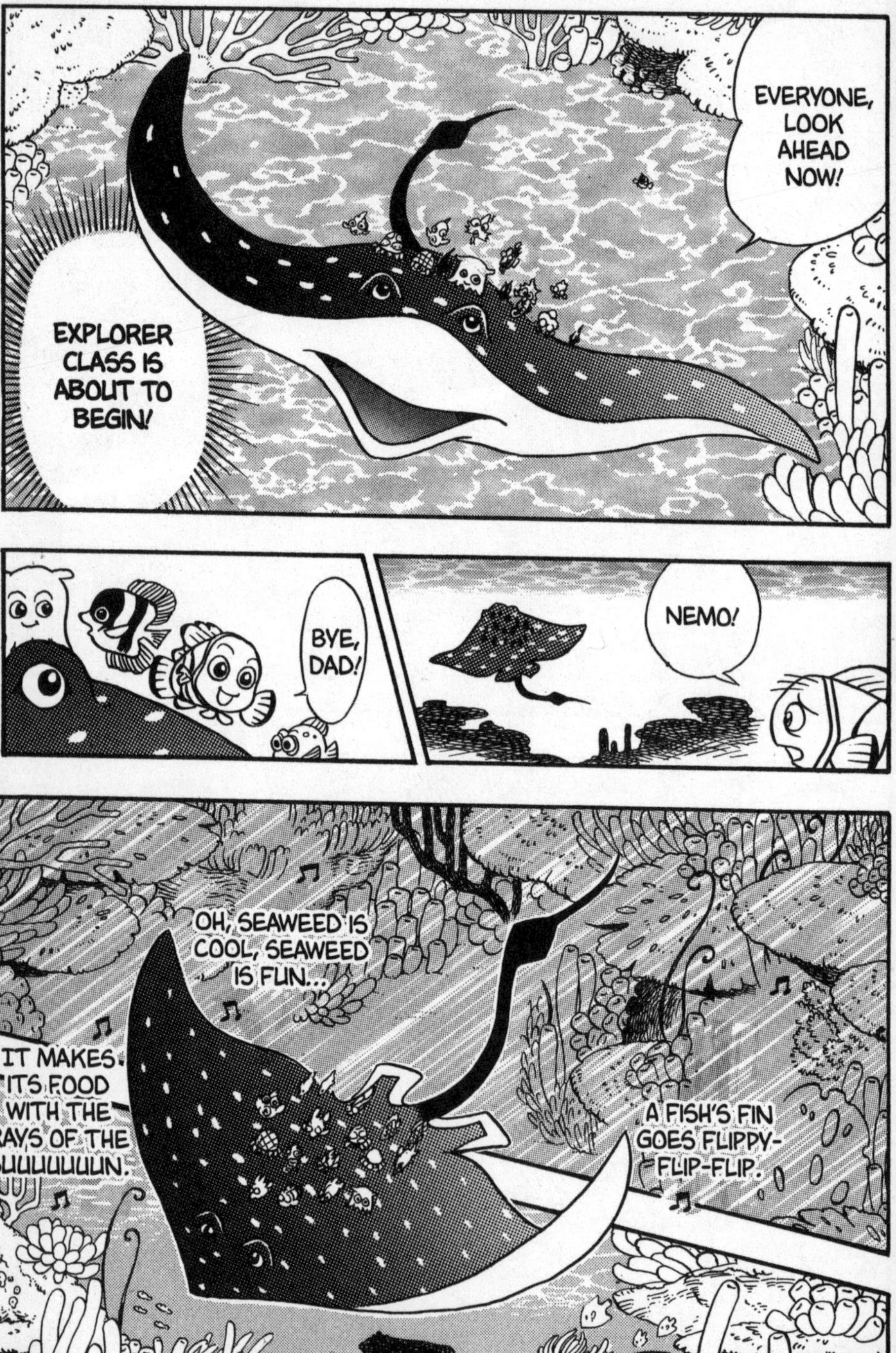
EVERYONE, LOOK AHEAD NOW!
EXPLORER CLASS IS ABOUT TO BEGIN!
NEMO!
BYE, DAD!
OH, SEAWEED IS COOL, SEAWEED IS FUN...
IT MAKES ITS FOOD WITH THE RAYS OF THE SUUUUUUUN.
A FISH'S FIN GOES FLIPPY-FLIP-FLIP.

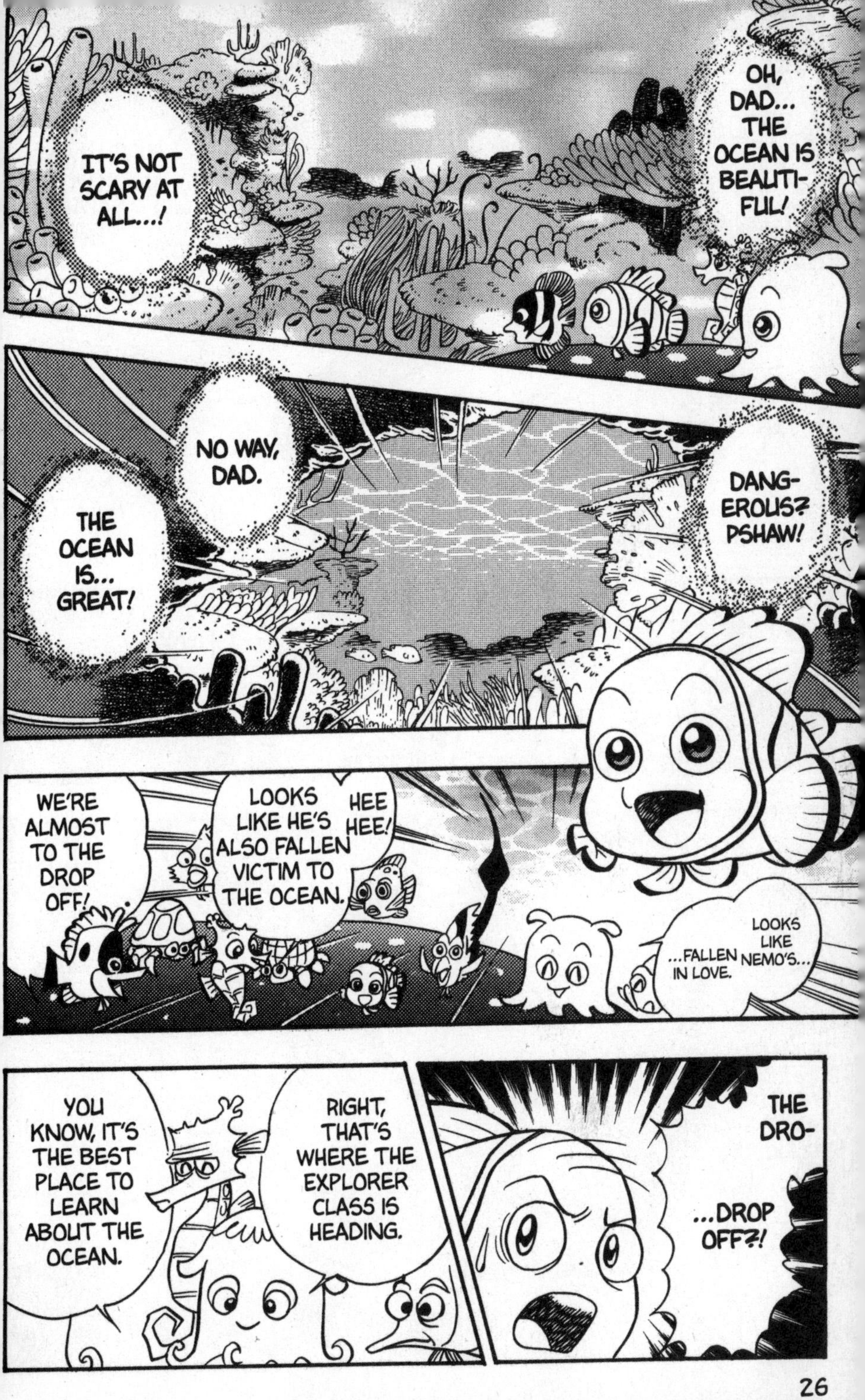
OH, DAD... THE OCEAN IS BEAUTIFUL!
IT'S NOT SCARY AT ALL...!
DANGEROUS? PSHAW!
NO WAY, DAD.
THE OCEAN IS... GREAT!
LOOKS LIKE NEMO'S...
...FALLEN IN LOVE.
HEE HEE!
LOOKS LIKE HE'S ALSO FALLEN VICTIM TO THE OCEAN.
WE'RE ALMOST TO THE DROP OFF!
THE DRO-
...DROP OFF?!
RIGHT, THAT'S WHERE THE EXPLORER CLASS IS HEADING.
YOU KNOW, IT'S THE BEST PLACE TO LEARN ABOUT THE OCEAN.

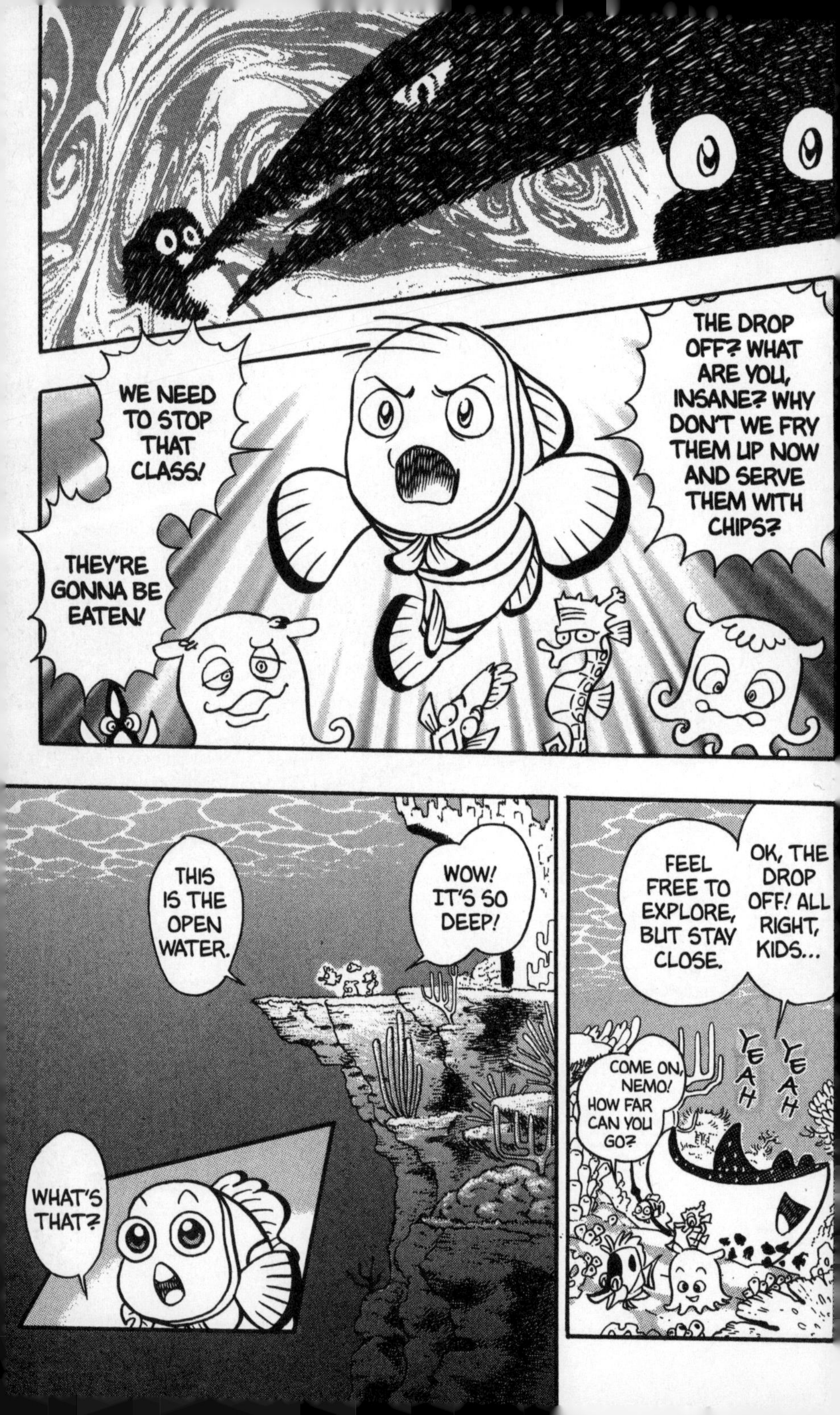
THE DROP OFF? WHAT ARE YOU, INSANE? WHY DON'T WE FRY THEM UP NOW AND SERVE THEM WITH CHIPS?
WE NEED TO STOP THAT CLASS!
THEY'RE GONNA BE EATEN!
OK, THE DROP OFF! ALL RIGHT, KIDS...
FEEL FREE TO EXPLORE, BUT STAY CLOSE.
YEAH
YEAH
COME ON, NEMO! HOW FAR CAN YOU GO?
WOW! IT'S SO DEEP!
THIS IS THE OPEN WATER.
WHAT'S THAT?

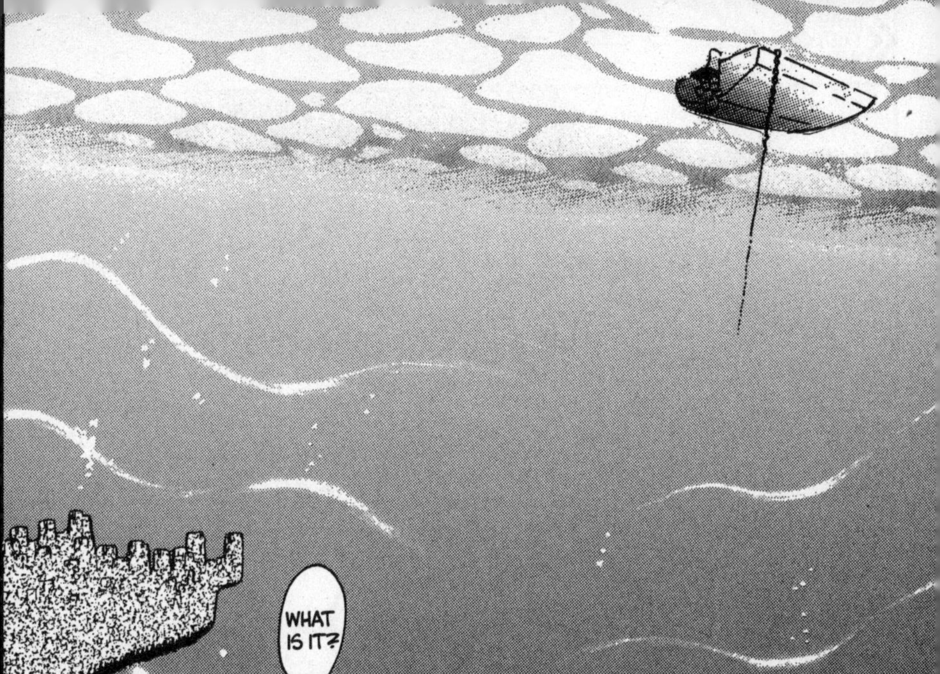
WHAT IS IT?

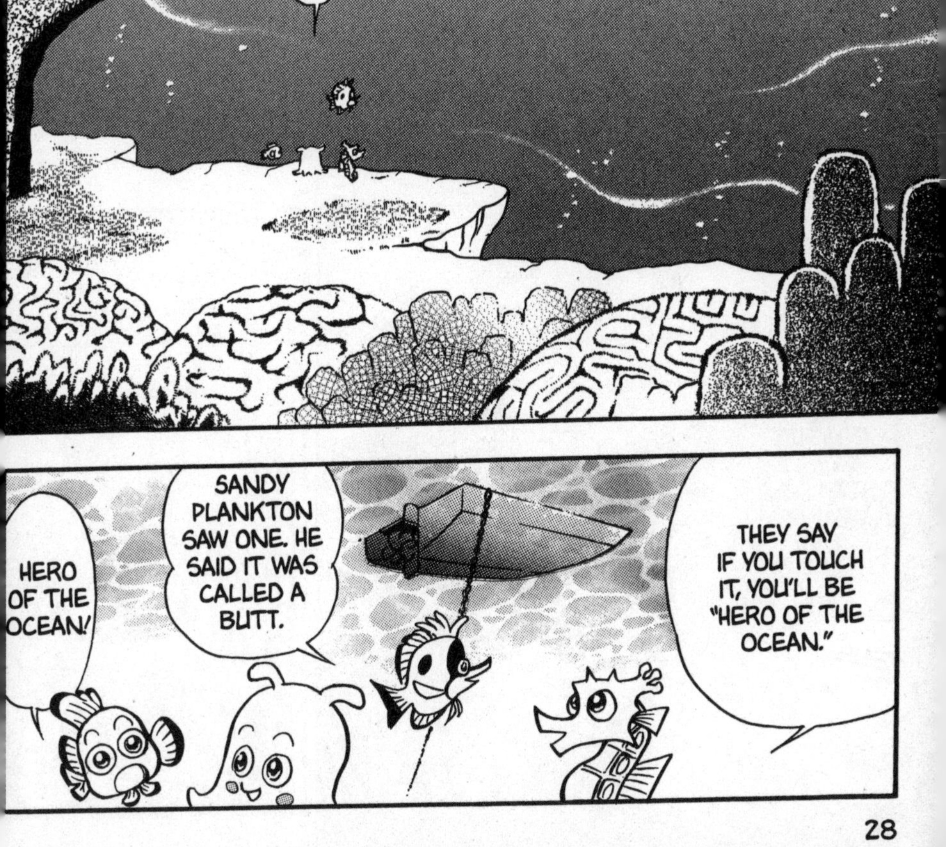
THEY SAY IF YOU TOUCH IT, YOU'LL BE "HERO OF THE OCEAN."
SANDY PLANKTON SAW ONE. HE SAID IT WAS CALLED A BUTT.
HERO OF THE OCEAN!

READ THIS WAY

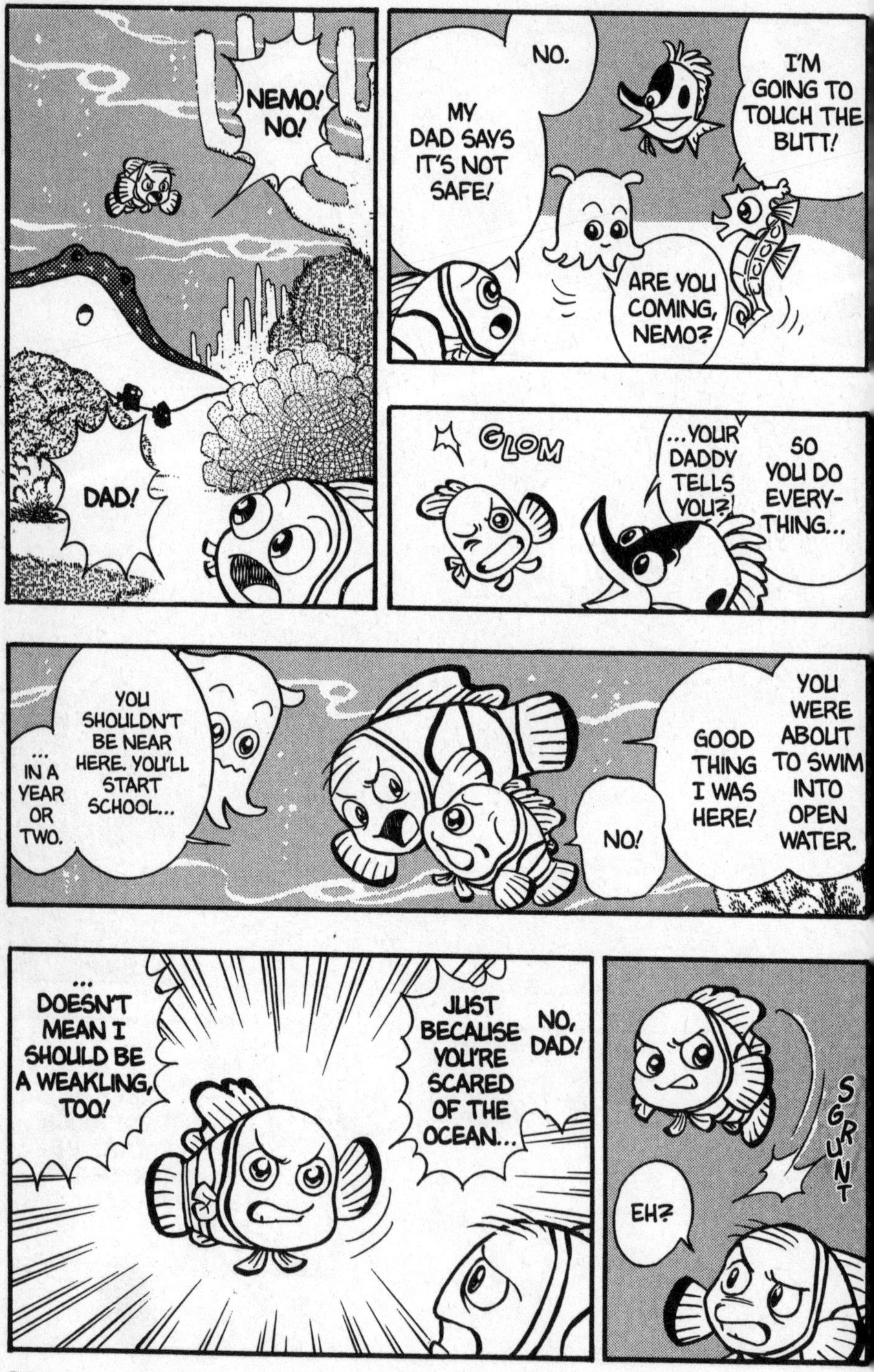

I'M GOING TO TOUCH THE BUTT!
ARE YOU COMING, NEMO?
NO.
MY DAD SAYS IT'S NOT SAFE!
SO YOU DO EVERY-THING...
...YOUR DADDY TELLS YOU?
GLOM
NEMO! NO!
DAD!
YOU WERE ABOUT TO SWIM INTO OPEN WATER.
GOOD THING I WAS HERE!
NO!
YOU SHOULDN'T BE NEAR HERE. YOU'LL START SCHOOL...
...IN A YEAR OR TWO.
SGRUNT
EH?
NO, DAD!
JUST BECAUSE YOU'RE SCARED OF THE OCEAN...
...DOESN'T MEAN I SHOULD BE A WEAKLING, TOO!

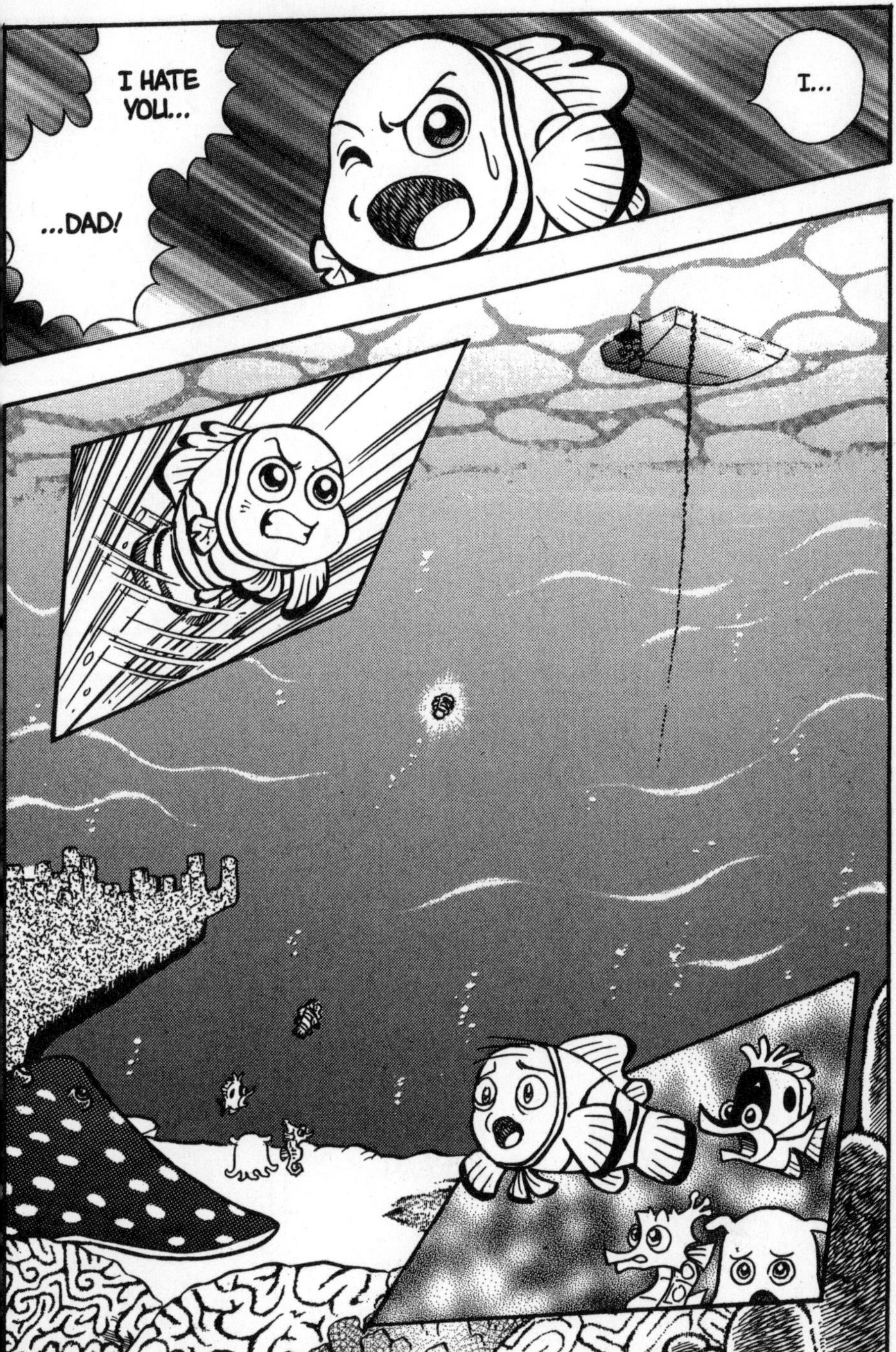
I...
I HATE YOU...
...DAD!

READ THIS WAY

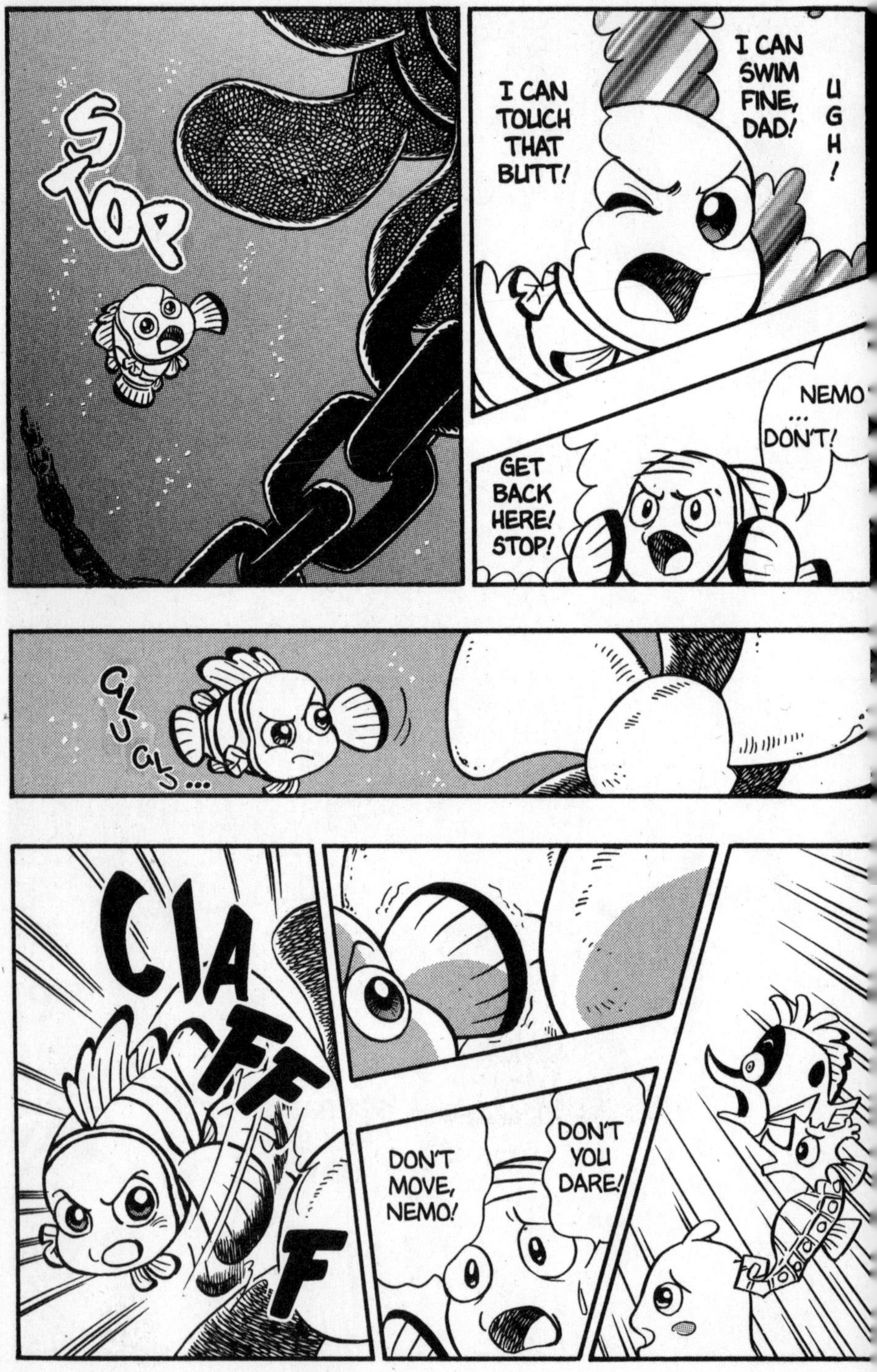

UGH!
I CAN SWIM FINE, DAD!
I CAN TOUCH THAT BUTT!
NEMO ... DON'T!
GET BACK HERE! STOP!
STOP
GLUG GLUG...
DON'T YOU DARE!
DON'T MOVE, NEMO!
CIAFFF

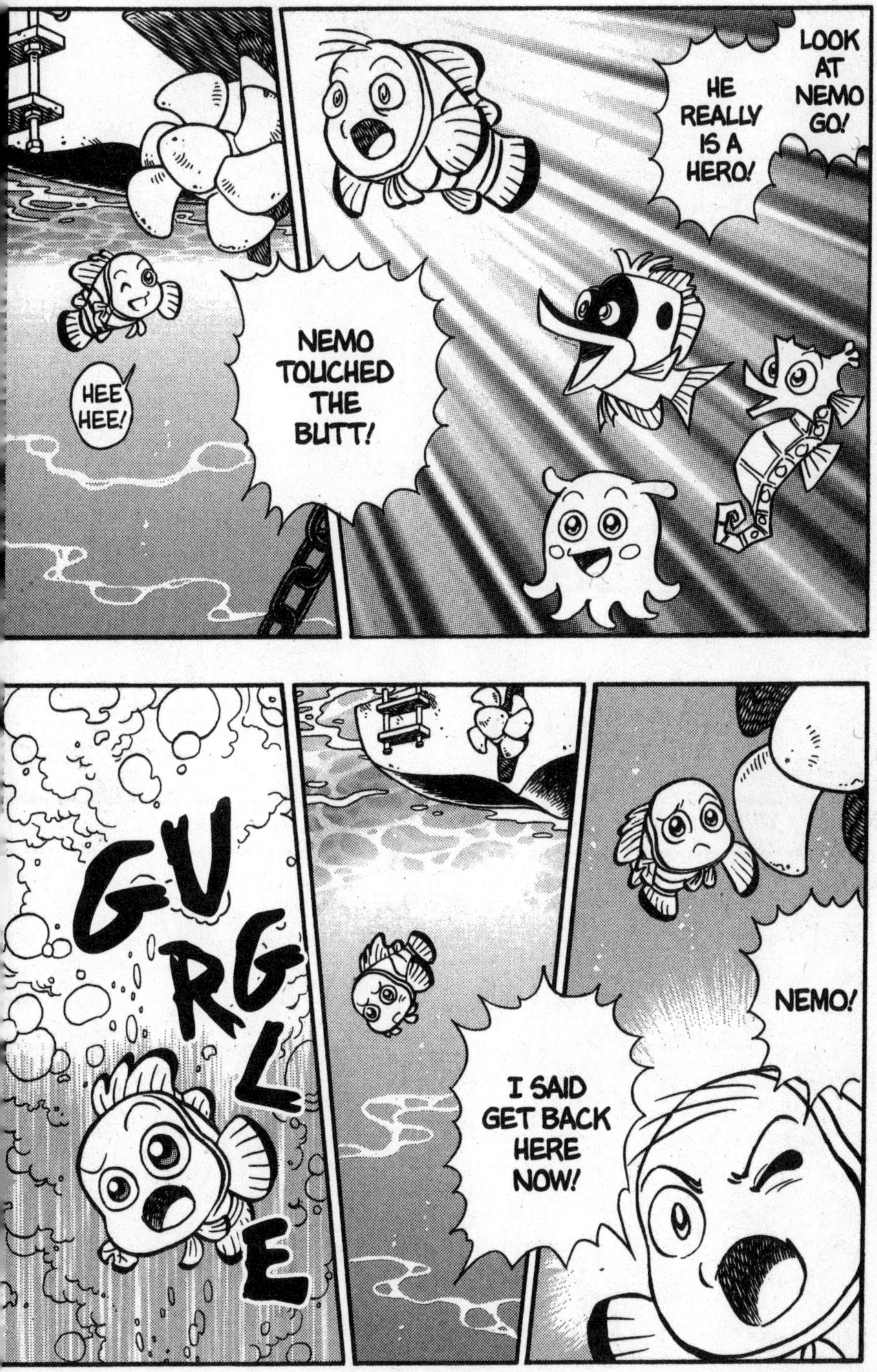
LOOK AT NEMO GO!
HE REALLY IS A HERO!
NEMO TOUCHED THE BUTT!
HEE HEE!
NEMO!
I SAID GET BACK HERE NOW!
GURGLE

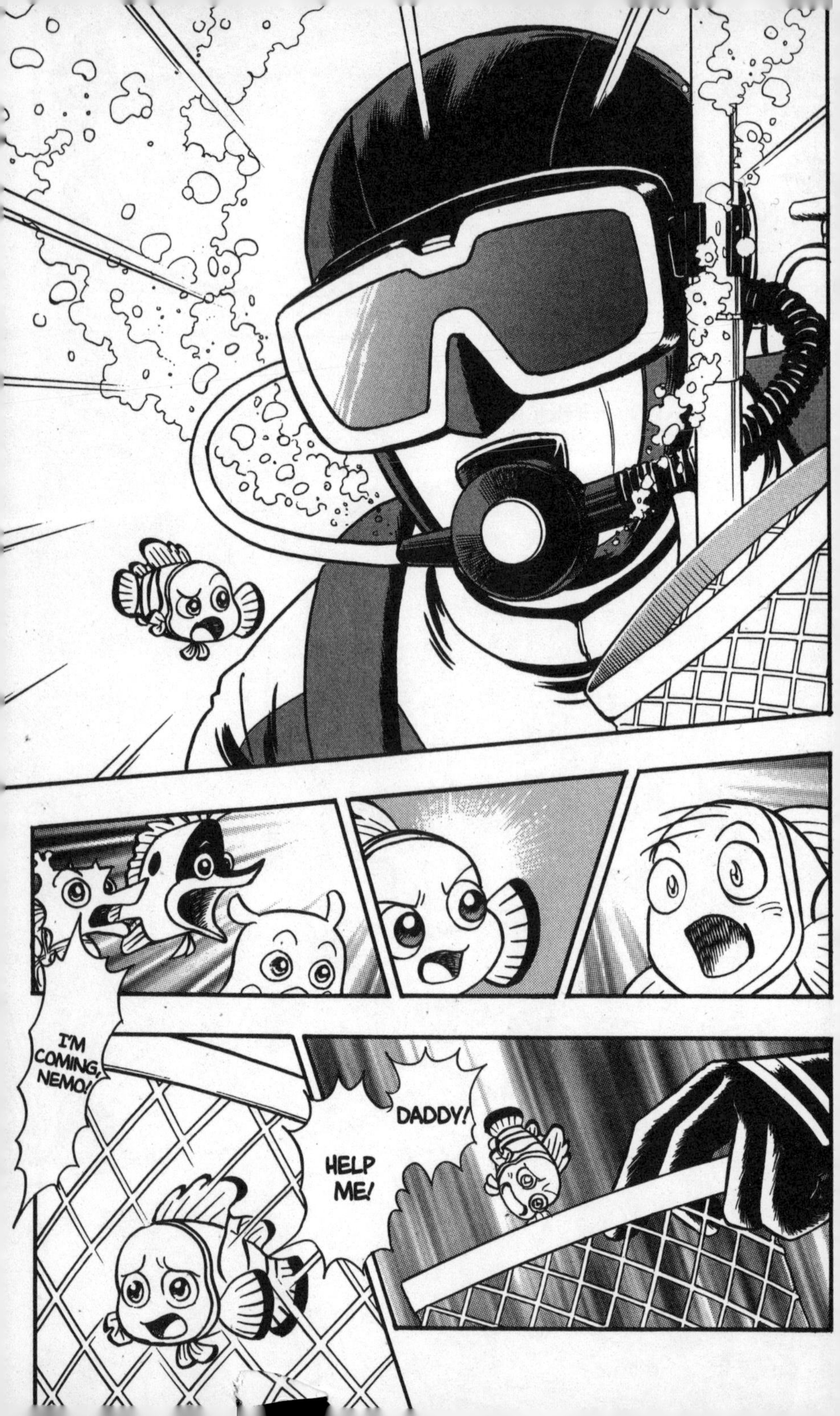
DADDY!
HELP ME!
I'M COMING, NEMO!

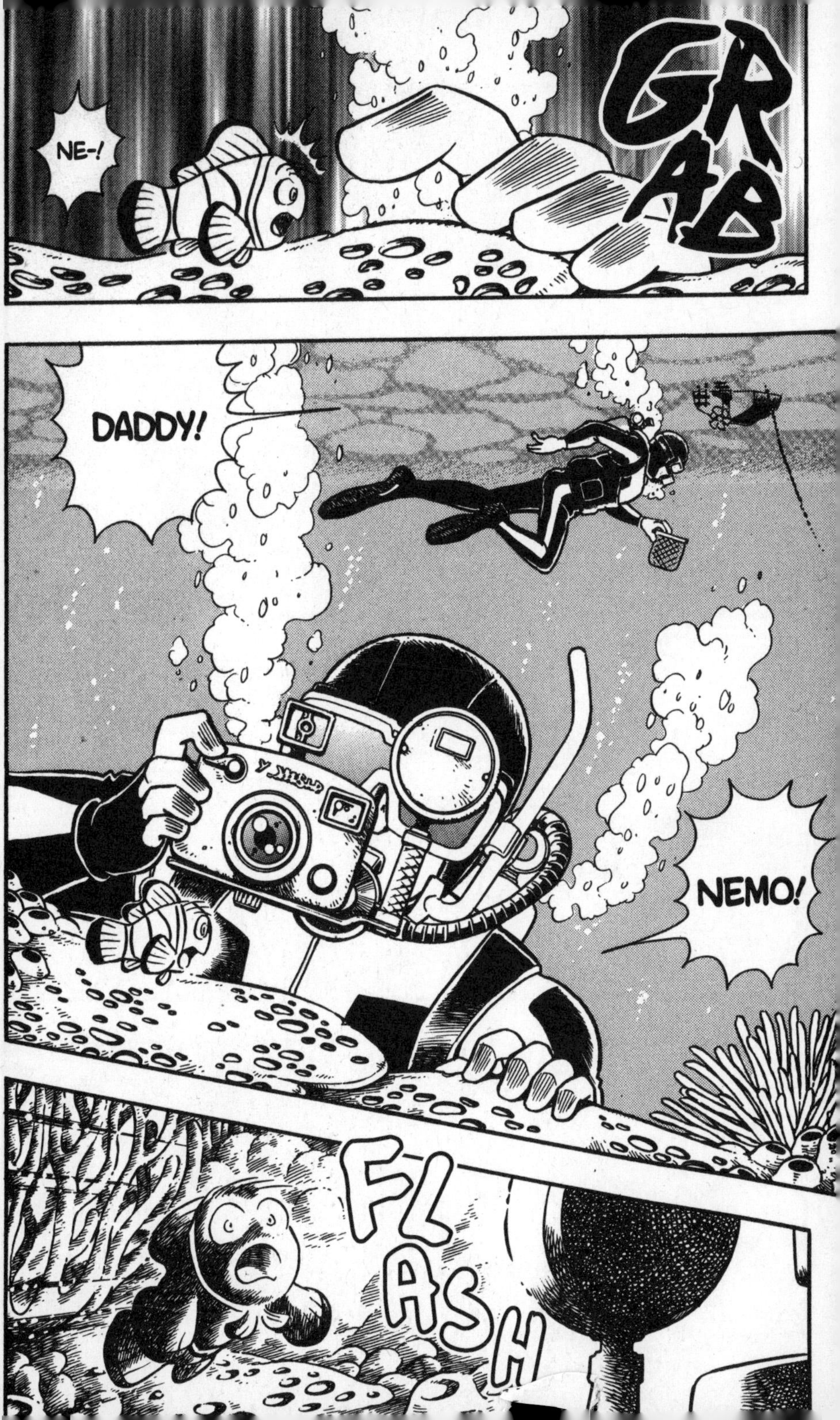
GRAB
NE-!
DADDY!
NEMO!
FLASH

READ THIS WAY

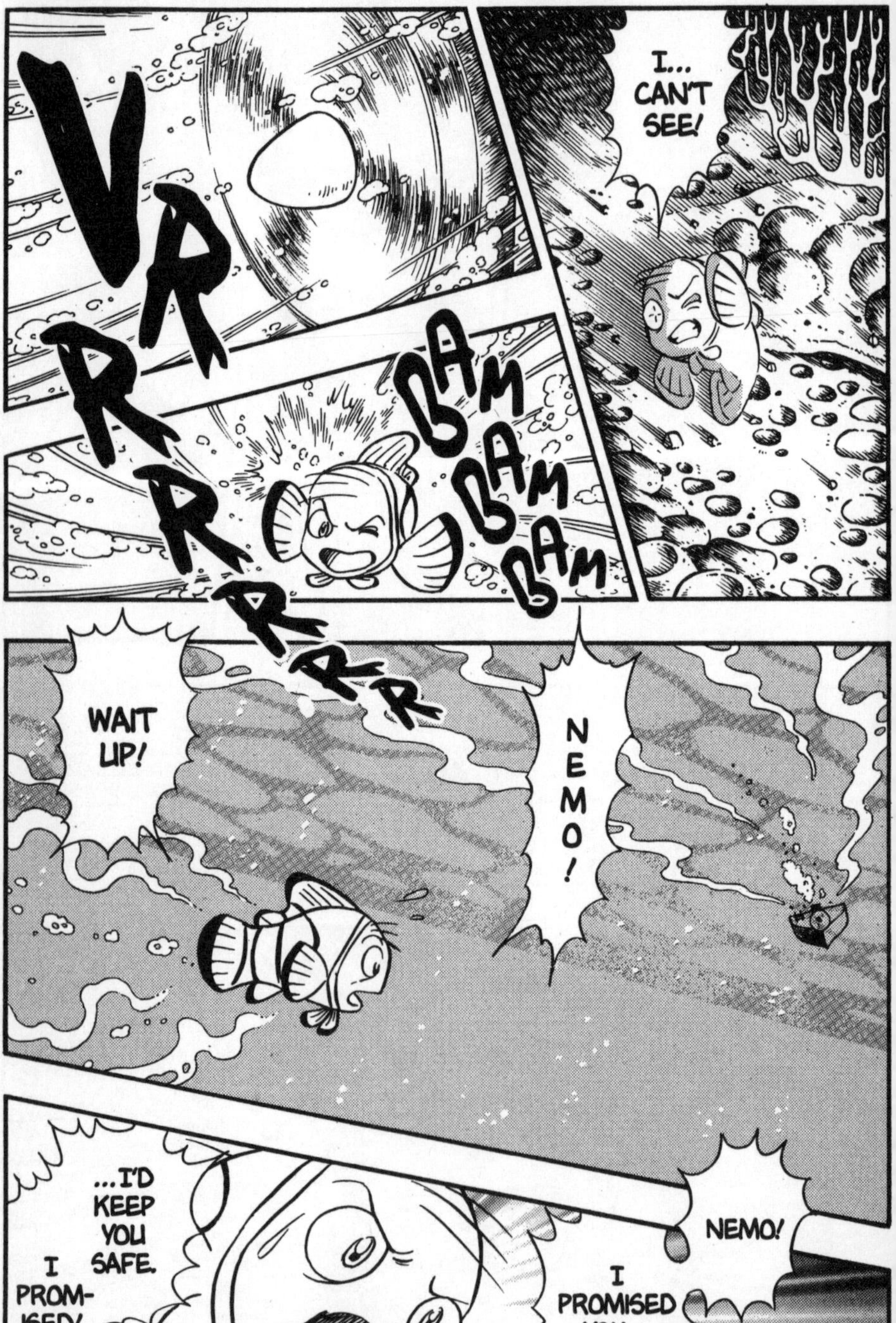
I... CAN'T SEE!
VRRRRRRR
BAM BAM BAM
NEMO!
WAIT UP!
NEMO!
I PROMISED YOU...
...I'D KEEP YOU SAFE.
I PROMISED!

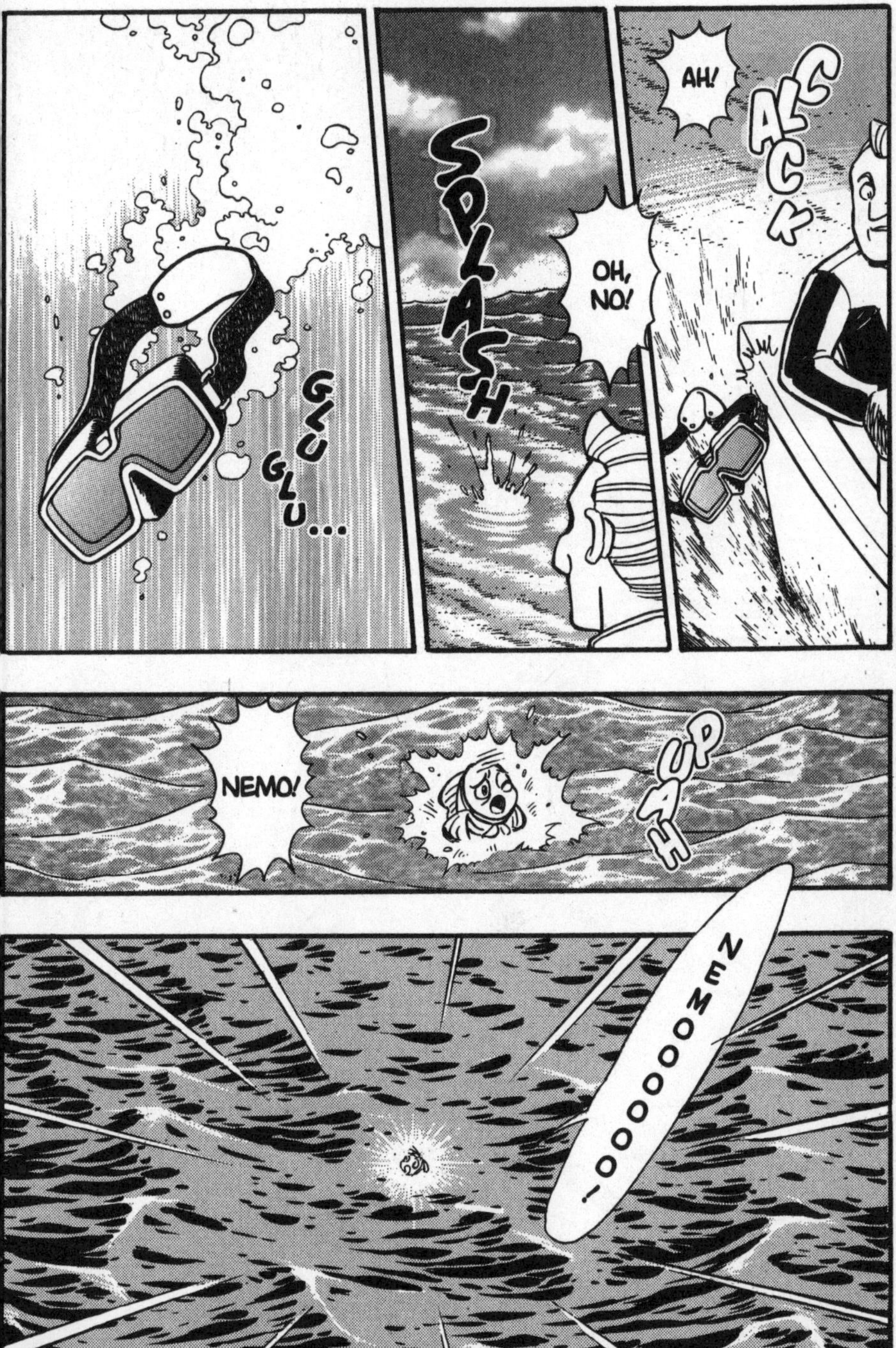
AH!
ALCCK
OH, NO!
SPLASH
GLU GLU...
UPAH
NEMO!
NEMOOOOOOO!

READ THIS WAY

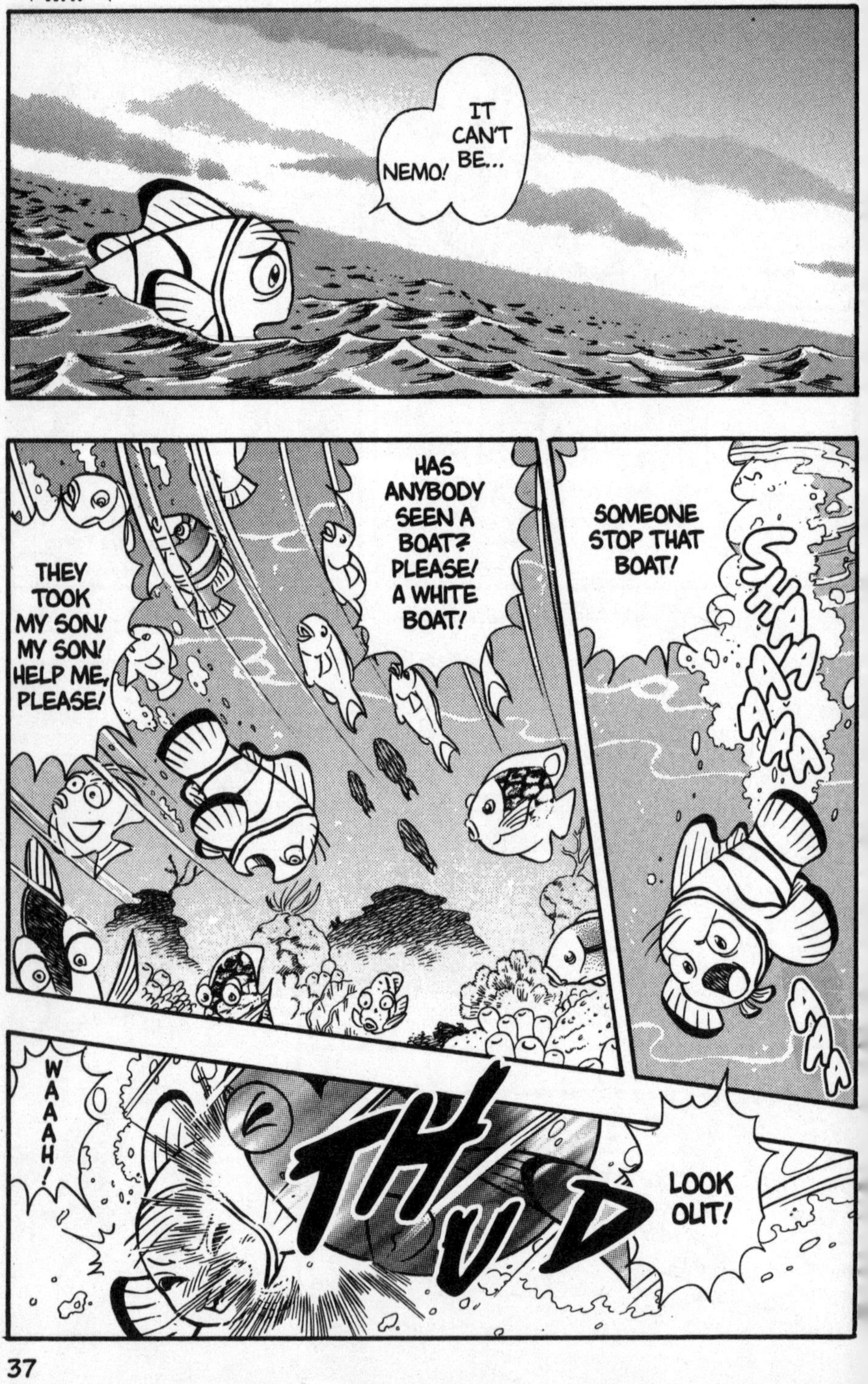

IT CAN'T BE...
NEMO!
SOMEONE STOP THAT BOAT!
SHAAAAAAA
AAA
HAS ANYBODY SEEN A BOAT? PLEASE! A WHITE BOAT!
THEY TOOK MY SON! MY SON! HELP ME, PLEASE!
LOOK OUT!
THUD
WAAAAH!

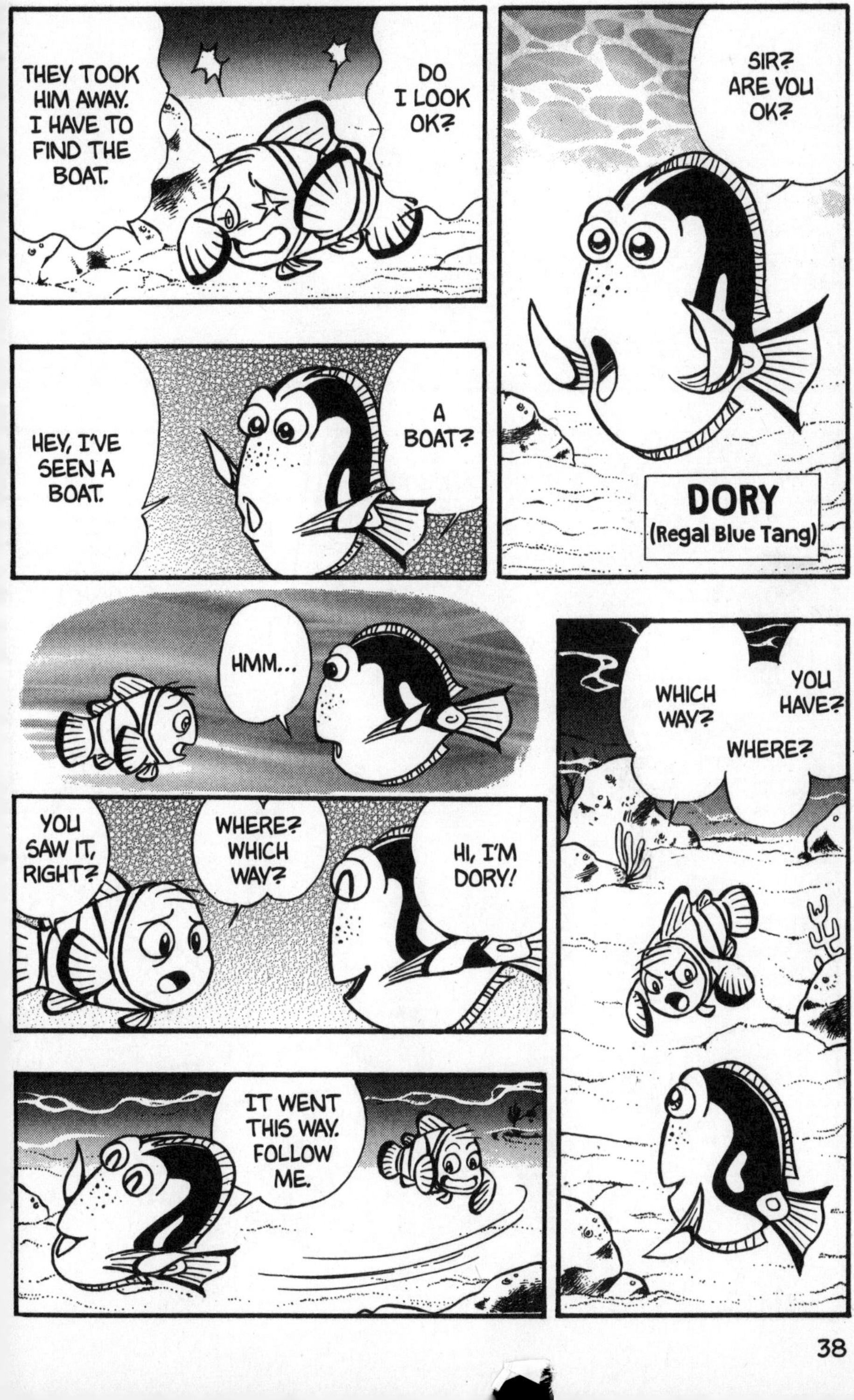
SIR? ARE YOU OK?
DORY (Regal Blue Tang)
DO I LOOK OK?
THEY TOOK HIM AWAY. I HAVE TO FIND THE BOAT.
A BOAT?
HEY, I'VE SEEN A BOAT.
YOU HAVE?
WHICH WAY?
WHERE?
HMM...
HI, I'M DORY!
WHERE? WHICH WAY?
YOU SAW IT, RIGHT?
IT WENT THIS WAY. FOLLOW ME.

READ THIS WAY

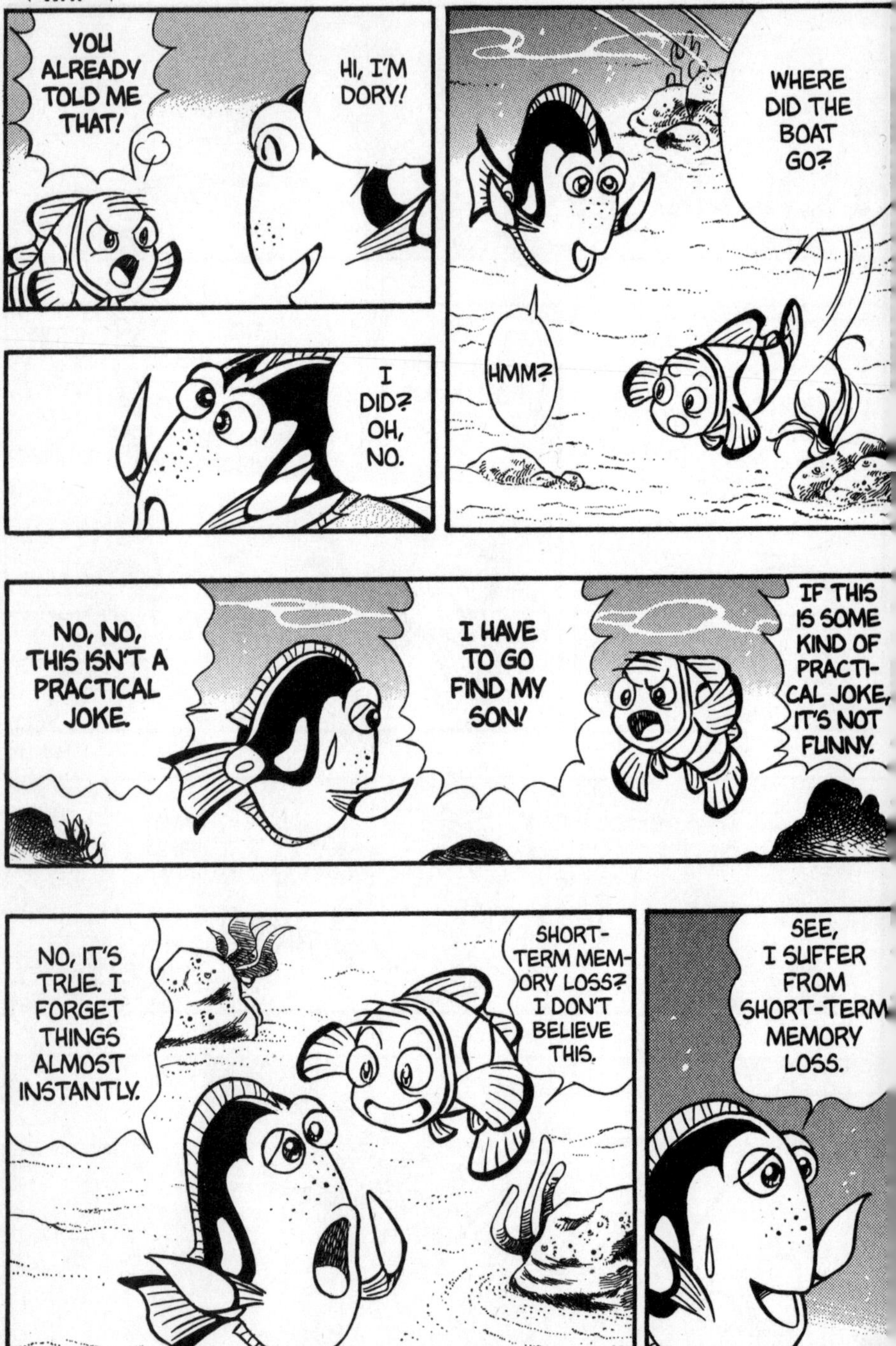

WHERE DID THE BOAT GO?
HMM?
HI, I'M DORY!
YOU ALREADY TOLD ME THAT!
I DID? OH, NO.
IF THIS IS SOME KIND OF PRACTICAL JOKE, IT'S NOT FUNNY.
I HAVE TO GO FIND MY SON!
NO, NO, THIS ISN'T A PRACTICAL JOKE.
SEE, I SUFFER FROM SHORT-TERM MEMORY LOSS.
SHORT-TERM MEMORY LOSS? I DON'T BELIEVE THIS.
NO, IT'S TRUE. I FORGET THINGS ALMOST INSTANTLY.

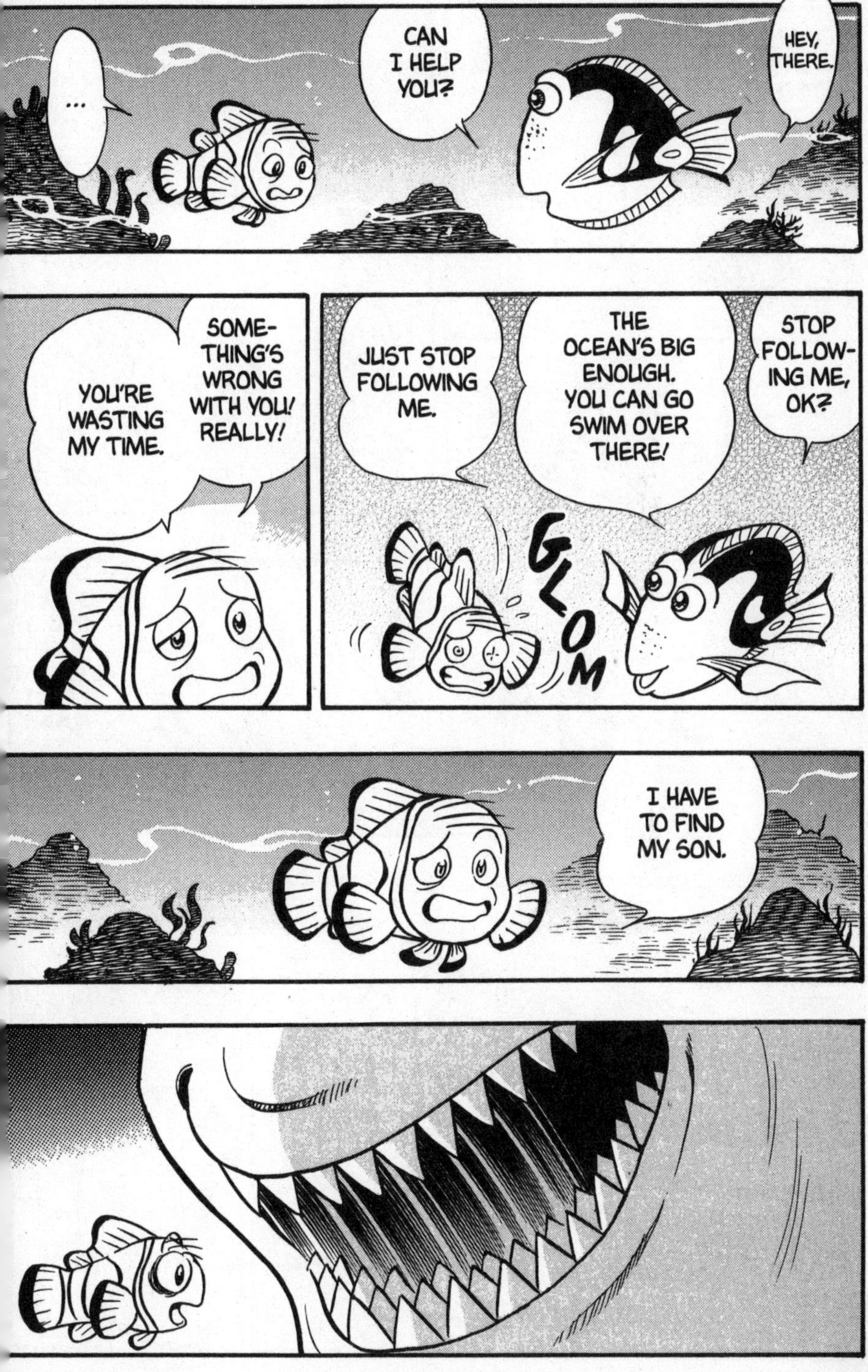
HEY, THERE.
CAN I HELP YOU?
...
STOP FOLLOWING ME, OK?
THE OCEAN'S BIG ENOUGH. YOU CAN GO SWIM OVER THERE!
JUST STOP FOLLOWING ME.
GLOM
SOMETHING'S WRONG WITH YOU! REALLY!
YOU'RE WASTING MY TIME.
I HAVE TO FIND MY SON.

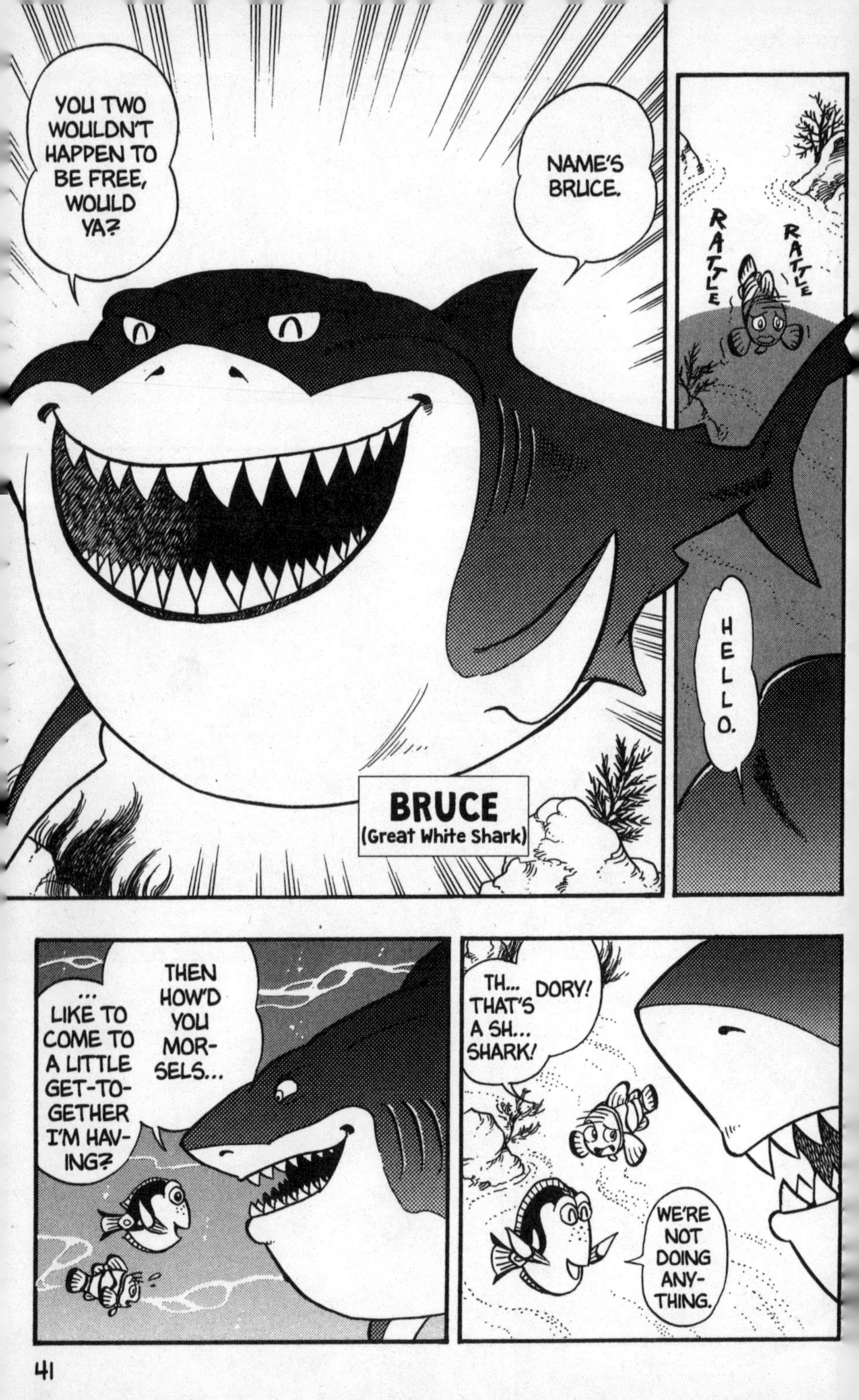
RATTLE RATTLE
HELLO.
NAME'S BRUCE.
YOU TWO WOULDN'T HAPPEN TO BE FREE, WOULD YA?
BRUCE
(Great White Shark)
DORY! TH... THAT'S A SH... SHARK!
WE'RE NOT DOING ANY-THING.
THEN HOW'D YOU MOR-SELS...
... LIKE TO COME TO A LITTLE GET-TO-GETHER I'M HAV-ING?

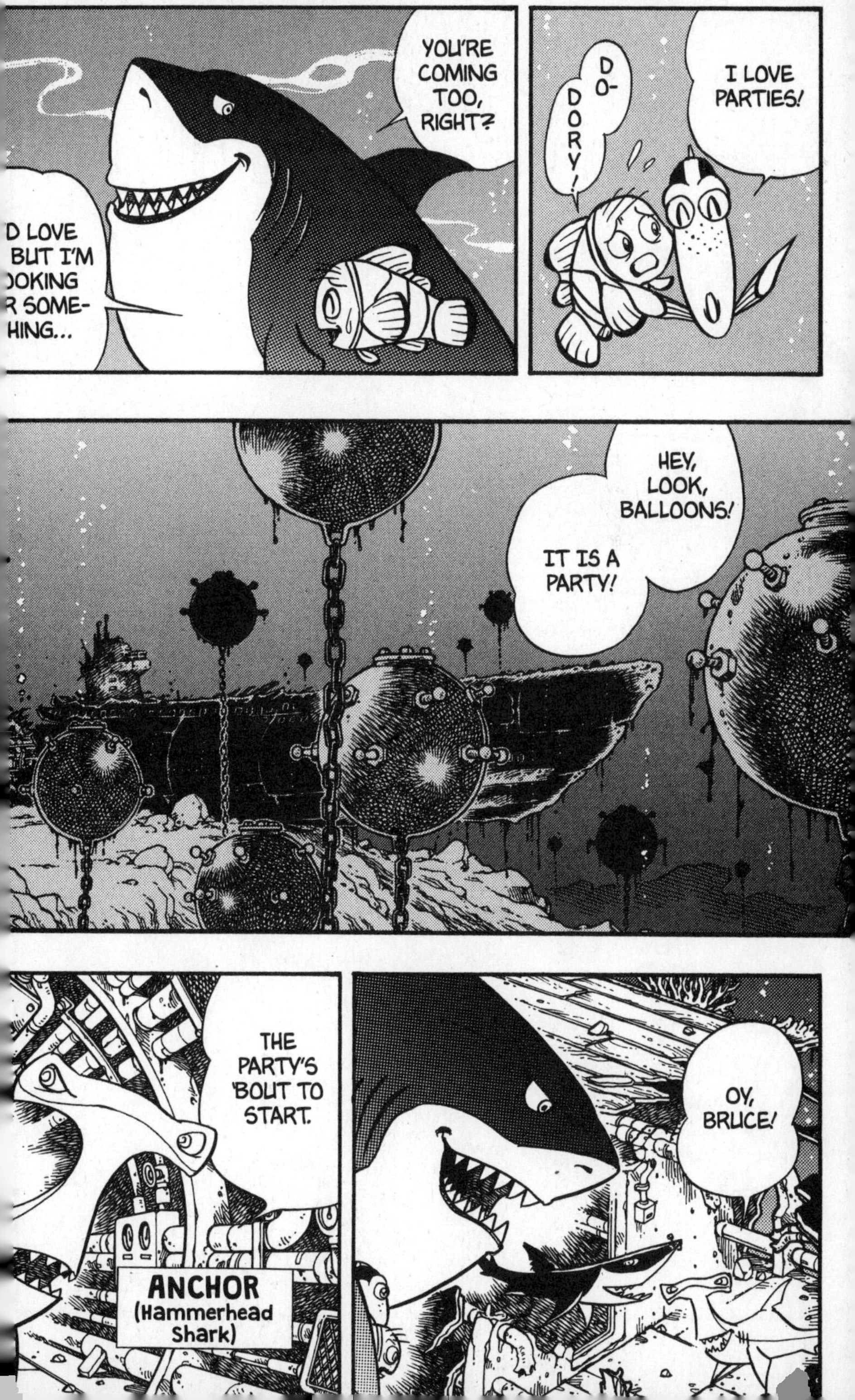

I LOVE PARTIES!
DO- DORY!
YOU'RE COMING TOO, RIGHT?
D LOVE BUT I'M OOKING R SOME- HING...
HEY, LOOK, BALLOONS!
IT IS A PARTY!
OY, BRUCE!
THE PARTY'S 'BOUT TO START.
ANCHOR (Hammerhead Shark)

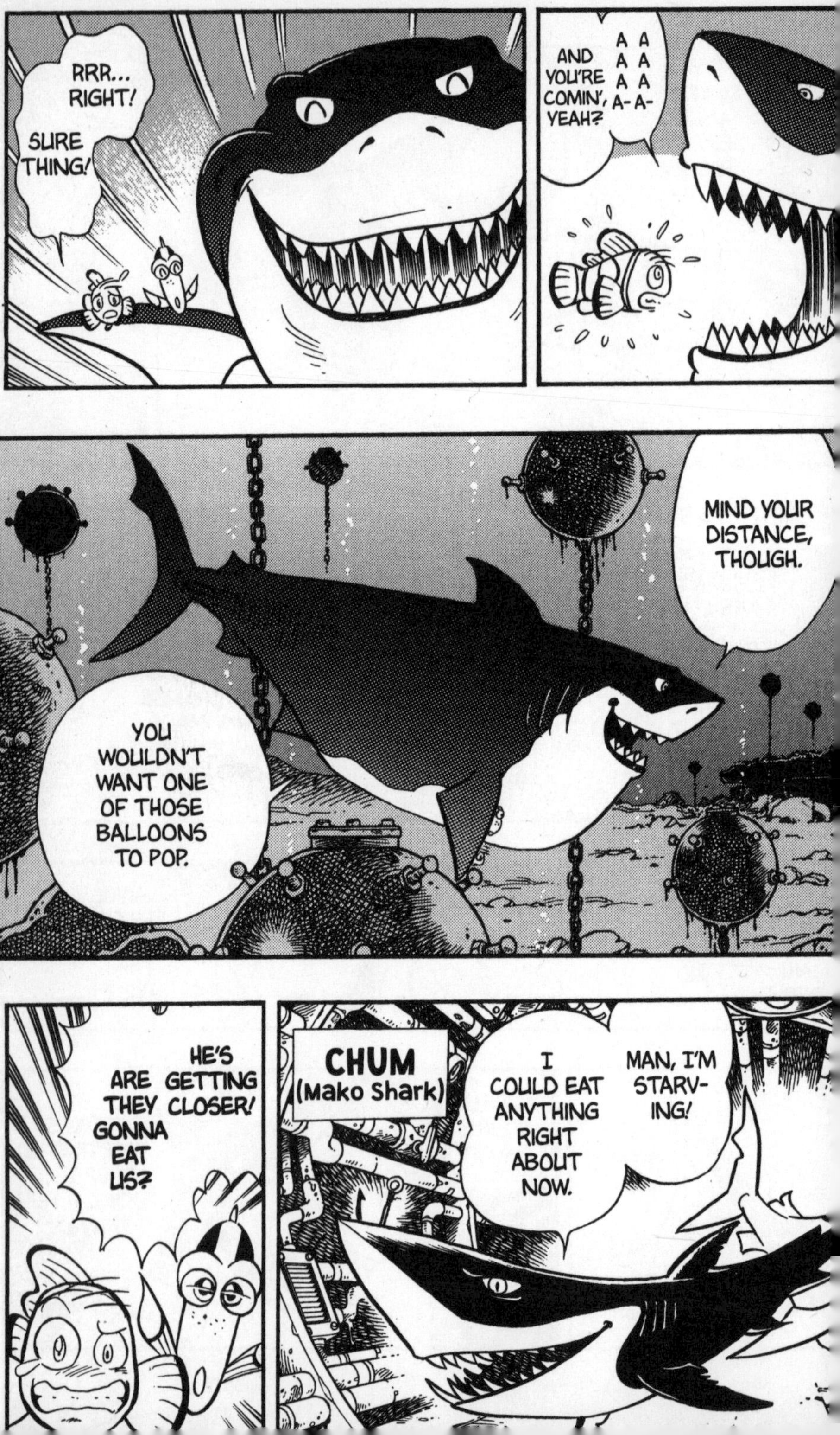
AND YOU'RE COMIN', YEAH?
A A A A A A A- A-
RRR... RIGHT!
SURE THING!
MIND YOUR DISTANCE, THOUGH.
YOU WOULDN'T WANT ONE OF THOSE BALLOONS TO POP.
CHUM (Mako Shark)
MAN, I'M STARV-ING!
I COULD EAT ANYTHING RIGHT ABOUT NOW.
HE'S GETTING CLOSER!
ARE THEY GONNA EAT US?

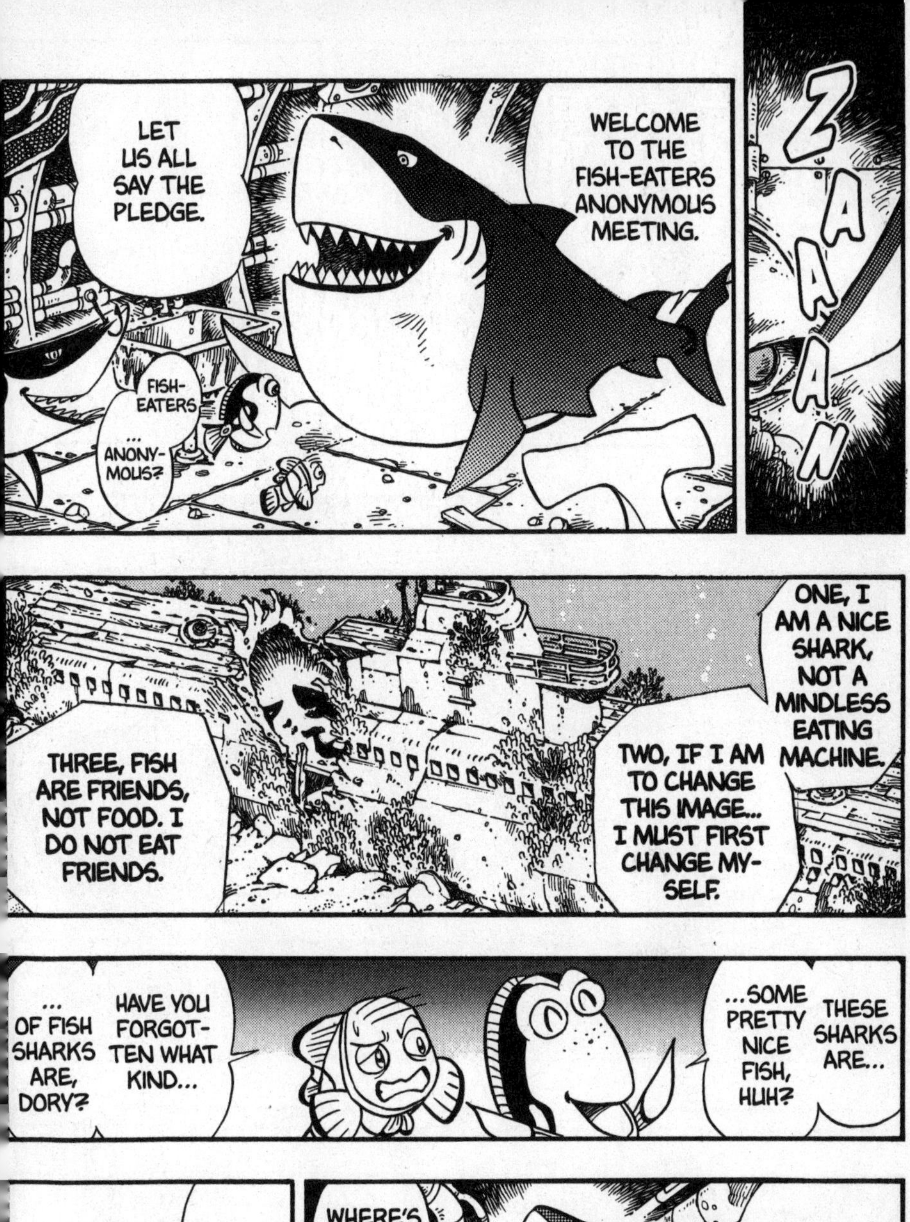
ZAAAAN
WELCOME TO THE FISH-EATERS ANONYMOUS MEETING.
LET US ALL SAY THE PLEDGE.
FISH-EATERS ... ANONYMOUS?
ONE, I AM A NICE SHARK, NOT A MINDLESS EATING MACHINE.
TWO, IF I AM TO CHANGE THIS IMAGE... I MUST FIRST CHANGE MYSELF.
THREE, FISH ARE FRIENDS, NOT FOOD. I DO NOT EAT FRIENDS.
THESE SHARKS ARE...
...SOME PRETTY NICE FISH, HUH?
HAVE YOU FORGOTTEN WHAT KIND...
... OF FISH SHARKS ARE, DORY?
TODAY'S MEETING IS STEP 5 ... "BRING A FISH FRIEND."
WHERE'S YOURS, CHUM?
OH, I SEEM TO HAVE...

READ THIS WAY

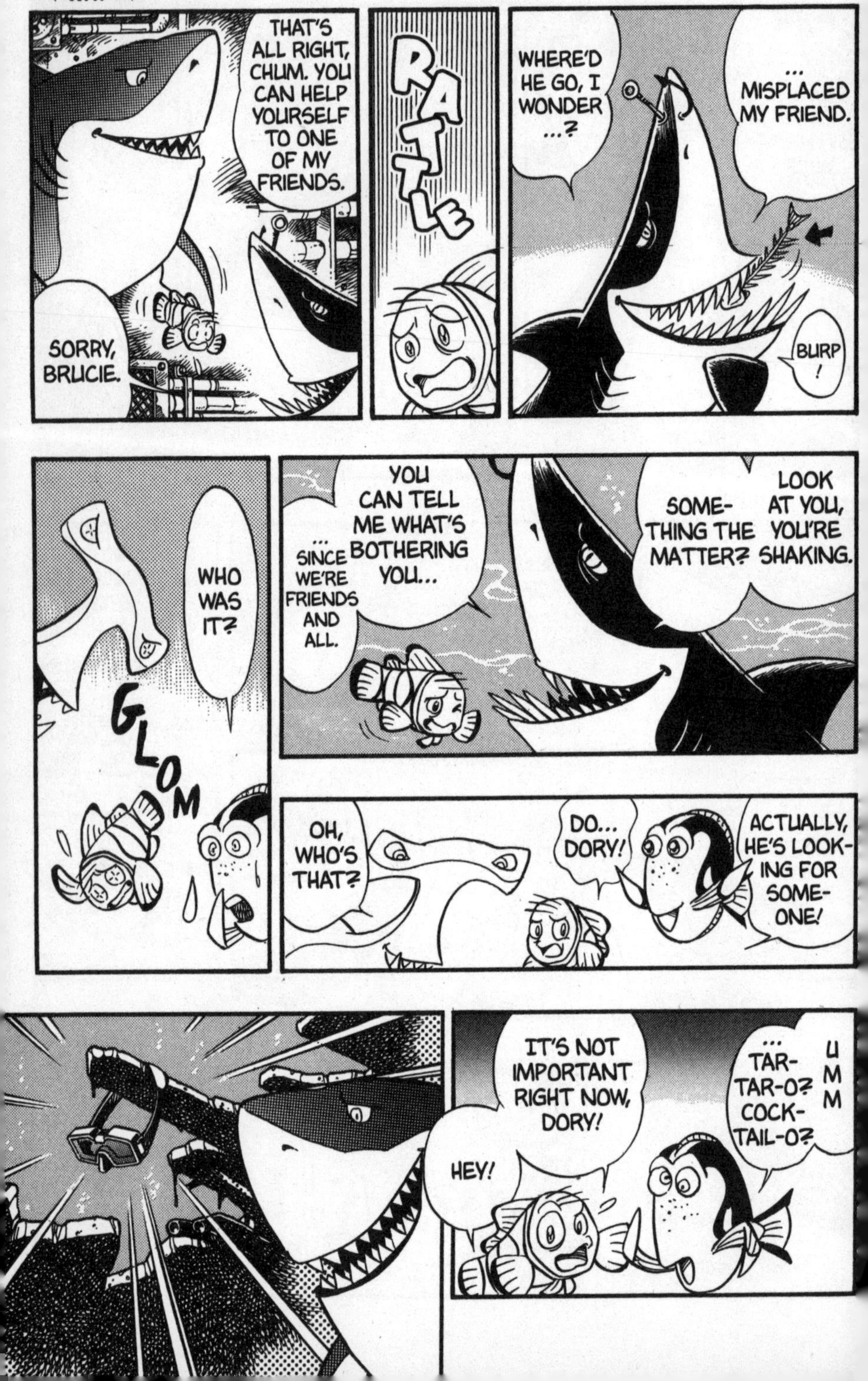

... MISPLACED MY FRIEND.
WHERE'D HE GO, I WONDER ...?
BURP!
RATTLE
THAT'S ALL RIGHT, CHUM. YOU CAN HELP YOURSELF TO ONE OF MY FRIENDS.
SORRY, BRUCIE.
LOOK AT YOU, YOU'RE SHAKING.
SOMETHING THE MATTER?
YOU CAN TELL ME WHAT'S BOTHERING YOU...
... SINCE WE'RE FRIENDS AND ALL.
ACTUALLY, HE'S LOOKING FOR SOMEONE!
DO... DORY!
OH, WHO'S THAT?
WHO WAS IT?
GLOM
UMM
... TAR-TAR-O? COCK-TAIL-O?
IT'S NOT IMPORTANT RIGHT NOW, DORY!
HEY!

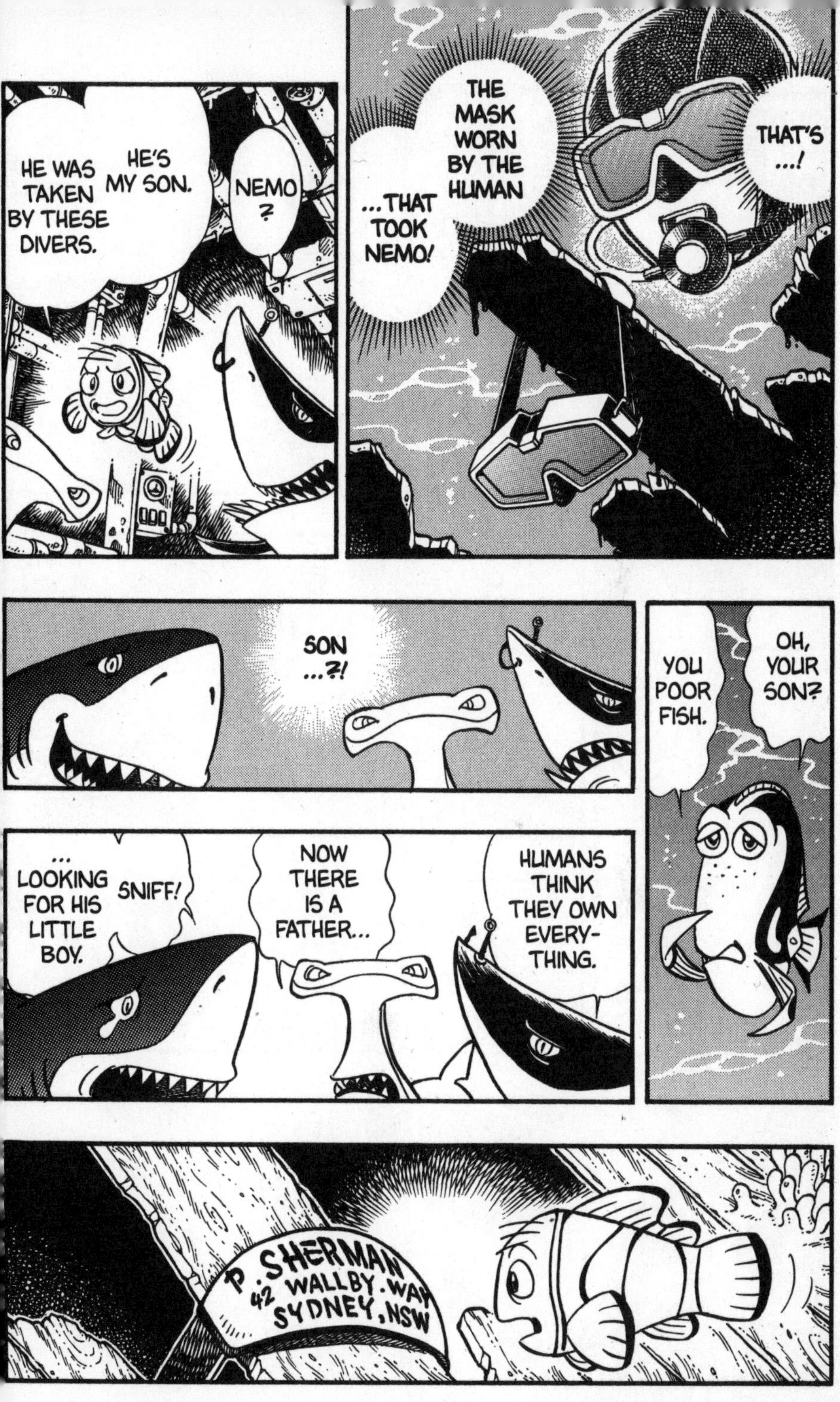
THAT'S ...!
THE MASK WORN BY THE HUMAN
...THAT TOOK NEMO!
NEMO?
HE'S MY SON.
HE WAS TAKEN BY THESE DIVERS.
OH, YOUR SON?
YOU POOR FISH.
SON ...?!
HUMANS THINK THEY OWN EVERY-THING.
NOW THERE IS A FATHER...
SNIFF!
...LOOKING FOR HIS LITTLE BOY.
P. SHERMAN 42 WALLBY. WAY SYDNEY, NSW

READ THIS WAY

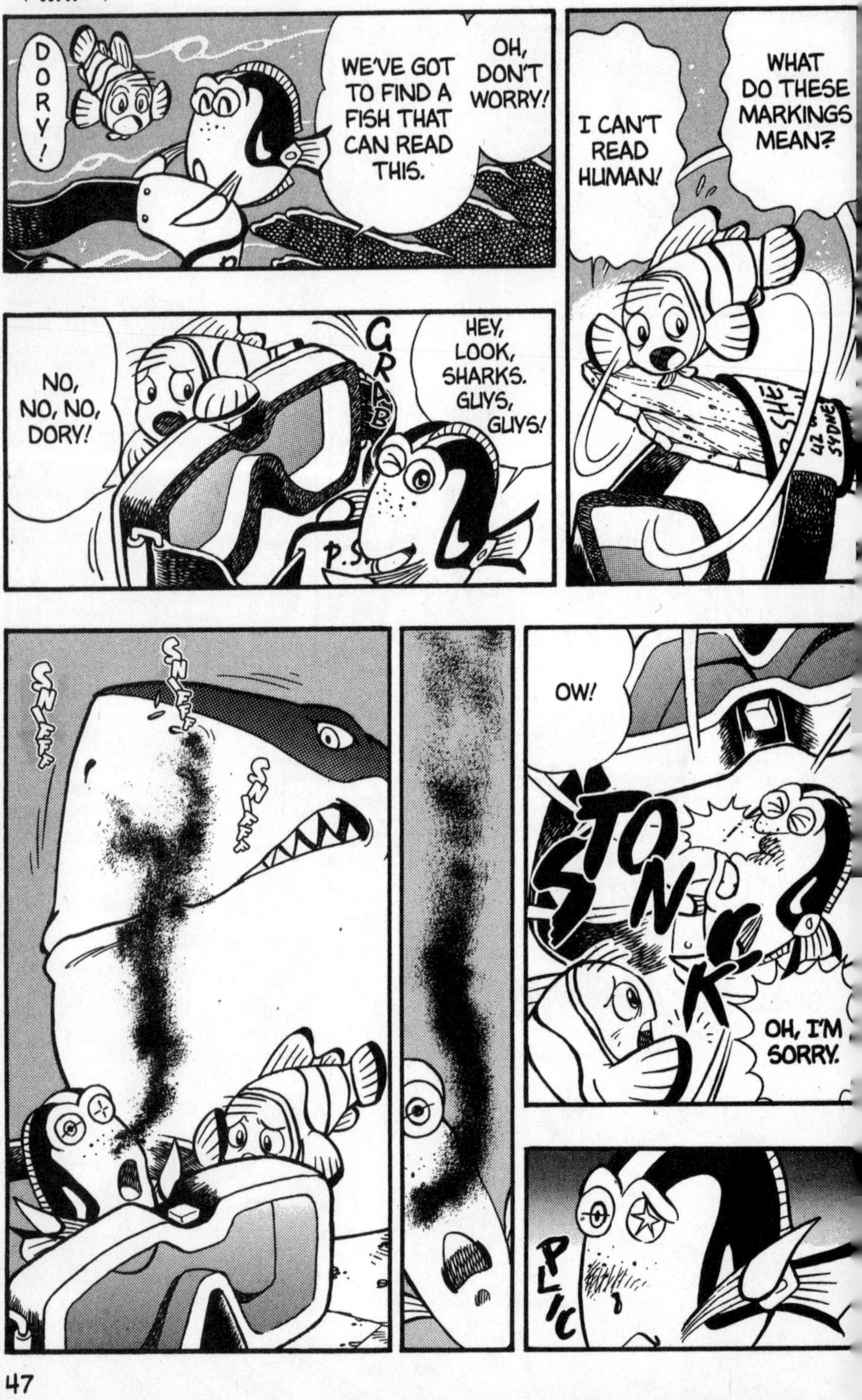
WHAT DO THESE MARKINGS MEAN?
I CAN'T READ HUMAN!
OH, DON'T WORRY!
WE'VE GOT TO FIND A FISH THAT CAN READ THIS.
DORY!
HEY, LOOK, SHARKS. GUYS, GUYS!
GRAB
NO, NO, NO, DORY!
OW!
STONK
OH, I'M SORRY.
PLIC
SNIFF
SNIFF
SNIFF

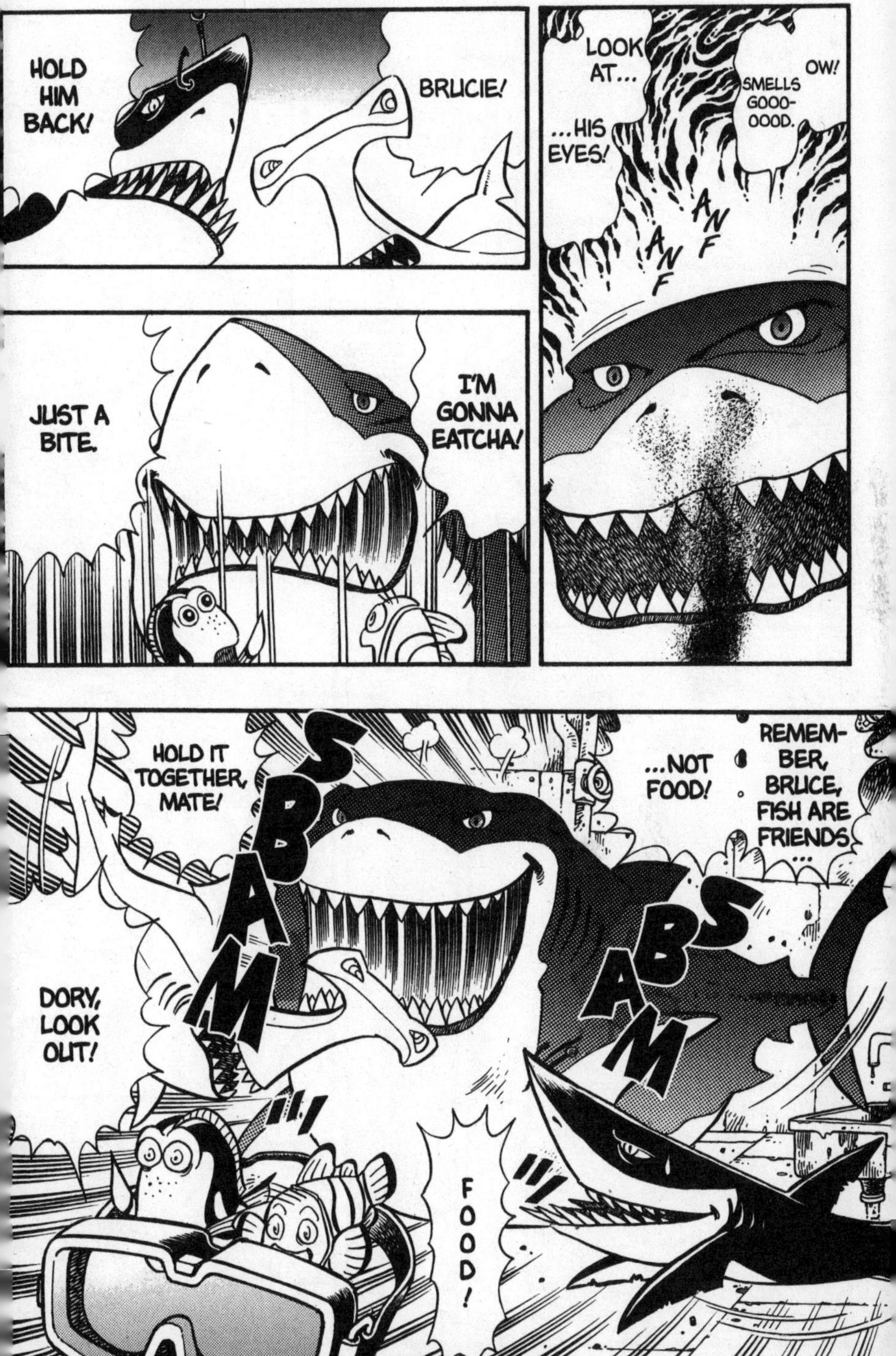
OW!
SMELLS GOOO-OOOD.
LOOK AT...
...HIS EYES!
ANF
ANF
BRUCIE!
HOLD HIM BACK!
I'M GONNA EATCHA!
JUST A BITE.
REMEM-BER, BRUCE, FISH ARE FRIENDS...
...NOT FOOD!
SBAM
HOLD IT TOGETHER, MATE!
SBAM
FOOD!
DORY, LOOK OUT!

READ THIS WAY

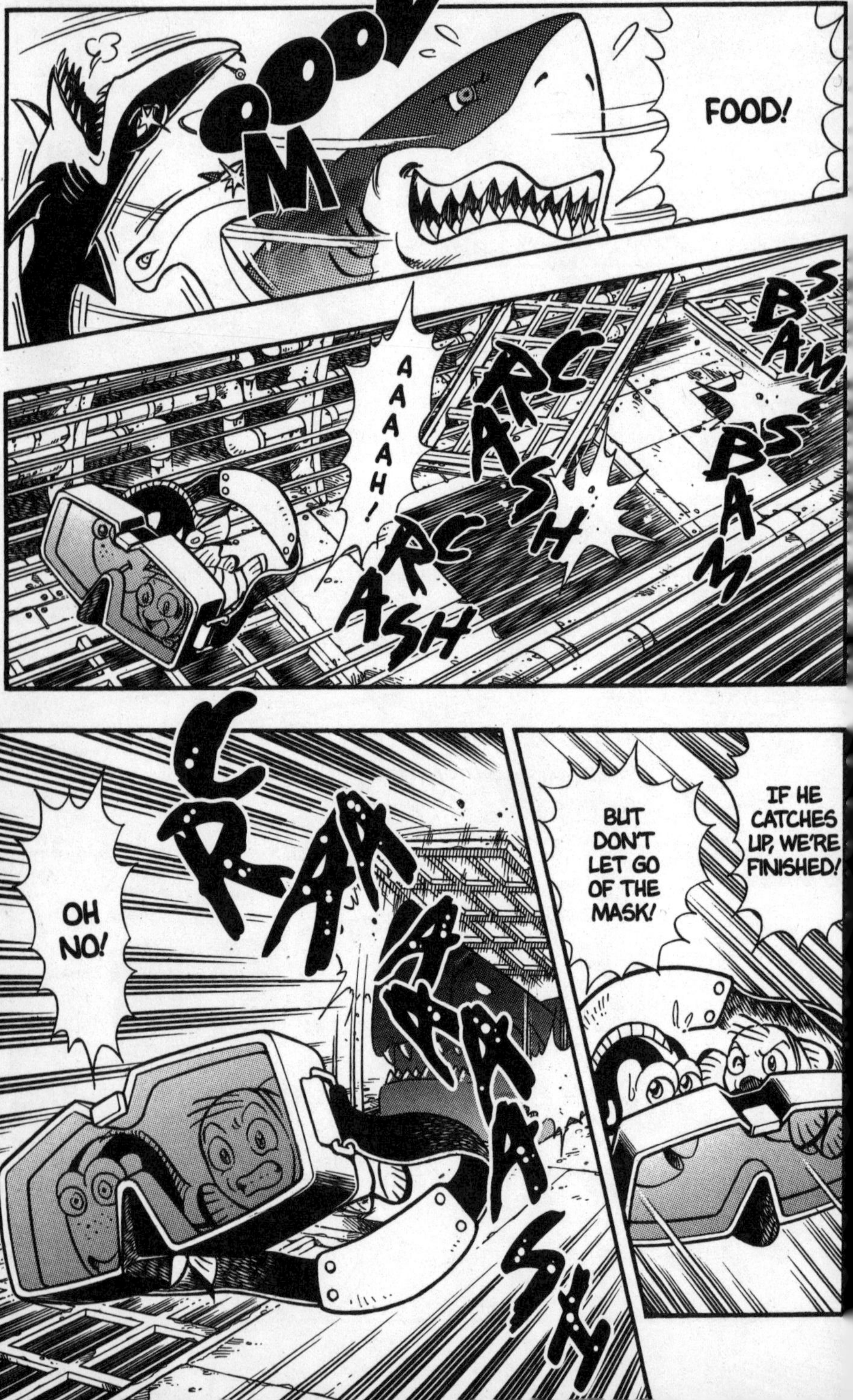

FOOD!
SBAM
SBAM
CRASH
CRASH
AAAAH!
IF HE CATCHES UP, WE'RE FINISHED!
BUT DON'T LET GO OF THE MASK!
OH NO!

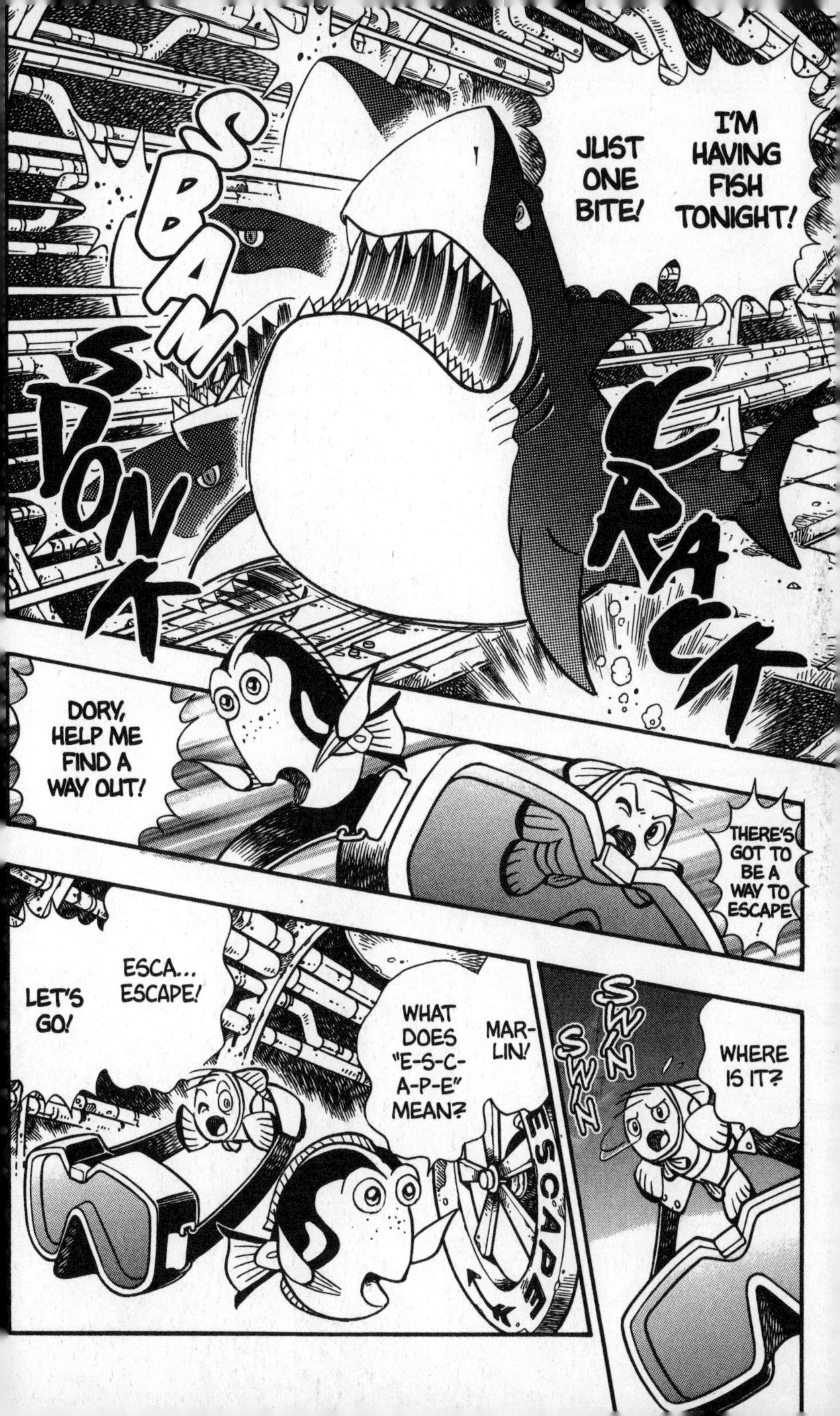

I'M HAVING FISH TONIGHT!
JUST ONE BITE!
CRACK
SBAM
DONK
THERE'S GOT TO BE A WAY TO ESCAPE!
DORY, HELP ME FIND A WAY OUT!
WHERE IS IT?
SWN SWN
MAR-LIN!
WHAT DOES "E-S-C-A-P-E" MEAN?
ESCA... ESCAPE!
LET'S GO!
ESCAPE

READ THIS WAY

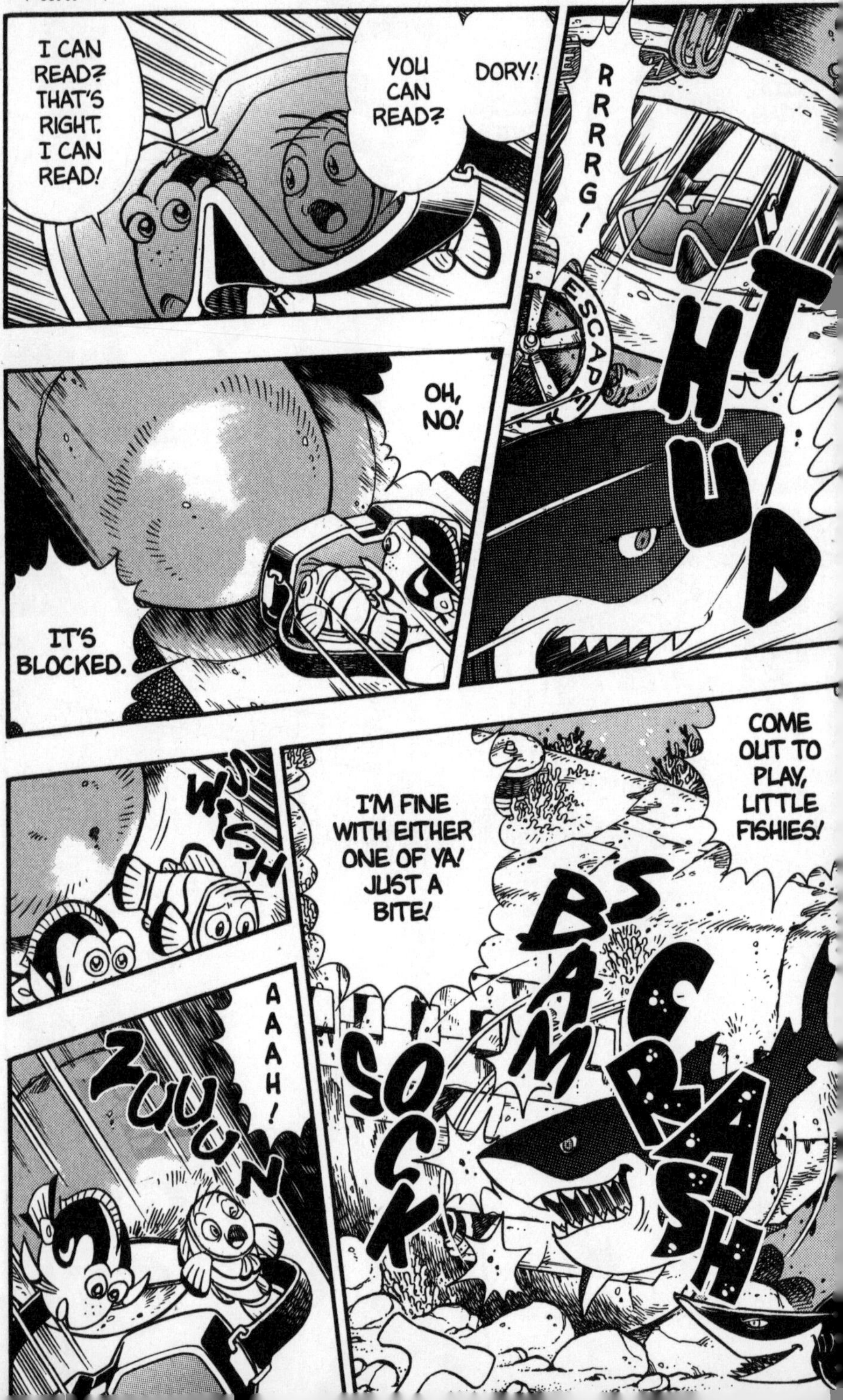

RRRRG!
THUD
DORY!
YOU CAN READ?
I CAN READ? THAT'S RIGHT. I CAN READ!
OH, NO!
IT'S BLOCKED.
COME OUT TO PLAY, LITTLE FISHIES!
I'M FINE WITH EITHER ONE OF YA! JUST A BITE!
BASH
CRASH
BAM
SOCK
SWISH
AAAAH!
ZUUUN

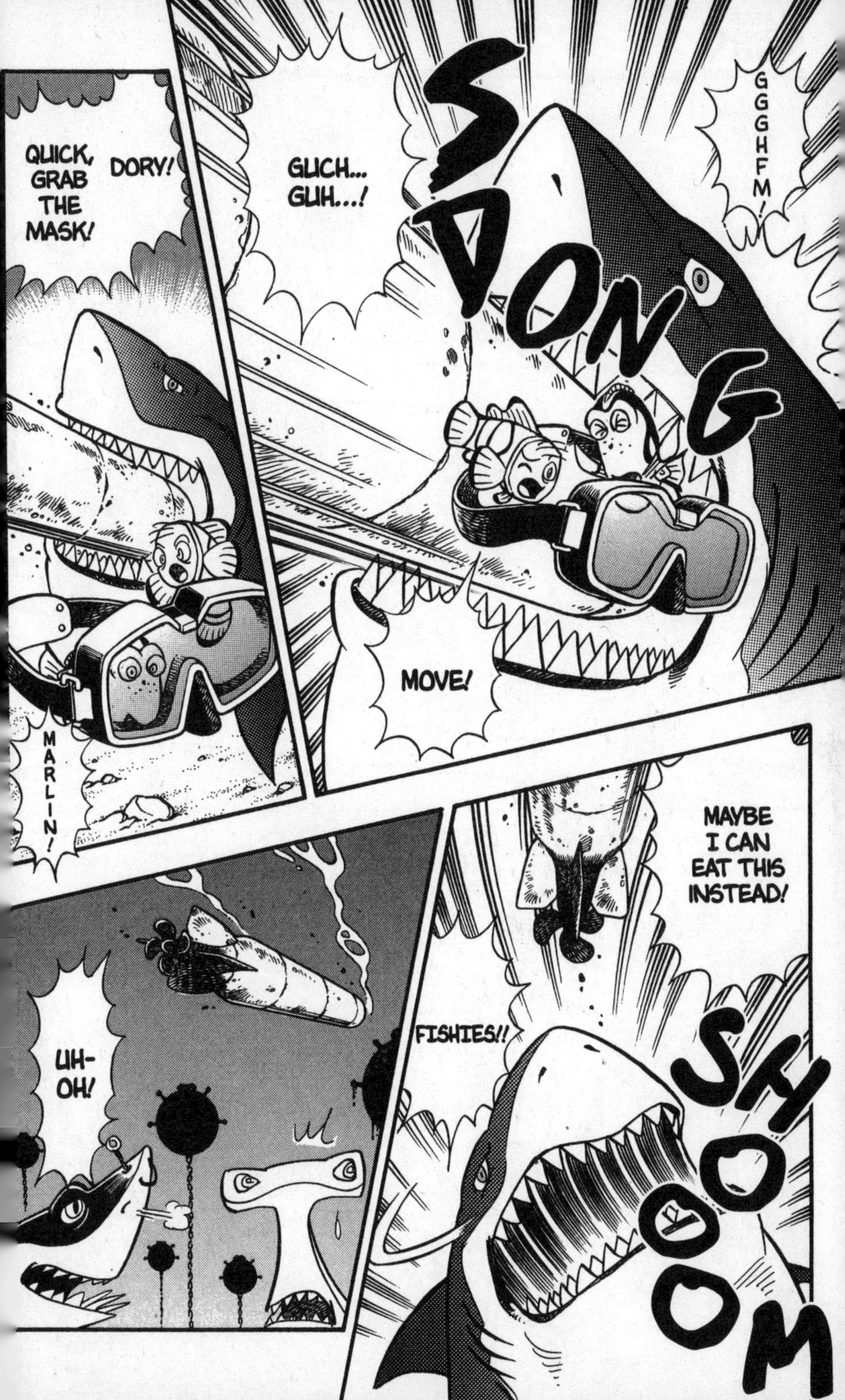
GGGHFM!
SDONG
GUCH... GUH...!
MOVE!
DORY!
QUICK, GRAB THE MASK!
MARLIN!
MAYBE I CAN EAT THIS INSTEAD!
SHOOOOM
FISHIES!!
UH-OH!

READ THIS WAY

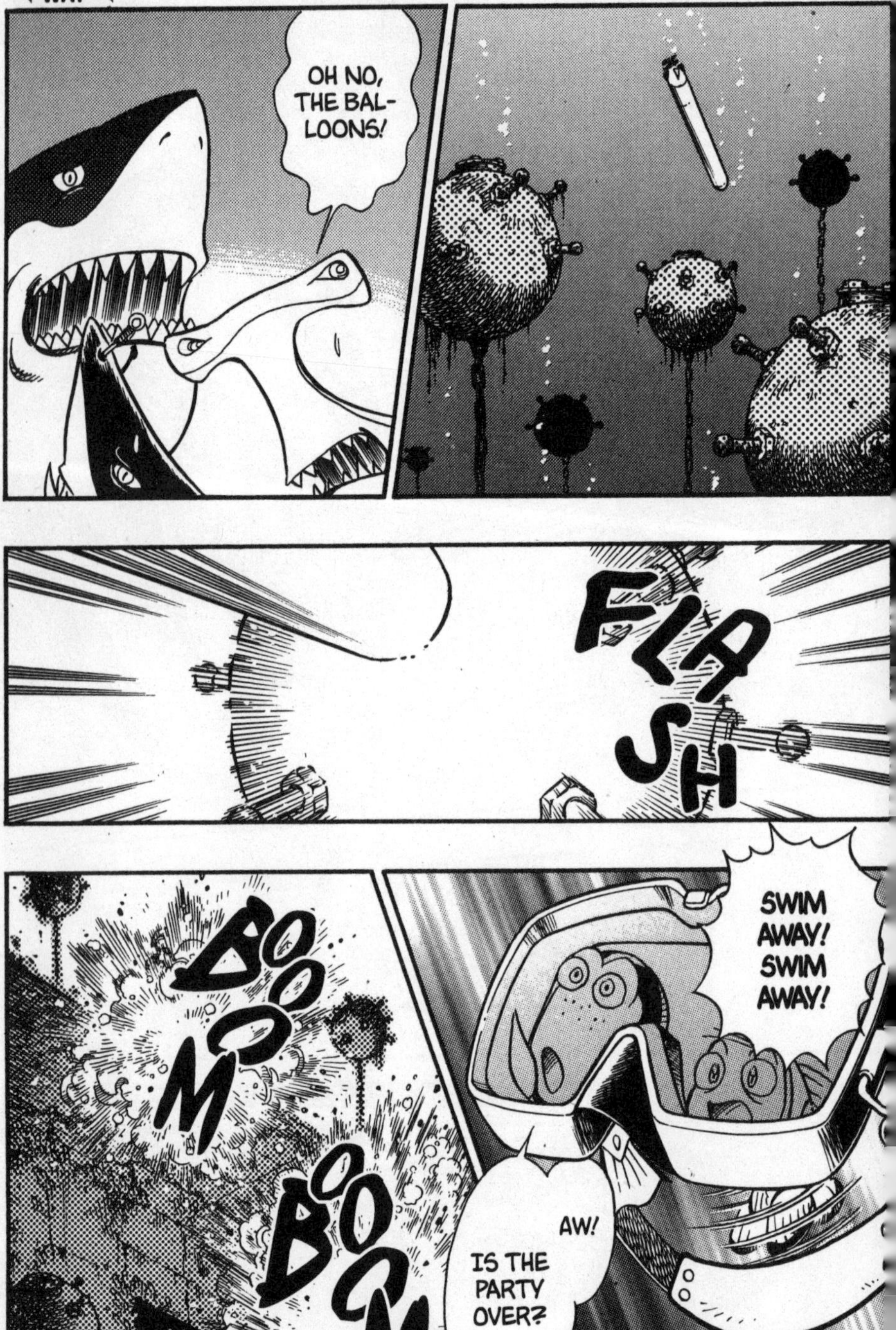
OH NO, THE BAL- LOONS!
FLASH
SWIM AWAY! SWIM AWAY!
AW! IS THE PARTY OVER?
BOOOM
BOOOM

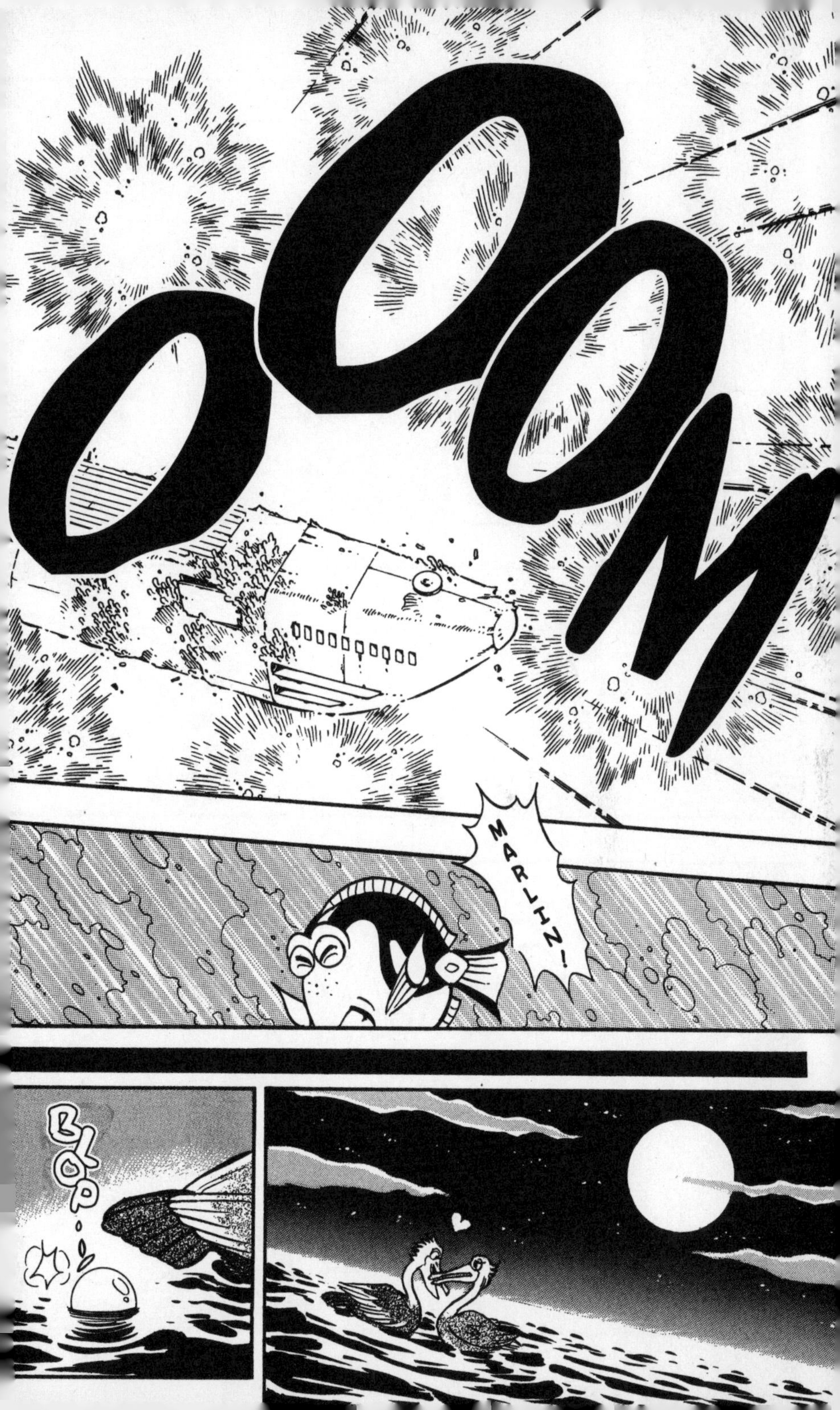
OOOM
MARLIN!
BLOP

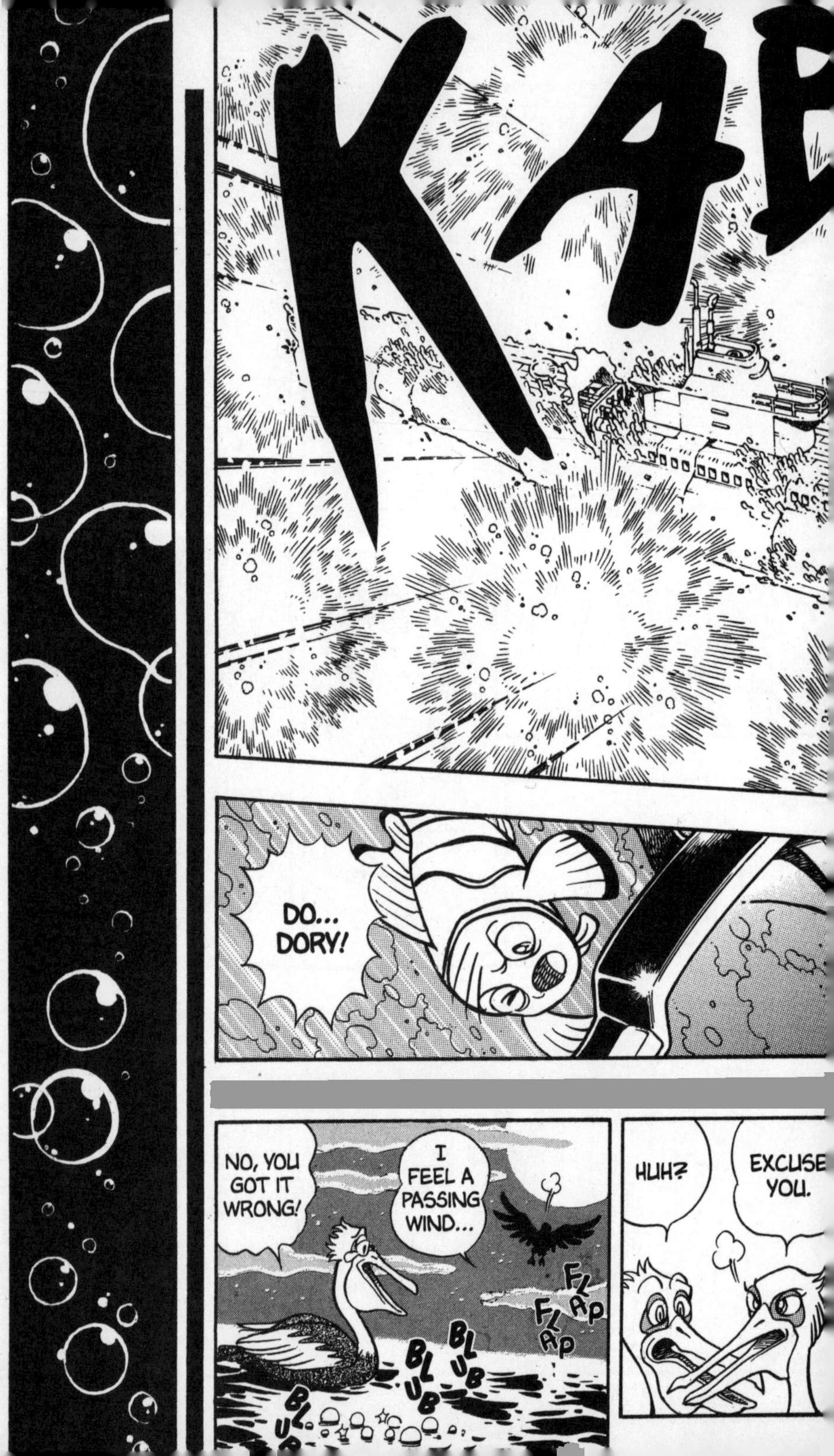
KA
DO... DORY!
EXCUSE YOU.
HUH?
I FEEL A PASSING WIND...
NO, YOU GOT IT WRONG!
FLAP
FLAP
BLUB
BLUB
BLU

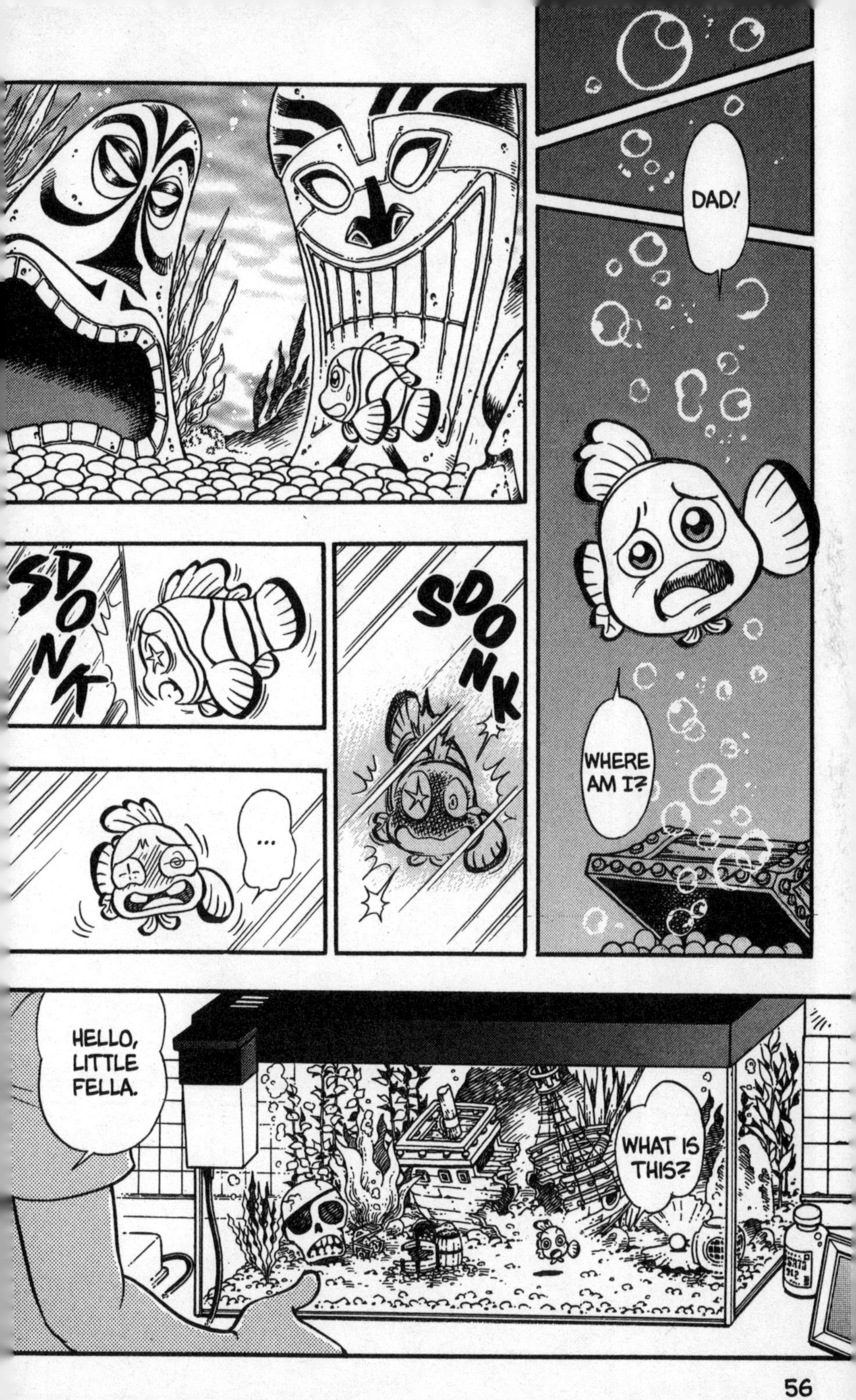
DAD!
WHERE AM I?
SDONK
SDONK
...
WHAT IS THIS?
HELLO, LITTLE FELLA.

READ THIS WAY

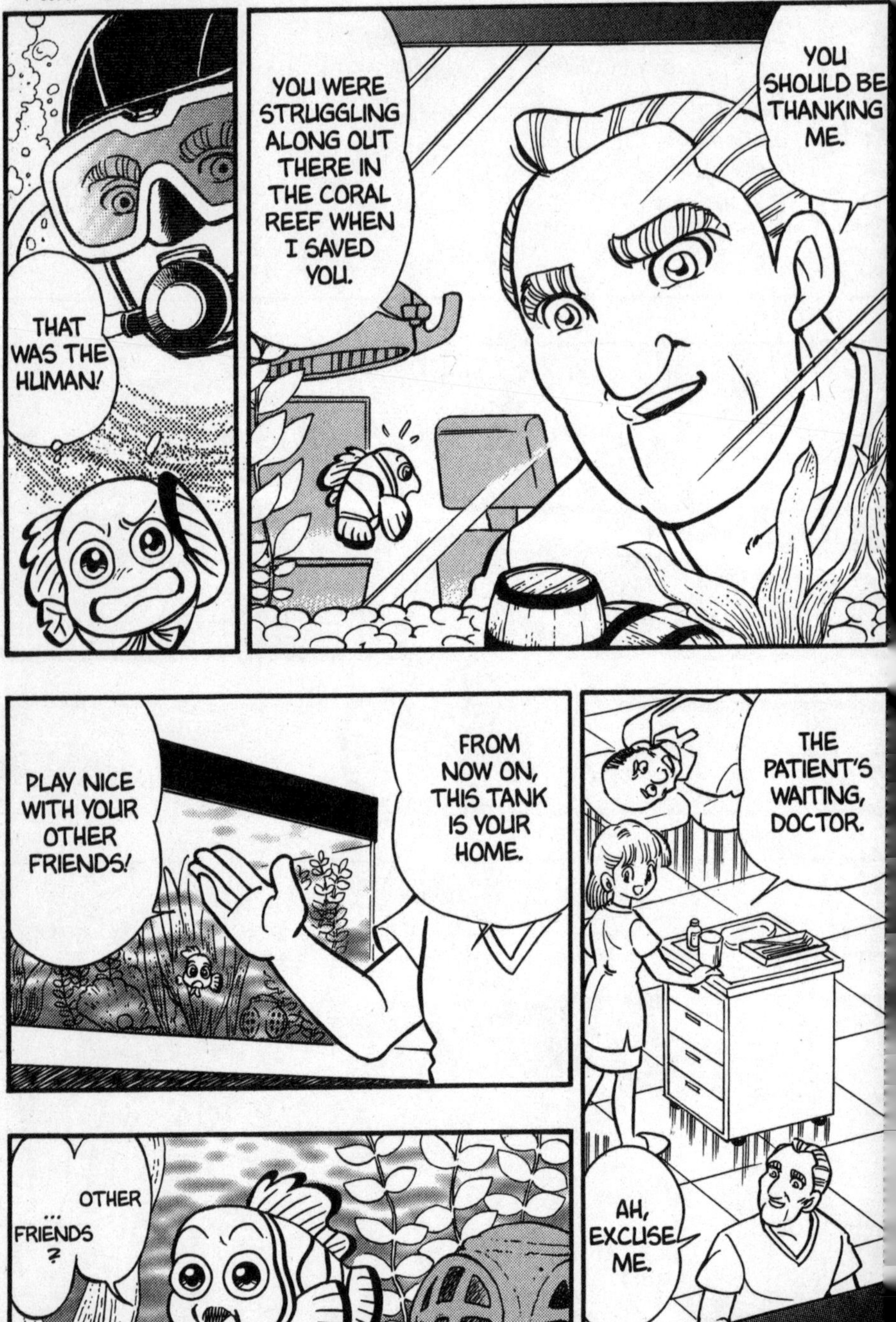

YOU SHOULD BE THANKING ME.
YOU WERE STRUGGLING ALONG OUT THERE IN THE CORAL REEF WHEN I SAVED YOU.
THAT WAS THE HUMAN!
THE PATIENT'S WAITING, DOCTOR.
AH, EXCUSE ME.
FROM NOW ON, THIS TANK IS YOUR HOME.
PLAY NICE WITH YOUR OTHER FRIENDS!
OTHER ... FRIENDS?

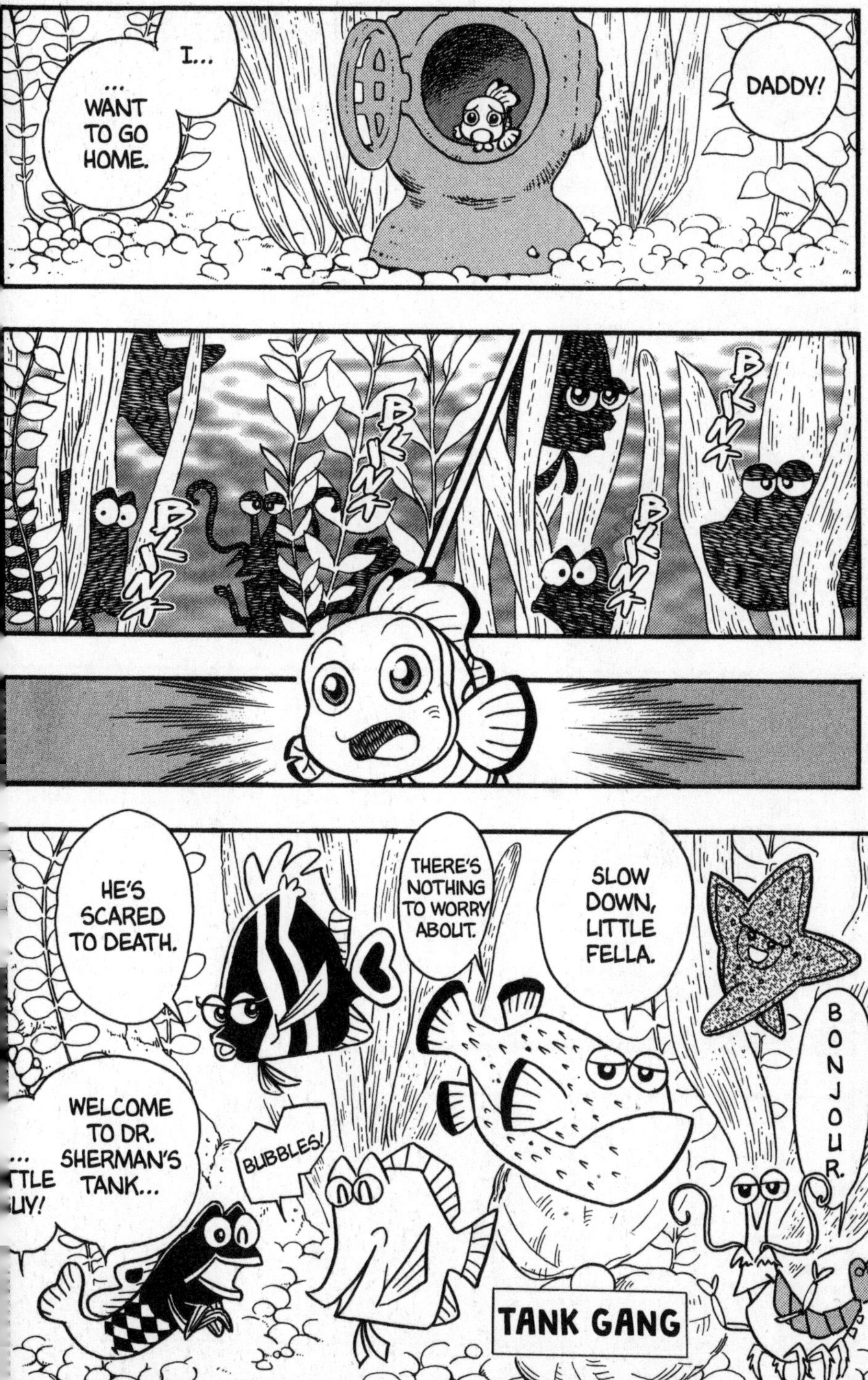
DADDY!
I... ...WANT TO GO HOME.
BLINK
BLINK
BLINK
BLINK
BONJOUR.
SLOW DOWN, LITTLE FELLA.
THERE'S NOTHING TO WORRY ABOUT.
HE'S SCARED TO DEATH.
BUBBLES!
WELCOME TO DR. SHERMAN'S TANK...
TANK GANG

READ THIS WAY

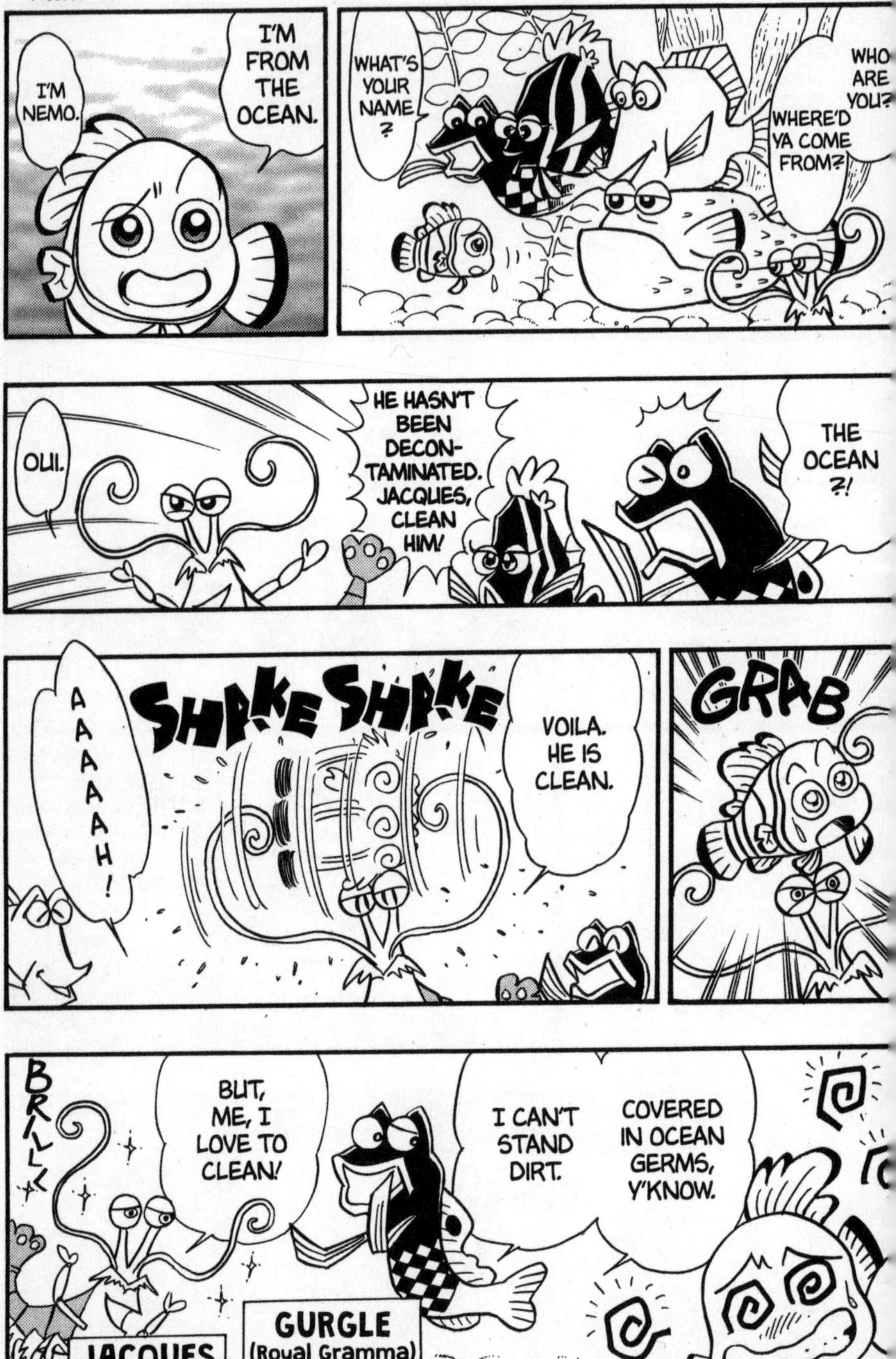
WHO ARE YOU?
WHERE'D YA COME FROM?
WHAT'S YOUR NAME?
I'M FROM THE OCEAN.
I'M NEMO.
THE OCEAN?!
HE HASN'T BEEN DECON-TAMINATED. JACQUES, CLEAN HIM!
OUI.
GRAB
VOILA. HE IS CLEAN.
SHAKE SHAKE
AAAAAAH!
COVERED IN OCEAN GERMS, Y'KNOW.
I CAN'T STAND DIRT.
BUT, ME, I LOVE TO CLEAN!
GURGLE
(Royal Gramma)
BRILL
JACQUES
(Scarlet Cleaner Shrimp)

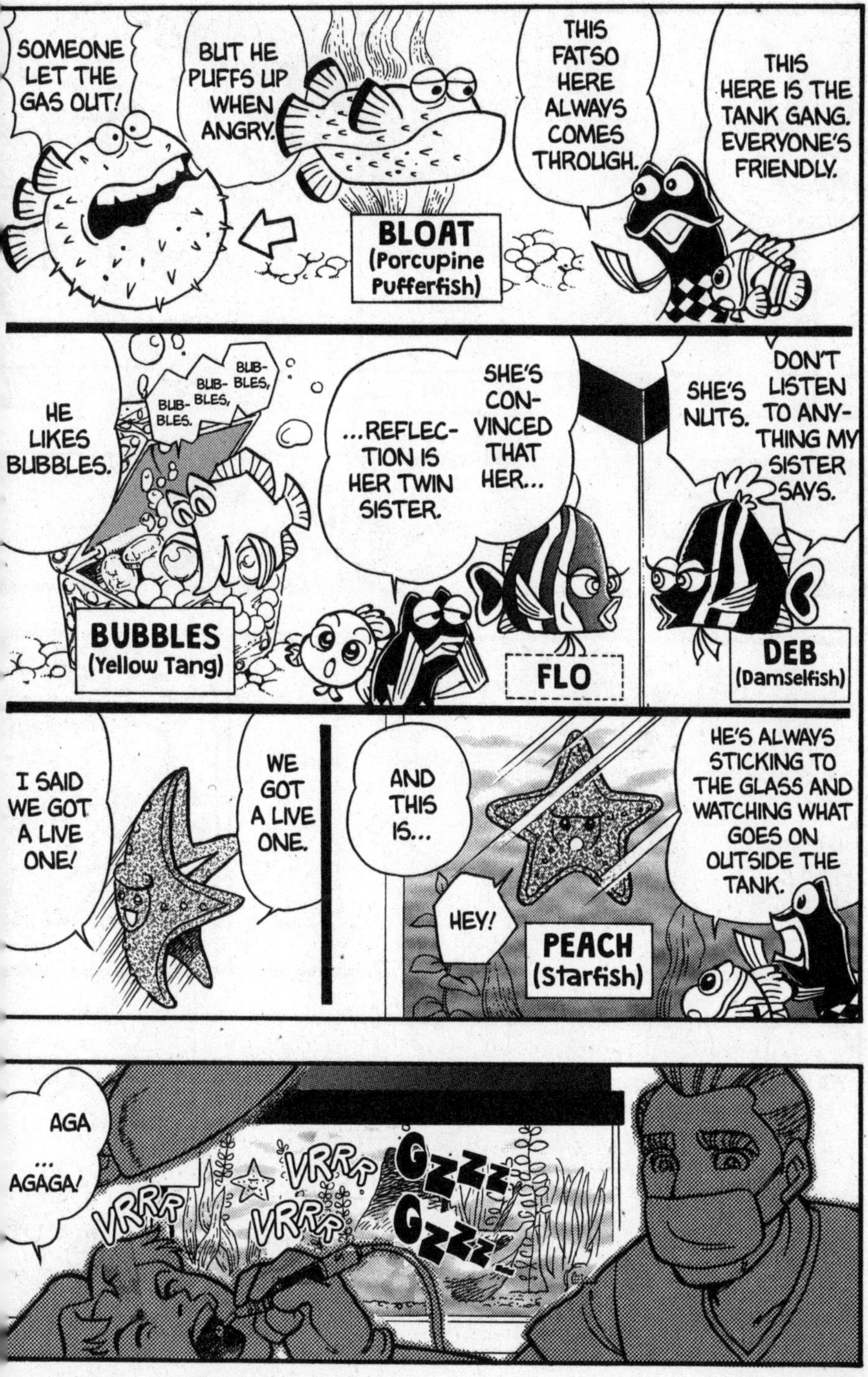
THIS HERE IS THE TANK GANG. EVERYONE'S FRIENDLY.
THIS FATSO HERE ALWAYS COMES THROUGH.
BLOAT (Porcupine Pufferfish)
BUT HE PUFFS UP WHEN ANGRY.
SOMEONE LET THE GAS OUT!
DON'T LISTEN TO ANY-THING MY SISTER SAYS.
SHE'S NUTS.
DEB (Damselfish)
SHE'S CON-VINCED THAT HER...
...REFLEC-TION IS HER TWIN SISTER.
FLO
BUB-BLES, BUB-BLES, BUB-BLES.
HE LIKES BUBBLES.
BUBBLES (Yellow Tang)
HE'S ALWAYS STICKING TO THE GLASS AND WATCHING WHAT GOES ON OUTSIDE THE TANK.
AND THIS IS...
HEY!
PEACH (Starfish)
WE GOT A LIVE ONE.
I SAID WE GOT A LIVE ONE!
GZZZ GZZZ.
VRRR
VRRR
VRRR
AGA ... AGAGA!

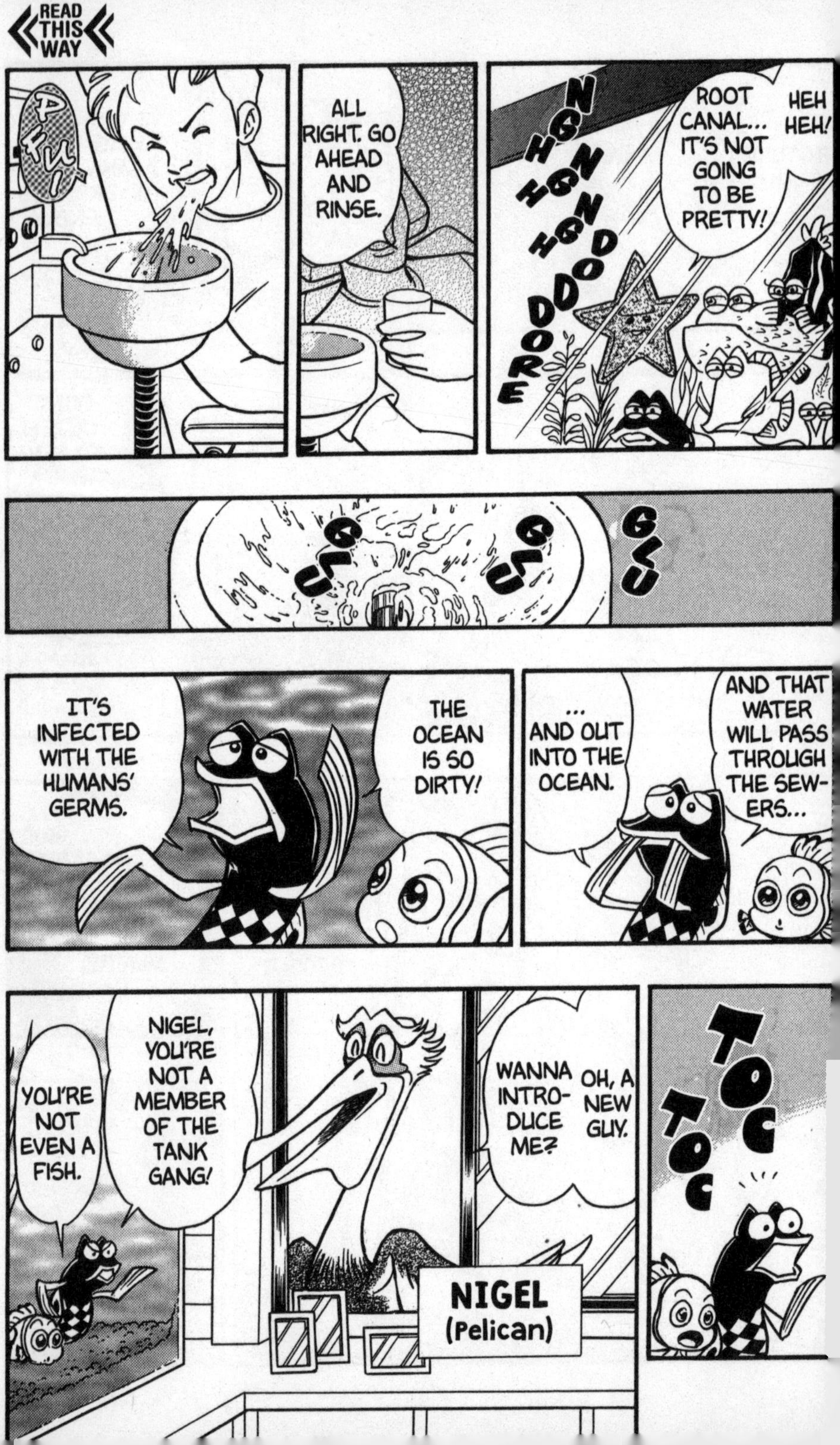
READ THIS WAY
HEH HEH!
ROOT CANAL... IT'S NOT GOING TO BE PRETTY!
ALL RIGHT. GO AHEAD AND RINSE.
GLU
GLU
GLU
AND THAT WATER WILL PASS THROUGH THE SEW-ERS...
... AND OUT INTO THE OCEAN.
THE OCEAN IS SO DIRTY!
IT'S INFECTED WITH THE HUMANS' GERMS.
TOC
TOC
OH, A NEW GUY.
WANNA INTRO-DUCE ME?
NIGEL (Pelican)
NIGEL, YOU'RE NOT A MEMBER OF THE TANK GANG!
YOU'RE NOT EVEN A FISH.

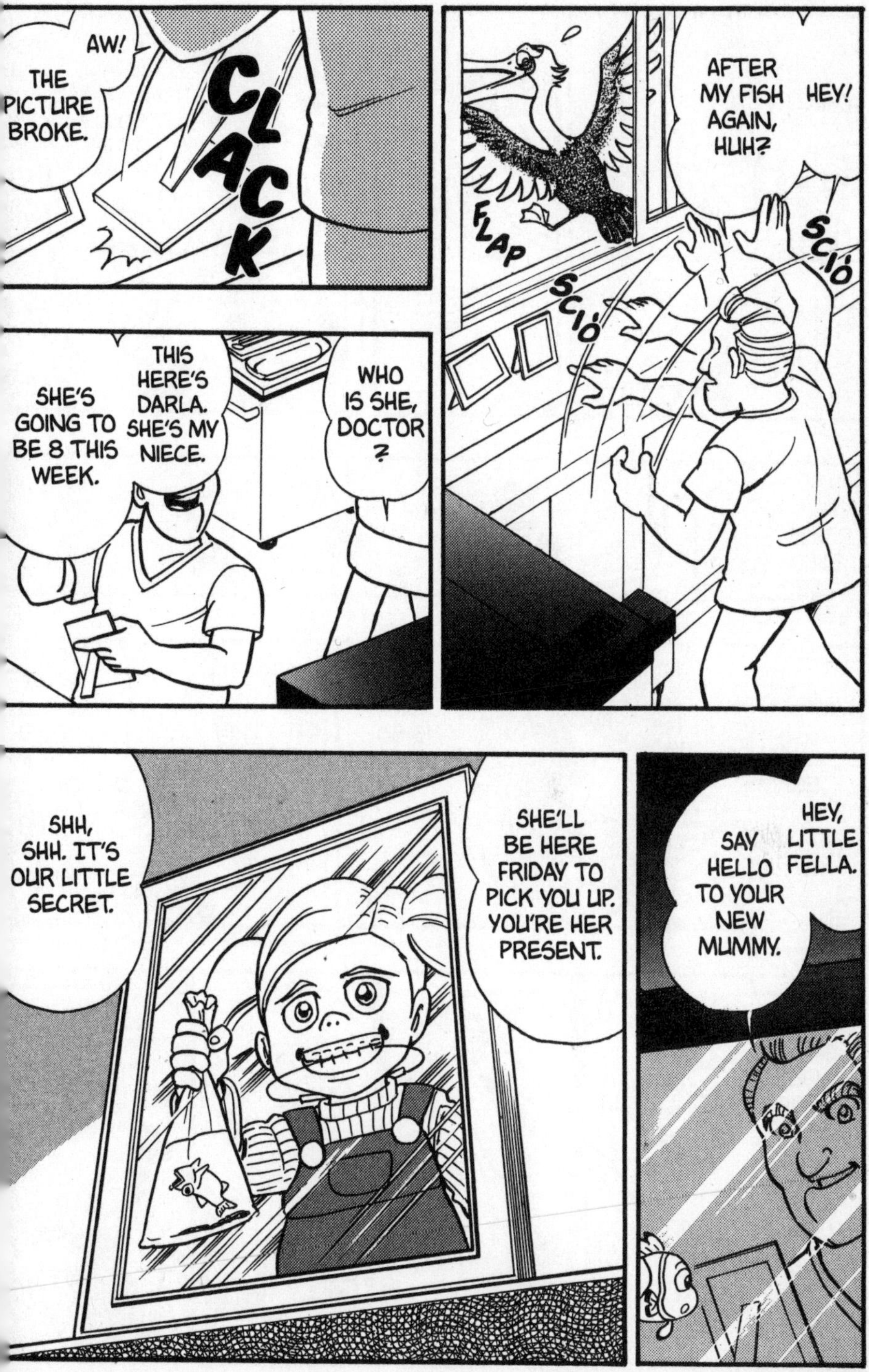
HEY!
AFTER MY FISH AGAIN, HUH?
FLAP
SCIÓ
SCIÓ
AW!
THE PICTURE BROKE.
CLACK
WHO IS SHE, DOCTOR?
THIS HERE'S DARLA. SHE'S MY NIECE.
SHE'S GOING TO BE 8 THIS WEEK.
HEY, LITTLE FELLA.
SAY HELLO TO YOUR NEW MUMMY.
SHE'LL BE HERE FRIDAY TO PICK YOU UP. YOU'RE HER PRESENT.
SHH, SHH. IT'S OUR LITTLE SECRET.

READ THIS WAY

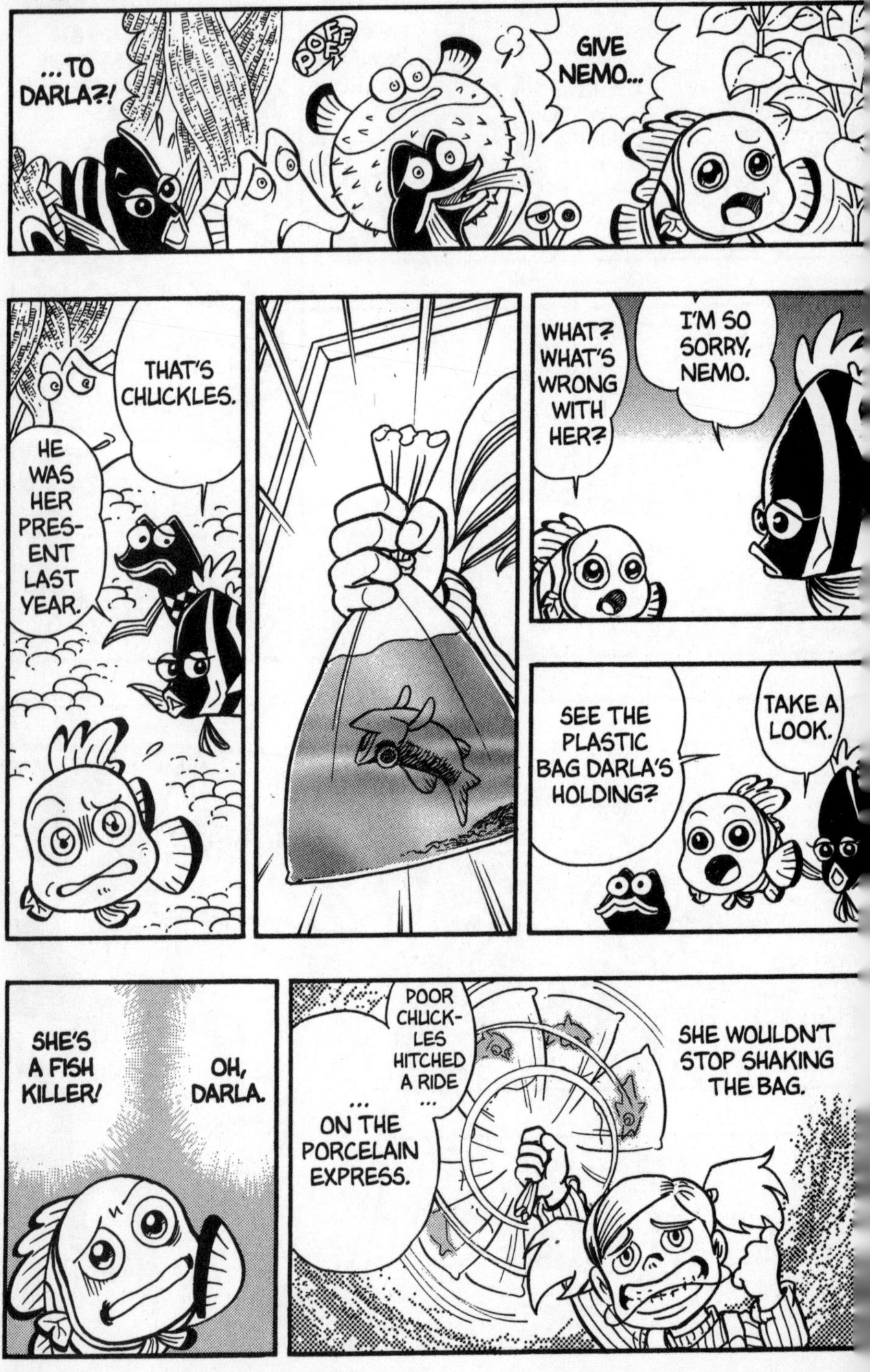
GIVE NEMO...
POFF
...TO DARLA?!
I'M SO SORRY, NEMO.
WHAT? WHAT'S WRONG WITH HER?
TAKE A LOOK.
SEE THE PLASTIC BAG DARLA'S HOLDING?
THAT'S CHUCKLES.
HE WAS HER PRESENT LAST YEAR.
SHE WOULDN'T STOP SHAKING THE BAG.
POOR CHUCKLES HITCHED A RIDE ...
... ON THE PORCELAIN EXPRESS.
OH, DARLA.
SHE'S A FISH KILLER!

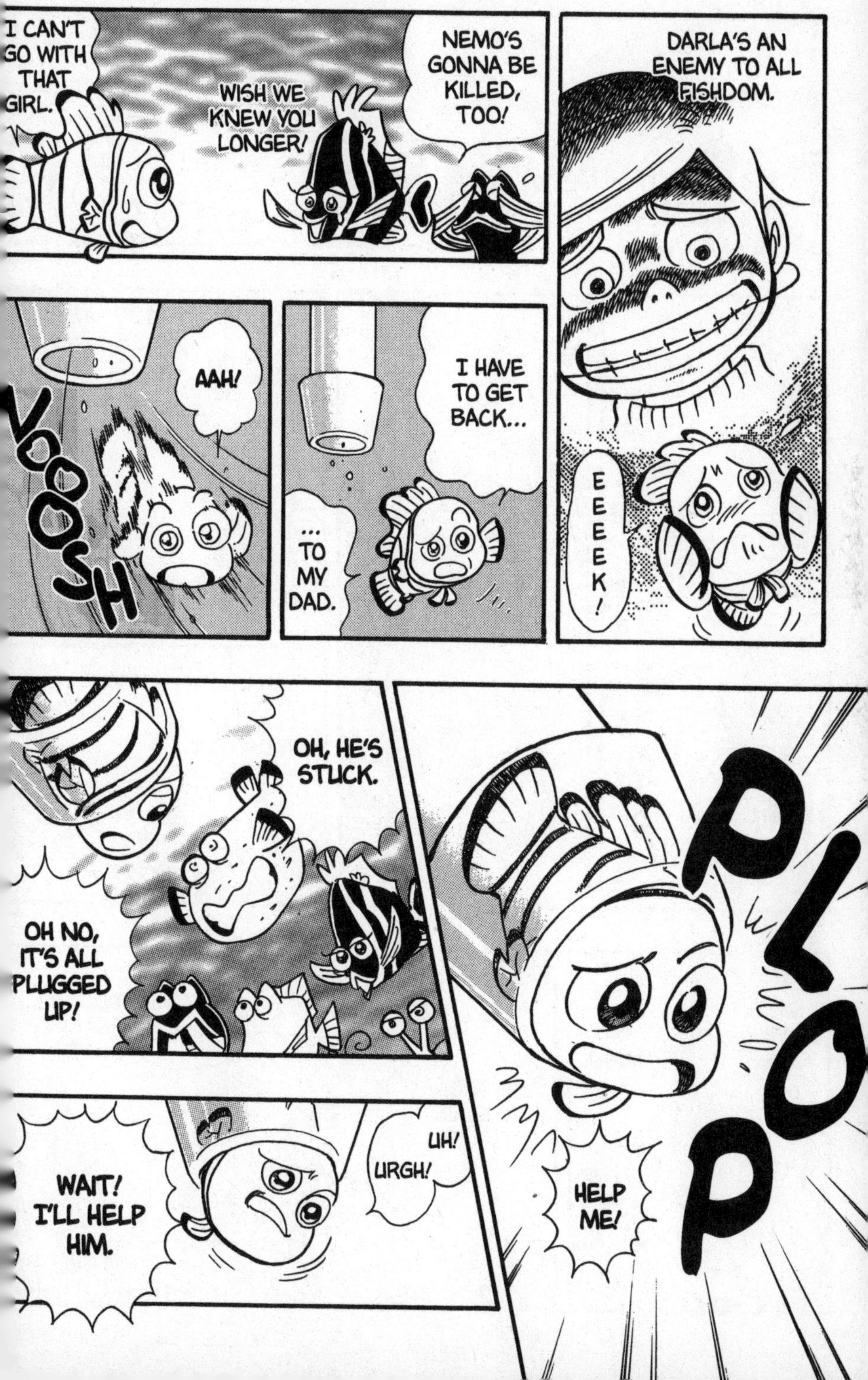

DARLA'S AN ENEMY TO ALL FISHDOM.
EEEEEK!
NEMO'S GONNA BE KILLED, TOO!
WISH WE KNEW YOU LONGER!
I CAN'T GO WITH THAT GIRL.
I HAVE TO GET BACK...
... TO MY DAD.
AAH!
VOOOSH
PLOP
HELP ME!
OH, HE'S STUCK.
OH NO, IT'S ALL PLUGGED UP!
UH!
URGH!
WAIT! I'LL HELP HIM.

READ THIS WAY

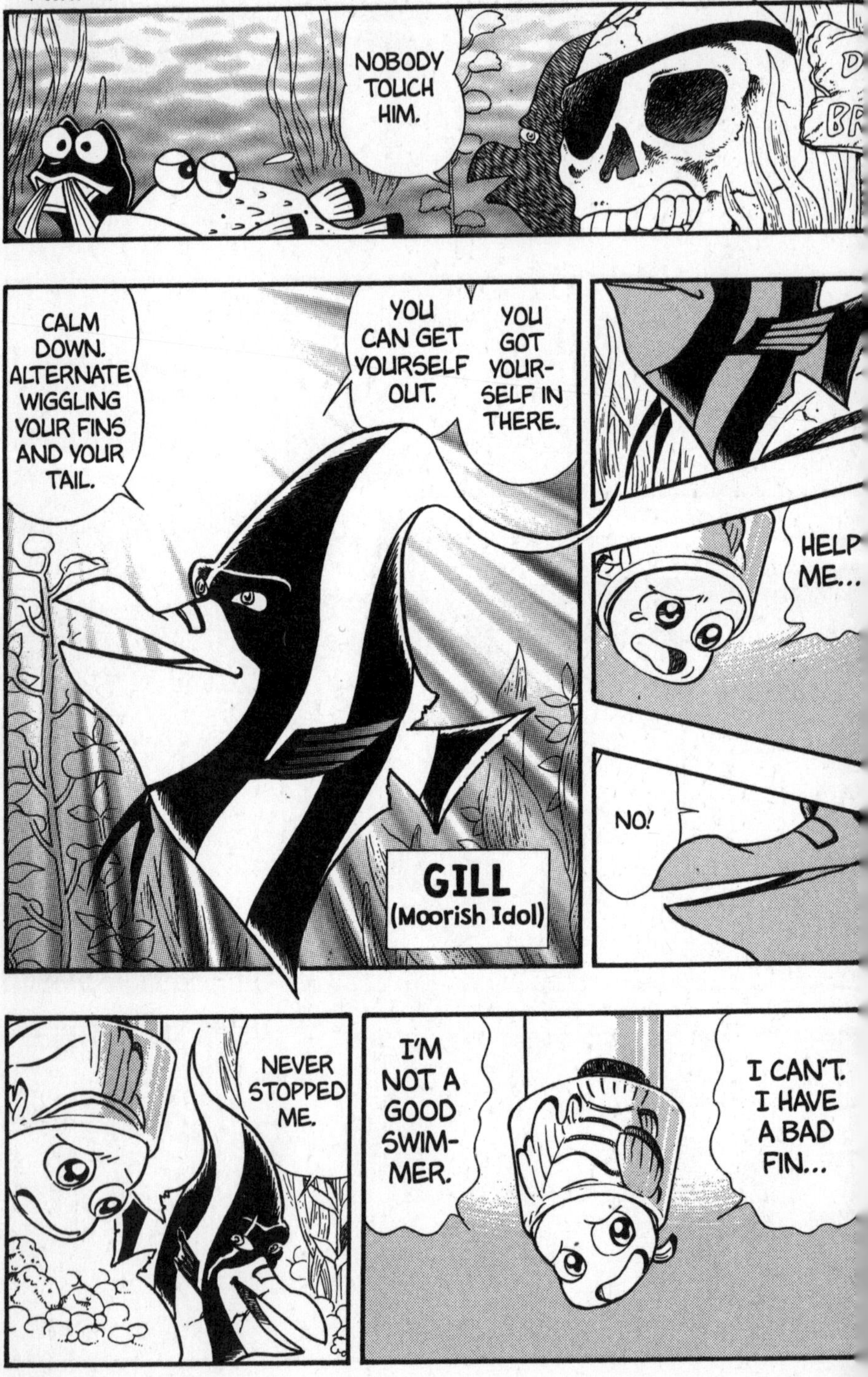
NOBODY TOUCH HIM.
HELP ME...
NO!
YOU GOT YOURSELF IN THERE.
YOU CAN GET YOURSELF OUT.
CALM DOWN. ALTERNATE WIGGLING YOUR FINS AND YOUR TAIL.
GILL (Moorish Idol)
I CAN'T. I HAVE A BAD FIN...
I'M NOT A GOOD SWIM-MER.
NEVER STOPPED ME.

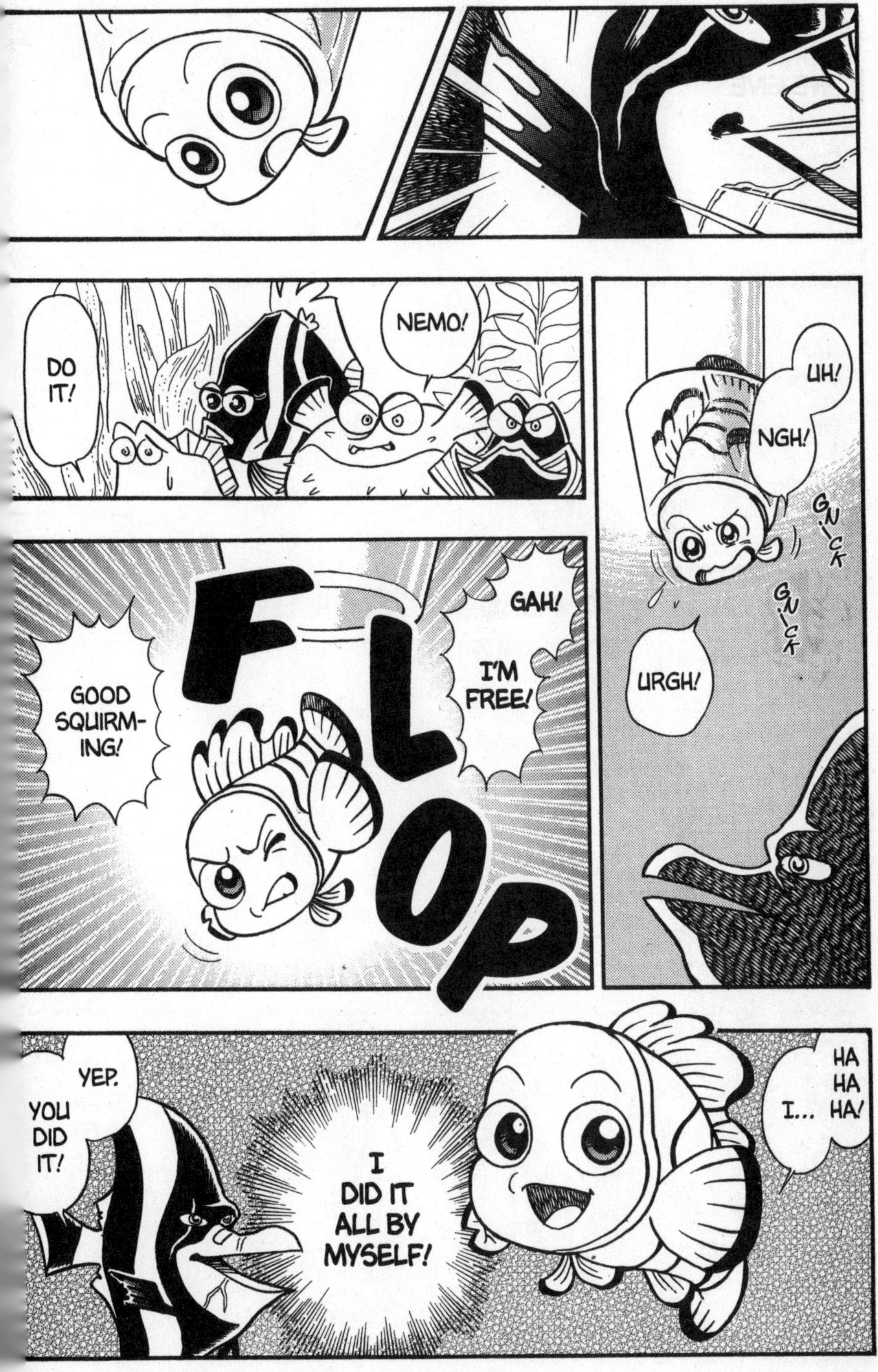
UH!
NGH!
GNICK
GNICK
URGH!
NEMO!
DO IT!
GAH!
I'M FREE!
FLOP
GOOD SQUIRMING!
HA HA HA!
I...
I DID IT ALL BY MYSELF!
YEP.
YOU DID IT!

READ THIS WAY

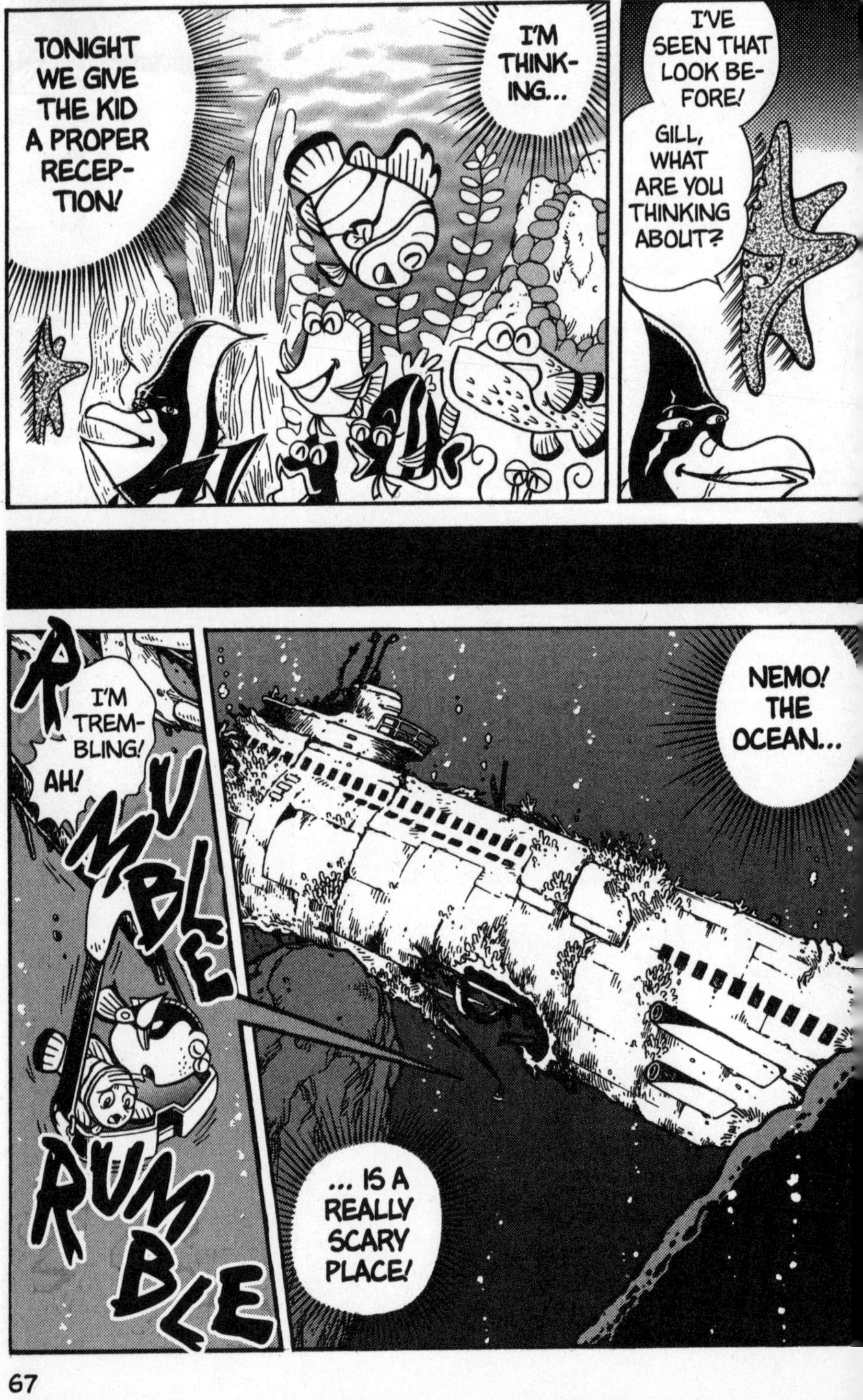

I'VE SEEN THAT LOOK BE-FORE!
GILL, WHAT ARE YOU THINKING ABOUT?
I'M THINK-ING...
TONIGHT WE GIVE THE KID A PROPER RECEP-TION!
NEMO! THE OCEAN...
... IS A REALLY SCARY PLACE!
RUMBLE
I'M TREM-BLING!
AH!
RUMBLE

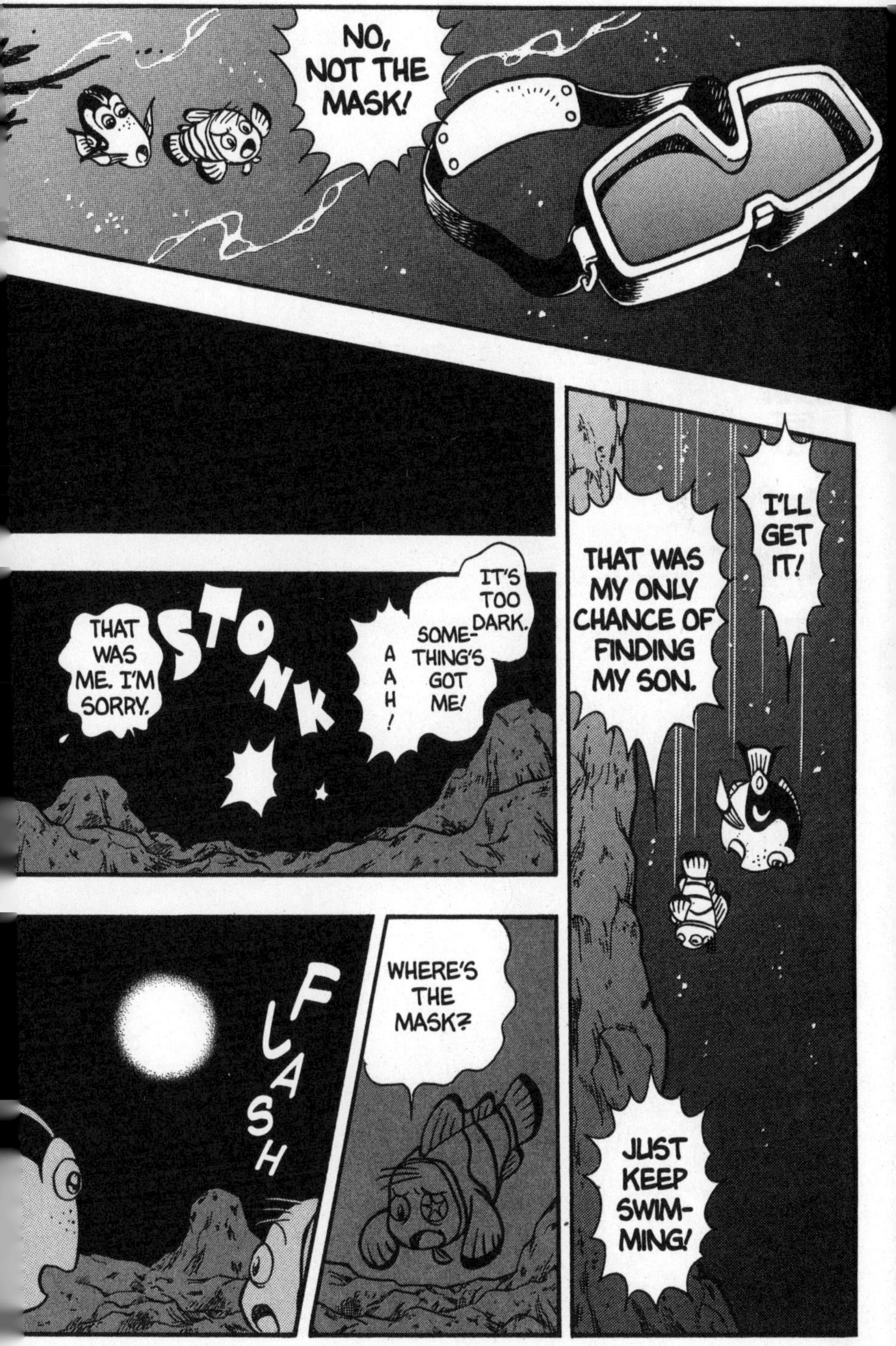

NO, NOT THE MASK!
I'LL GET IT!
THAT WAS MY ONLY CHANCE OF FINDING MY SON.
JUST KEEP SWIMMING!
IT'S TOO DARK.
SOME-THING'S GOT ME!
AAH!
STONK
THAT WAS ME. I'M SORRY.
WHERE'S THE MASK?
FLASH

READ THIS WAY

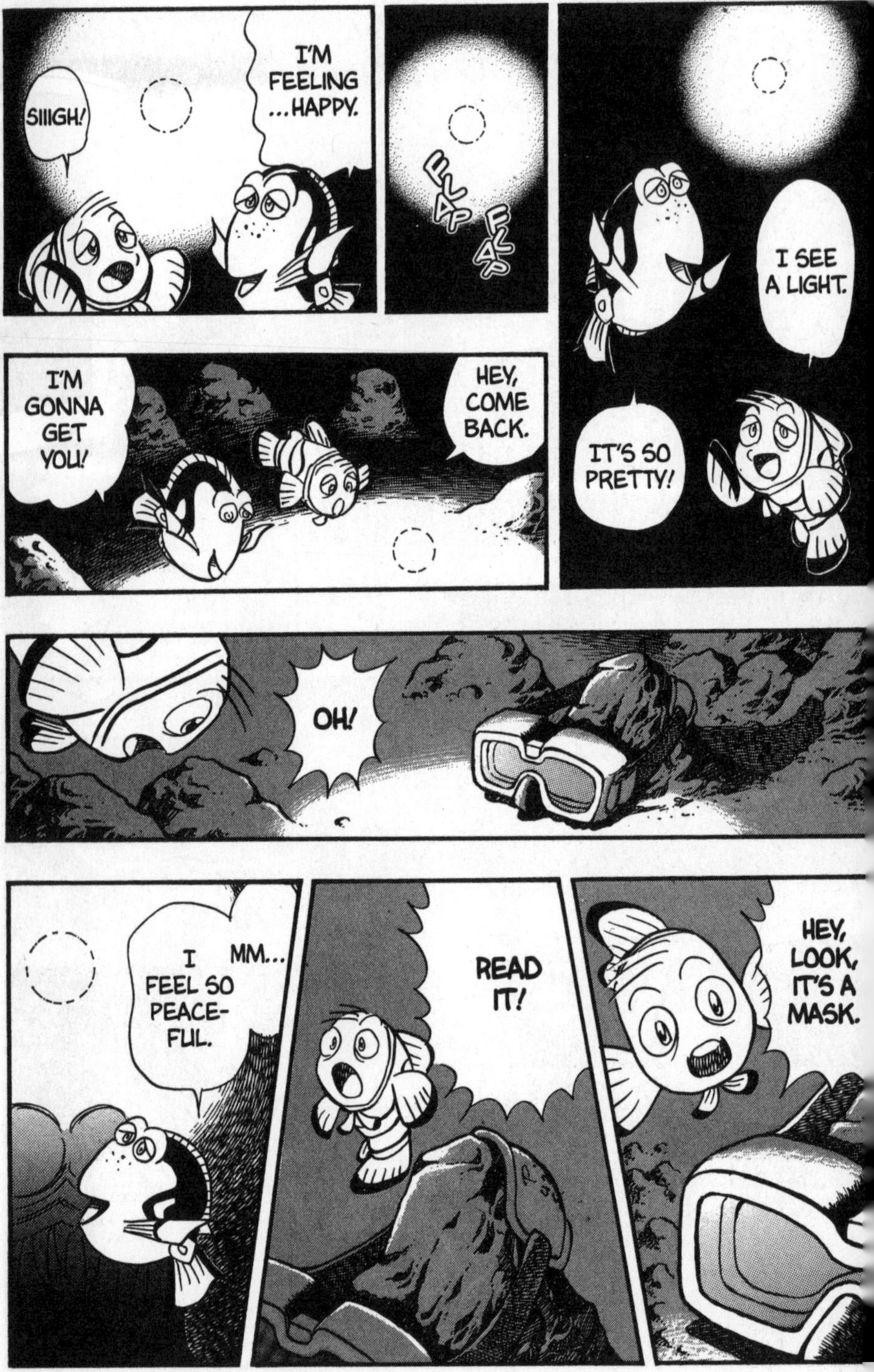
I SEE A LIGHT.
IT'S SO PRETTY!
FLAP FLAP
I'M FEELING ...HAPPY.
SIIIGH!
HEY, COME BACK.
I'M GONNA GET YOU!
OH!
HEY, LOOK, IT'S A MASK.
READ IT!
MM... I FEEL SO PEACE-FUL.

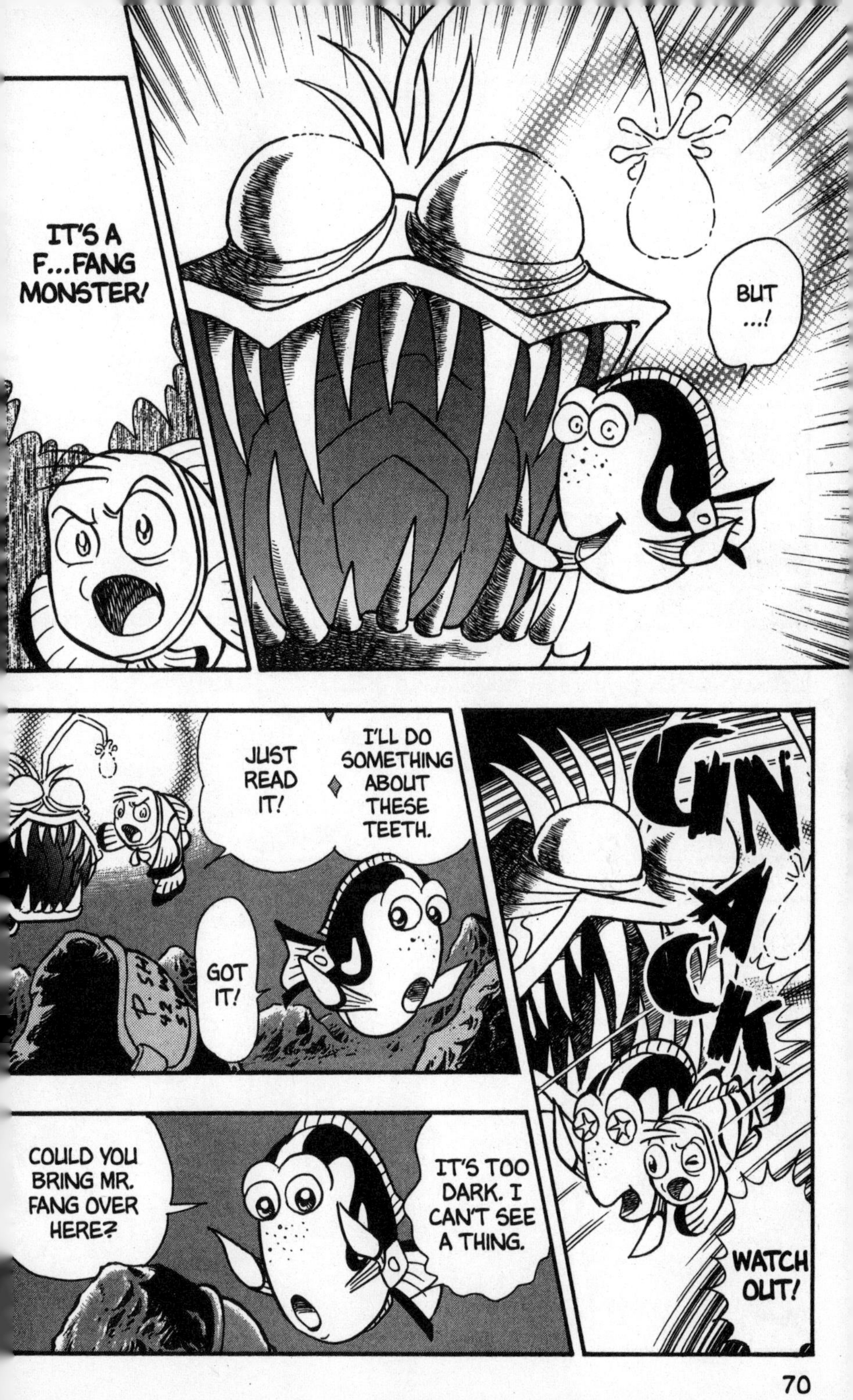
BUT ...!
IT'S A F...FANG MONSTER!
GINACK
WATCH OUT!
JUST READ IT! ◆ I'LL DO SOMETHING ABOUT THESE TEETH.
GOT IT!
IT'S TOO DARK. I CAN'T SEE A THING.
COULD YOU BRING MR. FANG OVER HERE?

READ THIS WAY

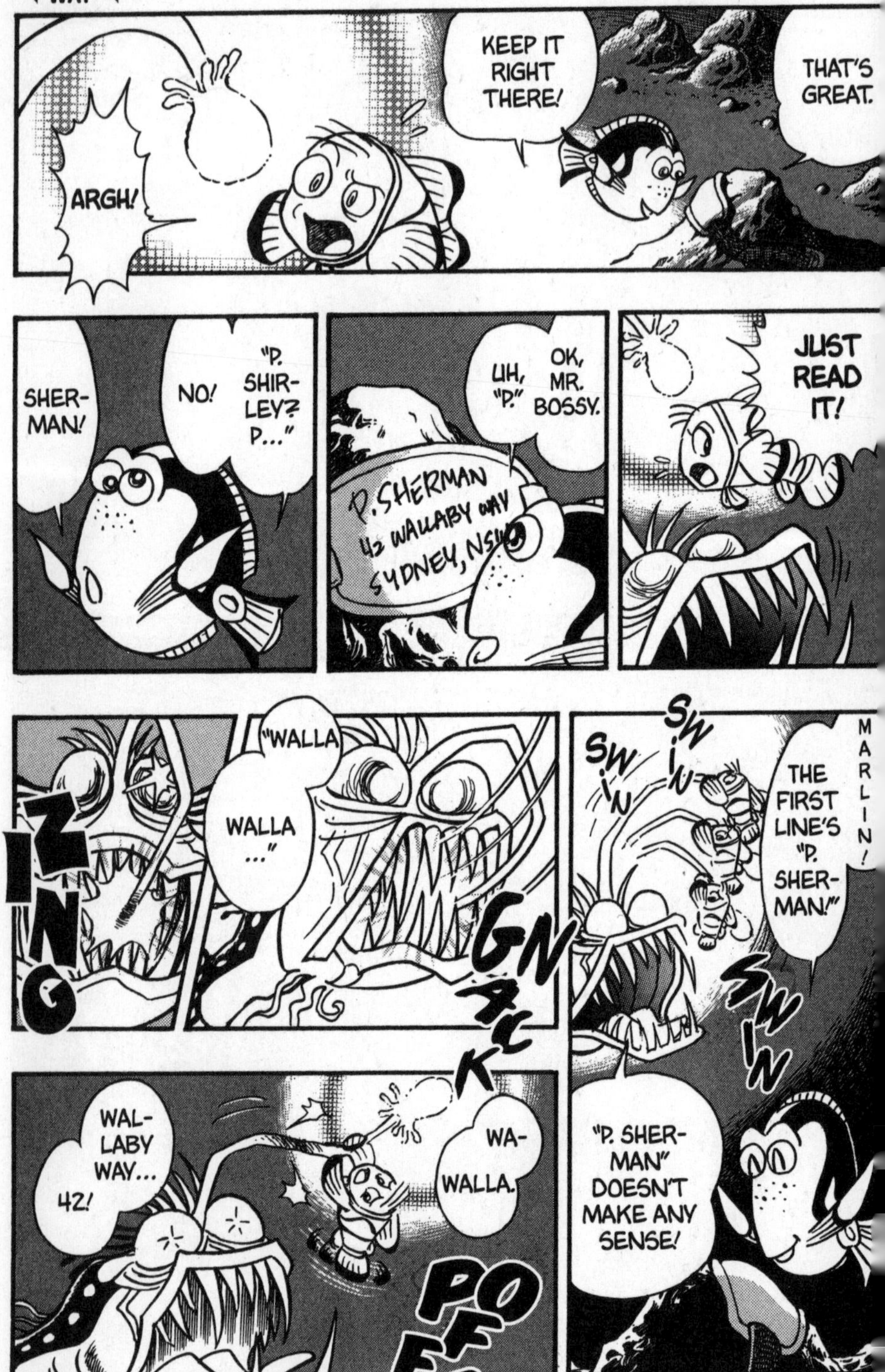
THAT'S GREAT.
KEEP IT RIGHT THERE!
ARGH!
JUST READ IT!
OK, MR. BOSSY.
UH, "P."
P. SHERMAN 42 WALLABY WAY SYDNEY, NS
"P. SHIRLEY? P..."
NO!
SHER-MAN!
MARLIN!
THE FIRST LINE'S "P. SHERMAN!"
SWIN
SWIN
"WALLA WALLA..."
GNACK
ZING
"P. SHER-MAN" DOESN'T MAKE ANY SENSE!
SWIN
WA-WALLA.
POFFF
WAL-LABY WAY... 42!

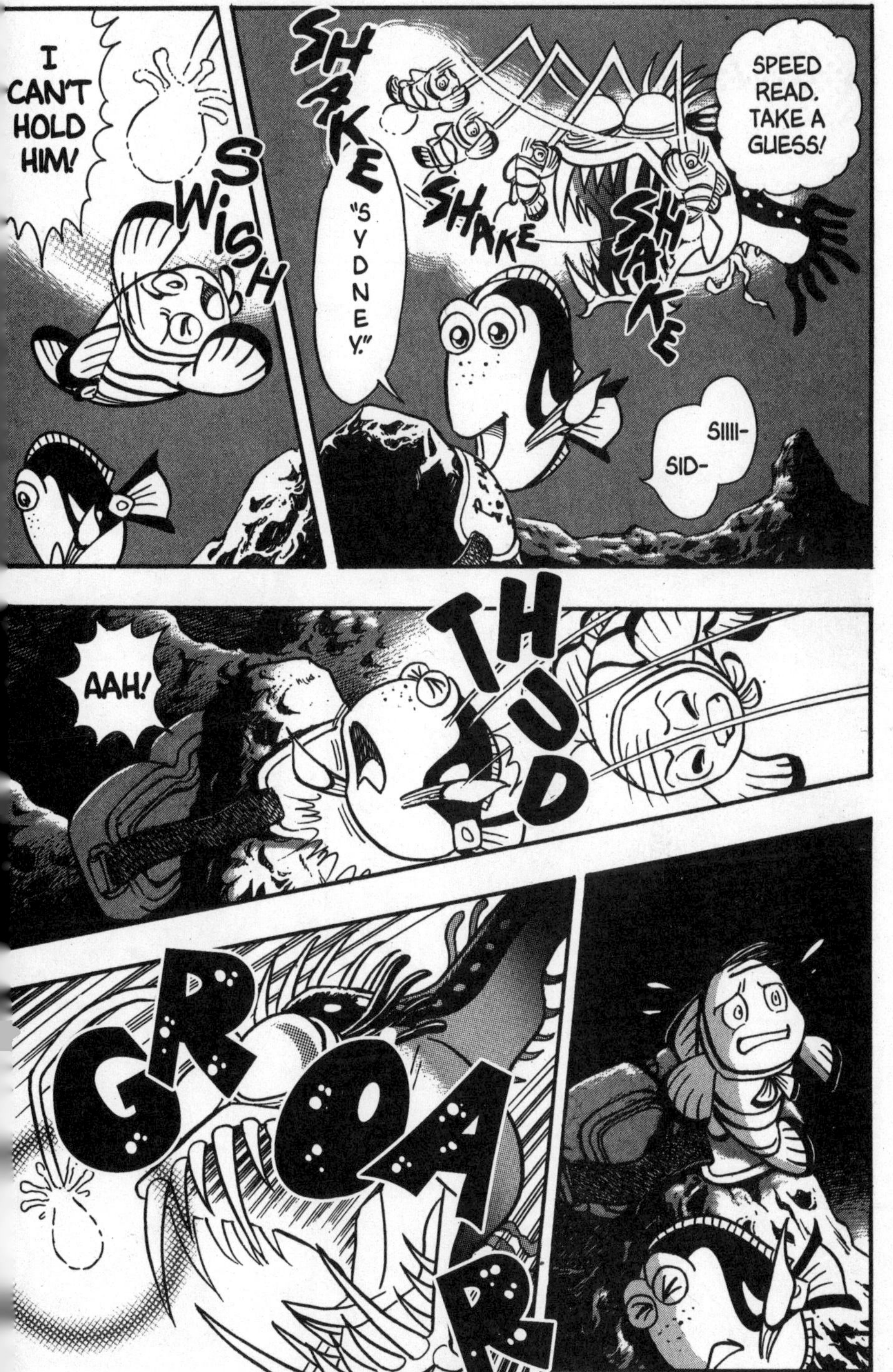
SPEED READ. TAKE A GUESS!
SHAKE
SHAKE
SHAKE
"SYDNEY."
SIIII-
SID-
I CAN'T HOLD HIM!
SWISH
THUD
AAH!
GROAAR

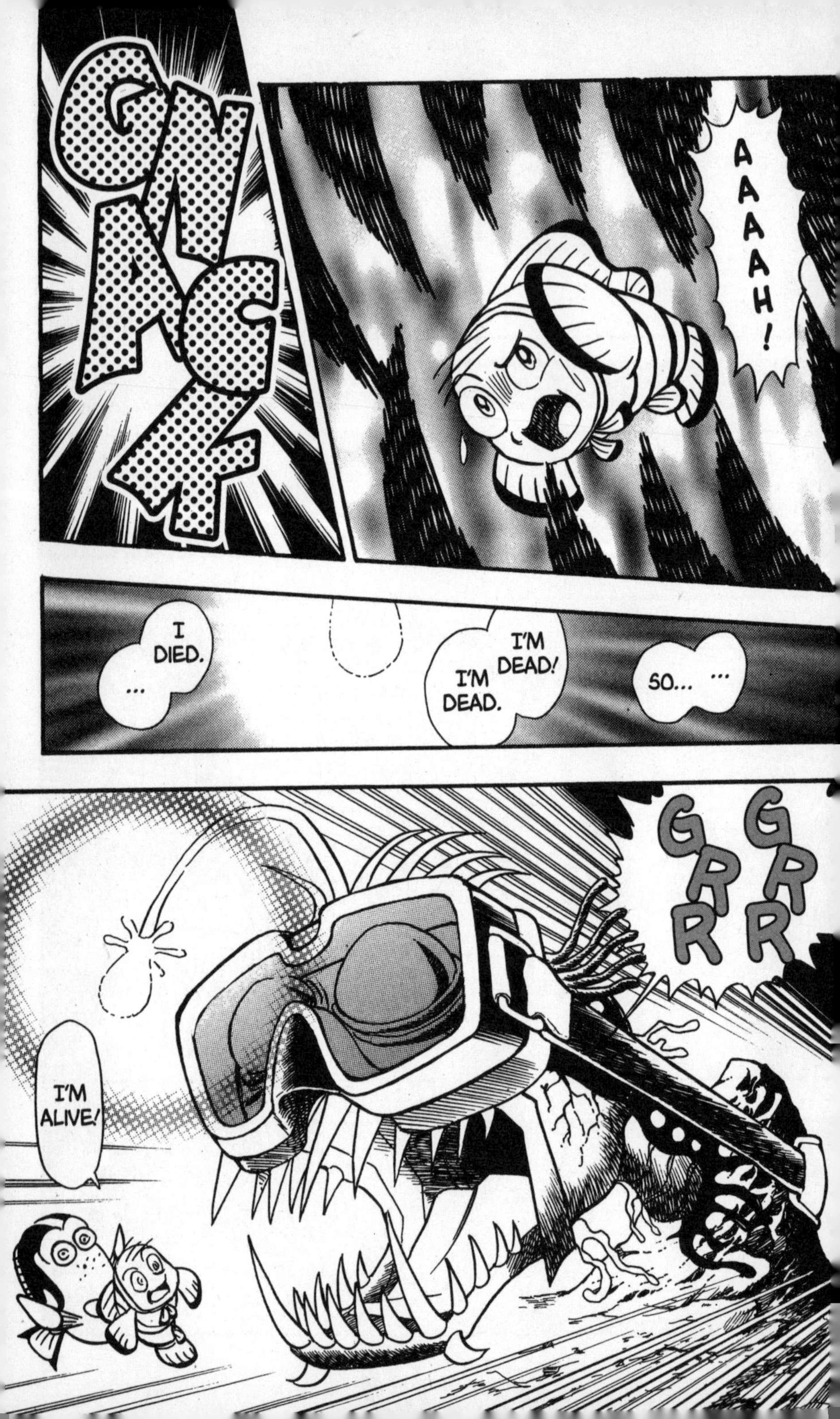
AAAAH!
SO... ...
I'M DEAD! I'M DEAD.
I DIED. ...
GRRR GRRR
I'M ALIVE!

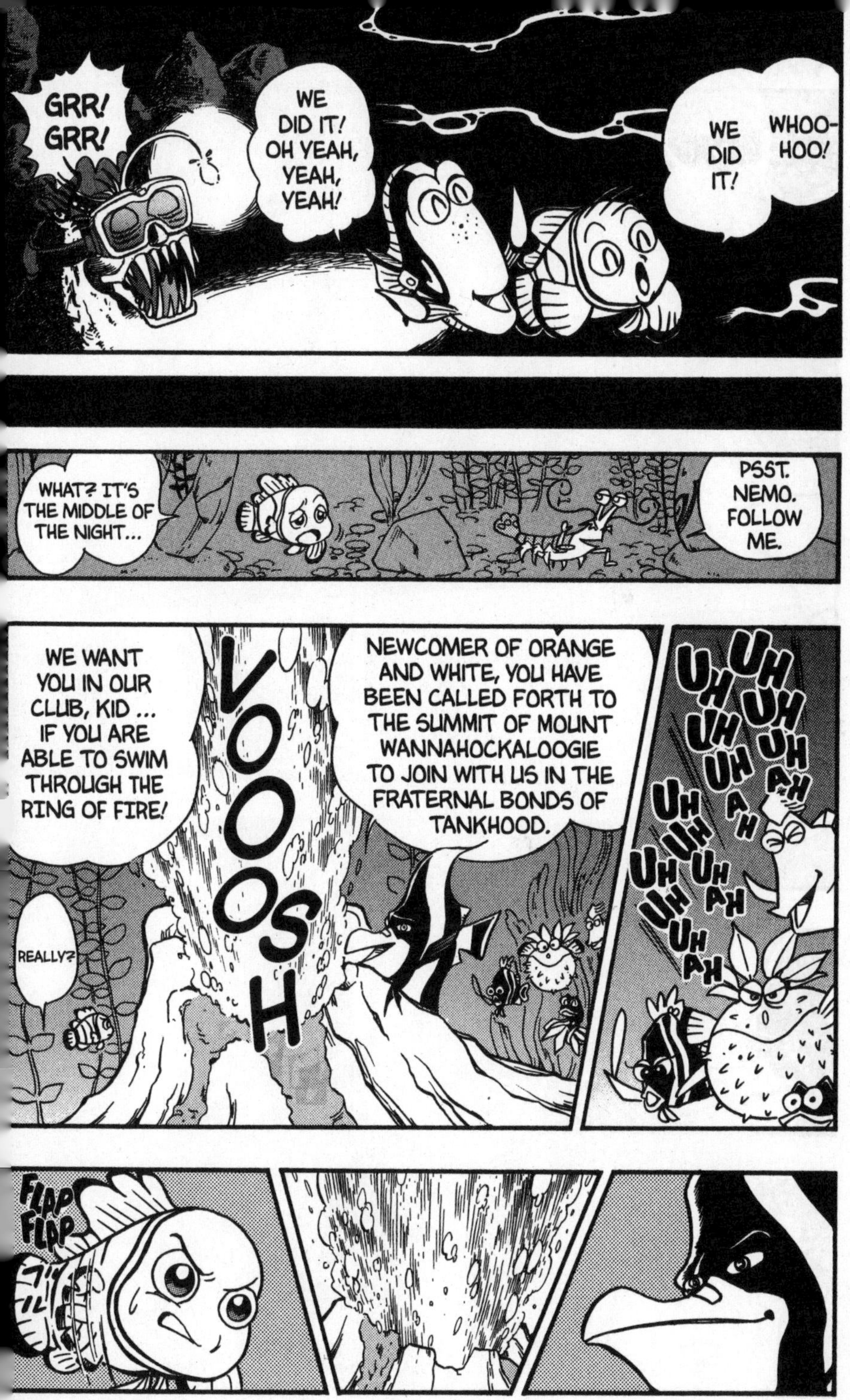
WHOO-HOO! WE DID IT!
WE DID IT! OH YEAH, YEAH, YEAH!
GRR! GRR!
PSST. NEMO. FOLLOW ME.
WHAT? IT'S THE MIDDLE OF THE NIGHT...
UH UH UH UH UH UH AH UH UH UH UH AH UH UH UH UH UH AH UH UH UH AH
NEWCOMER OF ORANGE AND WHITE, YOU HAVE BEEN CALLED FORTH TO THE SUMMIT OF MOUNT WANNAHOCKALOOGIE TO JOIN WITH US IN THE FRATERNAL BONDS OF TANKHOOD.
VOOOSH
WE WANT YOU IN OUR CLUB, KID ... IF YOU ARE ABLE TO SWIM THROUGH THE RING OF FIRE!
REALLY?
FLAP FLAP

READ THIS WAY

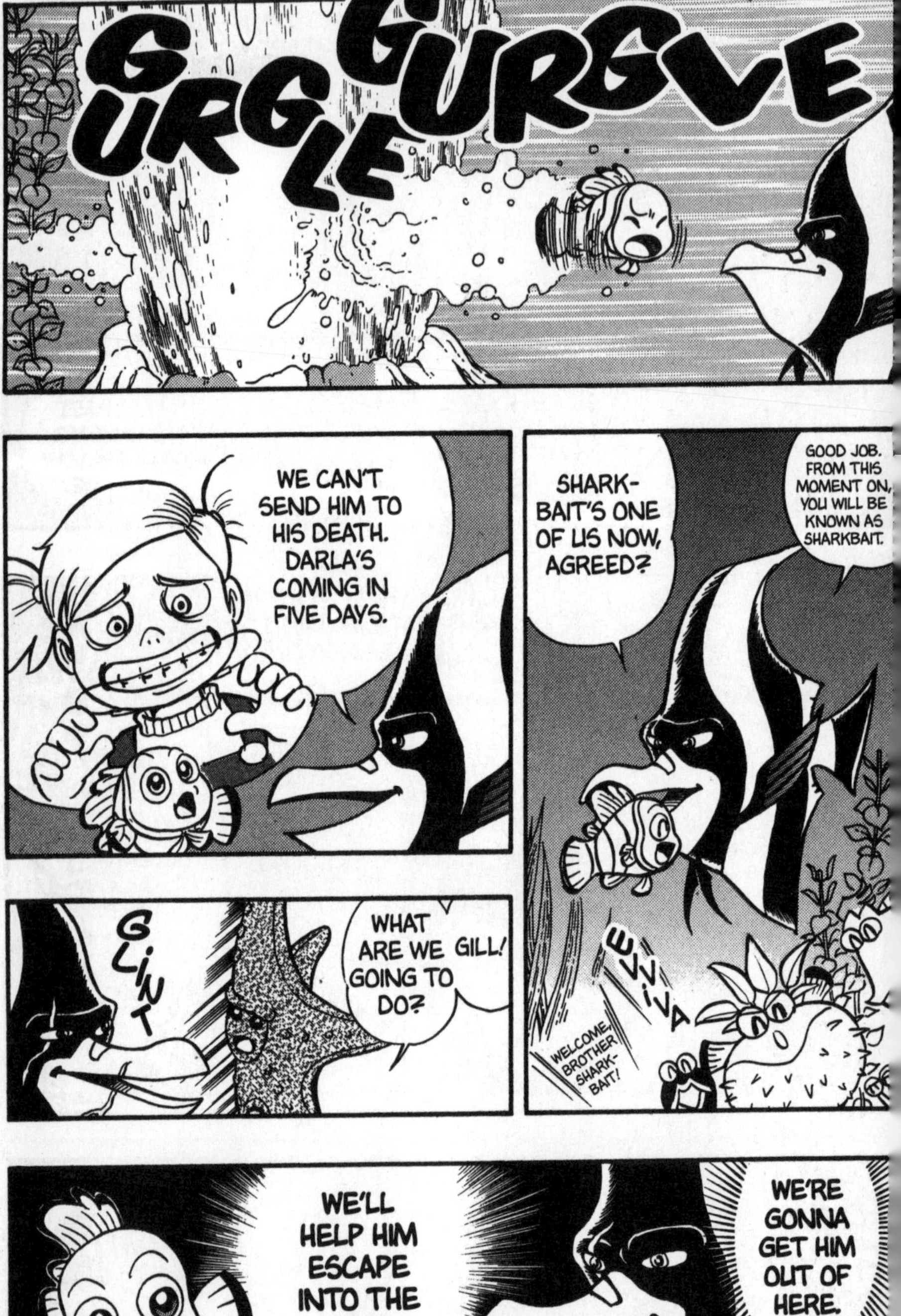
GURGLE GURGLE
GOOD JOB. FROM THIS MOMENT ON, YOU WILL BE KNOWN AS SHARKBAIT.
SHARK-BAIT'S ONE OF US NOW, AGREED?
EVVIVA
WELCOME, BROTHER SHARK-BAIT!
WE CAN'T SEND HIM TO HIS DEATH. DARLA'S COMING IN FIVE DAYS.
GILL!
WHAT ARE WE GOING TO DO?
GLINT
WE'RE GONNA GET HIM OUT OF HERE.
WE'LL HELP HIM ESCAPE INTO THE OCEAN!

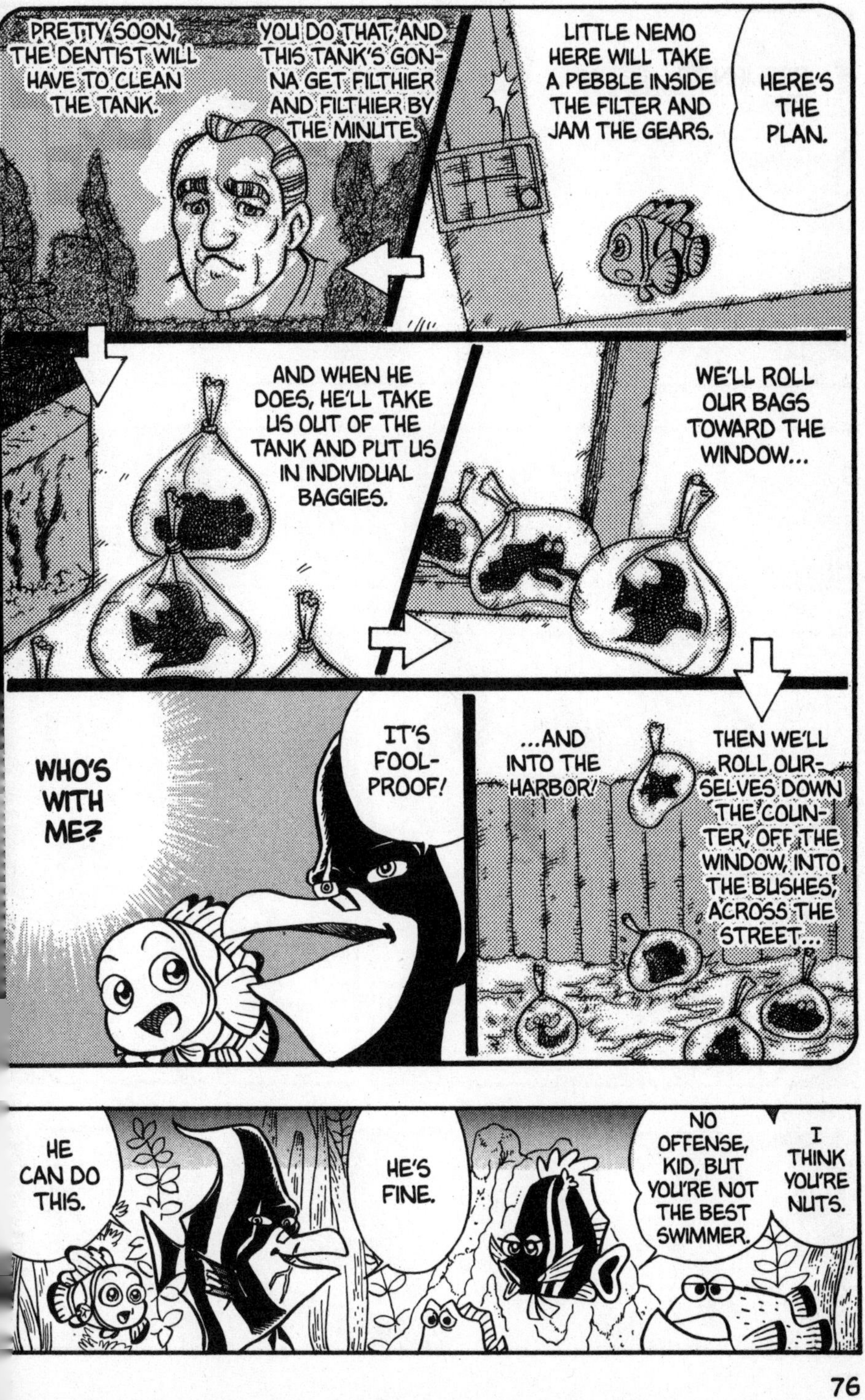
HERE'S THE PLAN.
LITTLE NEMO HERE WILL TAKE A PEBBLE INSIDE THE FILTER AND JAM THE GEARS.
YOU DO THAT, AND THIS TANK'S GONNA GET FILTHIER AND FILTHIER BY THE MINUTE.
PRETTY SOON, THE DENTIST WILL HAVE TO CLEAN THE TANK.
AND WHEN HE DOES, HE'LL TAKE US OUT OF THE TANK AND PUT US IN INDIVIDUAL BAGGIES.
WE'LL ROLL OUR BAGS TOWARD THE WINDOW...
THEN WE'LL ROLL OURSELVES DOWN THE COUNTER, OFF THE WINDOW, INTO THE BUSHES, ACROSS THE STREET...
...AND INTO THE HARBOR!
IT'S FOOLPROOF!
WHO'S WITH ME?
I THINK YOU'RE NUTS.
NO OFFENSE, KID, BUT YOU'RE NOT THE BEST SWIMMER.
HE'S FINE.
HE CAN DO THIS.

READ THIS WAY

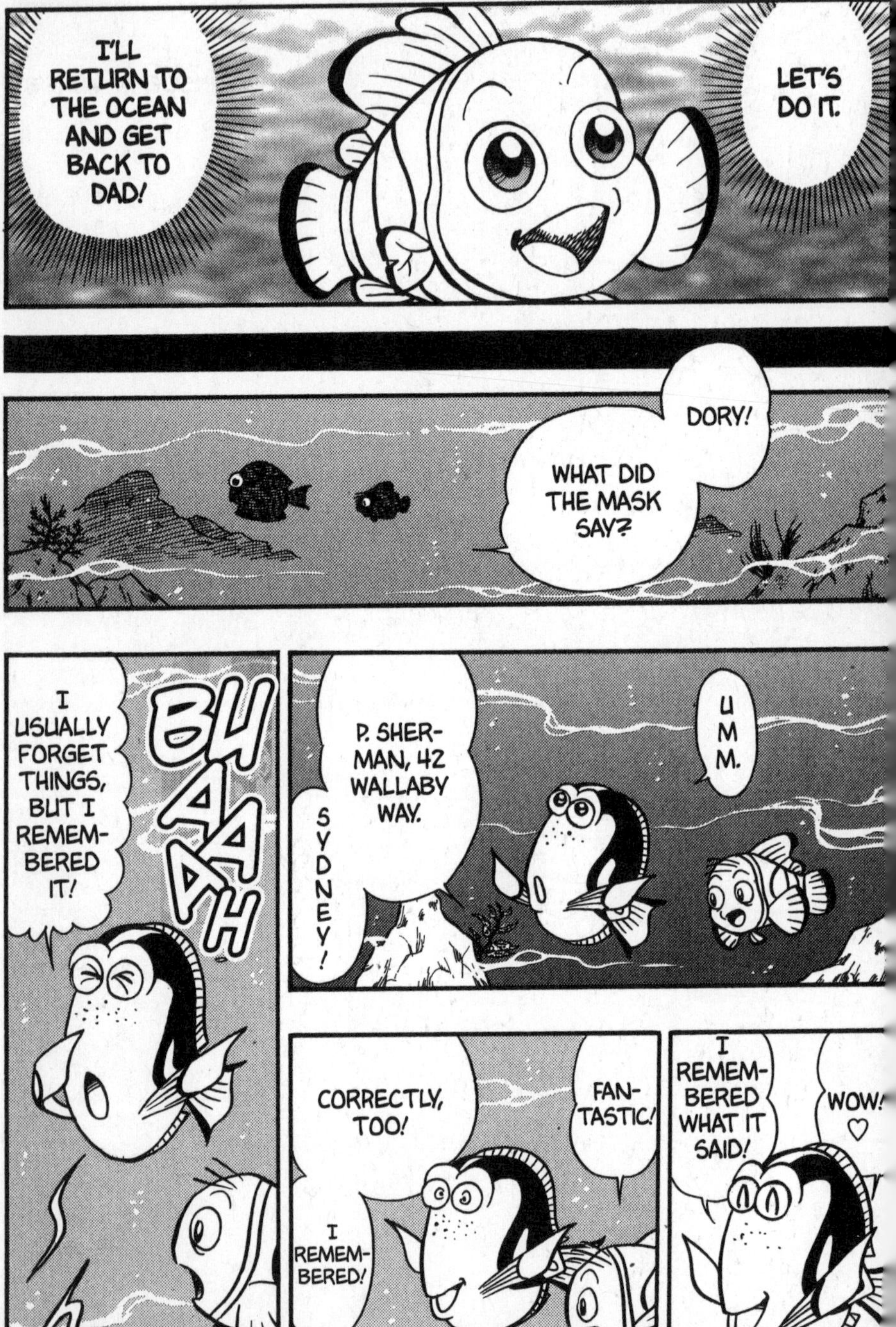
LET'S DO IT.
I'LL RETURN TO THE OCEAN AND GET BACK TO DAD!
DORY!
WHAT DID THE MASK SAY?
UMM.
P. SHERMAN, 42 WALLABY WAY.
SYDNEY!
WOW! ♡
I REMEMBERED WHAT IT SAID!
FANTASTIC!
CORRECTLY, TOO!
I REMEMBERED!
BUAAAH
I USUALLY FORGET THINGS, BUT I REMEMBERED IT!

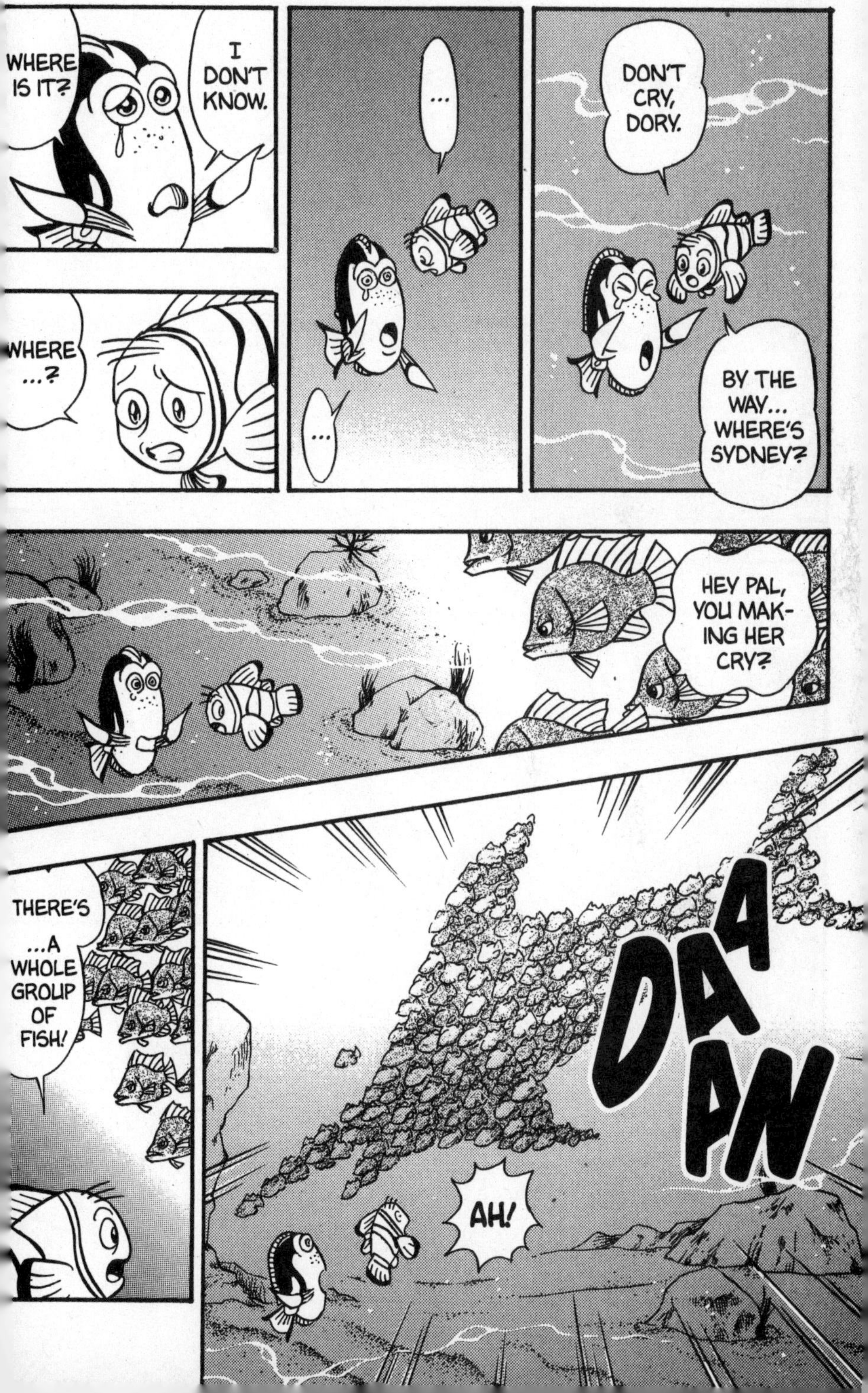
DON'T CRY, DORY.
BY THE WAY... WHERE'S SYDNEY?
...
...
I DON'T KNOW.
WHERE IS IT?
WHERE ...?
HEY PAL, YOU MAKING HER CRY?
DAAAN
AH!
THERE'S ...A WHOLE GROUP OF FISH!

READ THIS WAY

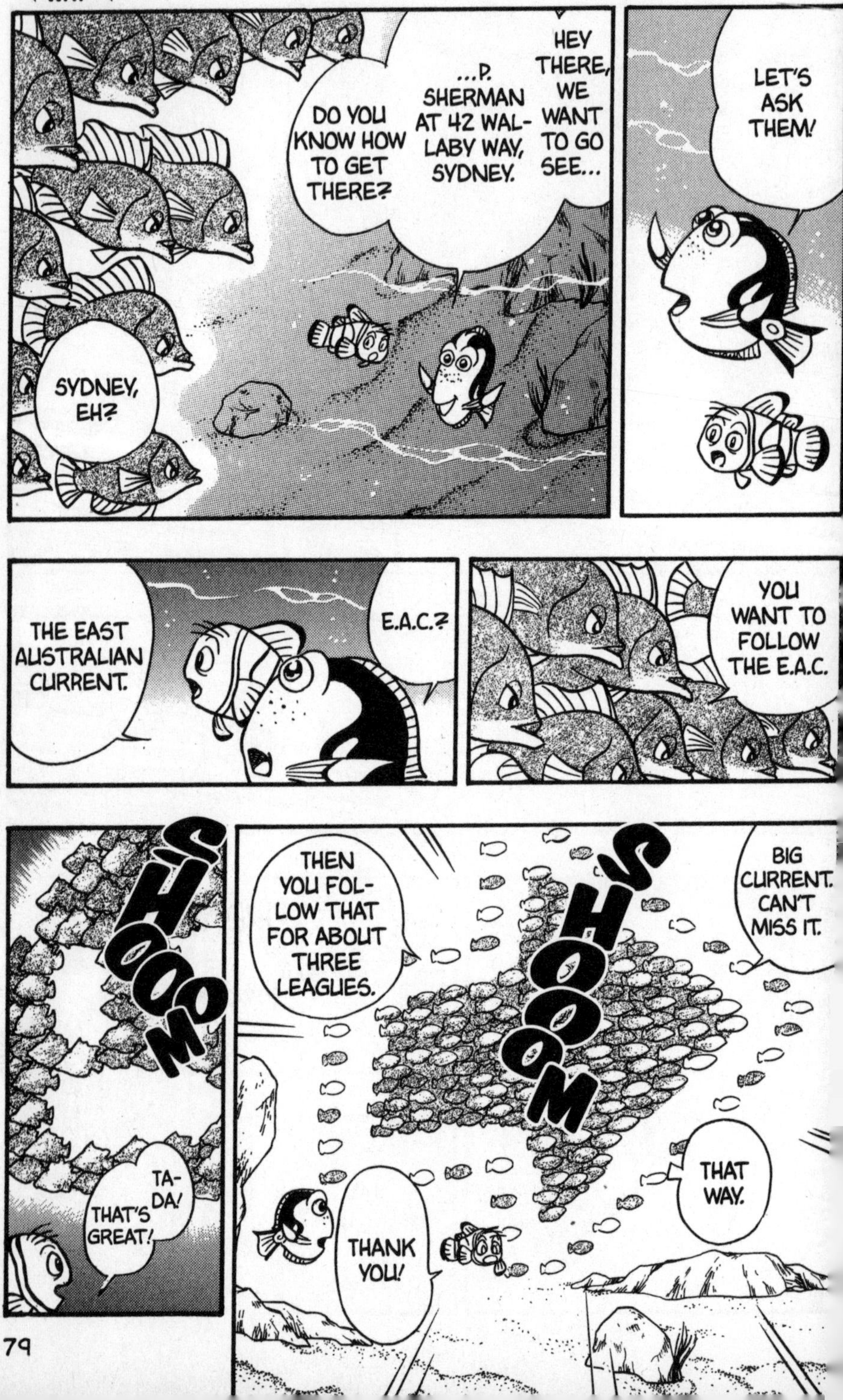
LET'S ASK THEM!
HEY THERE, WE WANT TO GO SEE...
...P. SHERMAN AT 42 WAL-LABY WAY, SYDNEY.
DO YOU KNOW HOW TO GET THERE?
SYDNEY, EH?
YOU WANT TO FOLLOW THE E.A.C.
E.A.C.?
THE EAST AUSTRALIAN CURRENT.
BIG CURRENT. CAN'T MISS IT.
SHOOOM
THEN YOU FOL-LOW THAT FOR ABOUT THREE LEAGUES.
THAT WAY.
THANK YOU!
SHOOOM
TA-DA!
THAT'S GREAT!

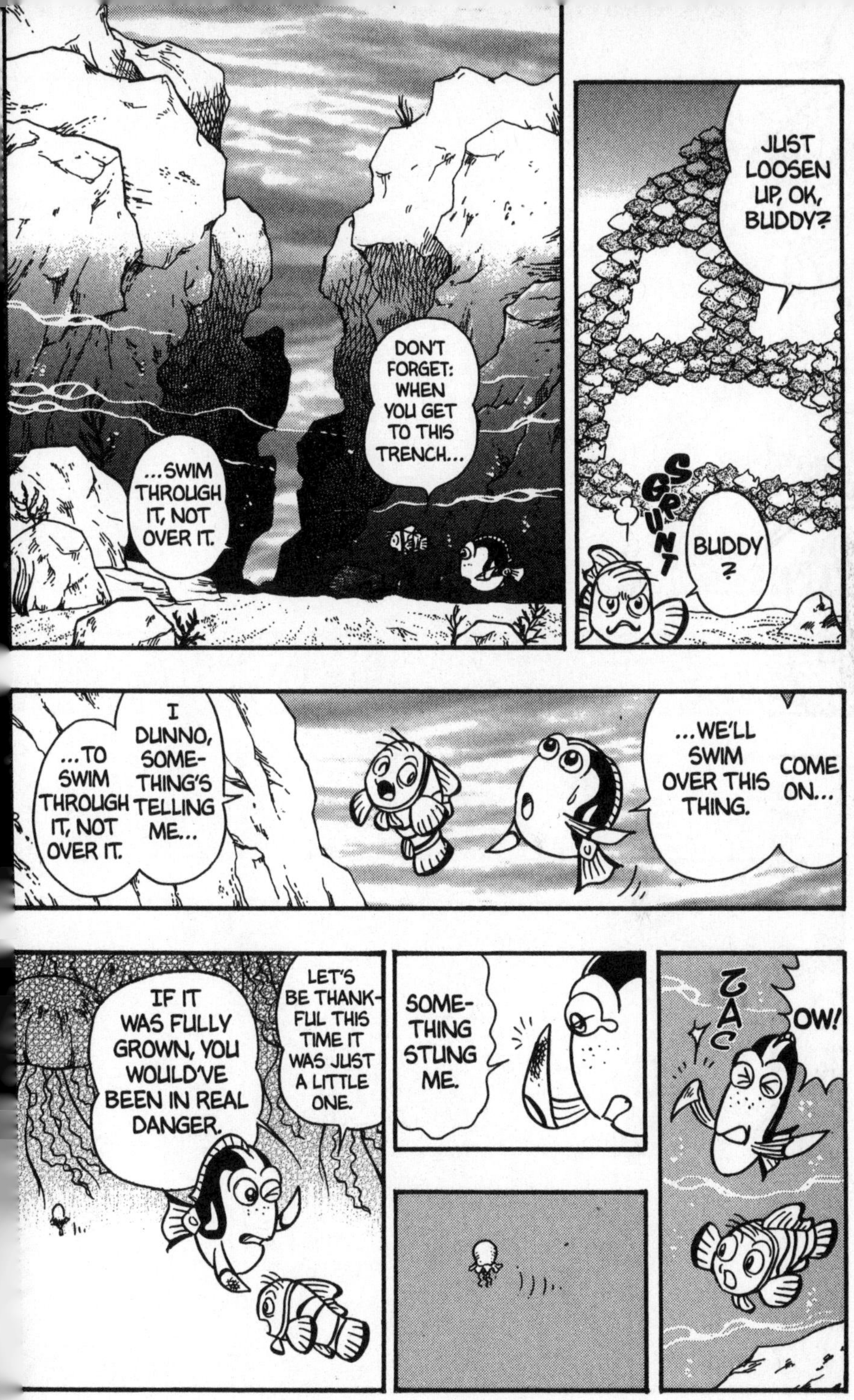
JUST LOOSEN UP, OK, BUDDY?
SGRUNT
BUDDY?
DON'T FORGET: WHEN YOU GET TO THIS TRENCH...
...SWIM THROUGH IT, NOT OVER IT.
COME ON...
...WE'LL SWIM OVER THIS THING.
I DUNNO, SOME-THING'S TELLING ME...
...TO SWIM THROUGH IT, NOT OVER IT.
ZAC
OW!
SOME-THING STUNG ME.
LET'S BE THANK-FUL THIS TIME IT WAS JUST A LITTLE ONE.
IF IT WAS FULLY GROWN, YOU WOULD'VE BEEN IN REAL DANGER.

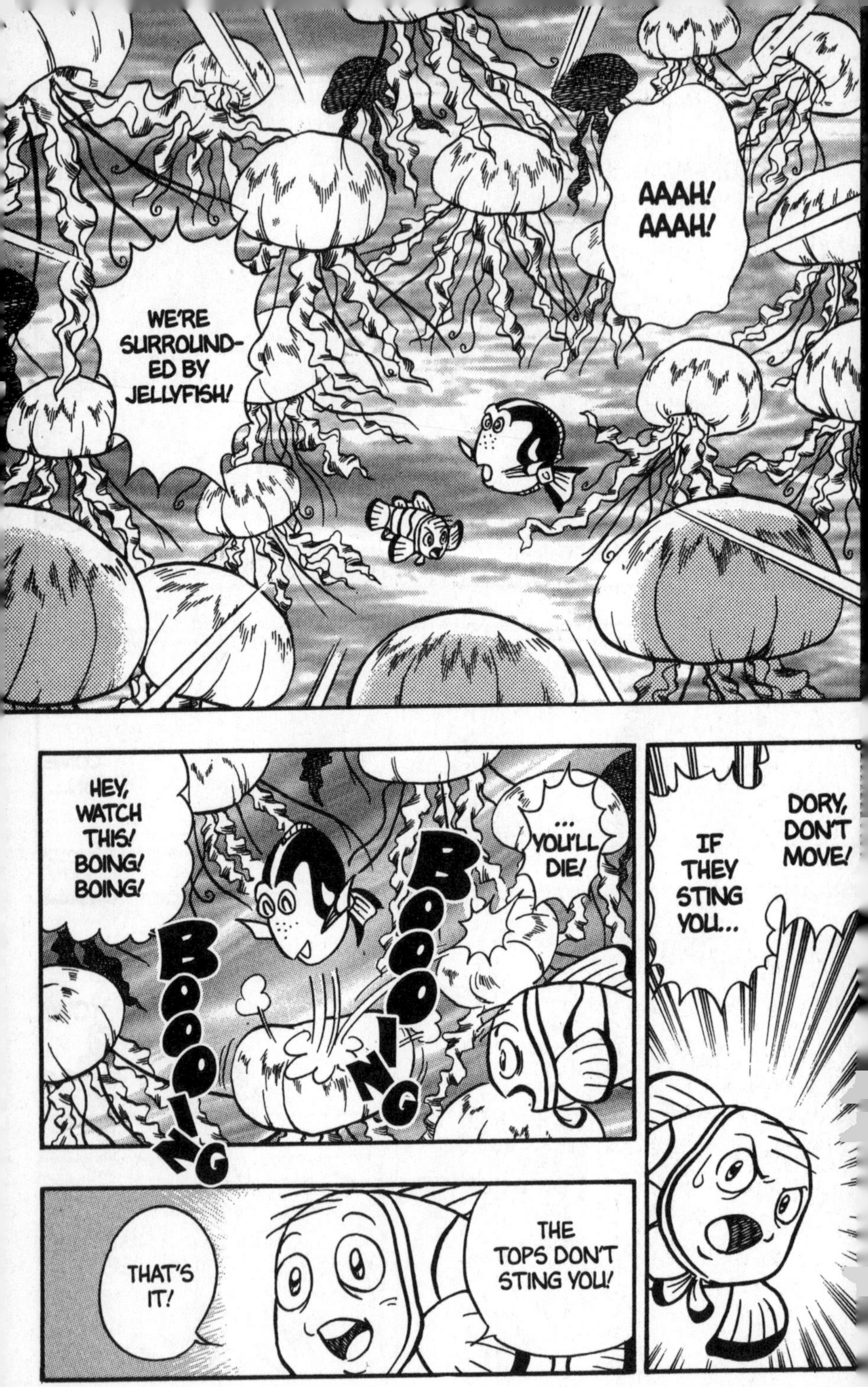
AAAH! AAAH!
WE'RE SURROUND-ED BY JELLYFISH!
DORY, DON'T MOVE!
IF THEY STING YOU...
... YOU'LL DIE!
HEY, WATCH THIS! BOING! BOING!
BOOOING
BOOOING
THE TOPS DON'T STING YOU!
THAT'S IT!

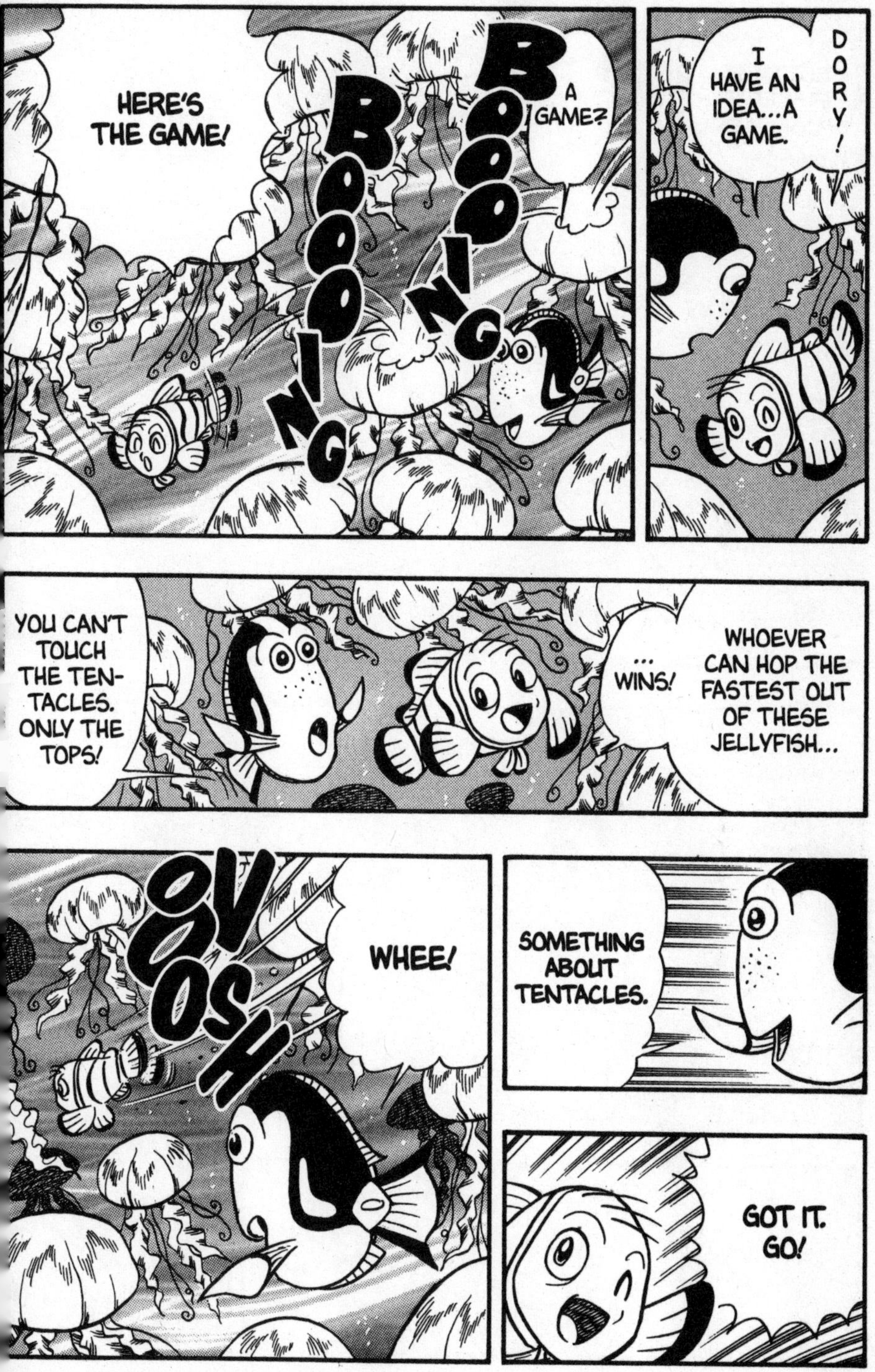
DORY!
I HAVE AN IDEA...A GAME.
A GAME?
BOOOING
BOOOOING
HERE'S THE GAME!
WHOEVER CAN HOP THE FASTEST OUT OF THESE JELLYFISH...
...WINS!
YOU CAN'T TOUCH THE TEN-TACLES. ONLY THE TOPS!
SOMETHING ABOUT TENTACLES.
GOT IT. GO!
WHEE!
WOOSH

READ THIS WAY

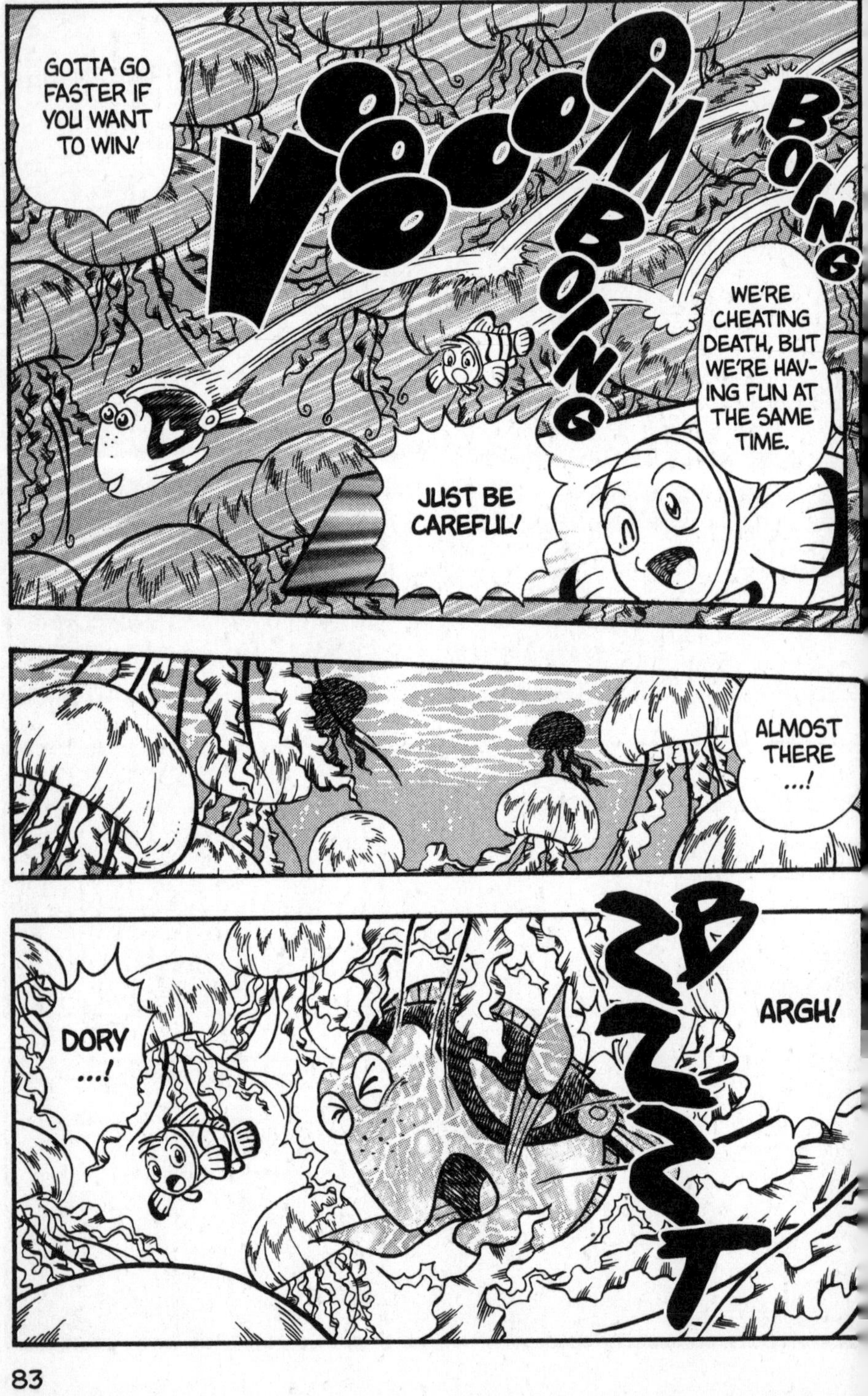
BOING
VOOOOOOOM
WE'RE CHEATING DEATH, BUT WE'RE HAVING FUN AT THE SAME TIME.
BOING BOING
JUST BE CAREFUL!
GOTTA GO FASTER IF YOU WANT TO WIN!
ALMOST THERE ...!
ARGH!
BZZZZT
DORY ...!

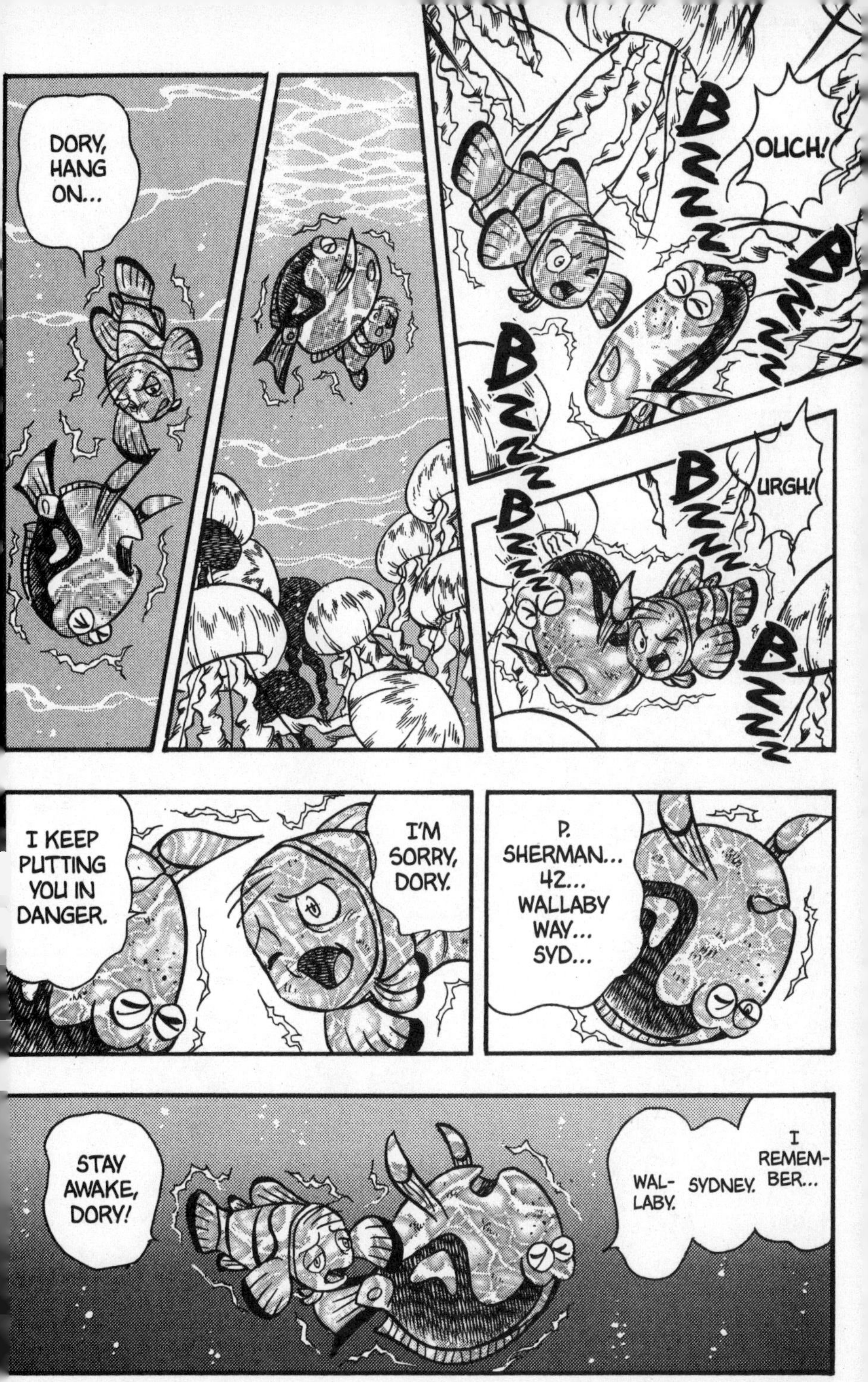
BZZZZ
OUCH!
BZZZZ
BZZZZ
URGH!
BZZZZ
BZZZZ
BZZZZ
DORY, HANG ON...
P. SHERMAN... 42... WALLABY WAY... SYD...
I'M SORRY, DORY.
I KEEP PUTTING YOU IN DANGER.
I REMEMBER...
SYDNEY.
WALLABY.
STAY AWAKE, DORY!

READ THIS WAY

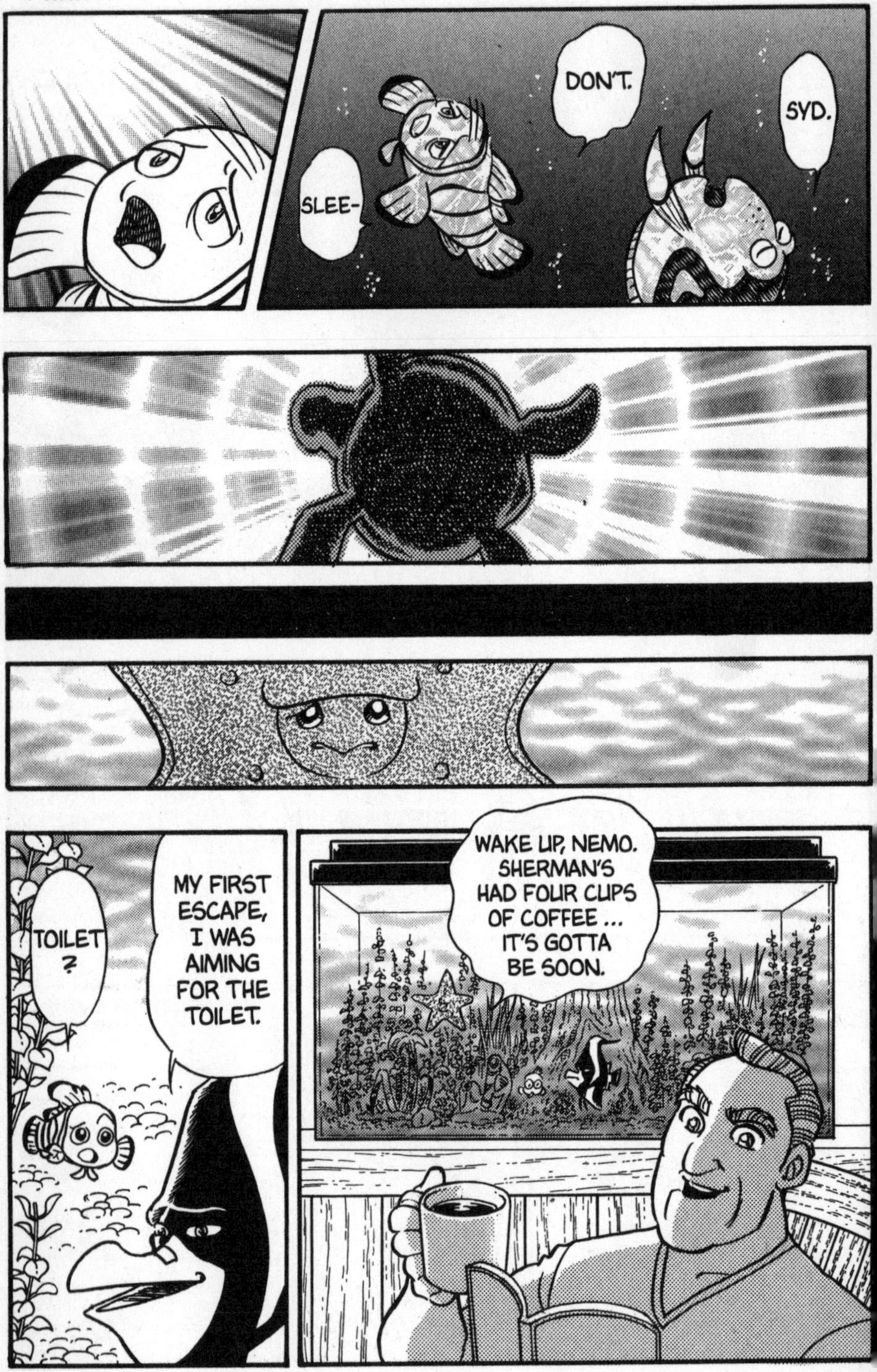

SYD.
DON'T.
SLEE-
WAKE UP, NEMO. SHERMAN'S HAD FOUR CUPS OF COFFEE ... IT'S GOTTA BE SOON.
MY FIRST ESCAPE, I WAS AIMING FOR THE TOILET.
TOILET?

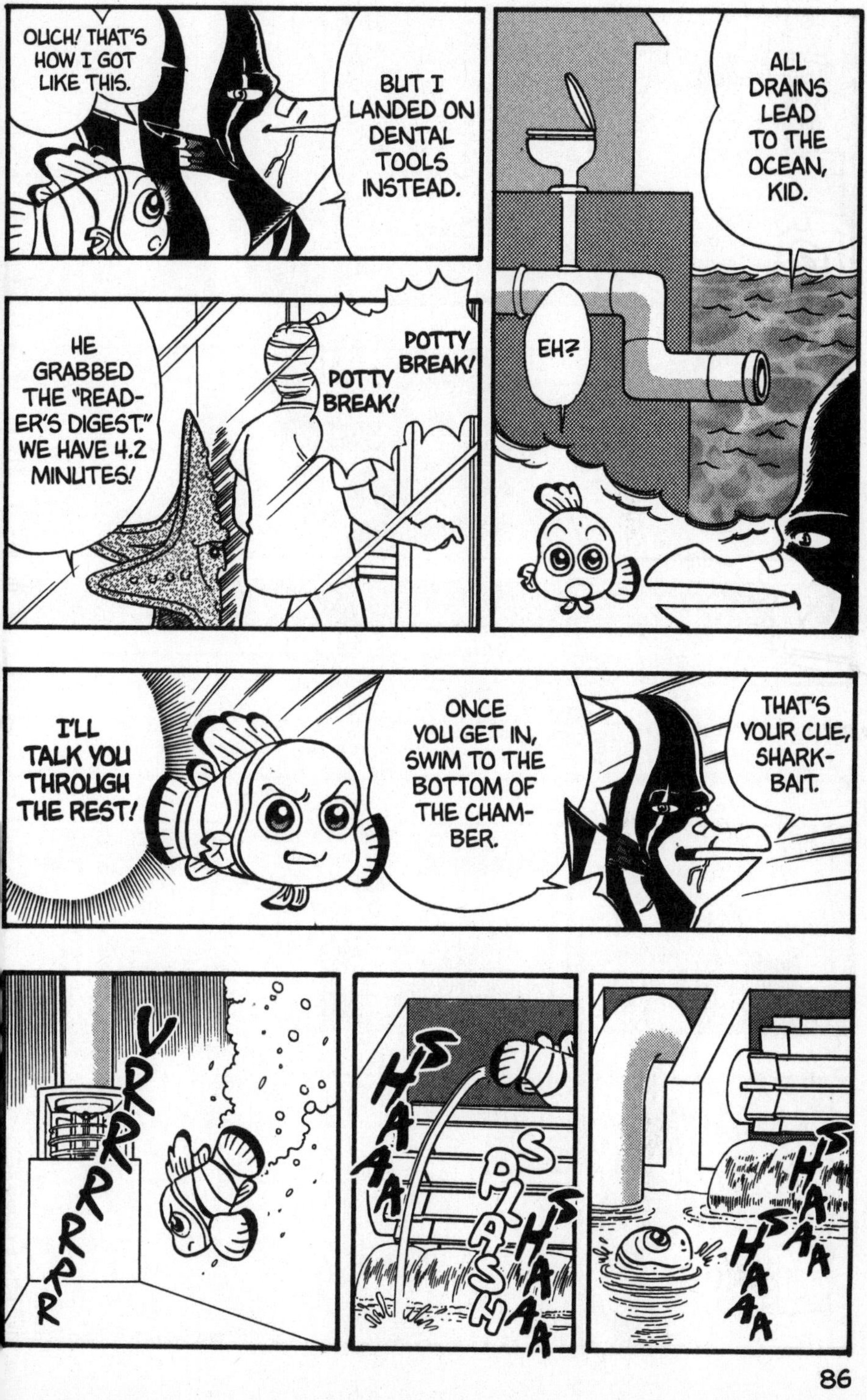
ALL DRAINS LEAD TO THE OCEAN, KID.
EH?
BUT I LANDED ON DENTAL TOOLS INSTEAD.
OUCH! THAT'S HOW I GOT LIKE THIS.
POTTY BREAK!
POTTY BREAK!
HE GRABBED THE "READER'S DIGEST." WE HAVE 4.2 MINUTES!
THAT'S YOUR CUE, SHARK-BAIT.
ONCE YOU GET IN, SWIM TO THE BOTTOM OF THE CHAMBER.
I'LL TALK YOU THROUGH THE REST!
SHAAA
SHAAAA
SHAAAA
SPLASH
SHAAAA
VRRRRRRRRR

READ THIS WAY

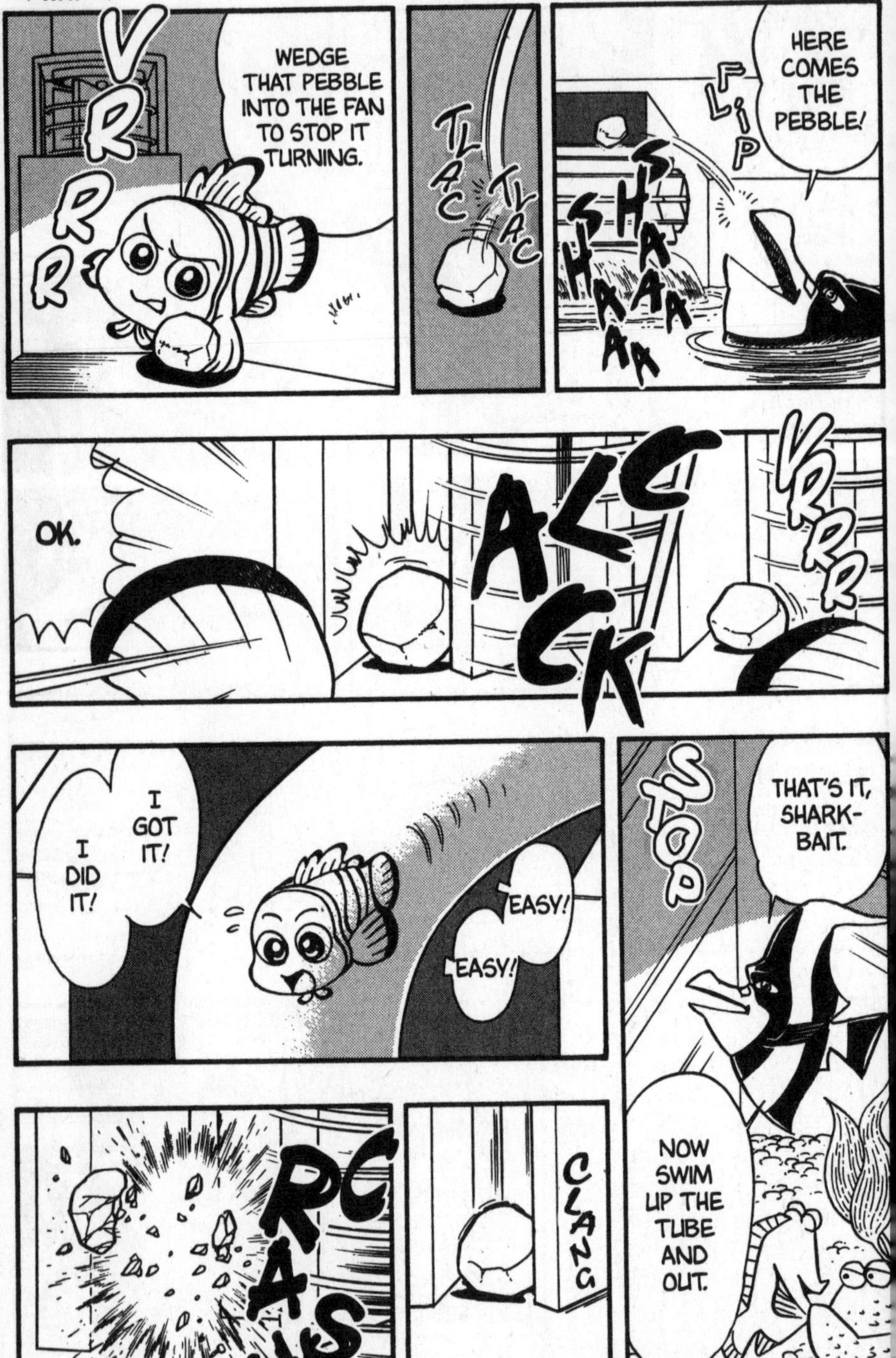

HERE COMES THE PEBBLE!
FLIP
SHAAAAA
SHAAAA
TLAC TLAC
WEDGE THAT PEBBLE INTO THE FAN TO STOP IT TURNING.
VRRRR
VRRRR
CLACK
OK.
THAT'S IT, SHARK-BAIT.
STOP
NOW SWIM UP THE TUBE AND OUT.
EASY!
EASY!
I GOT IT!
I DID IT!
CLANG
CRASH

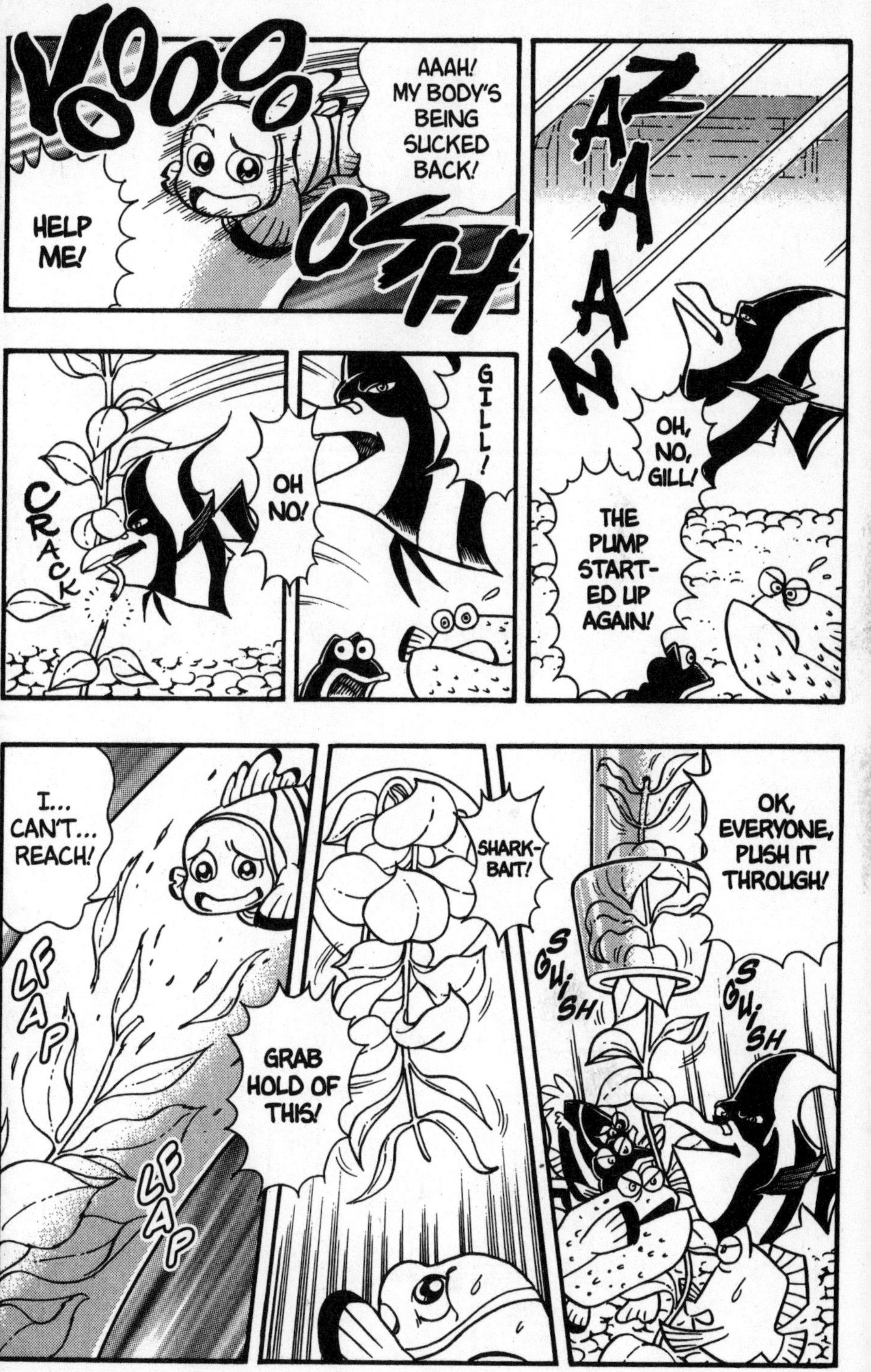
ZAAAN
OH, NO, GILL!
THE PUMP STARTED UP AGAIN!
AAAH! MY BODY'S BEING SUCKED BACK!
HELP ME!
YOOOOOOSH
GILL!
OH NO!
CRACK
OK, EVERYONE, PUSH IT THROUGH!
SQUISH
SQUISH
SHARK-BAIT!
GRAB HOLD OF THIS!
I... CAN'T... REACH!
FLAP
FLAP

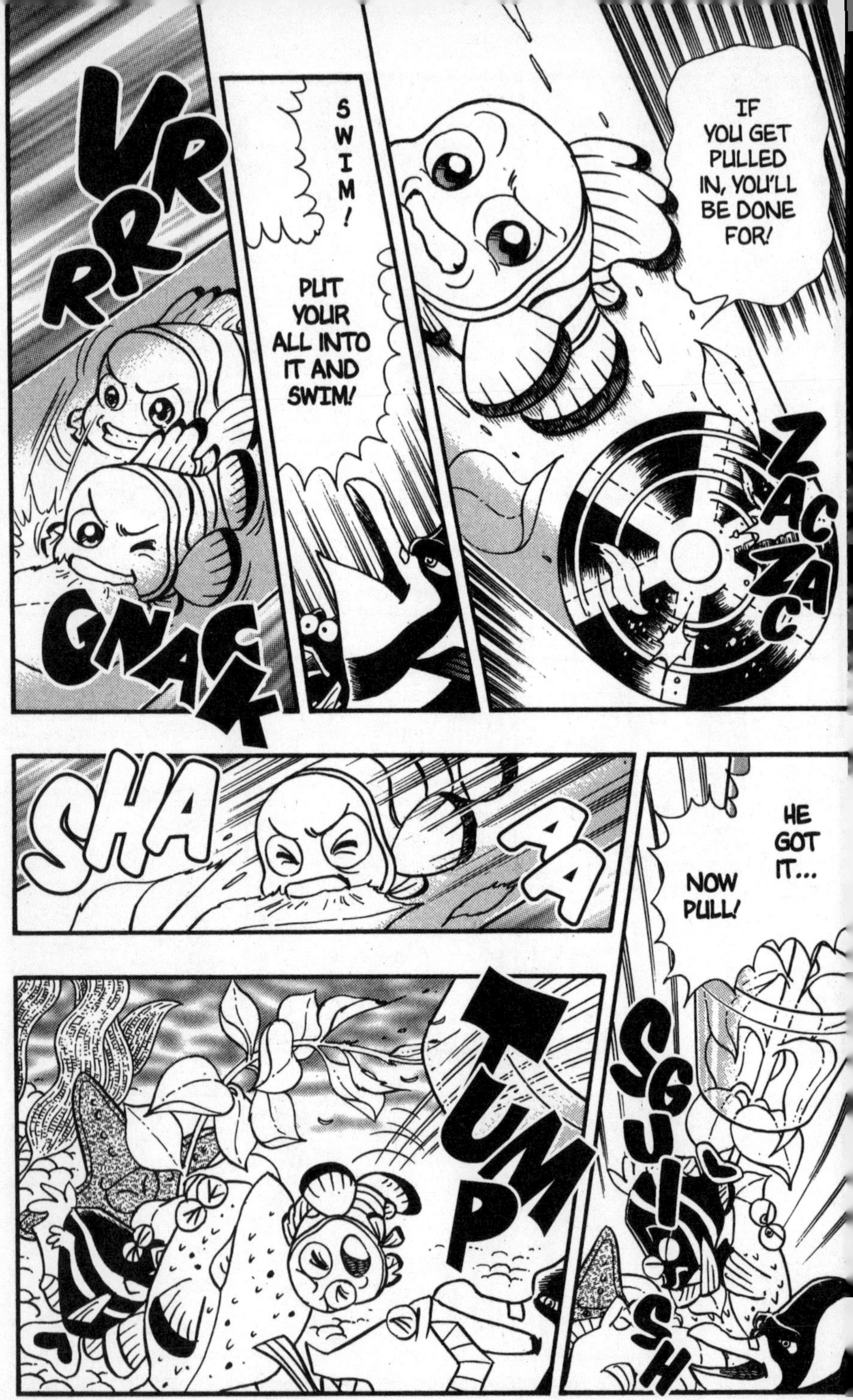
IF YOU GET PULLED IN, YOU'LL BE DONE FOR!
ZAC ZAC
SWIM!
PUT YOUR ALL INTO IT AND SWIM!
VRRRR
GNACK
HE GOT IT...
NOW PULL!
SGUISH
SHA
AA
TUMP

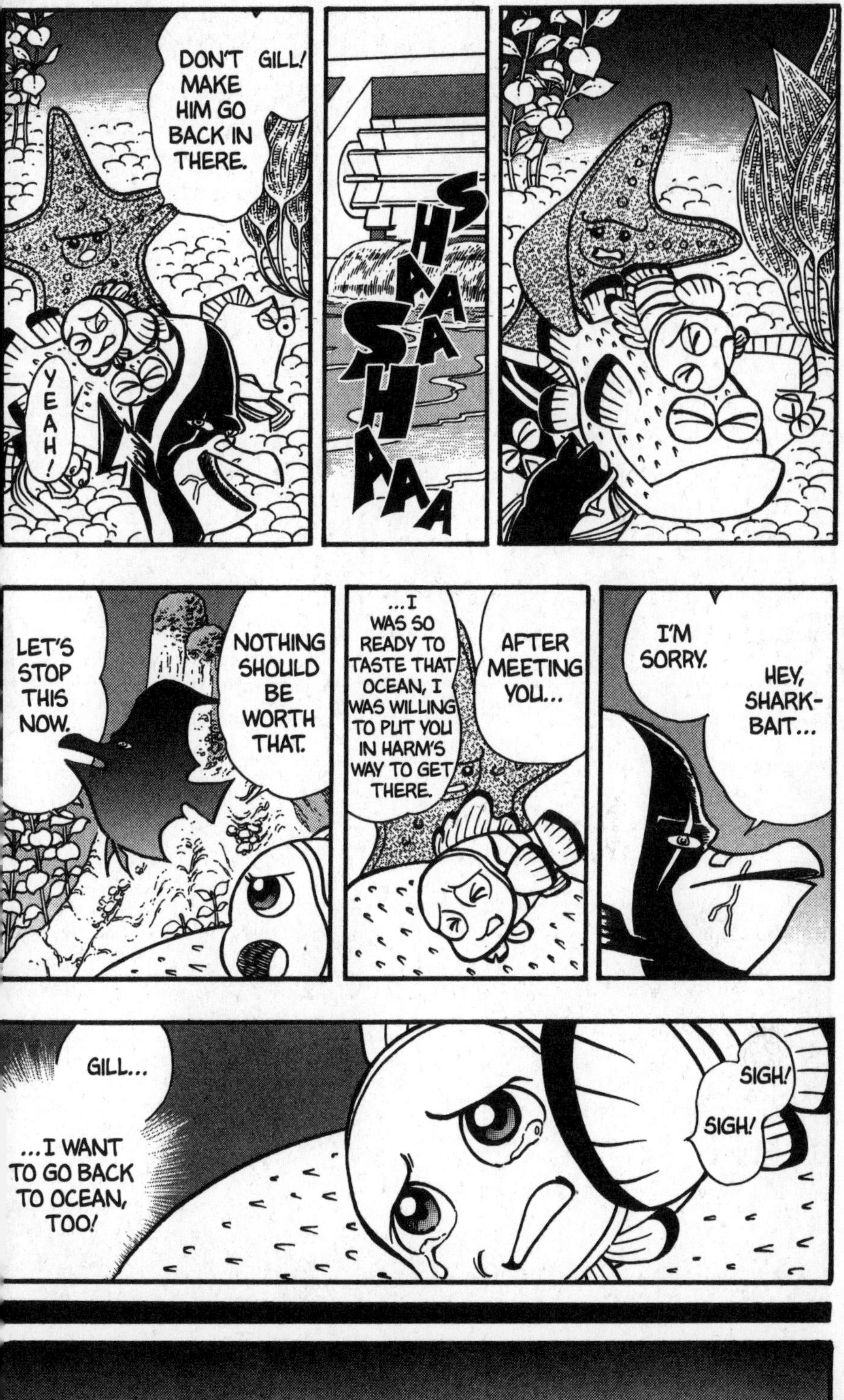
SHAAA
SHAAA
GILL! DON'T MAKE HIM GO BACK IN THERE.
YEAH!
HEY, SHARK-BAIT...
I'M SORRY.
AFTER MEETING YOU...
...I WAS SO READY TO TASTE THAT OCEAN, I WAS WILLING TO PUT YOU IN HARM'S WAY TO GET THERE.
NOTHING SHOULD BE WORTH THAT.
LET'S STOP THIS NOW.
SIGH!
SIGH!
GILL...
...I WANT TO GO BACK TO OCEAN, TOO!

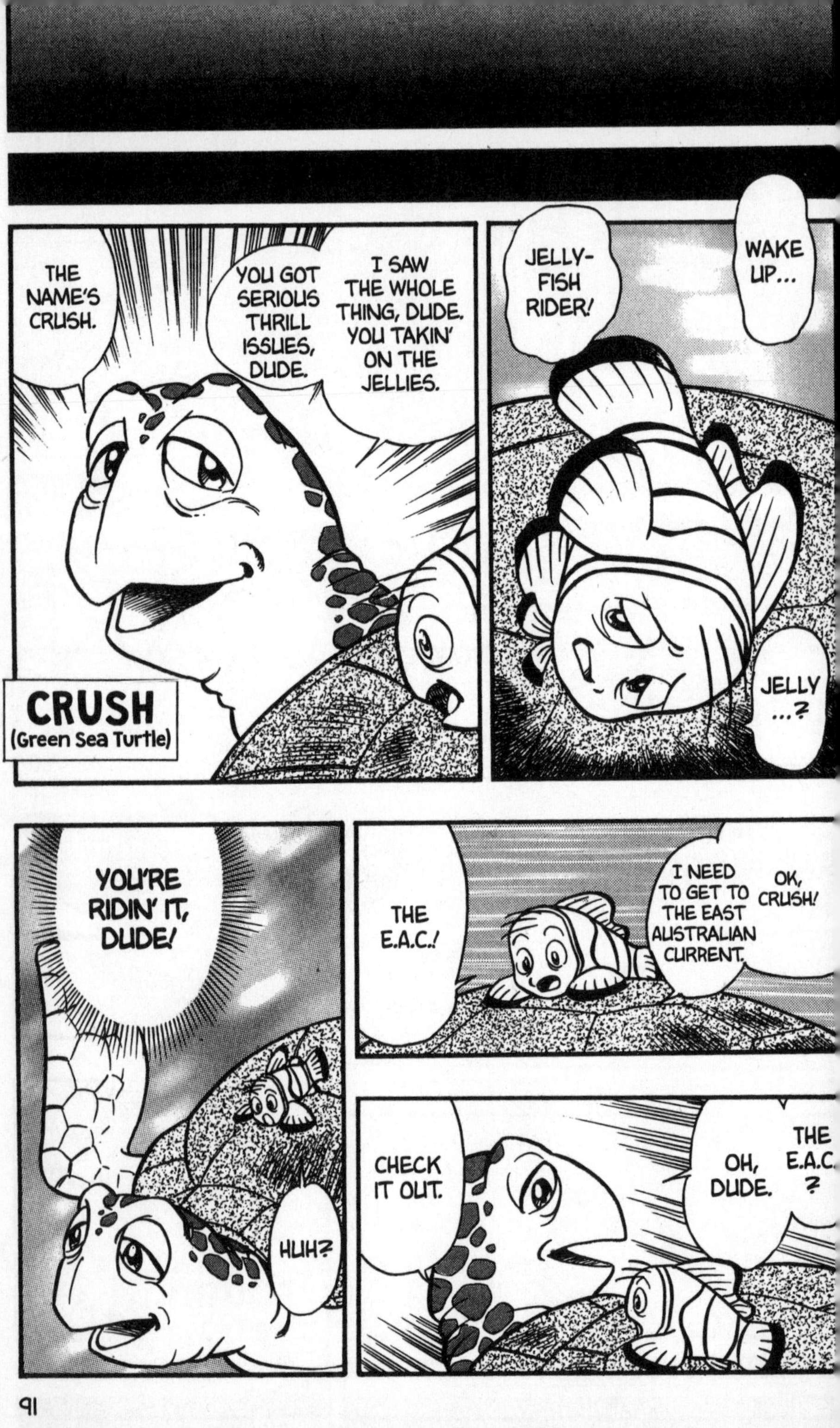
WAKE UP...
JELLY-FISH RIDER!
JELLY ...?
I SAW THE WHOLE THING, DUDE. YOU TAKIN' ON THE JELLIES.
YOU GOT SERIOUS THRILL ISSUES, DUDE.
THE NAME'S CRUSH.
CRUSH
(Green Sea Turtle)
OK, CRUSH!
I NEED TO GET TO THE EAST AUSTRALIAN CURRENT.
THE E.A.C.!
THE E.A.C.?
OH, DUDE.
CHECK IT OUT.
YOU'RE RIDIN' IT, DUDE!
HUH?

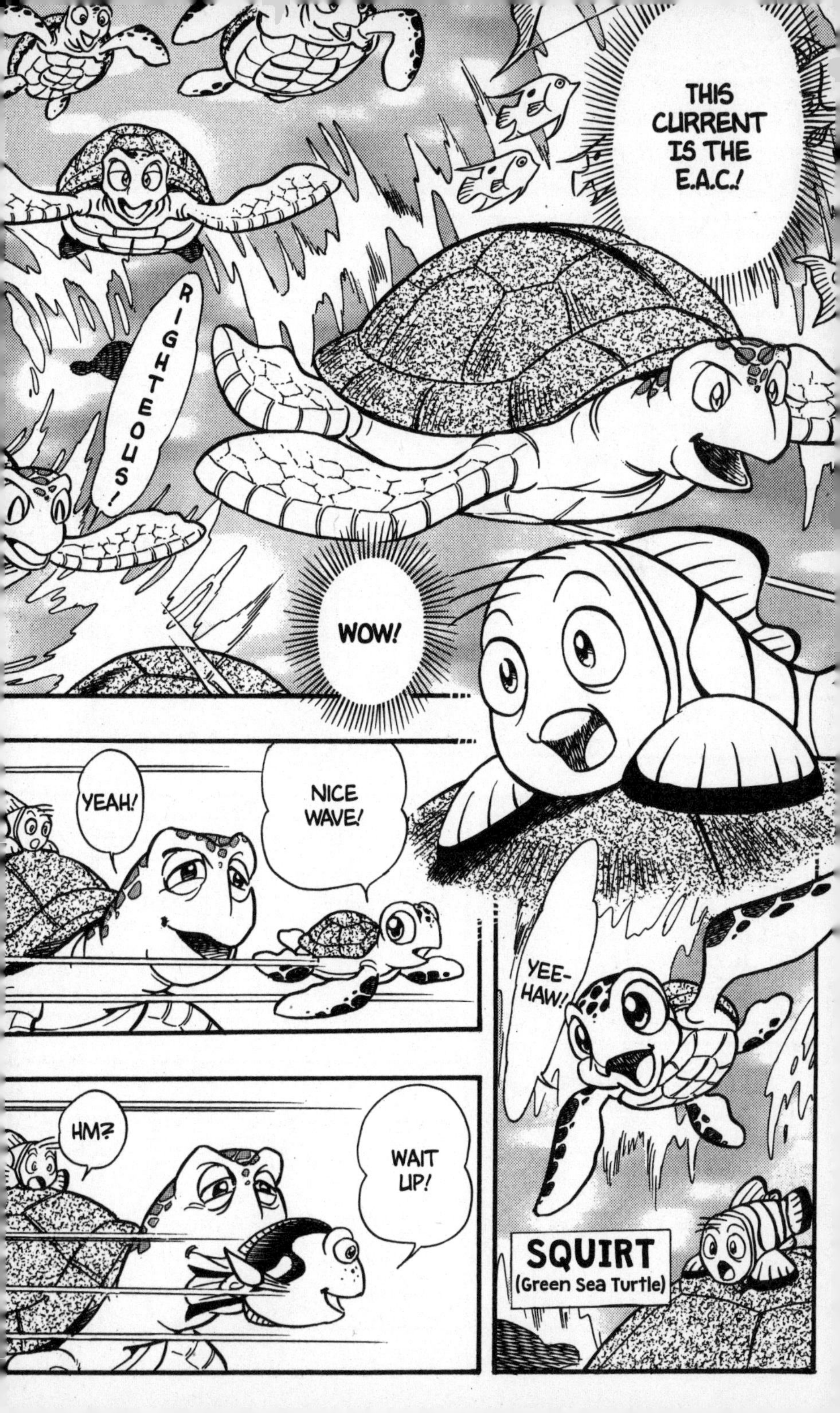
THIS CURRENT IS THE E.A.C.!
RIGHTEOUS!
WOW!
YEE-HAW!
SQUIRT
(Green Sea Turtle)
NICE WAVE!
YEAH!
WAIT UP!
HM?

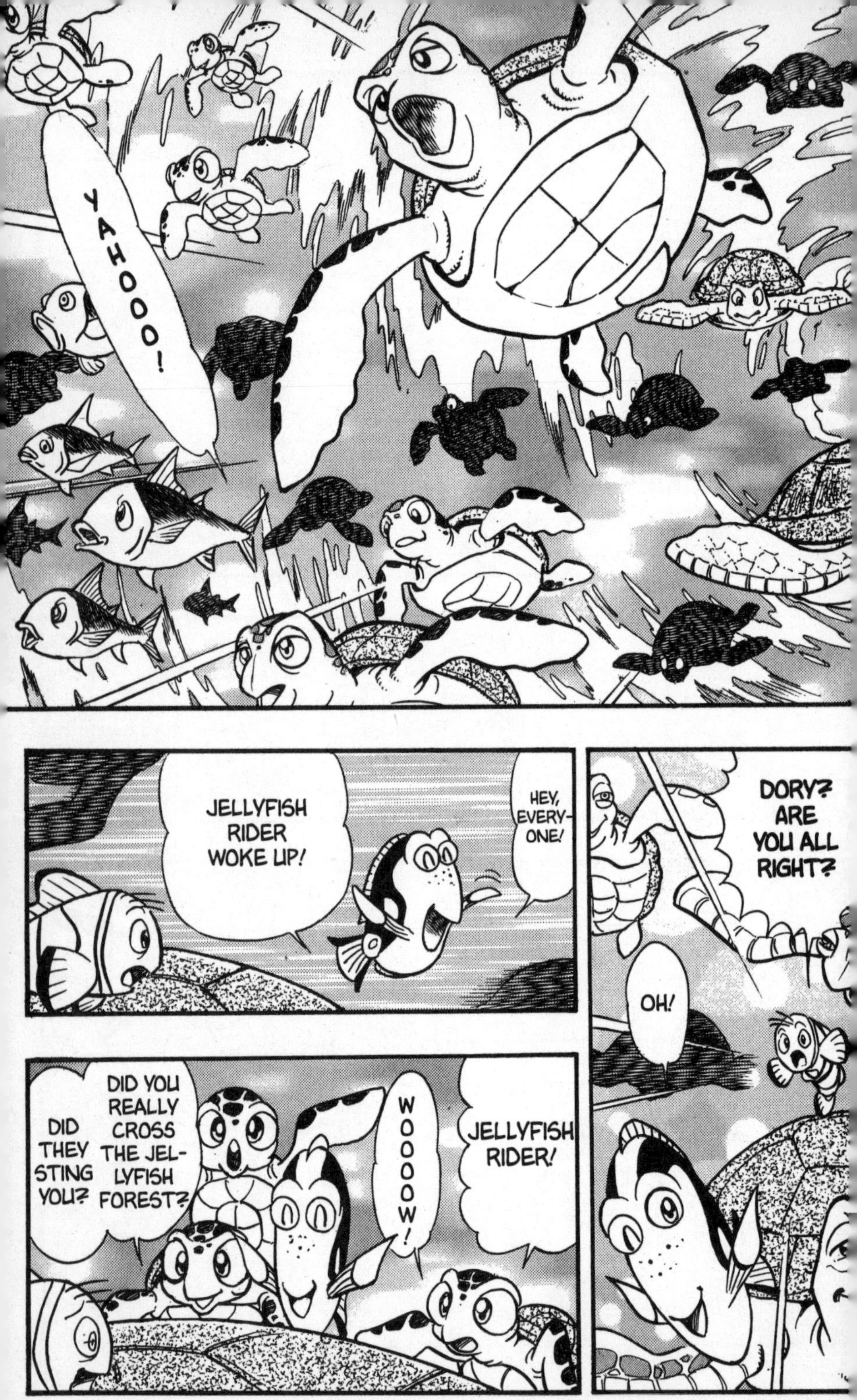
YAHOOOO!
DORY? ARE YOU ALL RIGHT?
OH!
HEY, EVERY-ONE!
JELLYFISH RIDER WOKE UP!
JELLYFISH RIDER!
WOOOOOW!
DID YOU REALLY CROSS THE JEL-LYFISH FOREST?
DID THEY STING YOU?

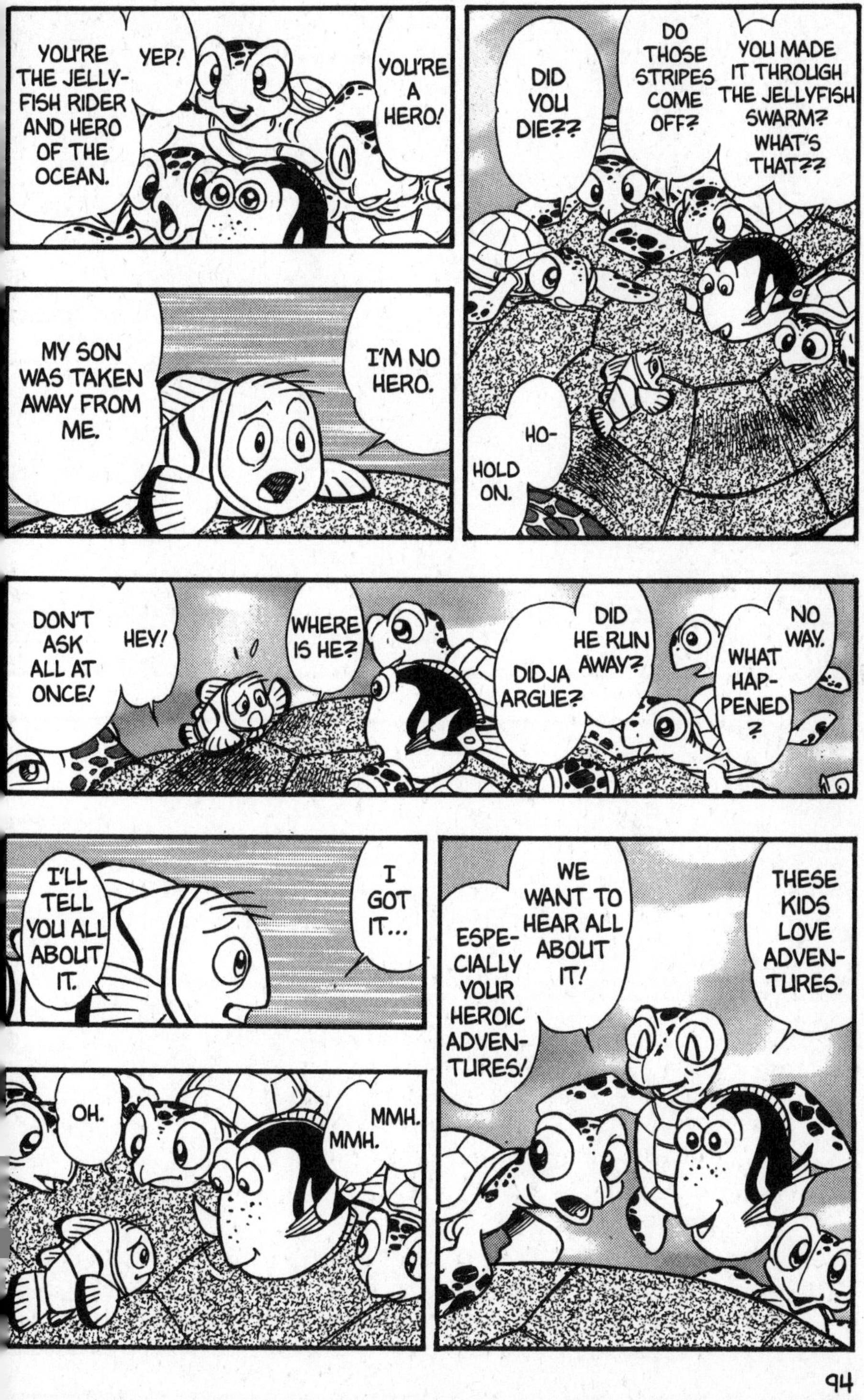
YOU MADE IT THROUGH THE JELLYFISH SWARM? WHAT'S THAT??
DO THOSE STRIPES COME OFF?
DID YOU DIE??
HO- HOLD ON.
YOU'RE A HERO!
YEP!
YOU'RE THE JELLY-FISH RIDER AND HERO OF THE OCEAN.
I'M NO HERO.
MY SON WAS TAKEN AWAY FROM ME.
NO WAY. WHAT HAP-PENED?
DID HE RUN AWAY?
DIDJA ARGUE?
WHERE IS HE?
HEY!
DON'T ASK ALL AT ONCE!
THESE KIDS LOVE ADVEN-TURES.
WE WANT TO HEAR ALL ABOUT IT!
ESPE-CIALLY YOUR HEROIC ADVEN-TURES!
I GOT IT...
I'LL TELL YOU ALL ABOUT IT.
MMH. MMH.
OH.

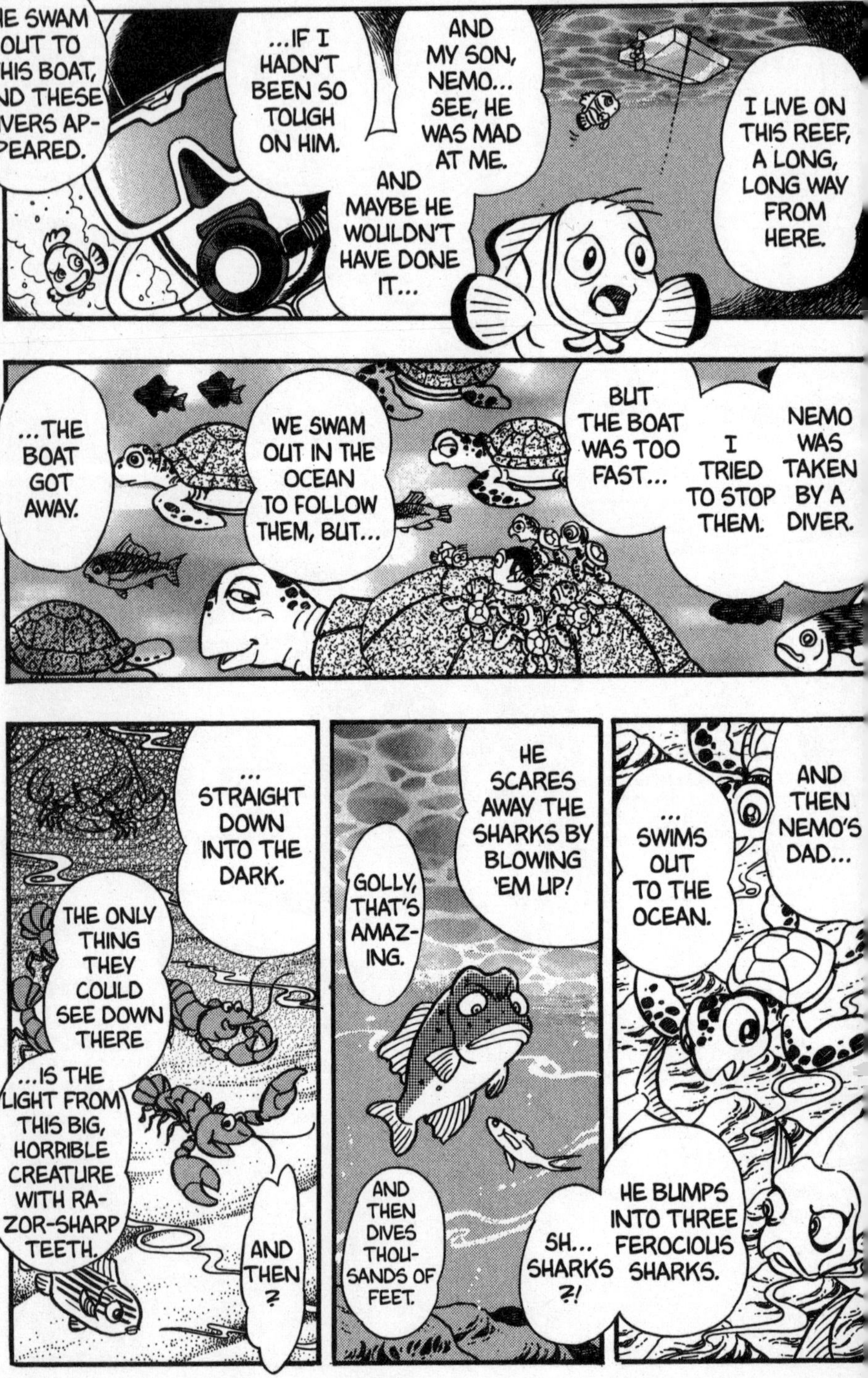
I LIVE ON THIS REEF, A LONG, LONG WAY FROM HERE.
AND MY SON, NEMO... SEE, HE WAS MAD AT ME.
AND MAYBE HE WOULDN'T HAVE DONE IT...
...IF I HADN'T BEEN SO TOUGH ON HIM.
HE SWAM OUT TO THIS BOAT, AND THESE DIVERS AP-PEARED.
NEMO WAS TAKEN BY A DIVER.
I TRIED TO STOP THEM.
BUT THE BOAT WAS TOO FAST...
WE SWAM OUT IN THE OCEAN TO FOLLOW THEM, BUT...
...THE BOAT GOT AWAY.
AND THEN NEMO'S DAD...
... SWIMS OUT TO THE OCEAN.
HE BUMPS INTO THREE FEROCIOUS SHARKS.
SH... SHARKS ?!
HE SCARES AWAY THE SHARKS BY BLOWING 'EM UP!
GOLLY, THAT'S AMAZ-ING.
AND THEN DIVES THOU-SANDS OF FEET.
... STRAIGHT DOWN INTO THE DARK.
THE ONLY THING THEY COULD SEE DOWN THERE
...IS THE LIGHT FROM THIS BIG, HORRIBLE CREATURE WITH RA-ZOR-SHARP TEETH.
AND THEN ?

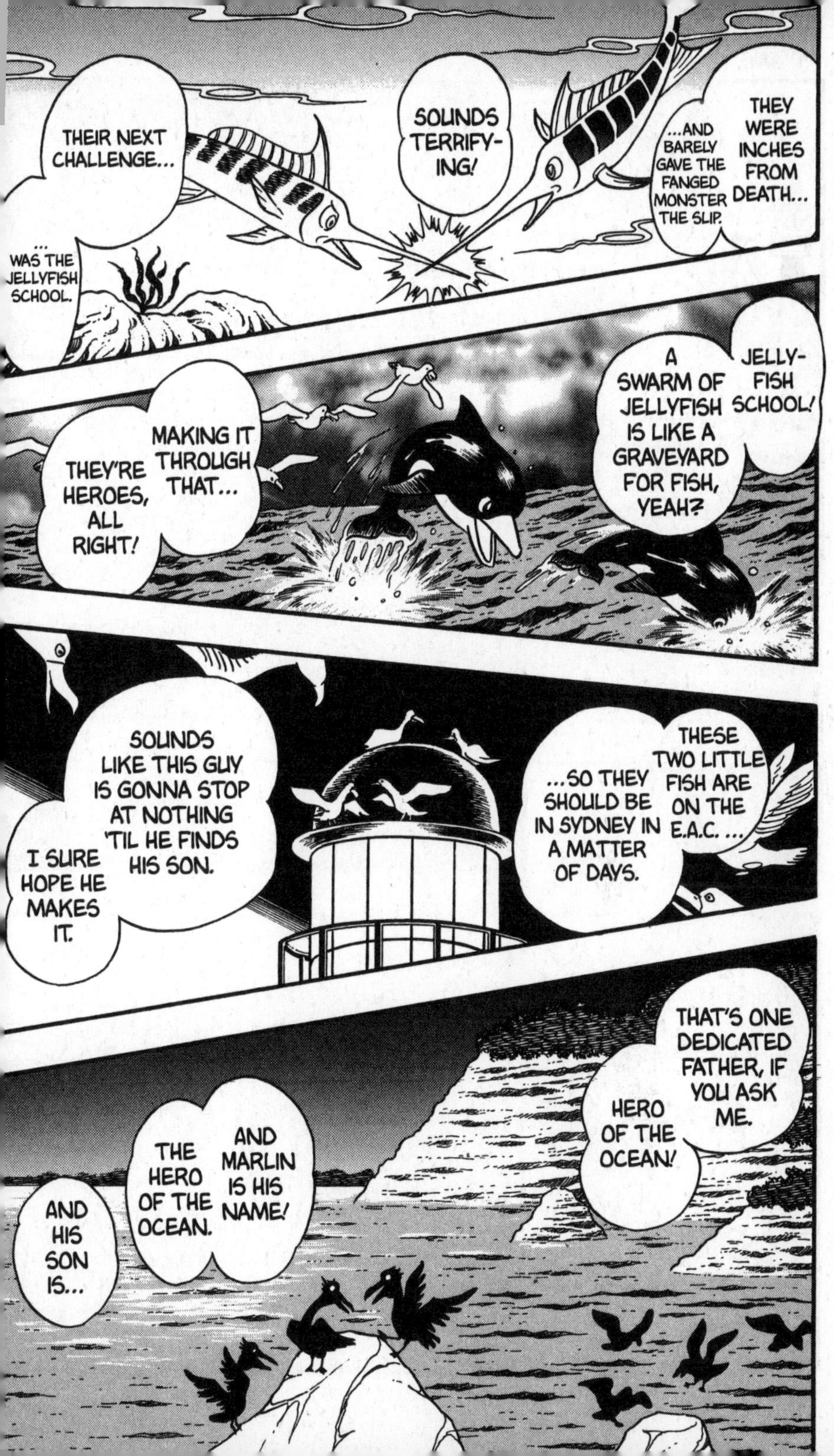
THEY WERE INCHES FROM DEATH...
...AND BARELY GAVE THE FANGED MONSTER THE SLIP.
SOUNDS TERRIFYING!
THEIR NEXT CHALLENGE...
...WAS THE JELLYFISH SCHOOL.
JELLYFISH SCHOOL!
A SWARM OF JELLYFISH IS LIKE A GRAVEYARD FOR FISH, YEAH?
MAKING IT THROUGH THAT...
THEY'RE HEROES, ALL RIGHT!
THESE TWO LITTLE FISH ARE ON THE E.A.C. ...
...SO THEY SHOULD BE IN SYDNEY IN A MATTER OF DAYS.
SOUNDS LIKE THIS GUY IS GONNA STOP AT NOTHING 'TIL HE FINDS HIS SON.
I SURE HOPE HE MAKES IT.
THAT'S ONE DEDICATED FATHER, IF YOU ASK ME.
HERO OF THE OCEAN!
AND MARLIN IS HIS NAME!
THE HERO OF THE OCEAN.
AND HIS SON IS...

READ THIS WAY

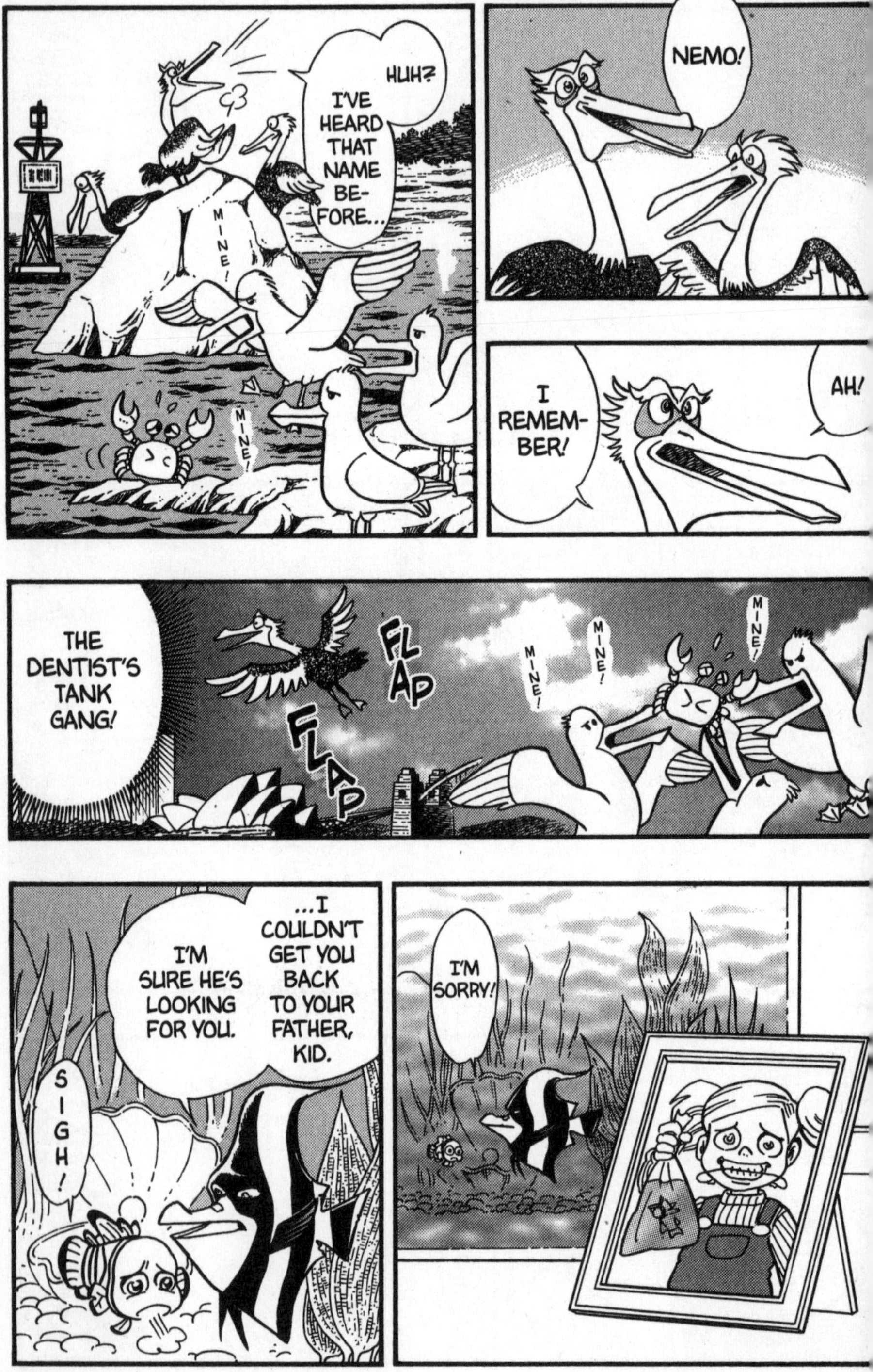
NEMO!
AH!
I REMEMBER!
HUH? I'VE HEARD THAT NAME BEFORE...
MINE!
MINE!
MINE!
MINE!
MINE!
FLAP
FLAP
THE DENTIST'S TANK GANG!
I'M SORRY!
...I COULDN'T GET YOU BACK TO YOUR FATHER, KID.
I'M SURE HE'S LOOKING FOR YOU.
SIGH!

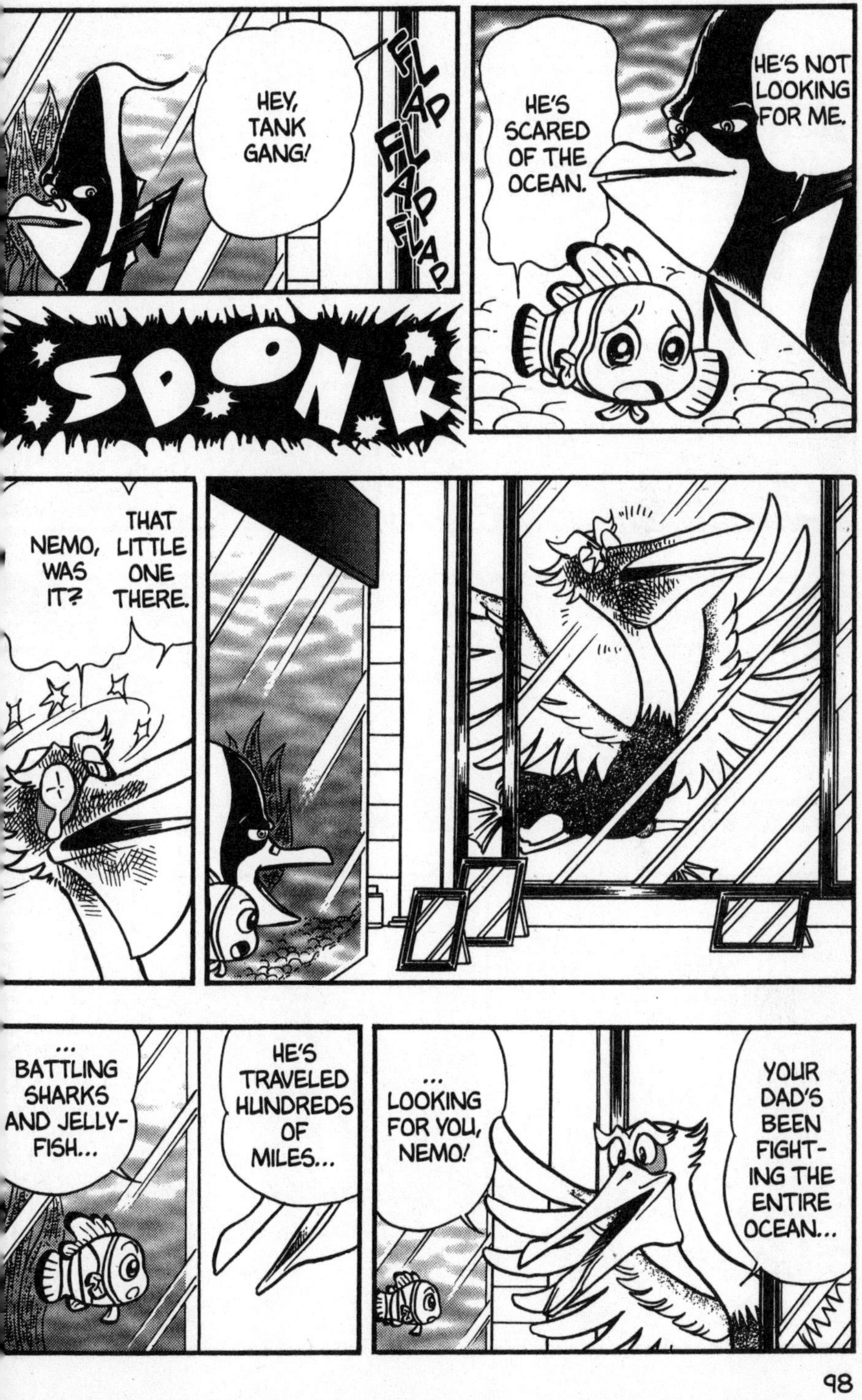
HE'S NOT LOOKING FOR ME.
HE'S SCARED OF THE OCEAN.
FLAP FLAP FLAP
HEY, TANK GANG!
SDONK
THAT LITTLE ONE THERE.
NEMO, WAS IT?
YOUR DAD'S BEEN FIGHT-ING THE ENTIRE OCEAN...
... LOOKING FOR YOU, NEMO!
HE'S TRAVELED HUNDREDS OF MILES...
... BATTLING SHARKS AND JELLY-FISH...

READ THIS WAY

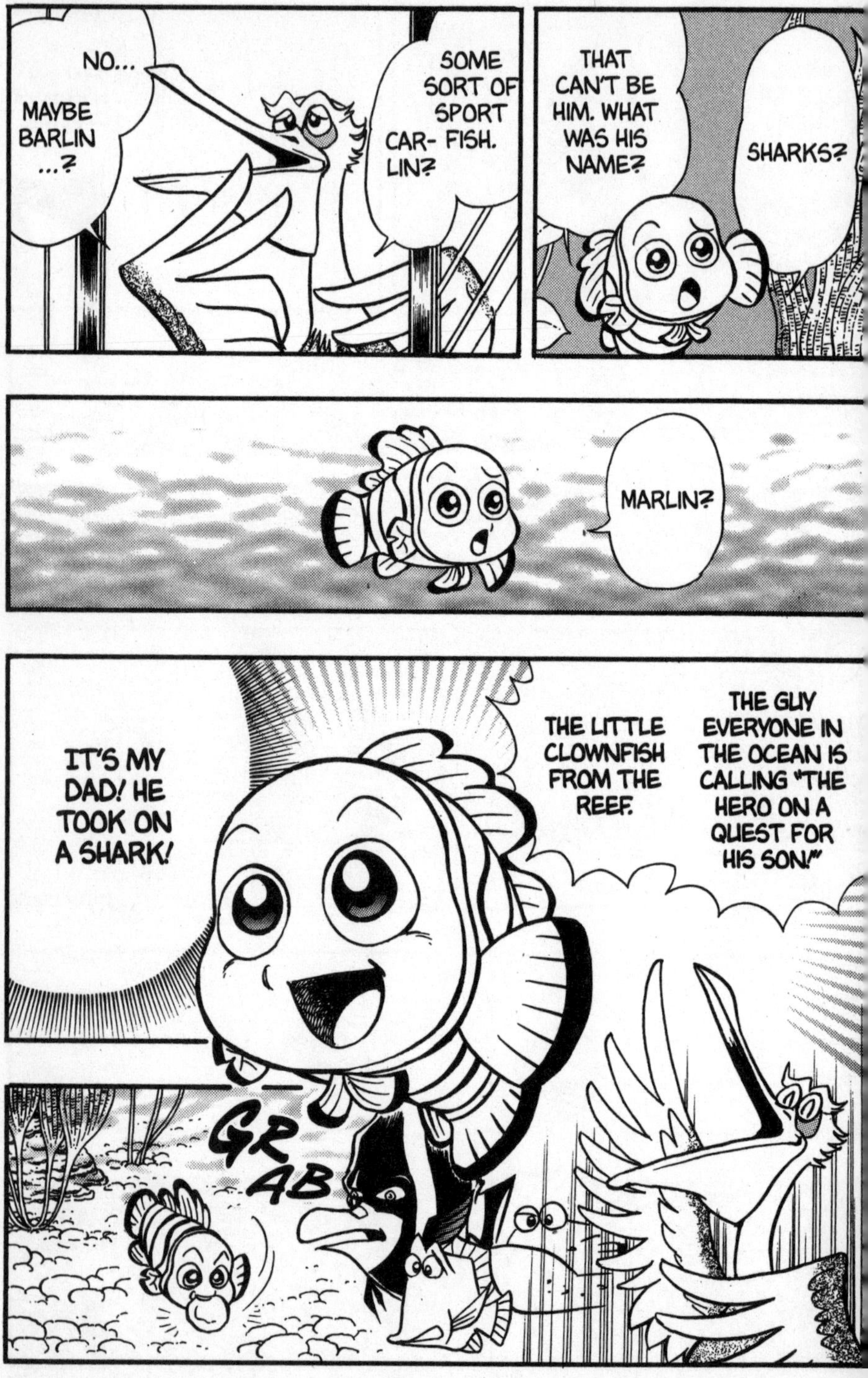

SHARKS?
THAT CAN'T BE HIM. WHAT WAS HIS NAME?
SOME SORT OF SPORT FISH.
CARLIN?
NO...
MAYBE BARLIN ...?
MARLIN?
THE GUY EVERYONE IN THE OCEAN IS CALLING "THE HERO ON A QUEST FOR HIS SON!"
THE LITTLE CLOWNFISH FROM THE REEF.
IT'S MY DAD! HE TOOK ON A SHARK!
GRAB

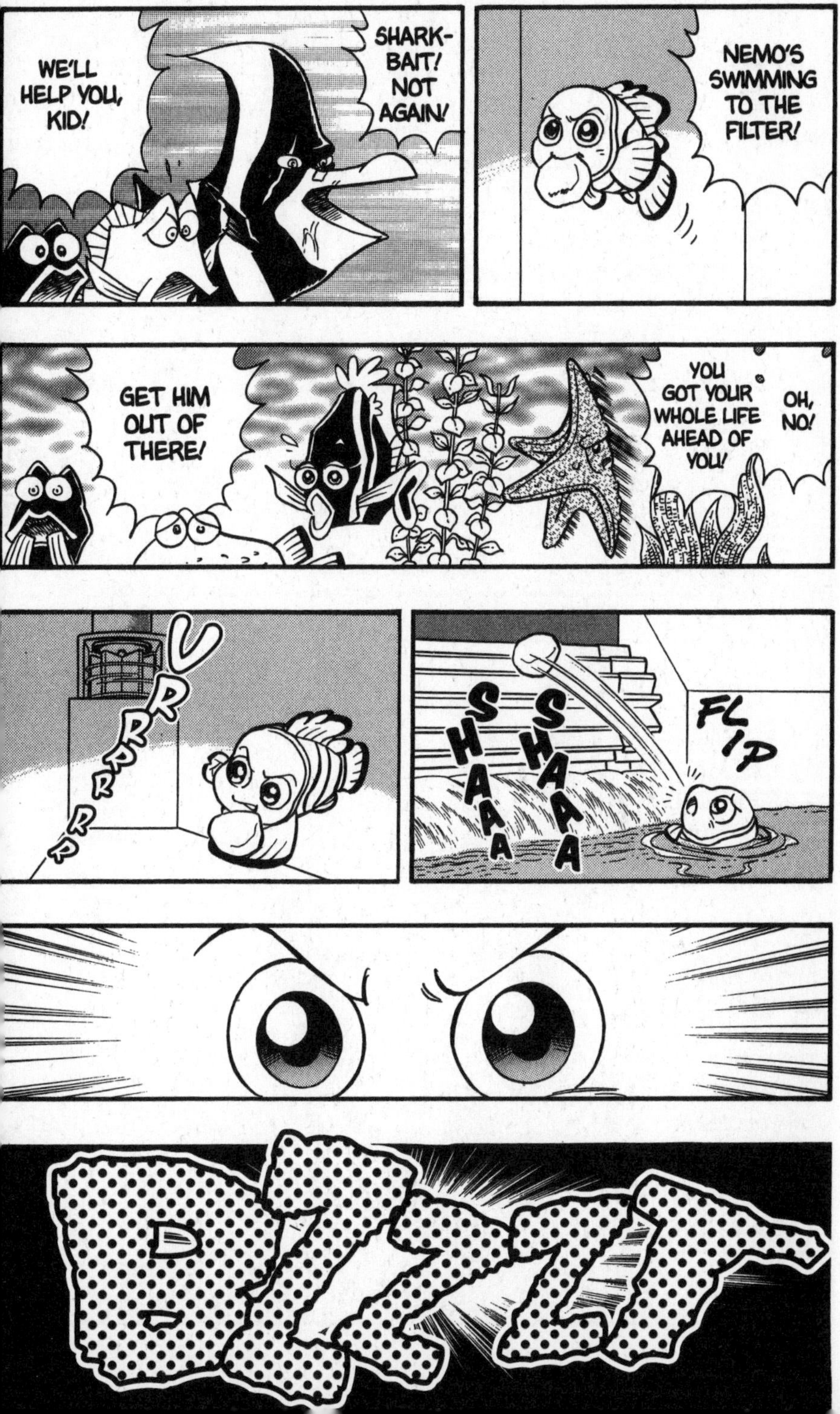
NEMO'S SWIMMING TO THE FILTER!
SHARK-BAIT! NOT AGAIN!
WE'LL HELP YOU, KID!
OH, NO!
YOU GOT YOUR WHOLE LIFE AHEAD OF YOU!
GET HIM OUT OF THERE!
FLIP
SHAAAA
SHAAAA
VRRRRRRR

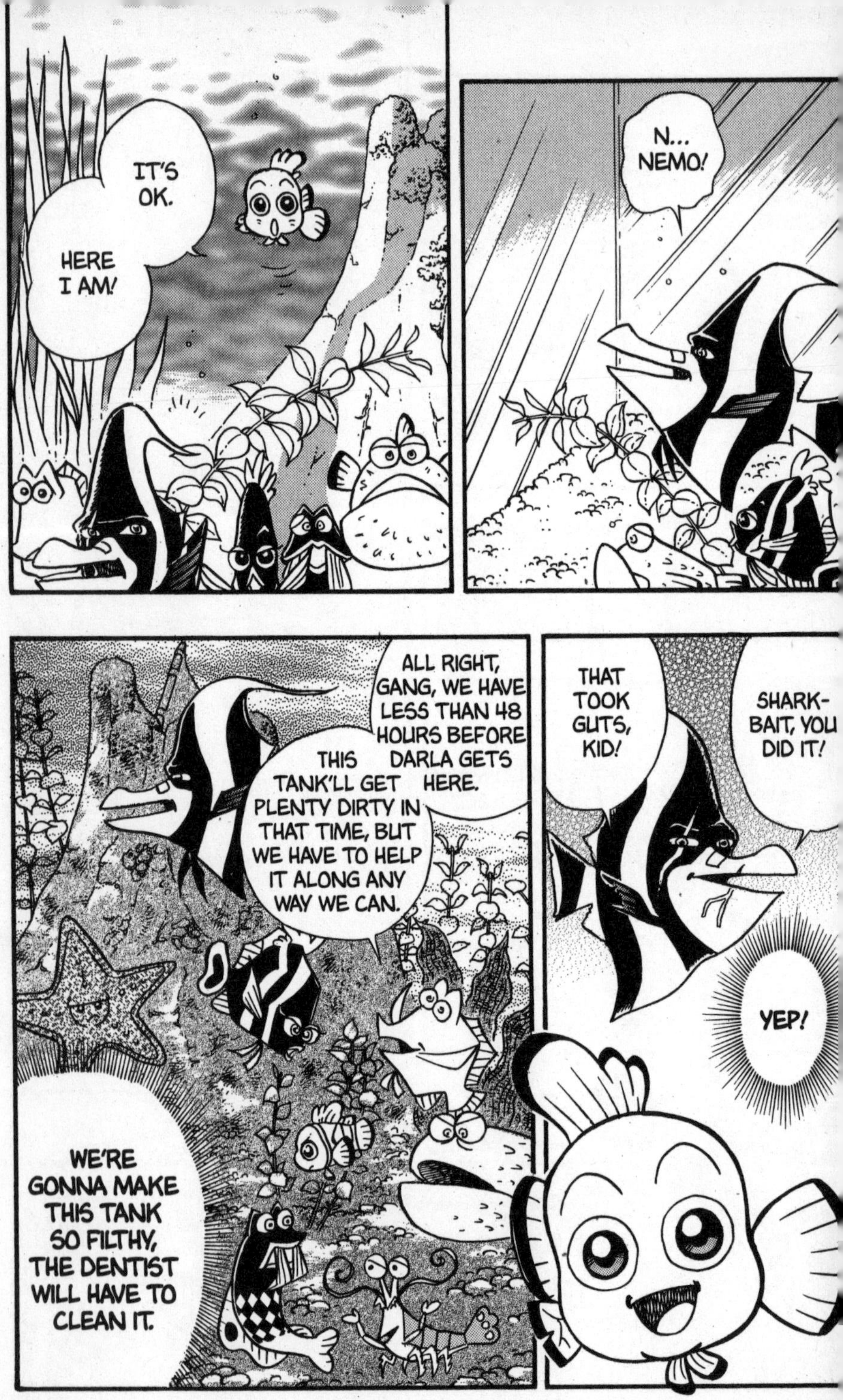
N... NEMO!
IT'S OK.
HERE I AM!
SHARK-BAIT, YOU DID IT!
THAT TOOK GUTS, KID!
YEP!
ALL RIGHT, GANG, WE HAVE LESS THAN 48 HOURS BEFORE DARLA GETS HERE.
THIS TANK'LL GET PLENTY DIRTY IN THAT TIME, BUT WE HAVE TO HELP IT ALONG ANY WAY WE CAN.
WE'RE GONNA MAKE THIS TANK SO FILTHY, THE DENTIST WILL HAVE TO CLEAN IT.

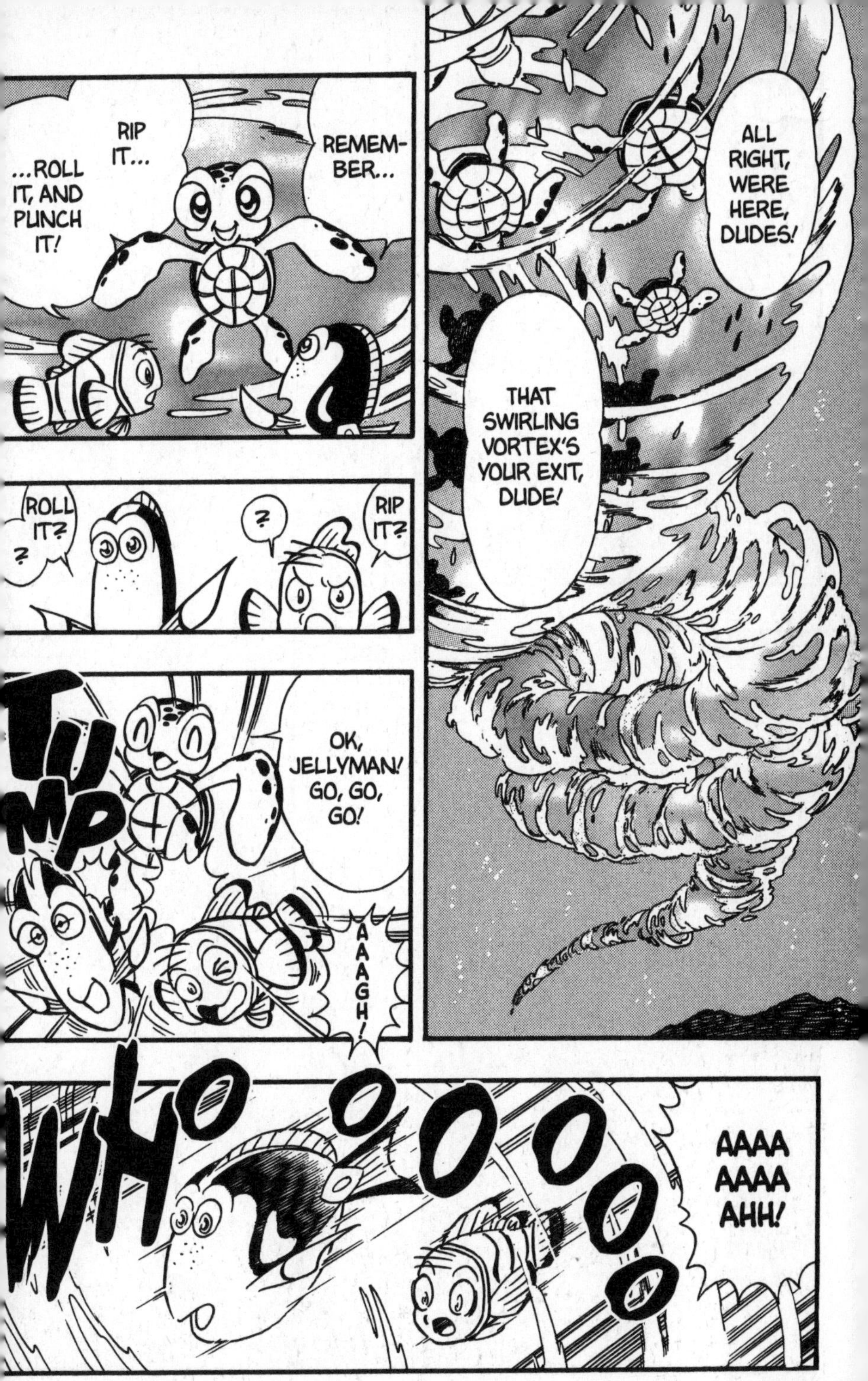
ALL RIGHT, WERE HERE, DUDES!
THAT SWIRLING VORTEX'S YOUR EXIT, DUDE!
REMEM-BER...
RIP IT...
...ROLL IT, AND PUNCH IT!
RIP IT?
?
ROLL IT?
?
OK, JELLYMAN! GO, GO, GO!
AAAAGH!
TUMP
AAAA AAAA AHH!
WHOOOOOOOO

READ THIS WAY

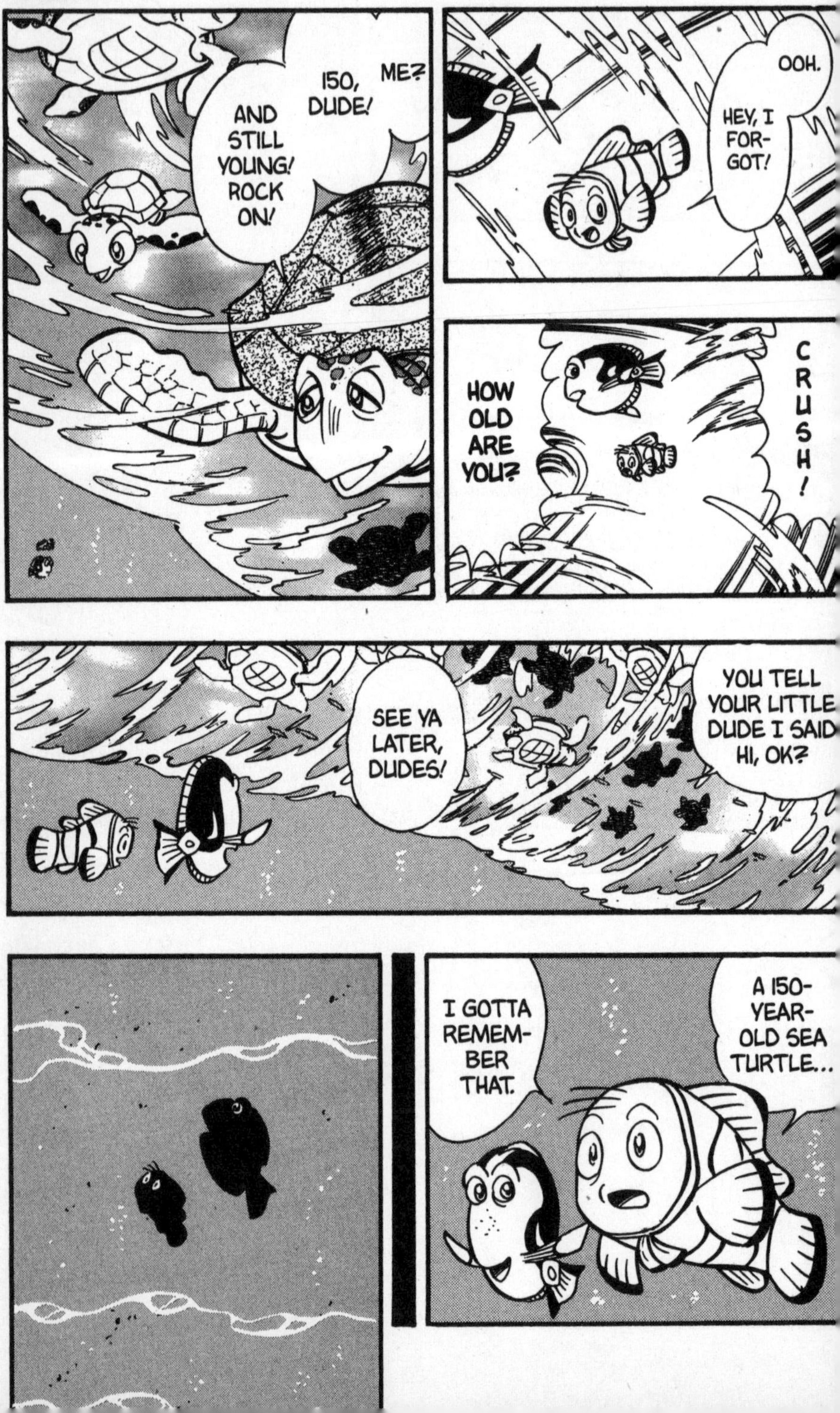
OOH.
HEY, I FOR-GOT!
CRUSH!
HOW OLD ARE YOU?
ME?
150, DUDE!
AND STILL YOUNG! ROCK ON!
YOU TELL YOUR LITTLE DUDE I SAID HI, OK?
SEE YA LATER, DUDES!
A 150-YEAR-OLD SEA TURTLE...
I GOTTA REMEM-BER THAT.

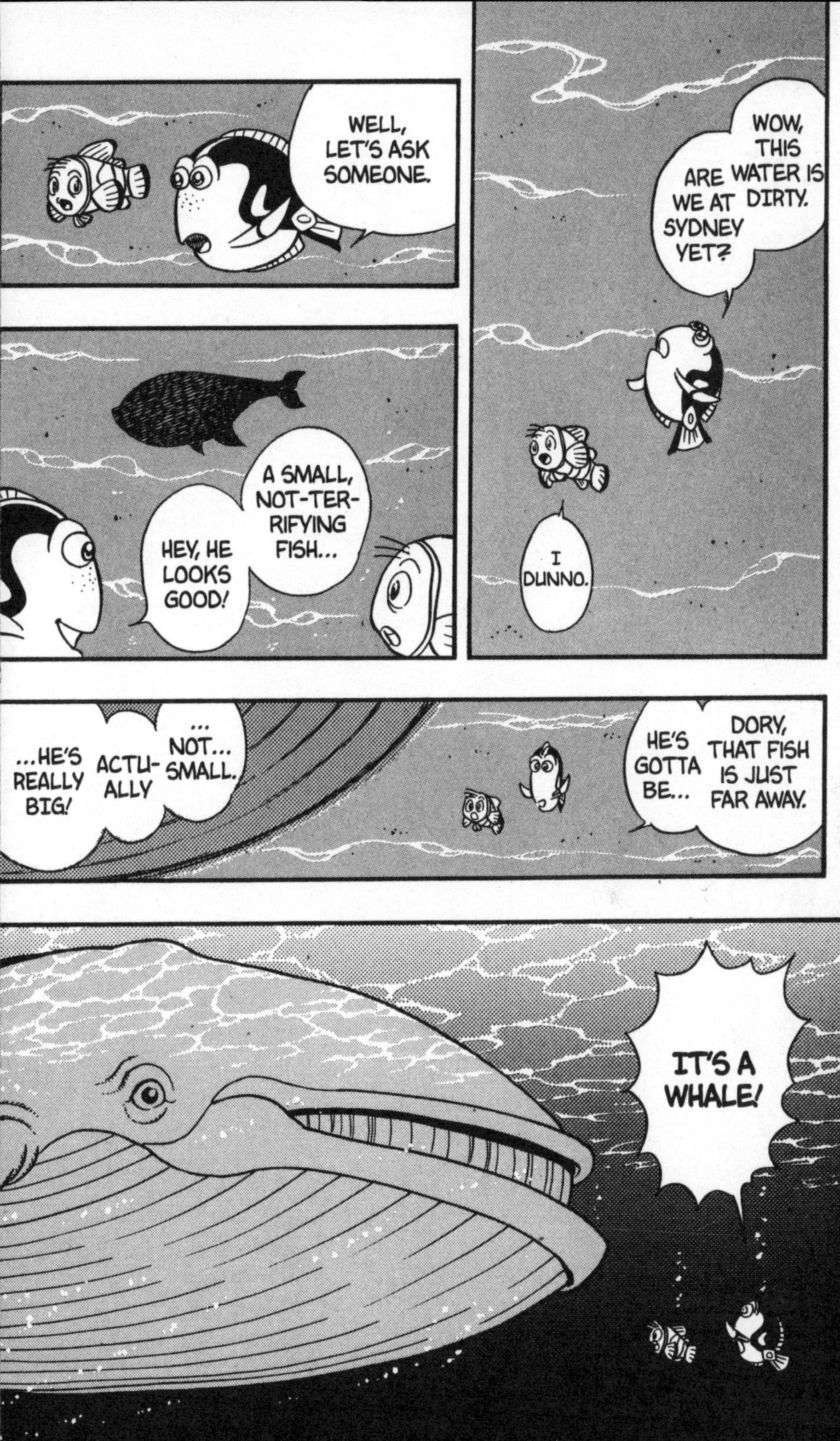
WOW, THIS WATER IS DIRTY.
ARE WE AT SYDNEY YET?
I DUNNO.
WELL, LET'S ASK SOMEONE.
A SMALL, NOT-TERRIFYING FISH...
HEY, HE LOOKS GOOD!
DORY, THAT FISH IS JUST FAR AWAY.
HE'S GOTTA BE...
... NOT... SMALL.
ACTU-ALLY
...HE'S REALLY BIG!
IT'S A WHALE!

READ THIS WAY

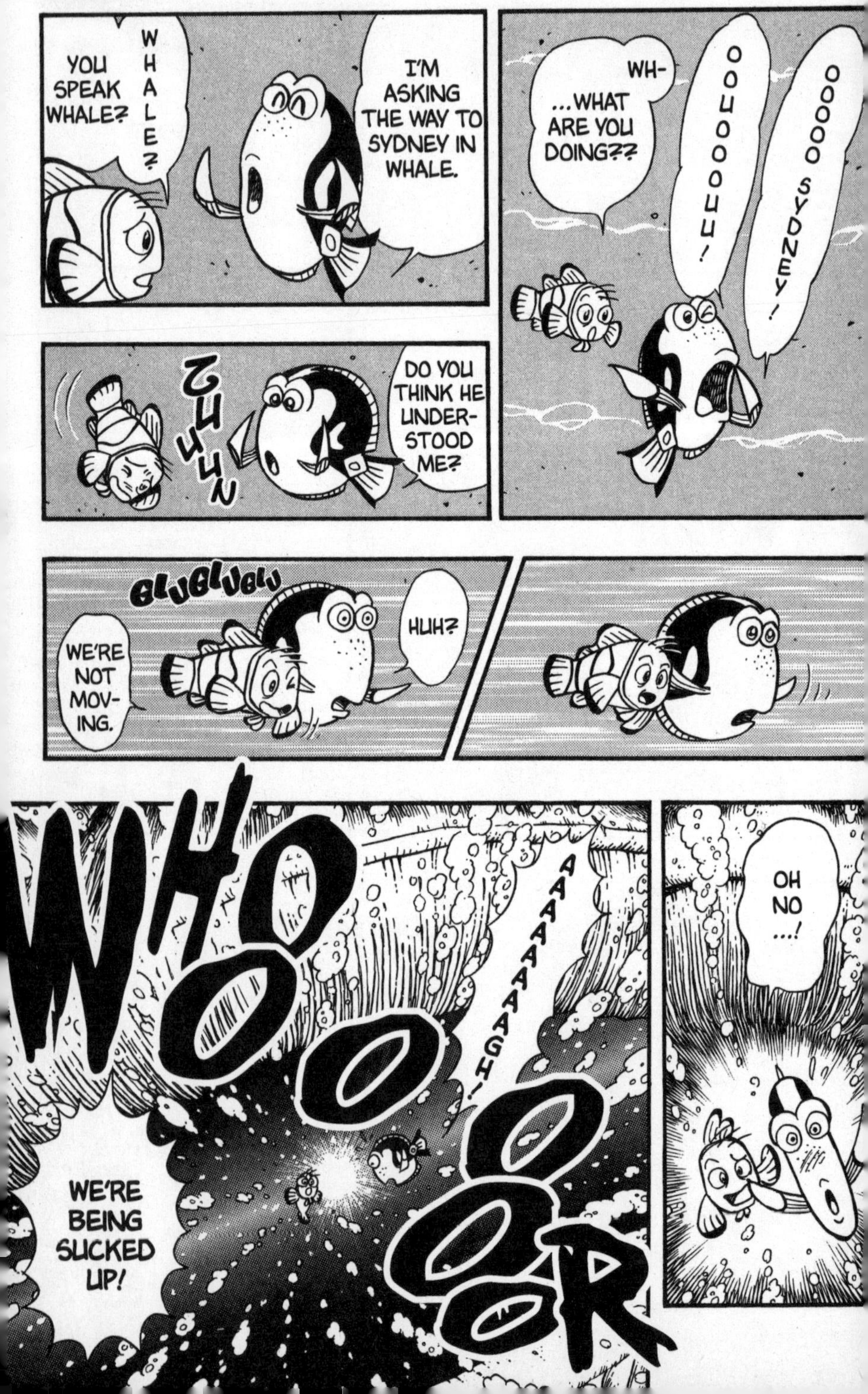
WH- ...WHAT ARE YOU DOING??
OOOOO SYDNEY!
OOUOOOUU!
I'M ASKING THE WAY TO SYDNEY IN WHALE.
YOU SPEAK WHALE?
WHALE?
DO YOU THINK HE UNDERSTOOD ME?
HUH?
GLUGLUGLU
WE'RE NOT MOV-ING.
OH NO...!
AAAAAAAAGH!
WE'RE BEING SUCKED UP!

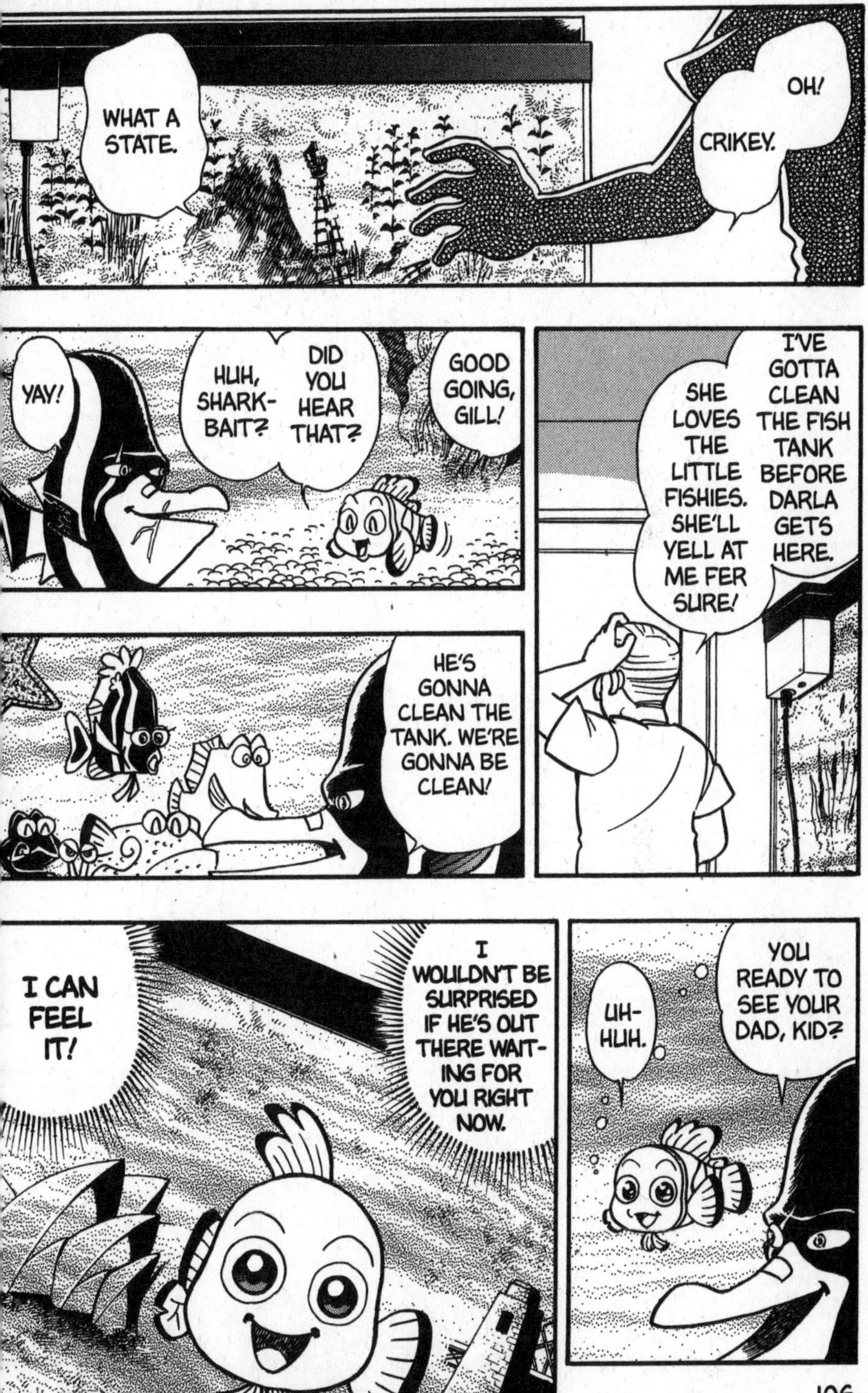
OH!
CRIKEY.
WHAT A STATE.
I'VE GOTTA CLEAN THE FISH TANK BEFORE DARLA GETS HERE.
SHE LOVES THE LITTLE FISHIES. SHE'LL YELL AT ME FER SURE!
GOOD GOING, GILL!
DID YOU HEAR THAT?
HUH, SHARK-BAIT?
YAY!
HE'S GONNA CLEAN THE TANK. WE'RE GONNA BE CLEAN!
YOU READY TO SEE YOUR DAD, KID?
UH-HUH.
I WOULDN'T BE SURPRISED IF HE'S OUT THERE WAIT-ING FOR YOU RIGHT NOW.
I CAN FEEL IT!

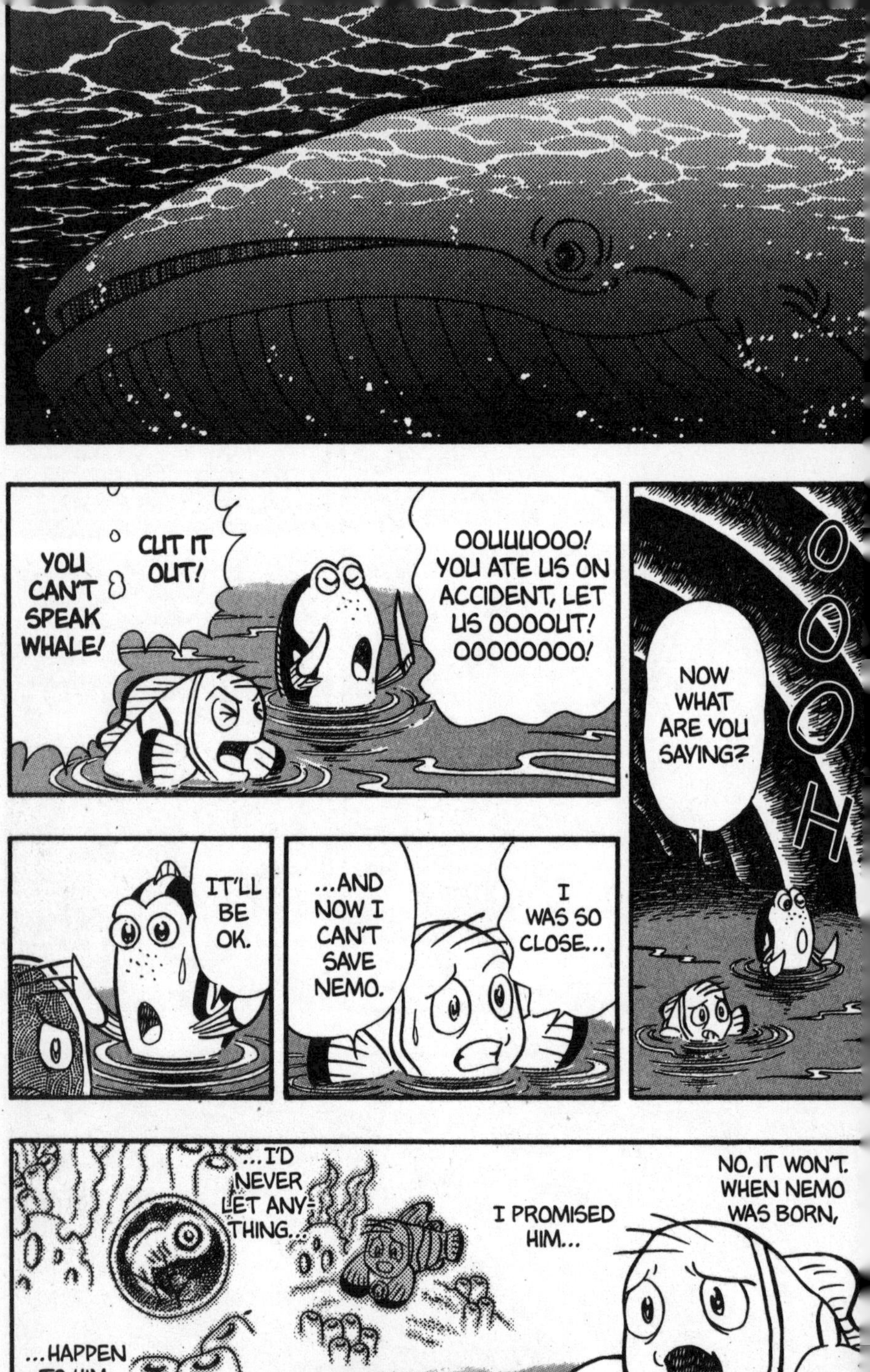
OOOOH
NOW WHAT ARE YOU SAYING?
OOUUUOOO! YOU ATE US ON ACCIDENT, LET US OOOOUT! OOOOOOOO!
CUT IT OUT!
YOU CAN'T SPEAK WHALE!
I WAS SO CLOSE...
...AND NOW I CAN'T SAVE NEMO.
IT'LL BE OK.
NO, IT WON'T. WHEN NEMO WAS BORN,
I PROMISED HIM...
...I'D NEVER LET ANY-THING...
...HAPPEN TO HIM.

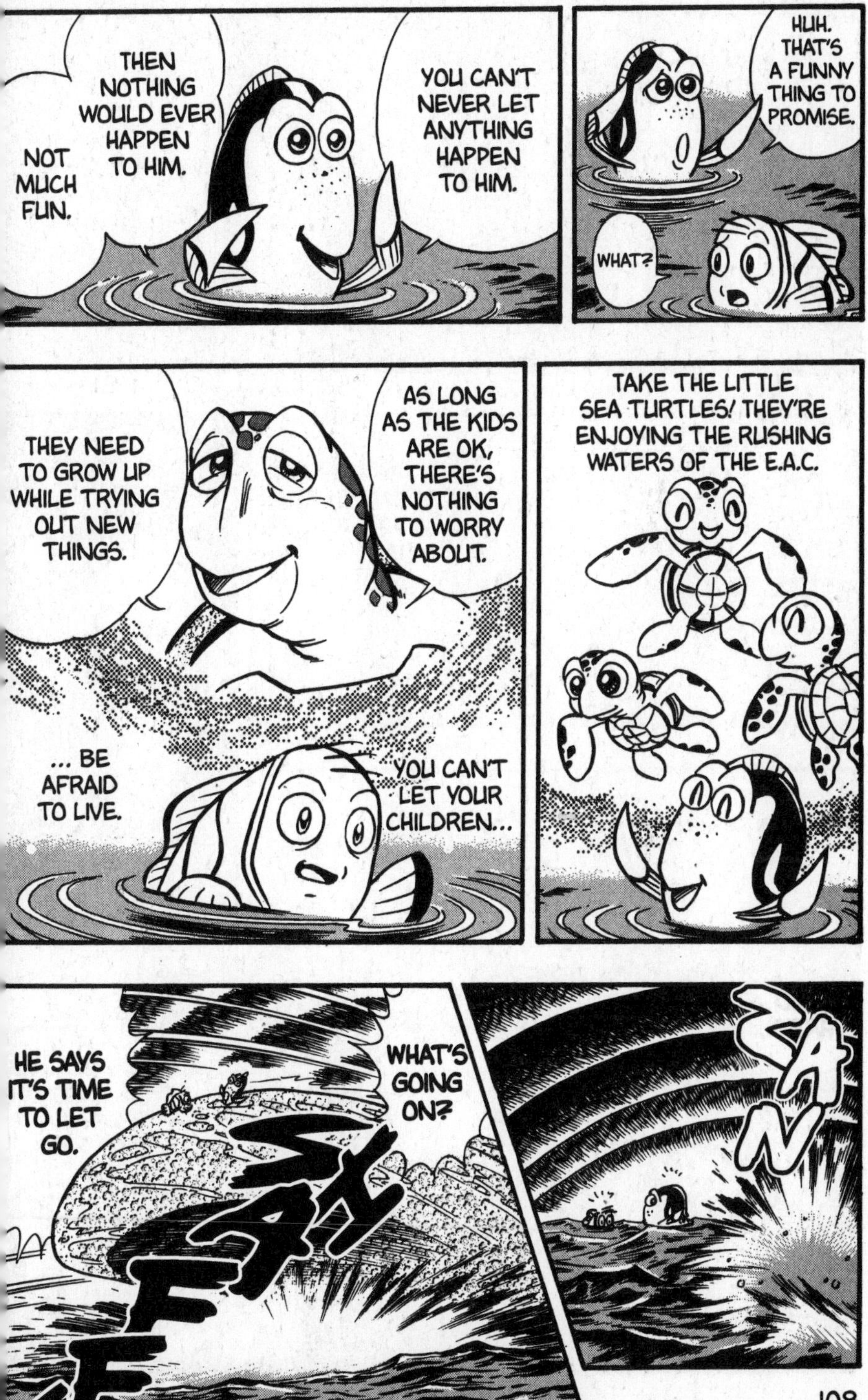
HUH. THAT'S A FUNNY THING TO PROMISE.
WHAT?
YOU CAN'T NEVER LET ANYTHING HAPPEN TO HIM.
THEN NOTHING WOULD EVER HAPPEN TO HIM.
NOT MUCH FUN.
TAKE THE LITTLE SEA TURTLES! THEY'RE ENJOYING THE RUSHING WATERS OF THE E.A.C.
AS LONG AS THE KIDS ARE OK, THERE'S NOTHING TO WORRY ABOUT.
THEY NEED TO GROW UP WHILE TRYING OUT NEW THINGS.
YOU CAN'T LET YOUR CHILDREN...
... BE AFRAID TO LIVE.
ZAN
WHAT'S GOING ON?
HE SAYS IT'S TIME TO LET GO.
ZAH
FFF

READ THIS WAY

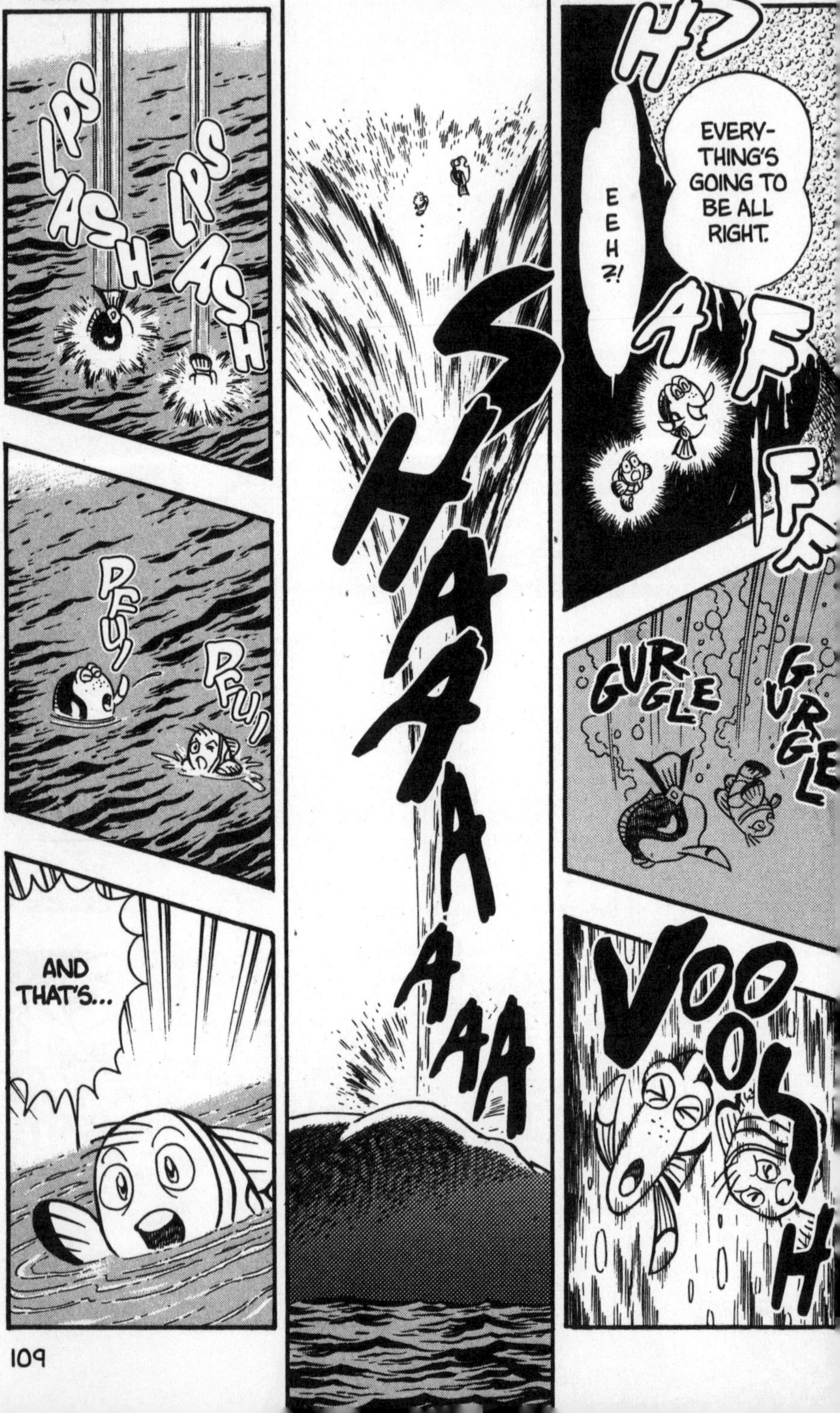
SHAFFF
EVERYTHING'S GOING TO BE ALL RIGHT.
EEH?!
GURGLE
GURGLE
VOOOSH
SHAAAAAAA
SPLASH
SPLASH
PFUI
PFUI
AND THAT'S...

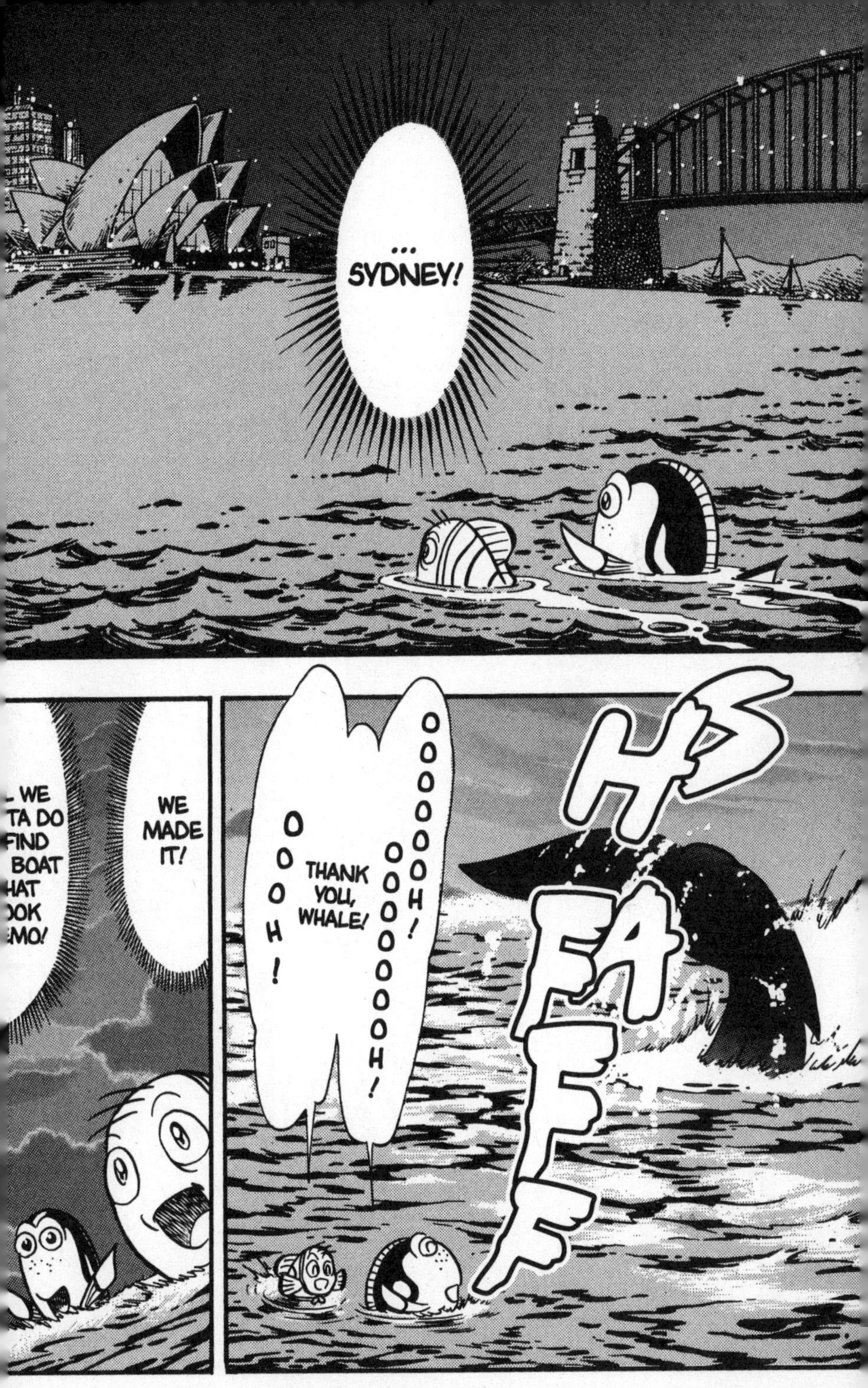

... SYDNEY!
OOOOOOH!
OOOOOOOH!
THANK YOU, WHALE!
OOOH!
HS
FA
FFF
WE MADE IT!
L WE TA DO FIND BOAT HAT OOK EMO!

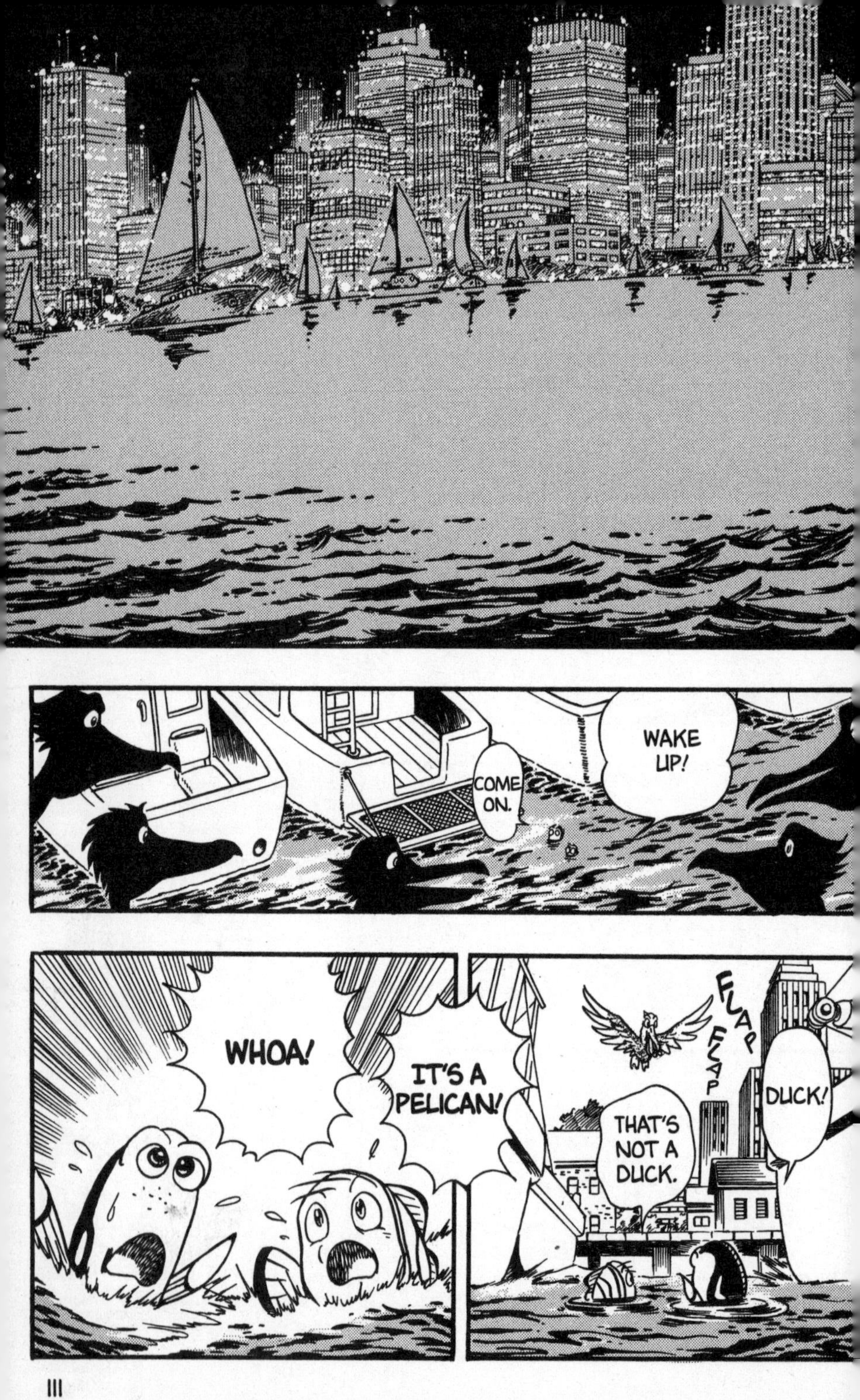
WAKE UP!
COME ON.
DUCK!
FLAP FLAP
THAT'S NOT A DUCK.
IT'S A PELICAN!
WHOA!

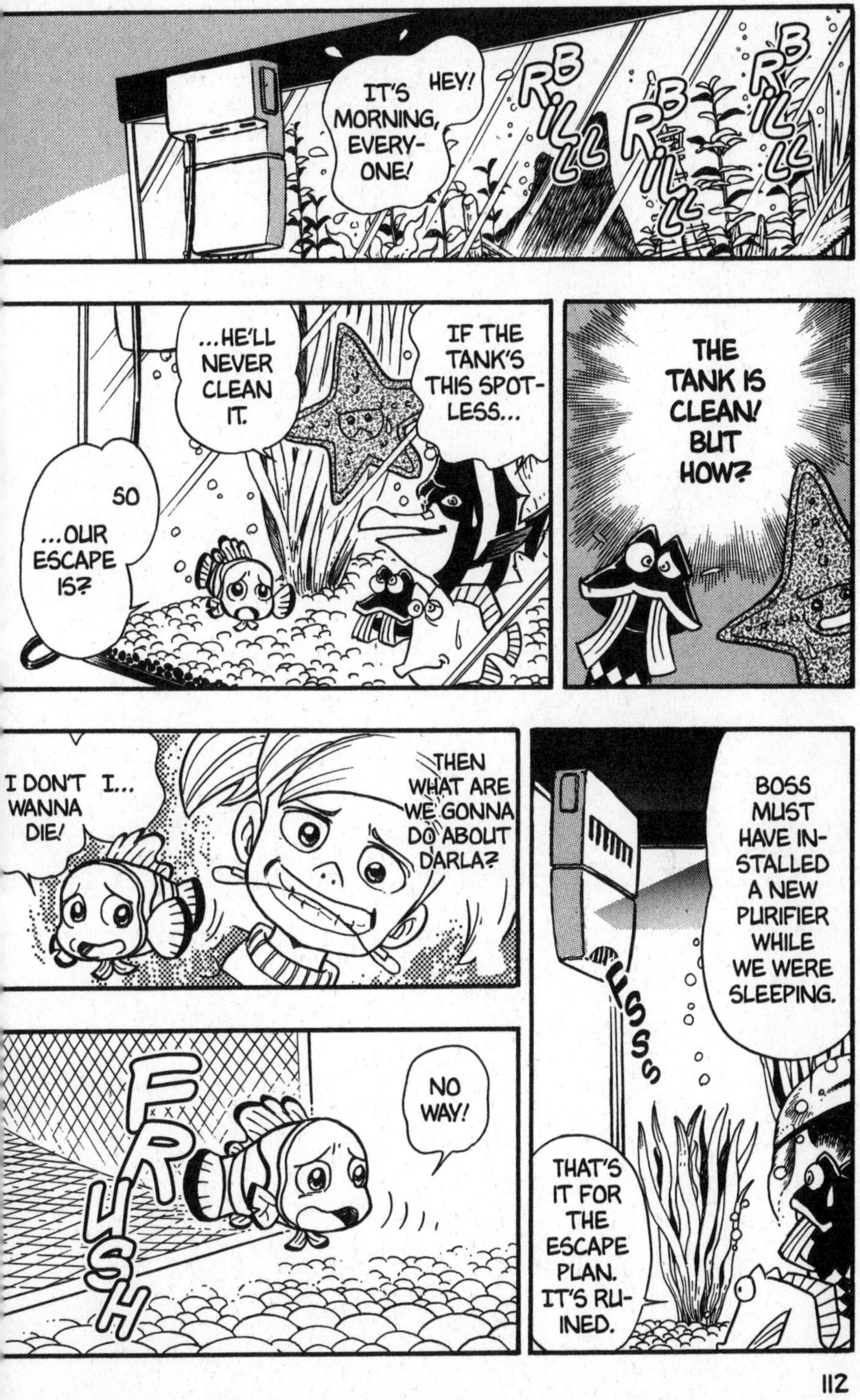
HEY! IT'S MORNING, EVERY-ONE!
RBiLL RBiLL RBiLL
THE TANK IS CLEAN! BUT HOW?
IF THE TANK'S THIS SPOT-LESS...
...HE'LL NEVER CLEAN IT.
SO ...OUR ESCAPE IS?
BOSS MUST HAVE IN-STALLED A NEW PURIFIER WHILE WE WERE SLEEPING.
SSSSS
THAT'S IT FOR THE ESCAPE PLAN. IT'S RU-INED.
THEN WHAT ARE WE GONNA DO ABOUT DARLA?
I... I DON'T WANNA DIE!
FRUSH
NO WAY!

READ THIS WAY

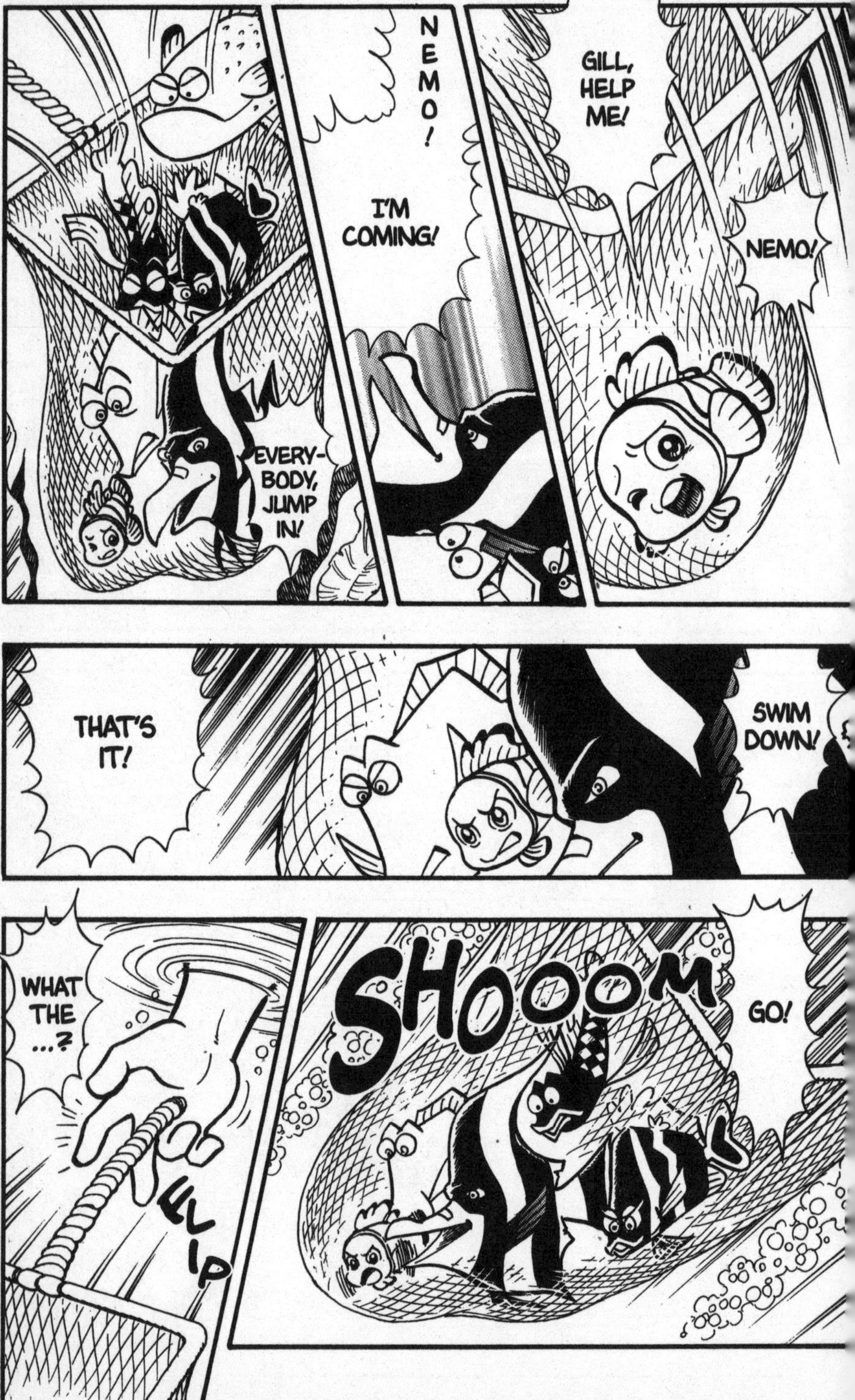
GILL, HELP ME!
NEMO!
NEMO!
I'M COMING!
EVERY-BODY, JUMP IN!
SWIM DOWN!
THAT'S IT!
GO!
SHOOOM
WHAT THE ...?

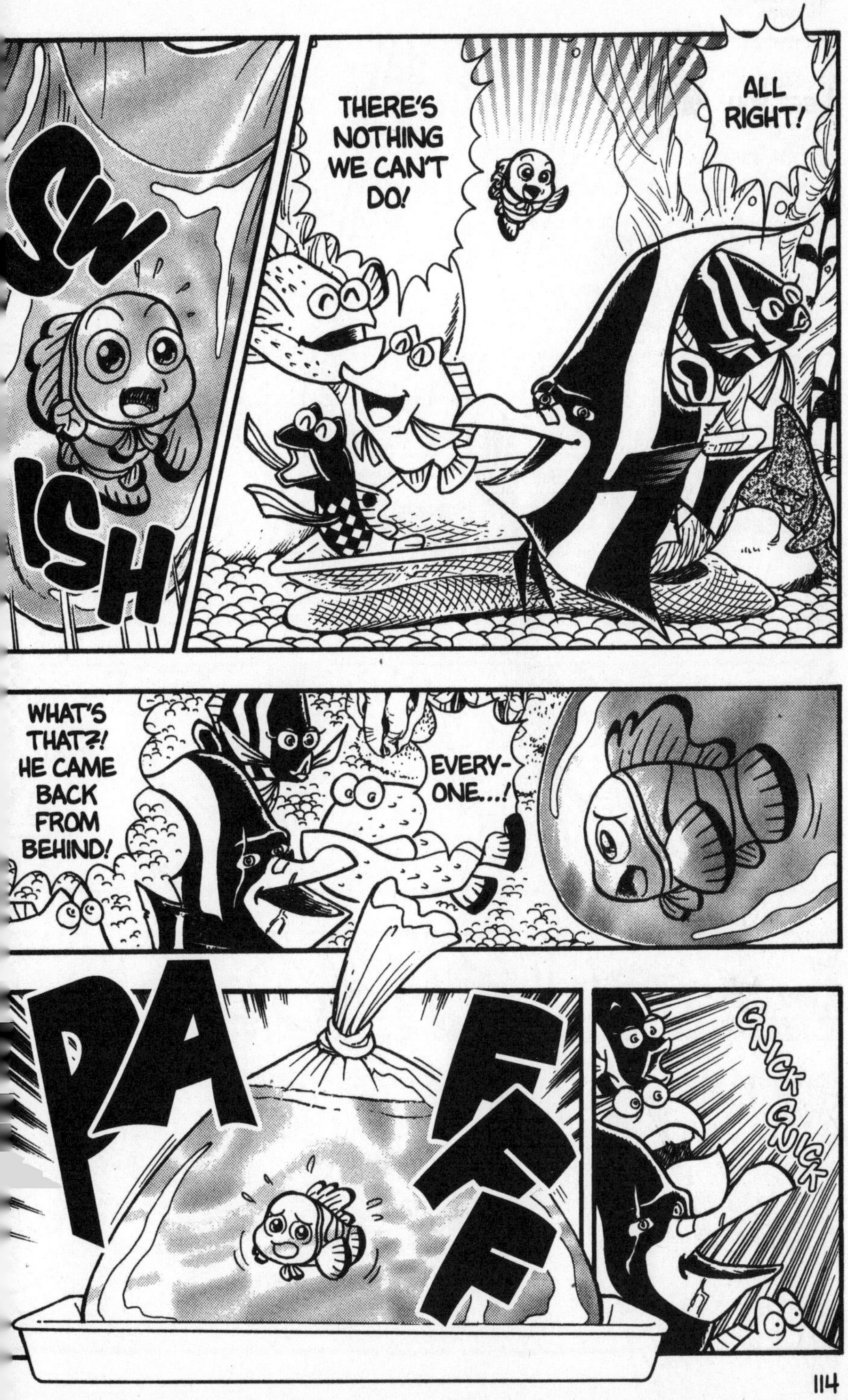

ALL RIGHT!
THERE'S NOTHING WE CAN'T DO!
SWISH
EVERY-ONE...!
WHAT'S THAT?! HE CAME BACK FROM BEHIND!
GNICK GNICK
PAFFF

READ THIS WAY

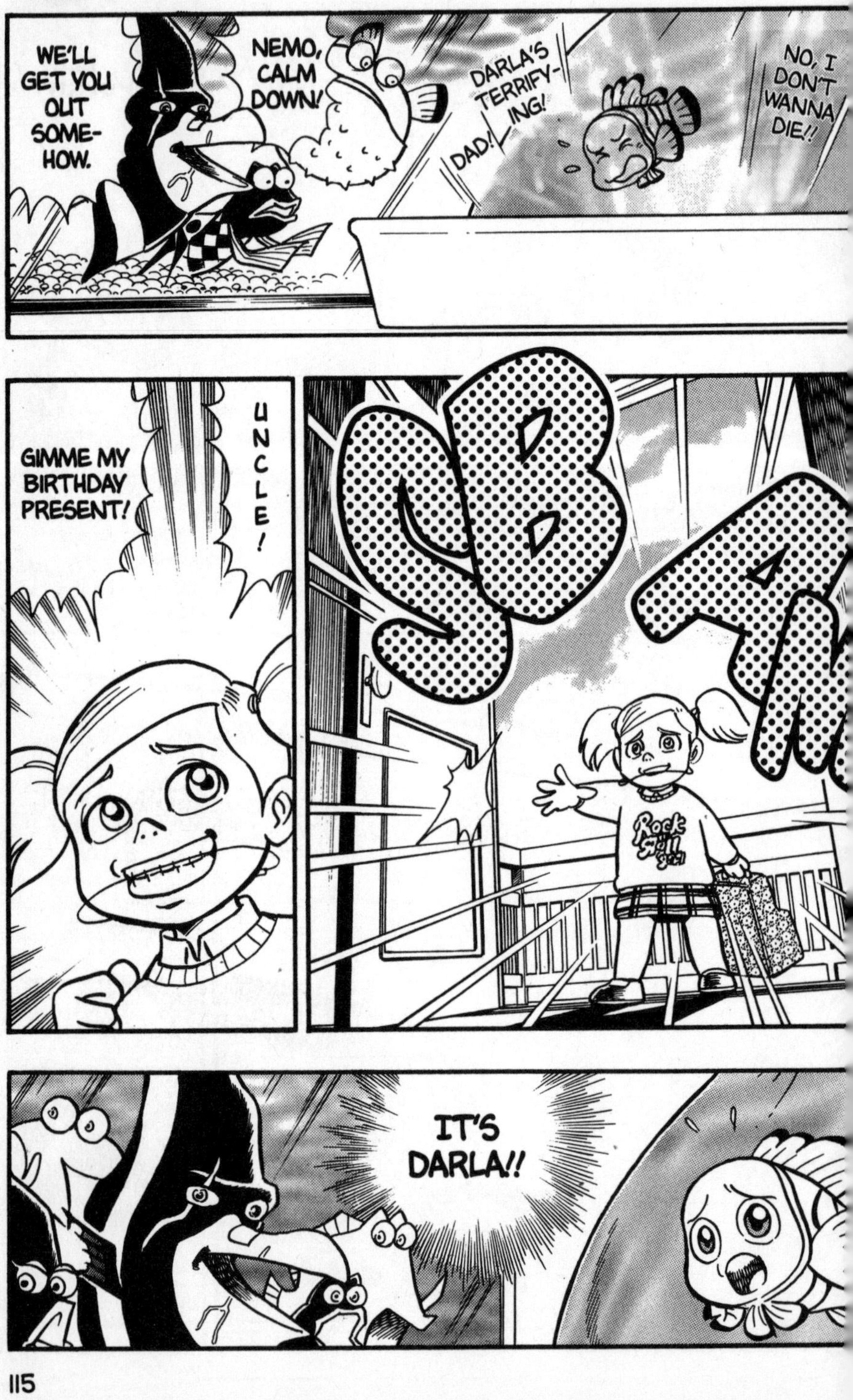
NO, I DON'T WANNA DIE!!
DARLA'S TERRIFY-ING!
DAD!
NEMO, CALM DOWN!
WE'LL GET YOU OUT SOME-HOW.
UNCLE!
GIMME MY BIRTHDAY PRESENT!
IT'S DARLA!!

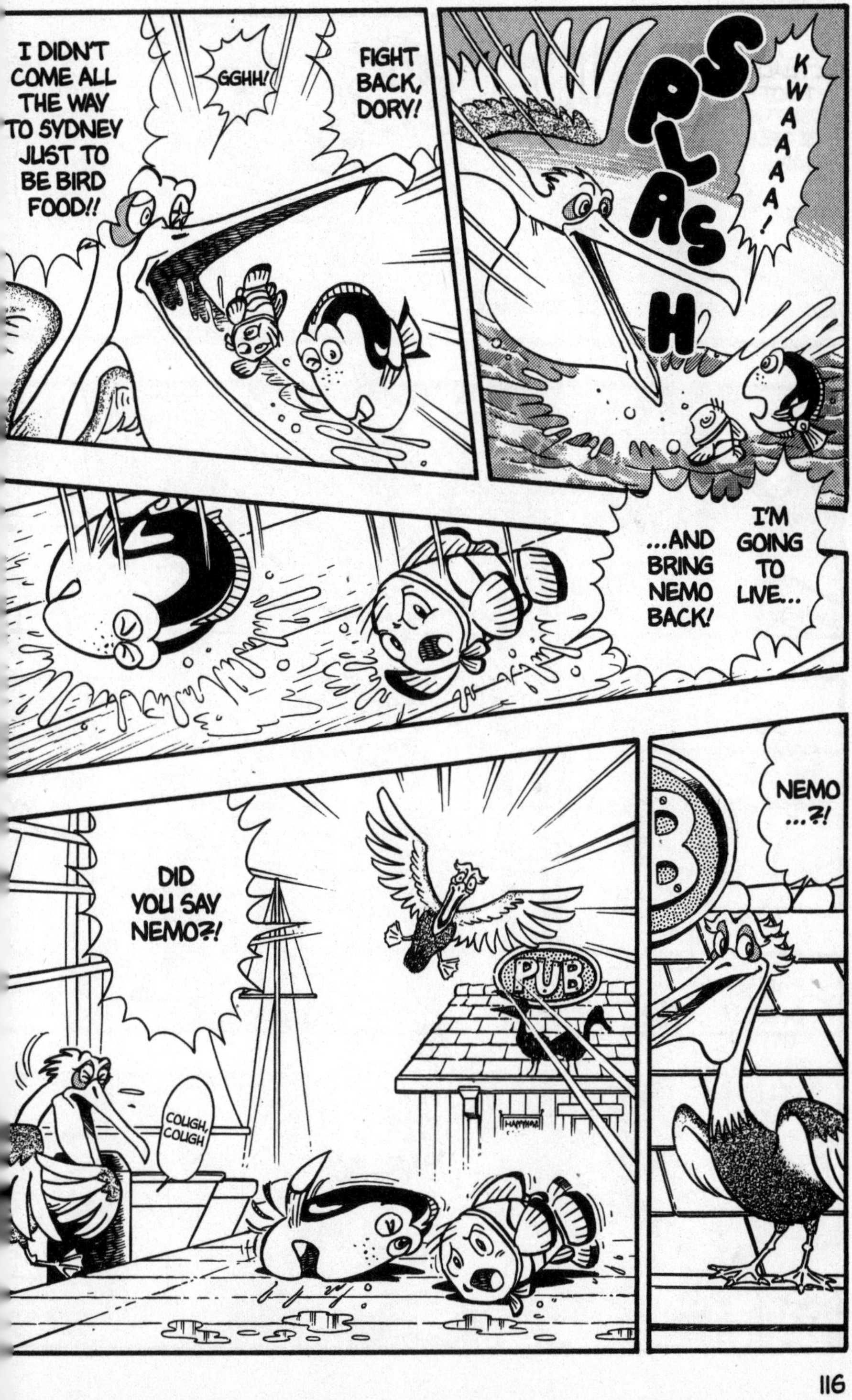
KWAAAA!
SPLASH
FIGHT BACK, DORY!
GGHH!
I DIDN'T COME ALL THE WAY TO SYDNEY JUST TO BE BIRD FOOD!!
I'M GOING TO LIVE...
...AND BRING NEMO BACK!
NEMO ...?!
DID YOU SAY NEMO?!
PUB
COUGH, COUGH

READ THIS WAY

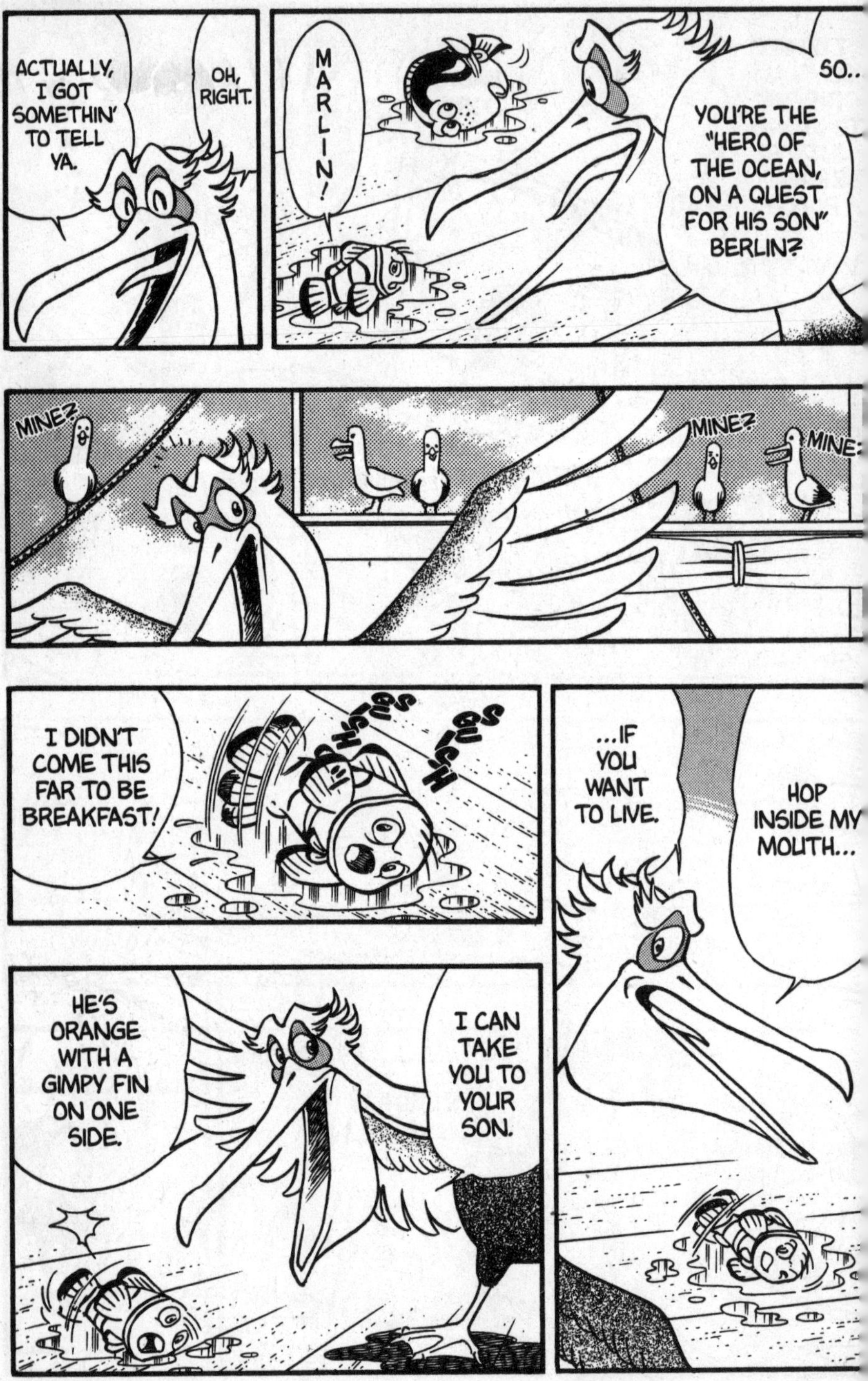

SO...
YOU'RE THE "HERO OF THE OCEAN, ON A QUEST FOR HIS SON" BERLIN?
MARLIN!
OH, RIGHT.
ACTUALLY, I GOT SOMETHIN' TO TELL YA.
MINE?
MINE?
MINE?
HOP INSIDE MY MOUTH...
...IF YOU WANT TO LIVE.
SQUISH
SQUISH
I DIDN'T COME THIS FAR TO BE BREAKFAST!
I CAN TAKE YOU TO YOUR SON.
HE'S ORANGE WITH A GIMPY FIN ON ONE SIDE.

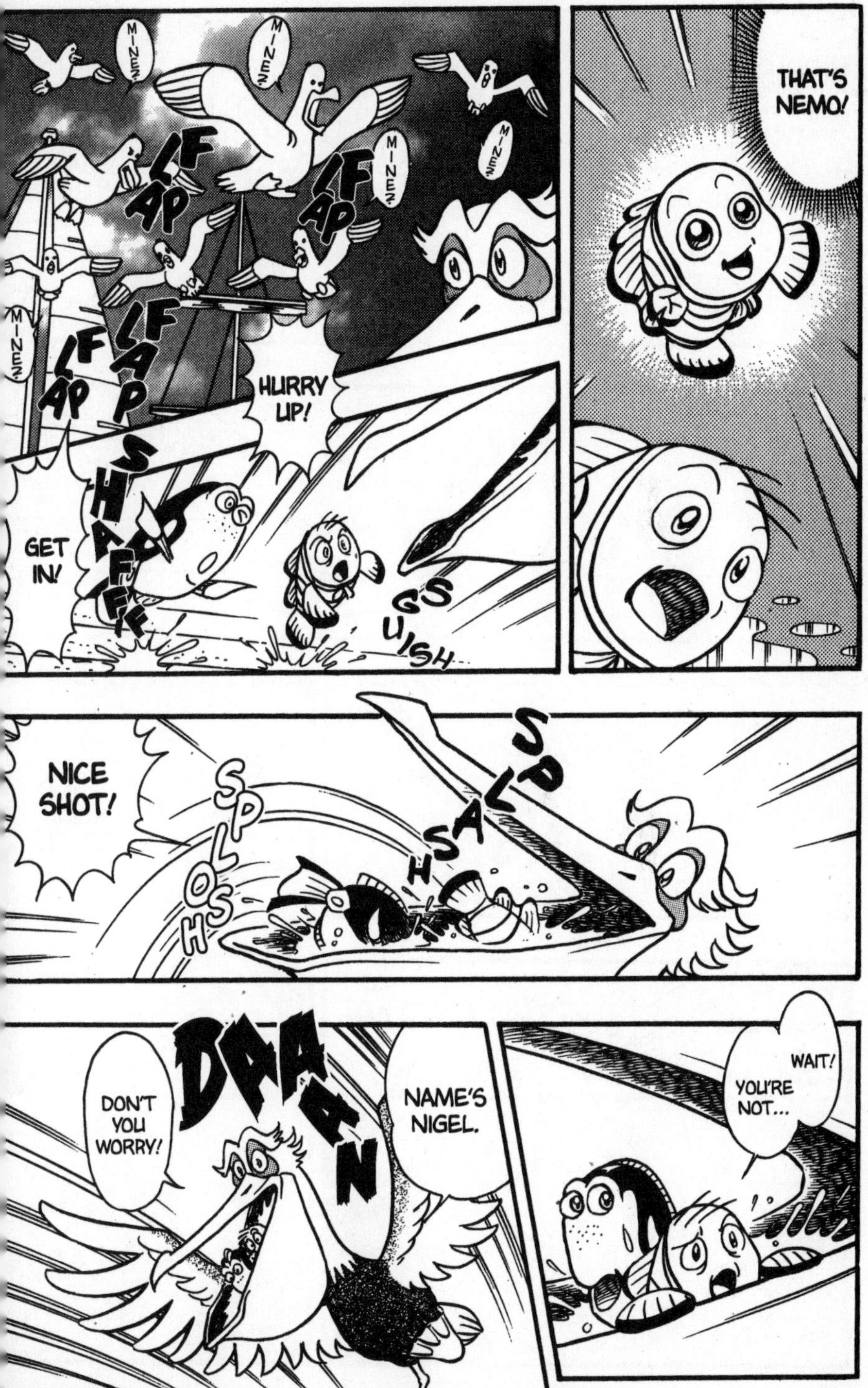
THAT'S NEMO!
MINE?
MINE?
MINE?
MINE?
MINE?
FLAP
FLAP
FLAP
FLAP
HURRY UP!
GET IN!
SQUISH
SPLASH
NICE SHOT!
SPLOSH
WAIT! YOU'RE NOT...
NAME'S NIGEL.
DAAN
DON'T YOU WORRY!

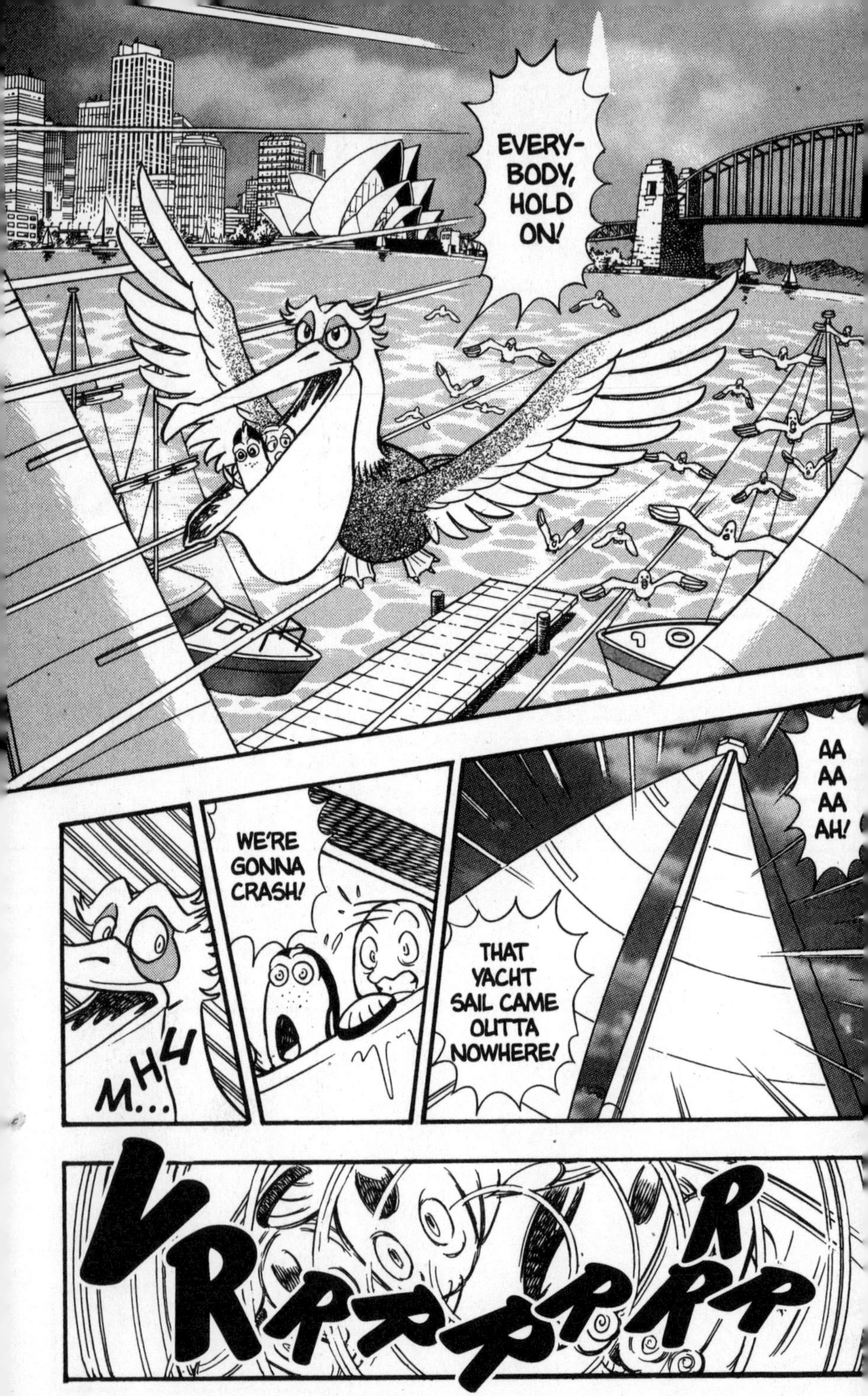
EVERY-BODY, HOLD ON!
AA AA AA AH!
THAT YACHT SAIL CAME OUTTA NOWHERE!
WE'RE GONNA CRASH!
UHM...
VRRRRRRRR

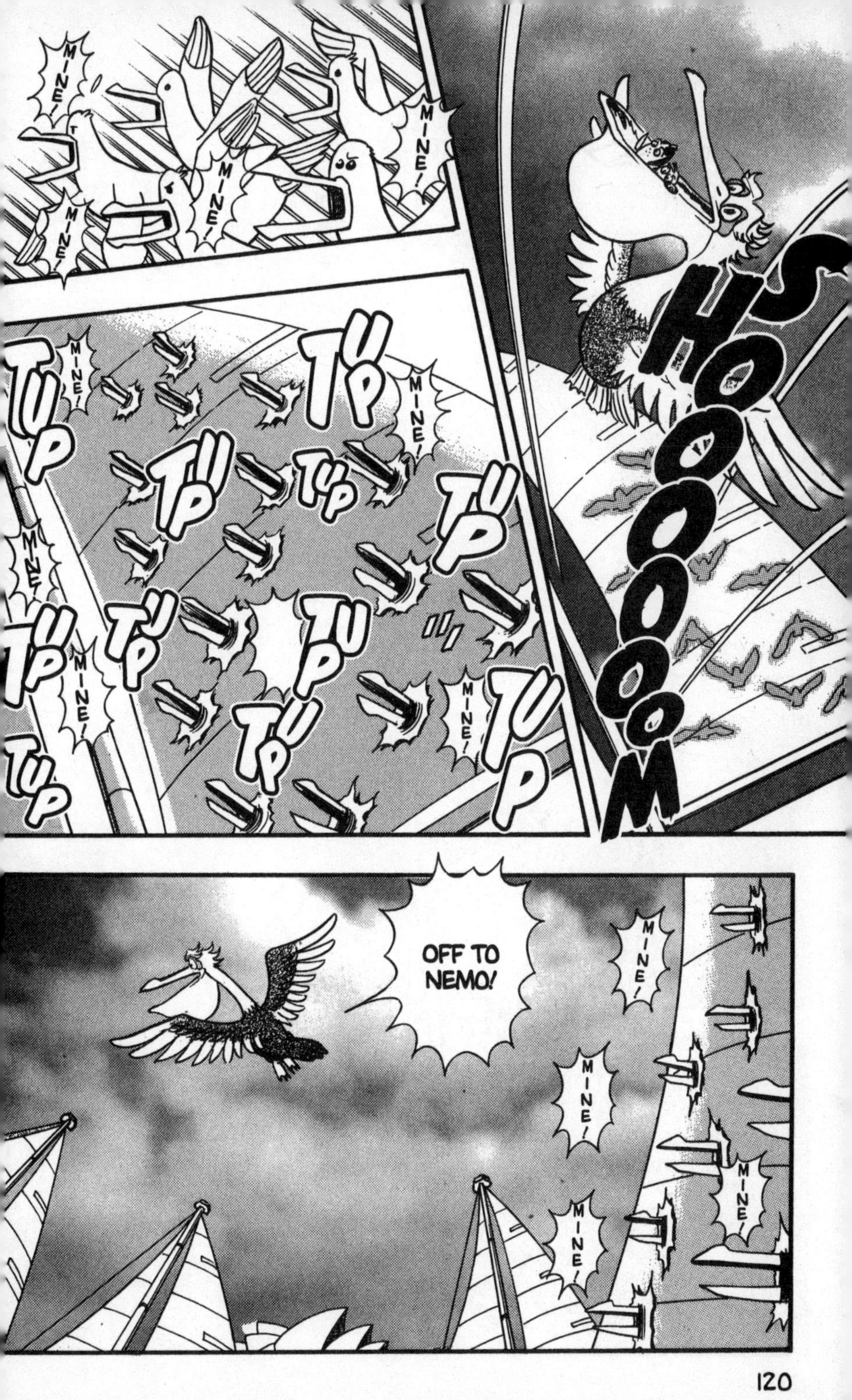
SHOOOOOOOM
MINE!
MINE!
MINE!
MINE!
TUP
MINE!
TUP
MINE!
TUP
TUP
TUP
TUP
MINE!
TUP
TUP
TUP
MINE!
TUP
TUP
MINE!
TUP
OFF TO NEMO!
MINE!
MINE!
MINE!
MINE!

READ THIS WAY

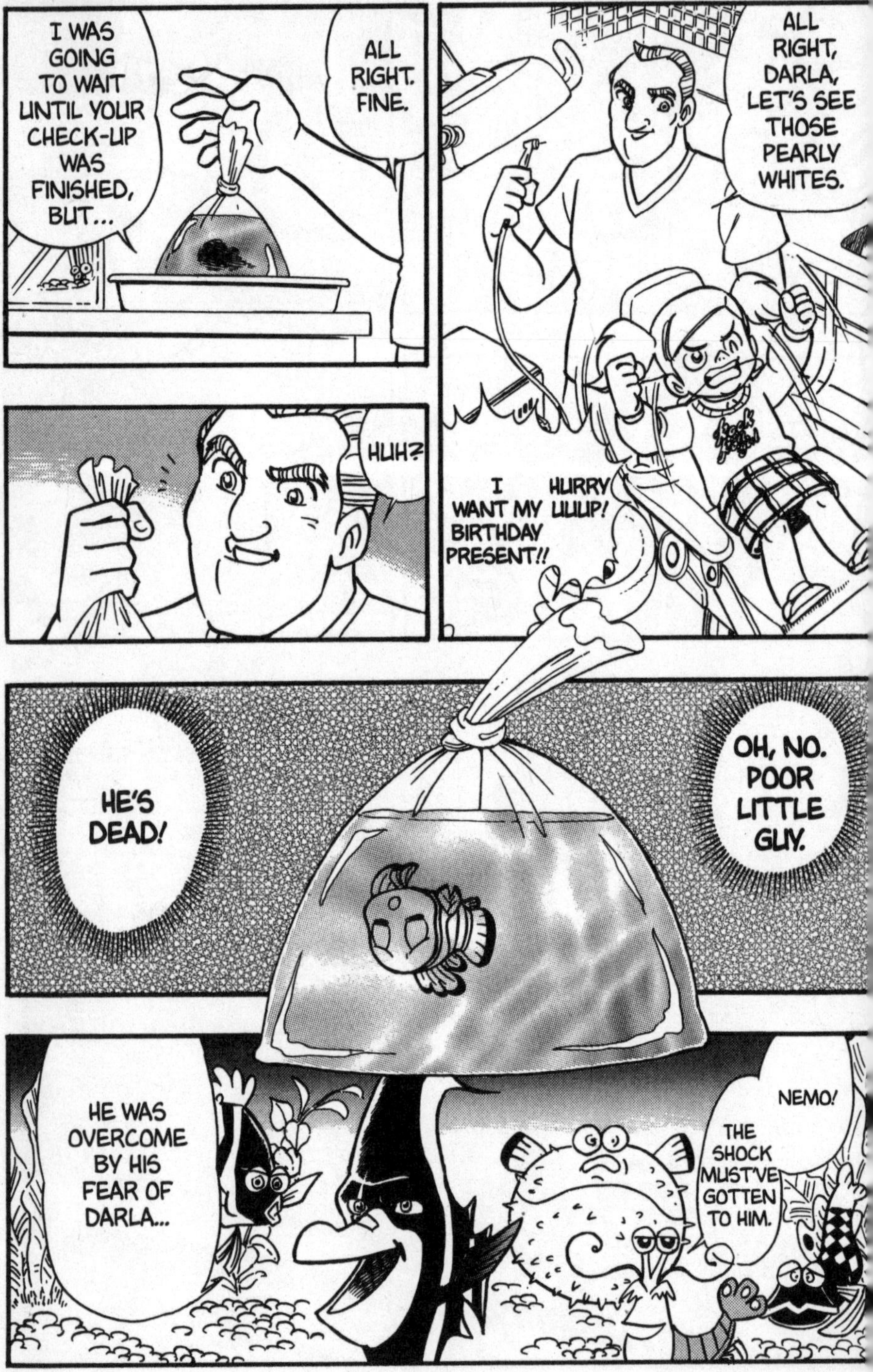
ALL RIGHT, DARLA, LET'S SEE THOSE PEARLY WHITES.
HURRY UUUP!
I WANT MY BIRTHDAY PRESENT!!
ALL RIGHT. FINE.
I WAS GOING TO WAIT UNTIL YOUR CHECK-UP WAS FINISHED, BUT...
HUH?
OH, NO. POOR LITTLE GUY.
HE'S DEAD!
NEMO!
THE SHOCK MUST'VE GOTTEN TO HIM.
HE WAS OVERCOME BY HIS FEAR OF DARLA...

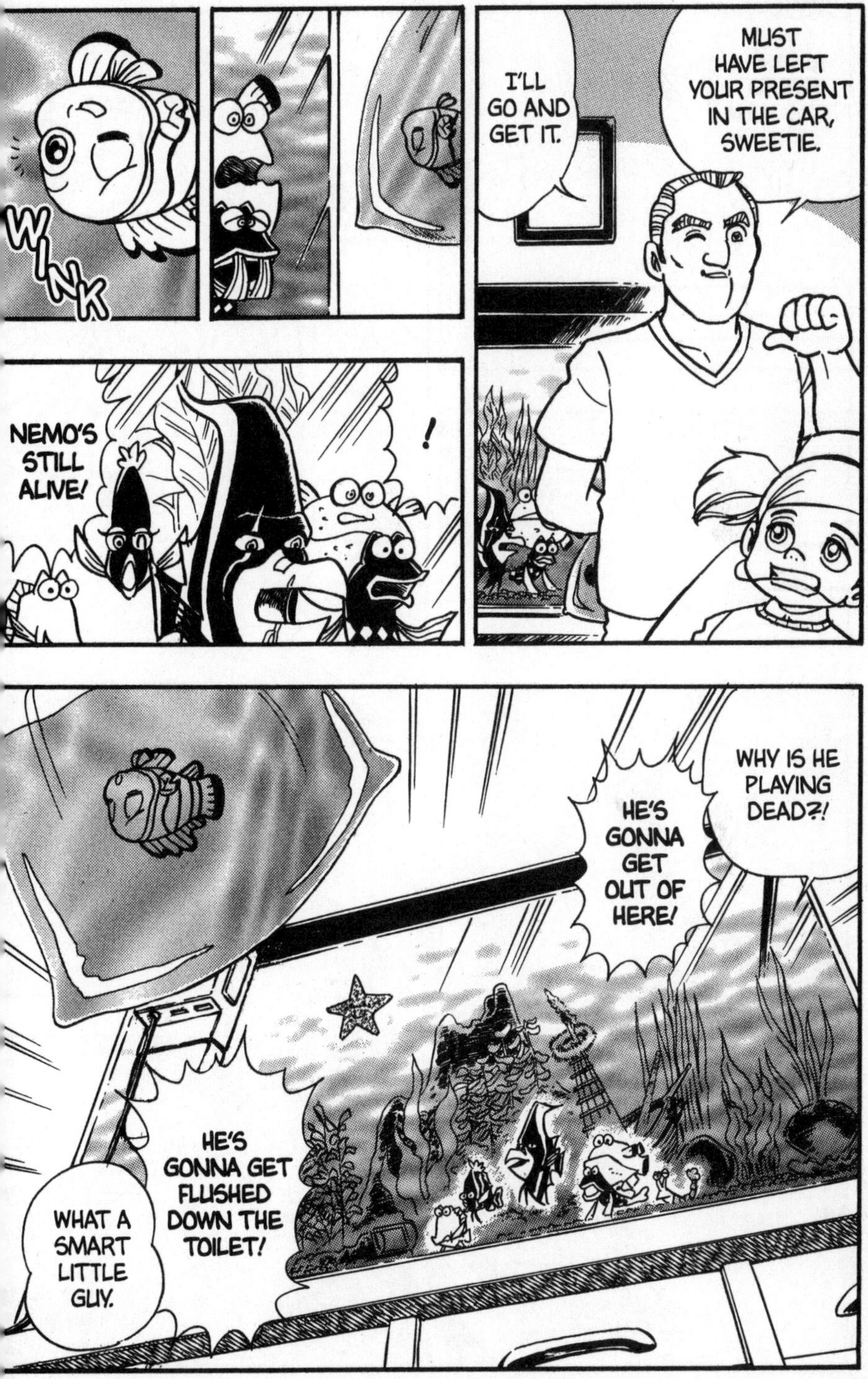
MUST HAVE LEFT YOUR PRESENT IN THE CAR, SWEETIE.
I'LL GO AND GET IT.
WINK
NEMO'S STILL ALIVE!
!
WHY IS HE PLAYING DEAD?!
HE'S GONNA GET OUT OF HERE!
HE'S GONNA GET FLUSHED DOWN THE TOILET!
WHAT A SMART LITTLE GUY.

READ THIS WAY

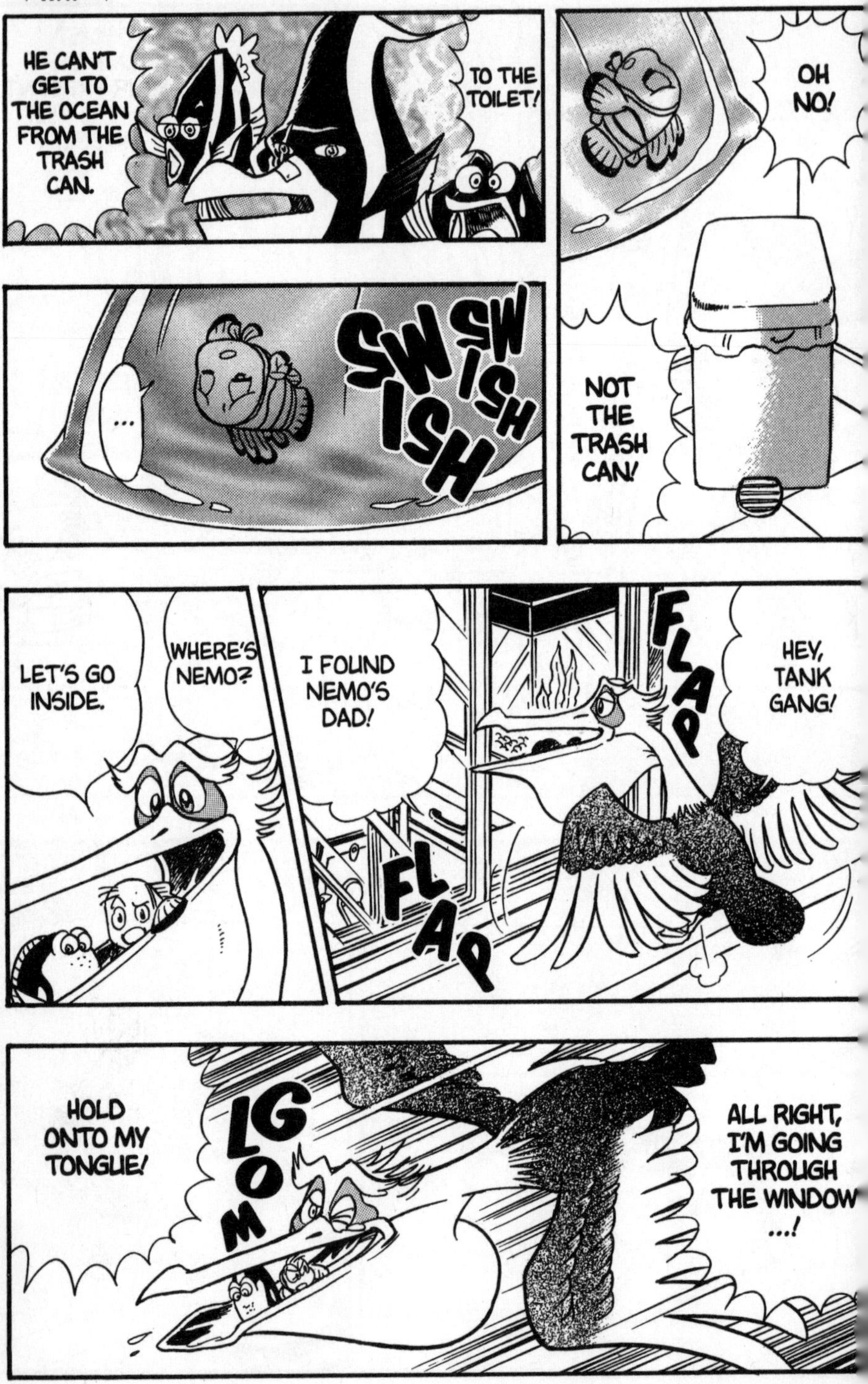
OH NO!
NOT THE TRASH CAN!
TO THE TOILET!
HE CAN'T GET TO THE OCEAN FROM THE TRASH CAN.
SWISH
SWISH
...
HEY, TANK GANG!
FLAP
I FOUND NEMO'S DAD!
FLAP
WHERE'S NEMO?
LET'S GO INSIDE.
ALL RIGHT, I'M GOING THROUGH THE WINDOW ...!
GLOM
HOLD ONTO MY TONGUE!

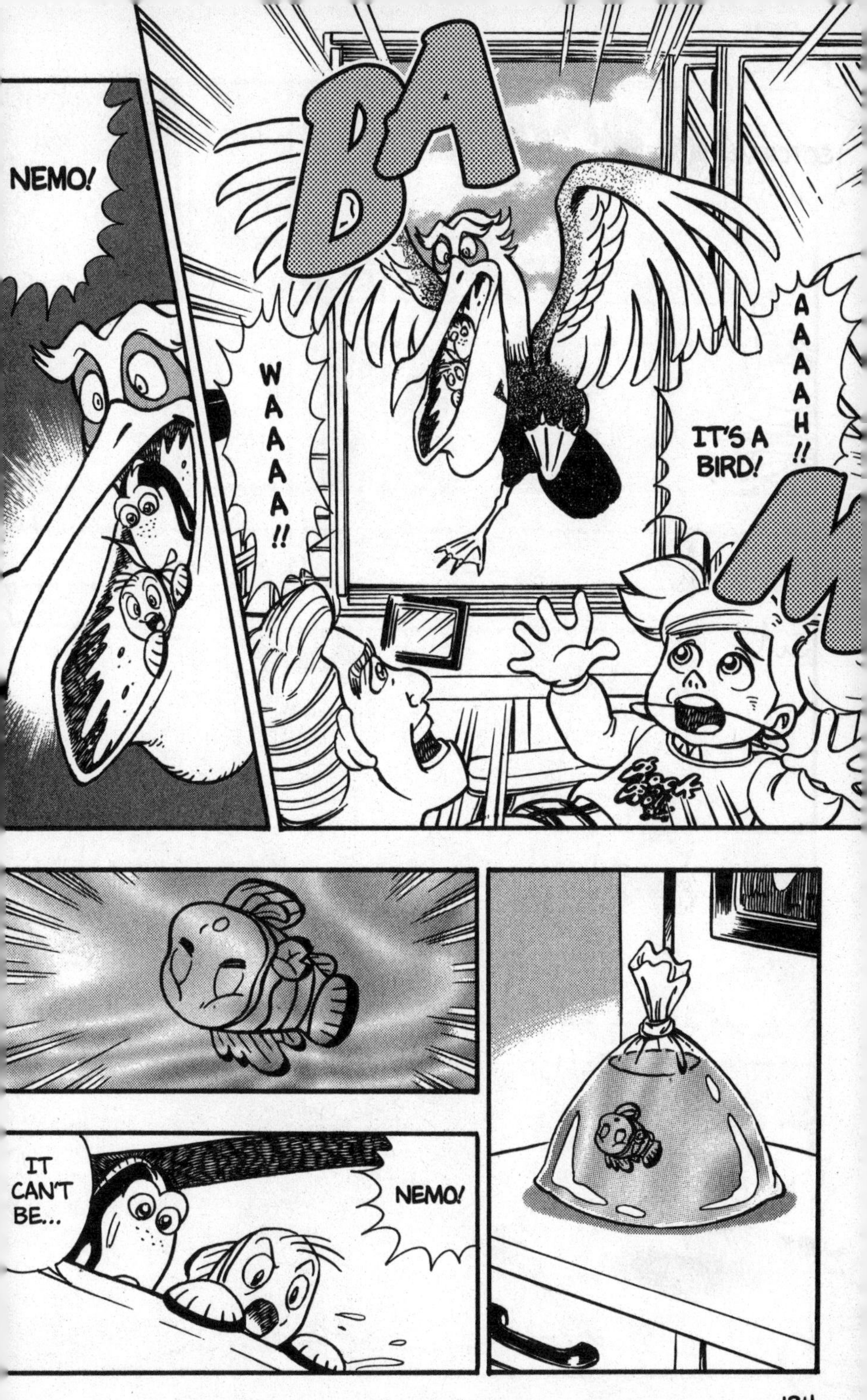
BAM
AAAAAH!!
IT'S A BIRD!
WAAAAA!!
NEMO!
NEMO!
IT CAN'T BE...

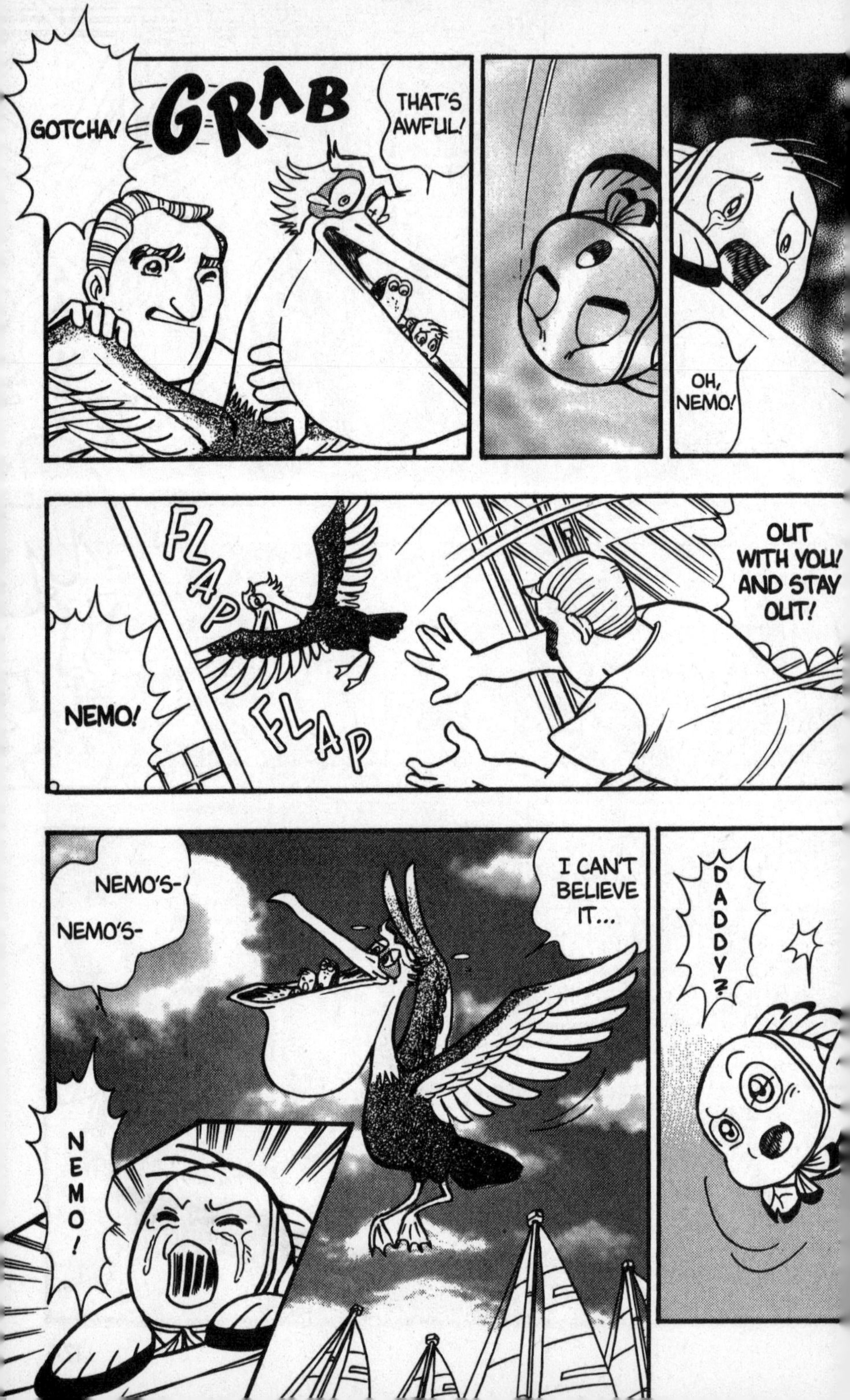
OH, NEMO!
THAT'S AWFUL!
GRAB
GOTCHA!
OUT WITH YOU! AND STAY OUT!
FLAP
FLAP
NEMO!
DADDY?
I CAN'T BELIEVE IT...
NEMO'S-
NEMO'S-
NEMO!

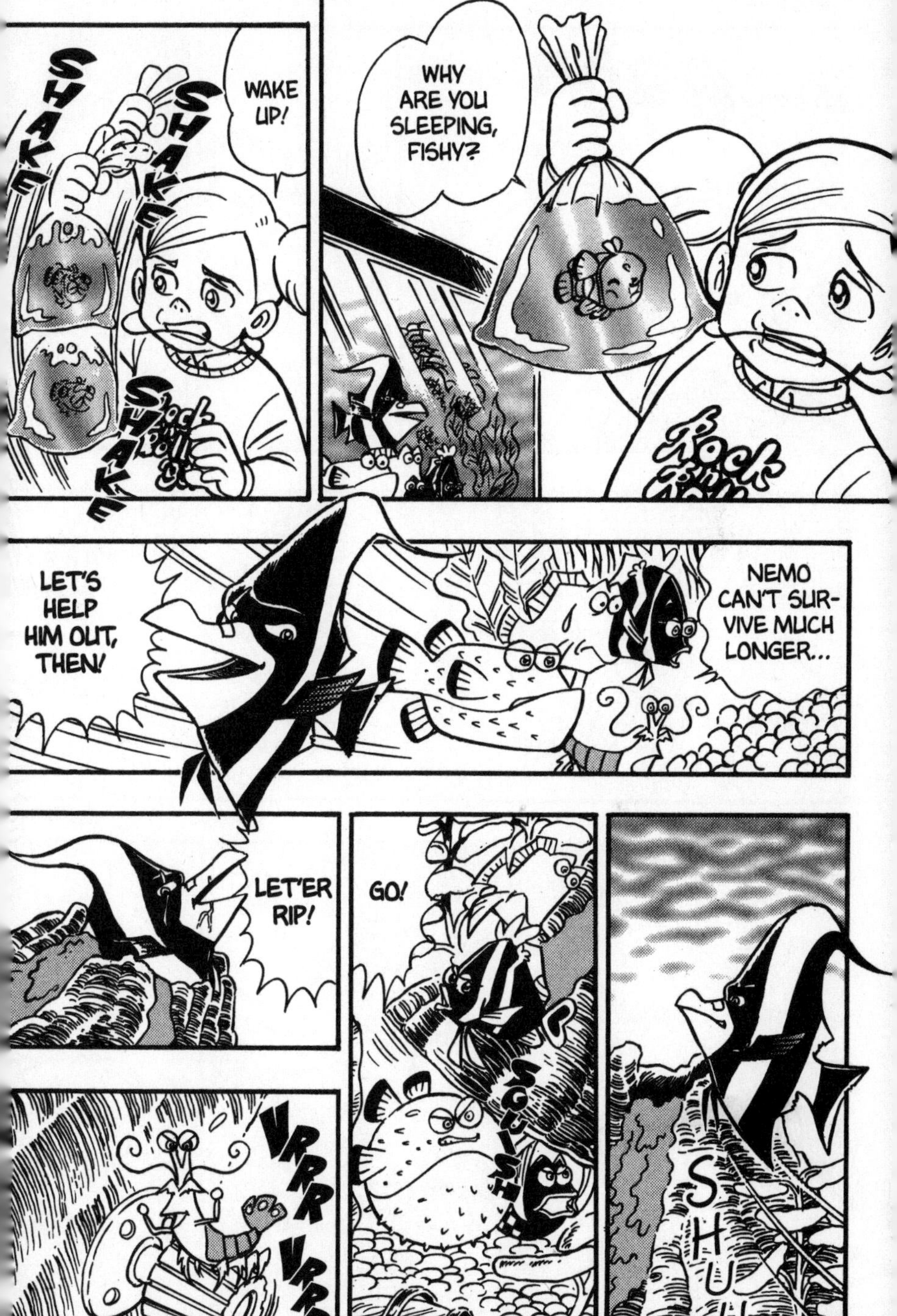
WHY ARE YOU SLEEPING, FISHY?
WAKE UP!
SHAKE
SHAKE
SHAKE
NEMO CAN'T SURVIVE MUCH LONGER...
LET'S HELP HIM OUT, THEN!
SHUUUU
GO!
SQUISH
LET'ER RIP!
VRRR
VRRR

READ THIS WAY

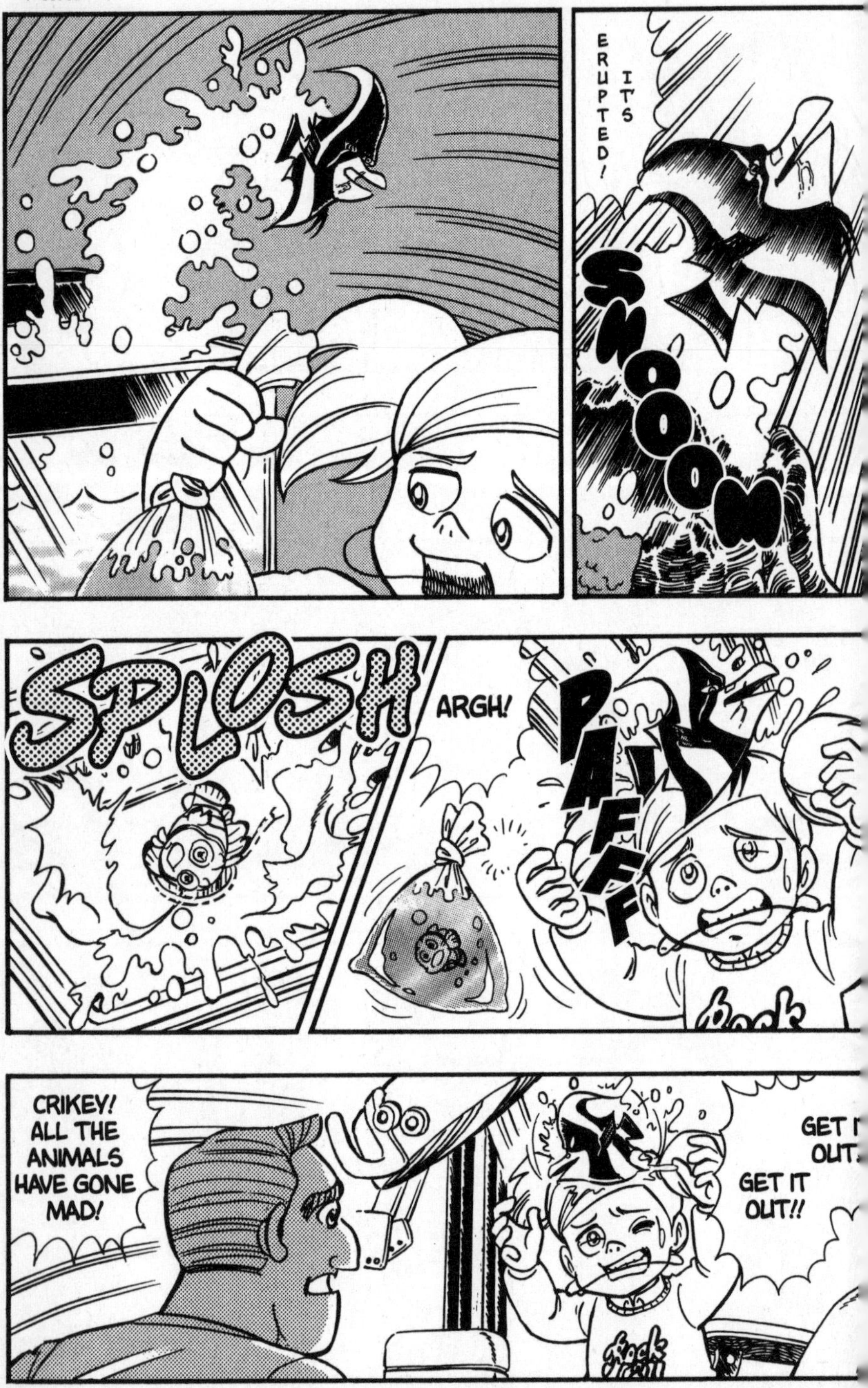
IT'S ERUPTED!
SHOOOOM
ARGH!
PAFFF
SPLOSH
GET I OUT.
GET IT OUT!!
CRIKEY! ALL THE ANIMALS HAVE GONE MAD!

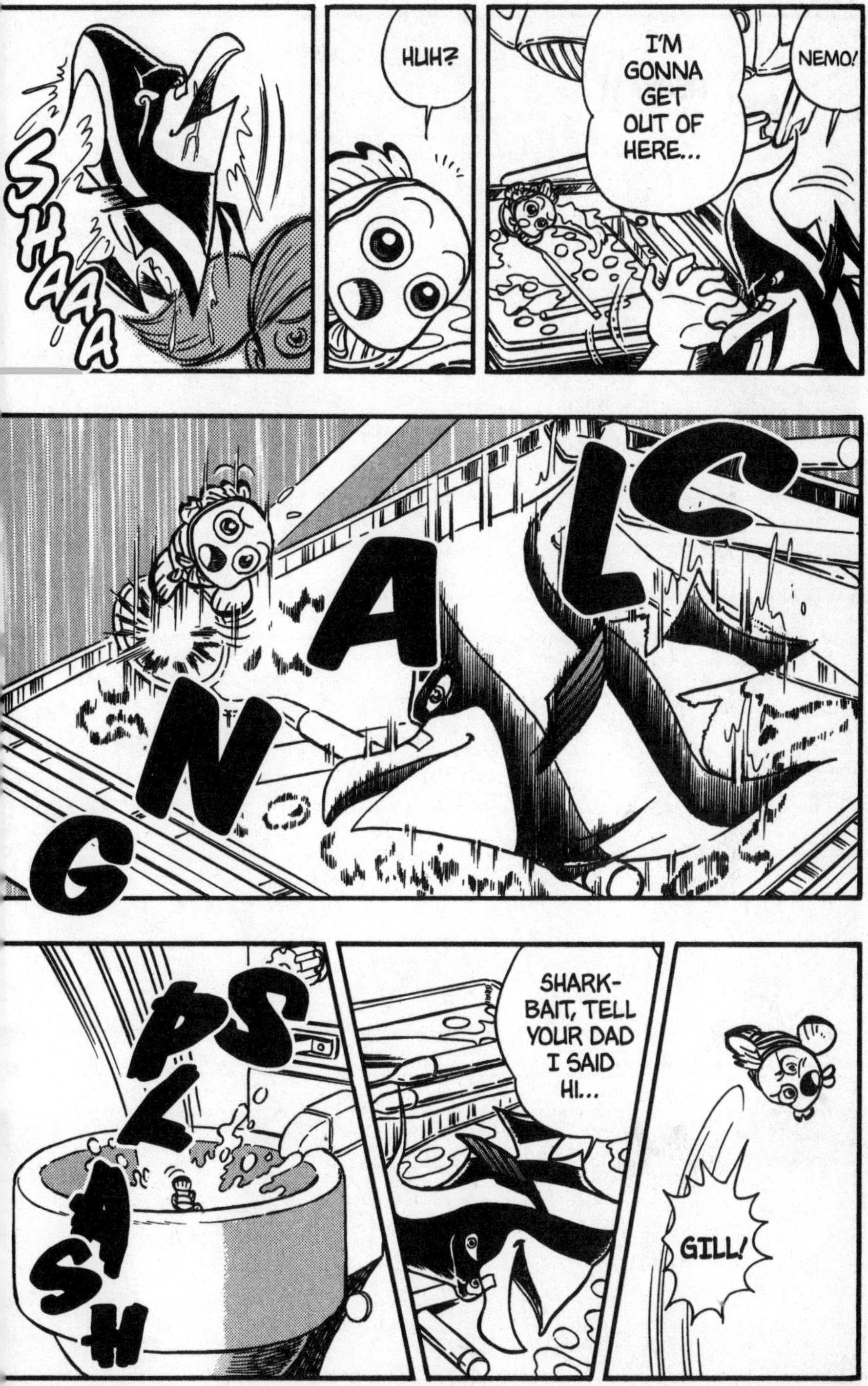
NEMO!
I'M GONNA GET OUT OF HERE...
HUH?
SHAAAA
CLANG
GILL!
SHARK-BAIT, TELL YOUR DAD I SAID HI...
SPLASH

READ THIS WAY

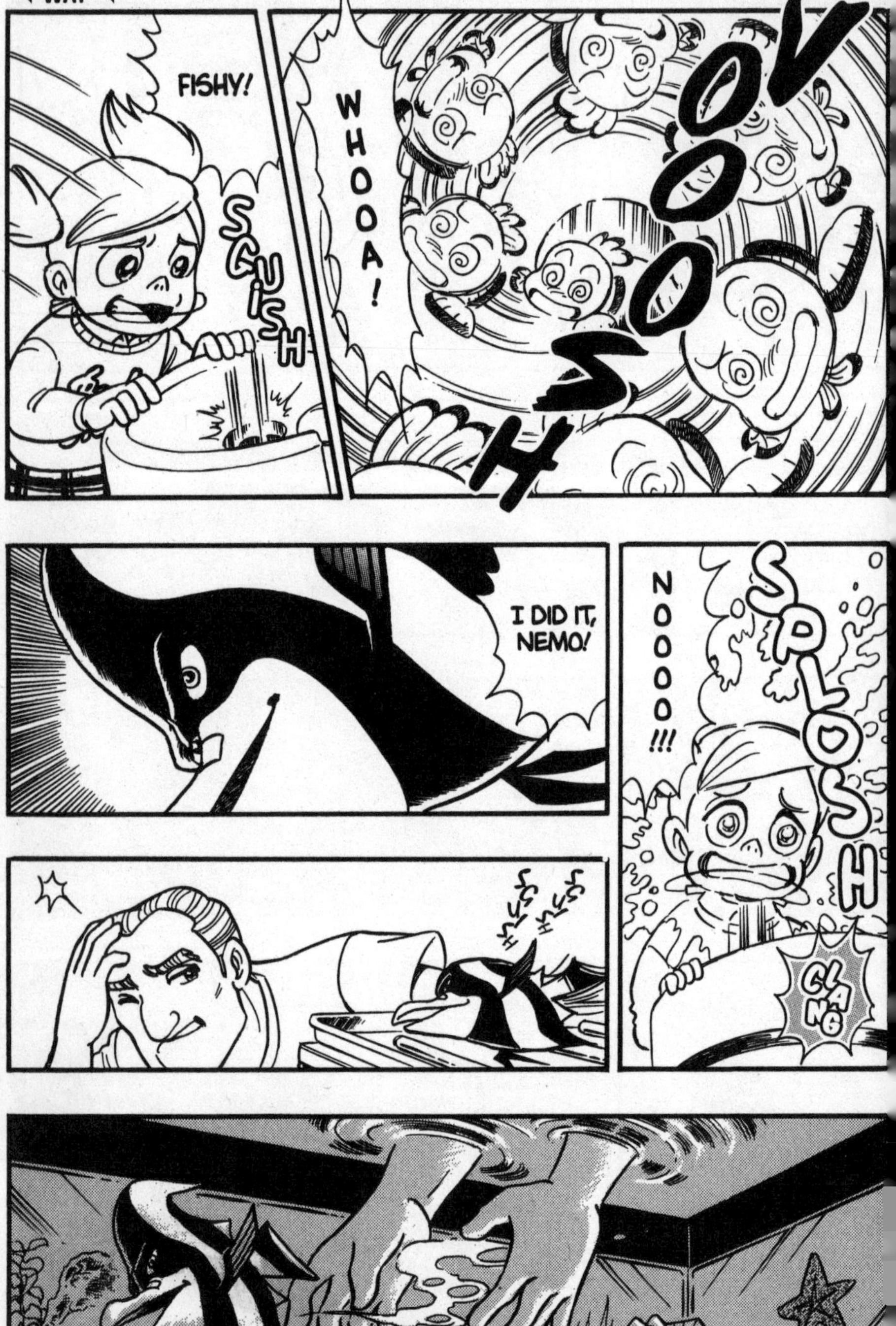
WHOOA!
VOOOOSH
FISHY!
SQUISH
NOOOOO!!!
SPLOSH
CLANG
I DID IT, NEMO!

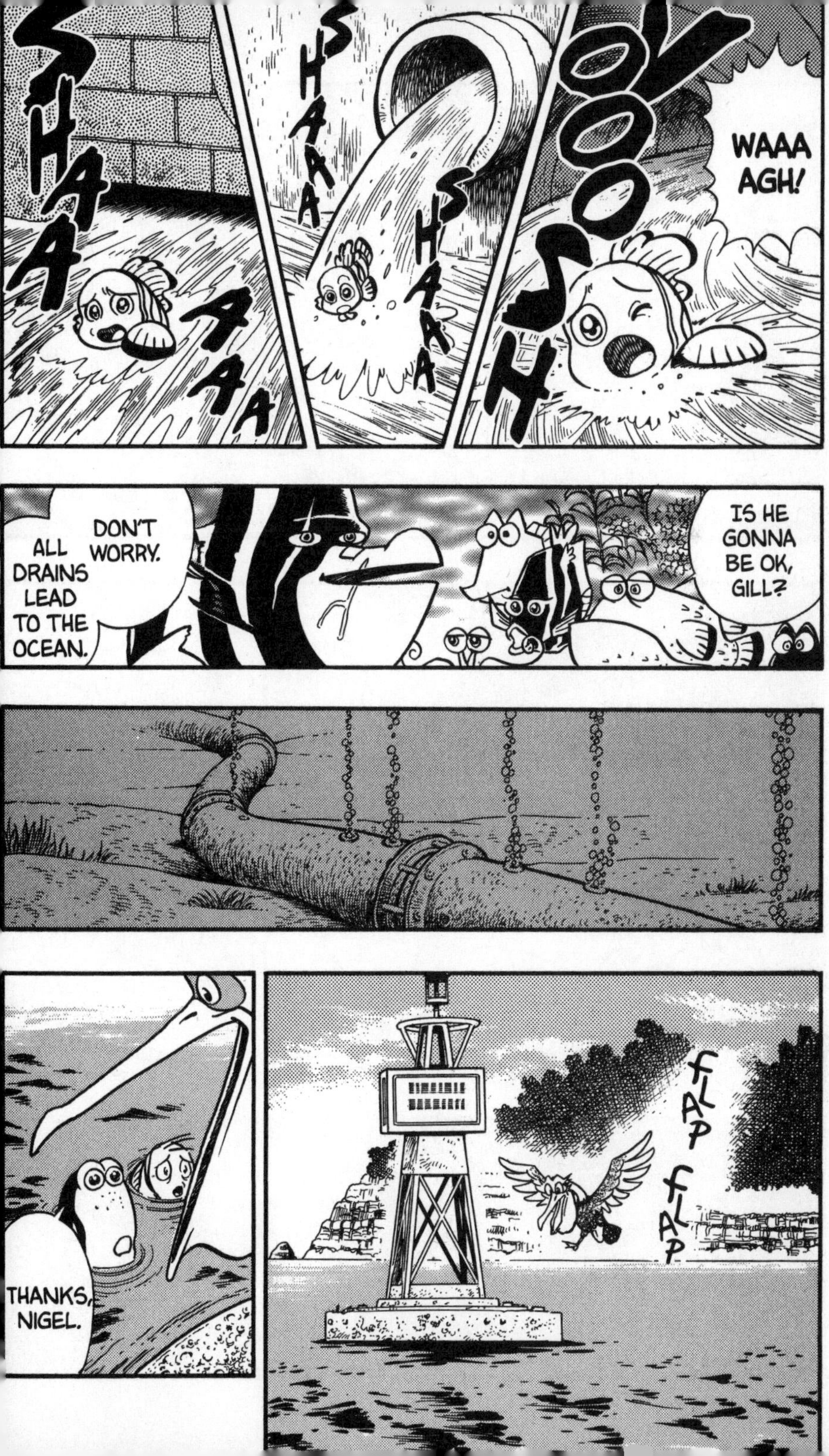
WAAA AGH!
WOOOSH
SHAAAA
SHAAAA
SHAAA
AAA
IS HE GONNA BE OK, GILL?
DON'T WORRY. ALL DRAINS LEAD TO THE OCEAN.
FLAP FLAP
THANKS, NIGEL.

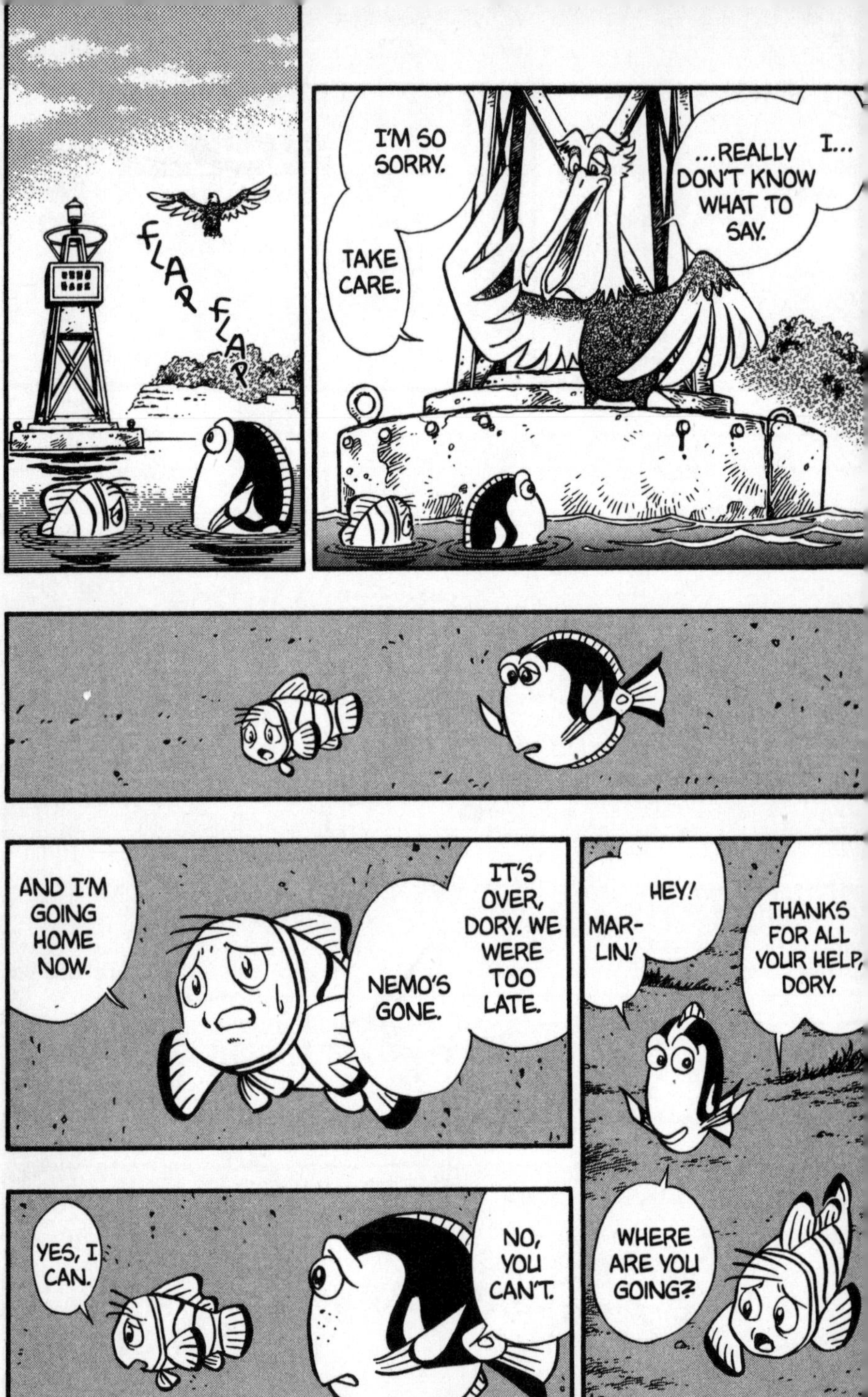
I... ...REALLY DON'T KNOW WHAT TO SAY.
I'M SO SORRY.
TAKE CARE.
FLAP FLAP
THANKS FOR ALL YOUR HELP, DORY.
HEY! MARLIN!
WHERE ARE YOU GOING?
IT'S OVER, DORY. WE WERE TOO LATE.
NEMO'S GONE.
AND I'M GOING HOME NOW.
NO, YOU CAN'T.
YES, I CAN.

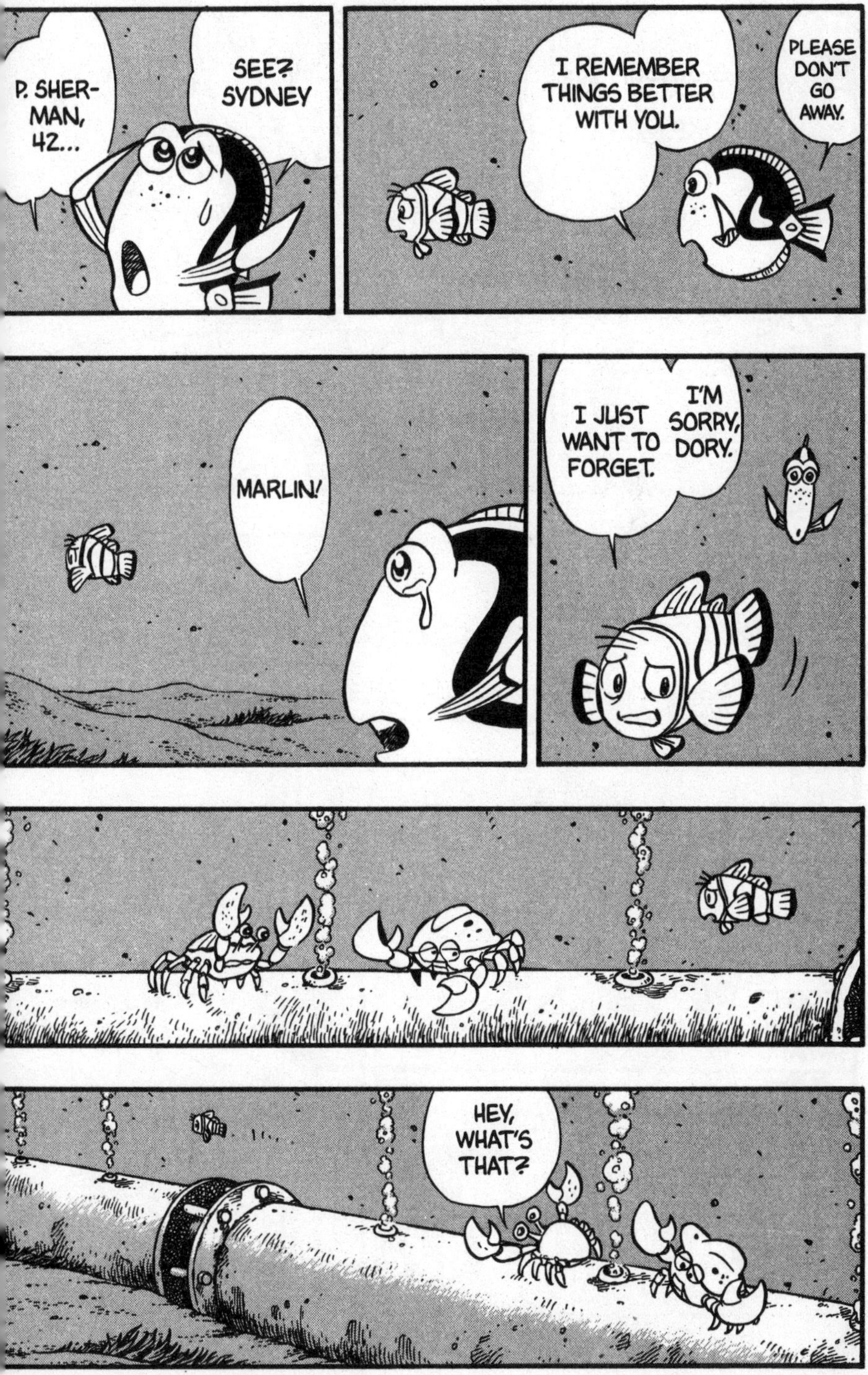
PLEASE DON'T GO AWAY.
I REMEMBER THINGS BETTER WITH YOU.
SEE? SYDNEY
P. SHER-MAN, 42...
I'M SORRY, DORY.
I JUST WANT TO FORGET.
MARLIN!
HEY, WHAT'S THAT?

READ THIS WAY

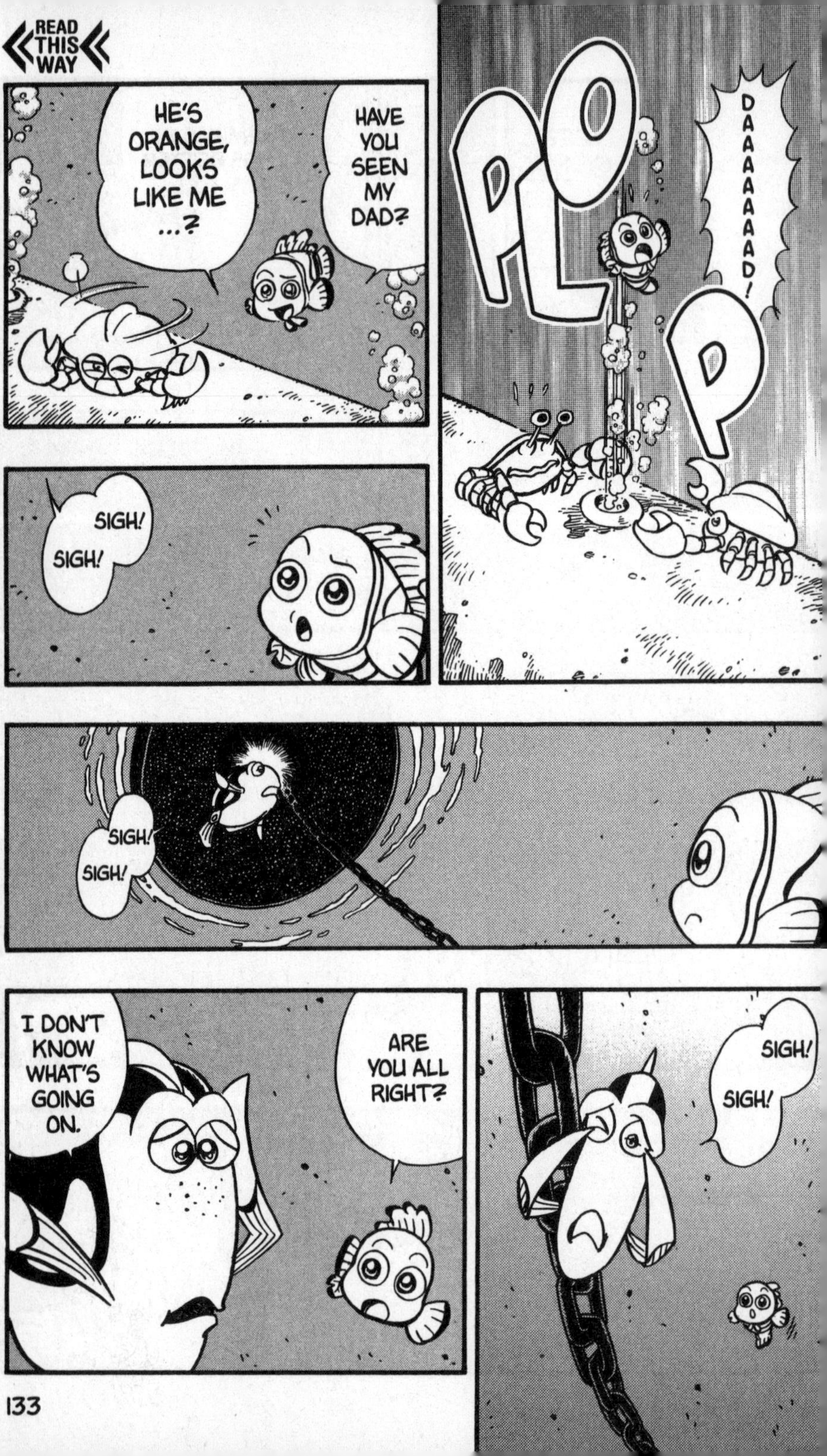
DAAAAAAAD!
PLOP
HAVE YOU SEEN MY DAD?
HE'S ORANGE, LOOKS LIKE ME ...?
SIGH! SIGH!
SIGH! SIGH!
SIGH! SIGH!
ARE YOU ALL RIGHT?
I DON'T KNOW WHAT'S GOING ON.

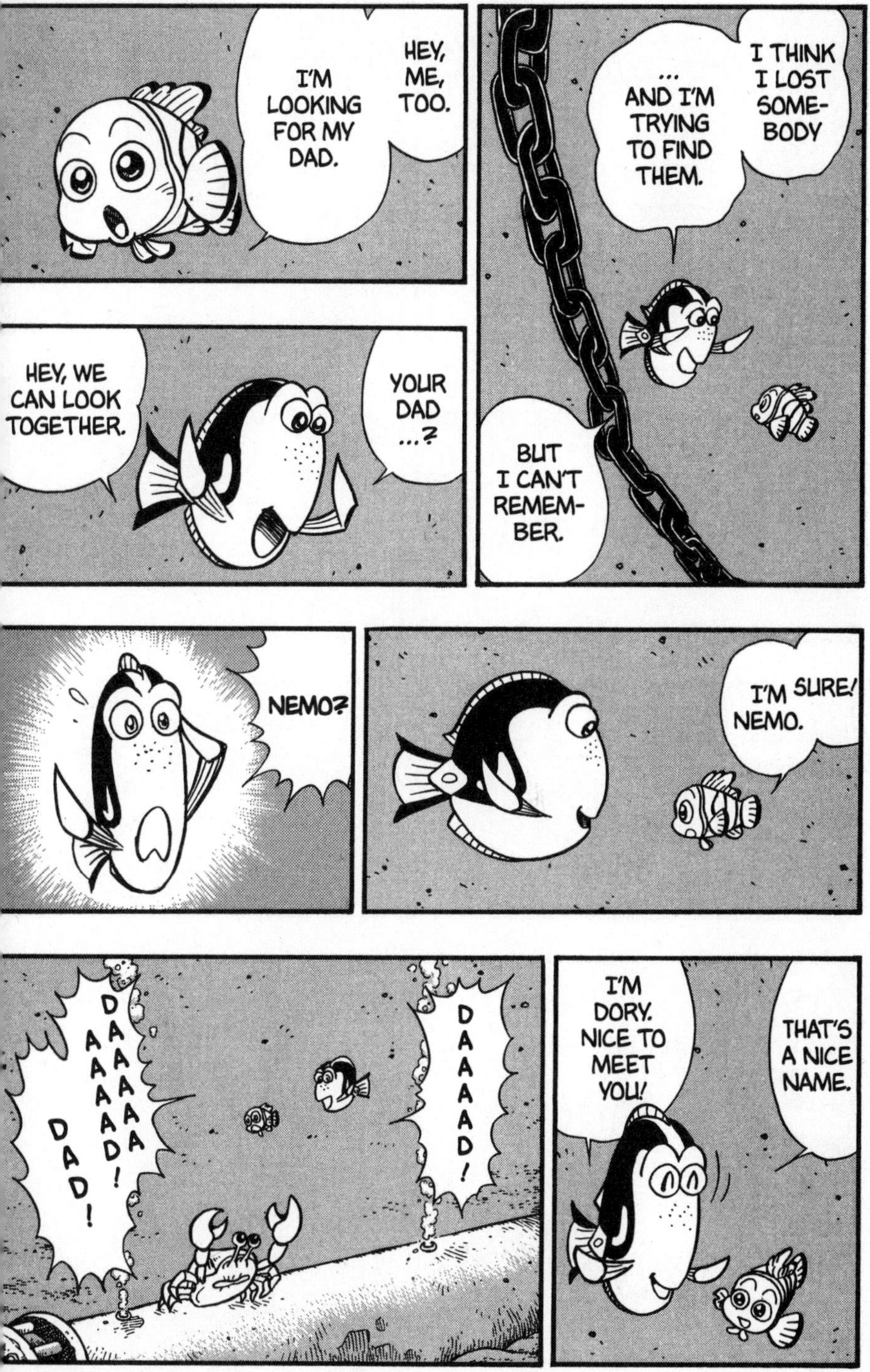
I THINK I LOST SOME-BODY
... AND I'M TRYING TO FIND THEM.
BUT I CAN'T REMEM-BER.
HEY, ME, TOO.
I'M LOOKING FOR MY DAD.
YOUR DAD ...?
HEY, WE CAN LOOK TOGETHER.
I'M SURE! NEMO.
NEMO?
THAT'S A NICE NAME.
I'M DORY. NICE TO MEET YOU!
DAAAAAD!
DAAAAAAAAAAAD! DAD!

READ THIS WAY

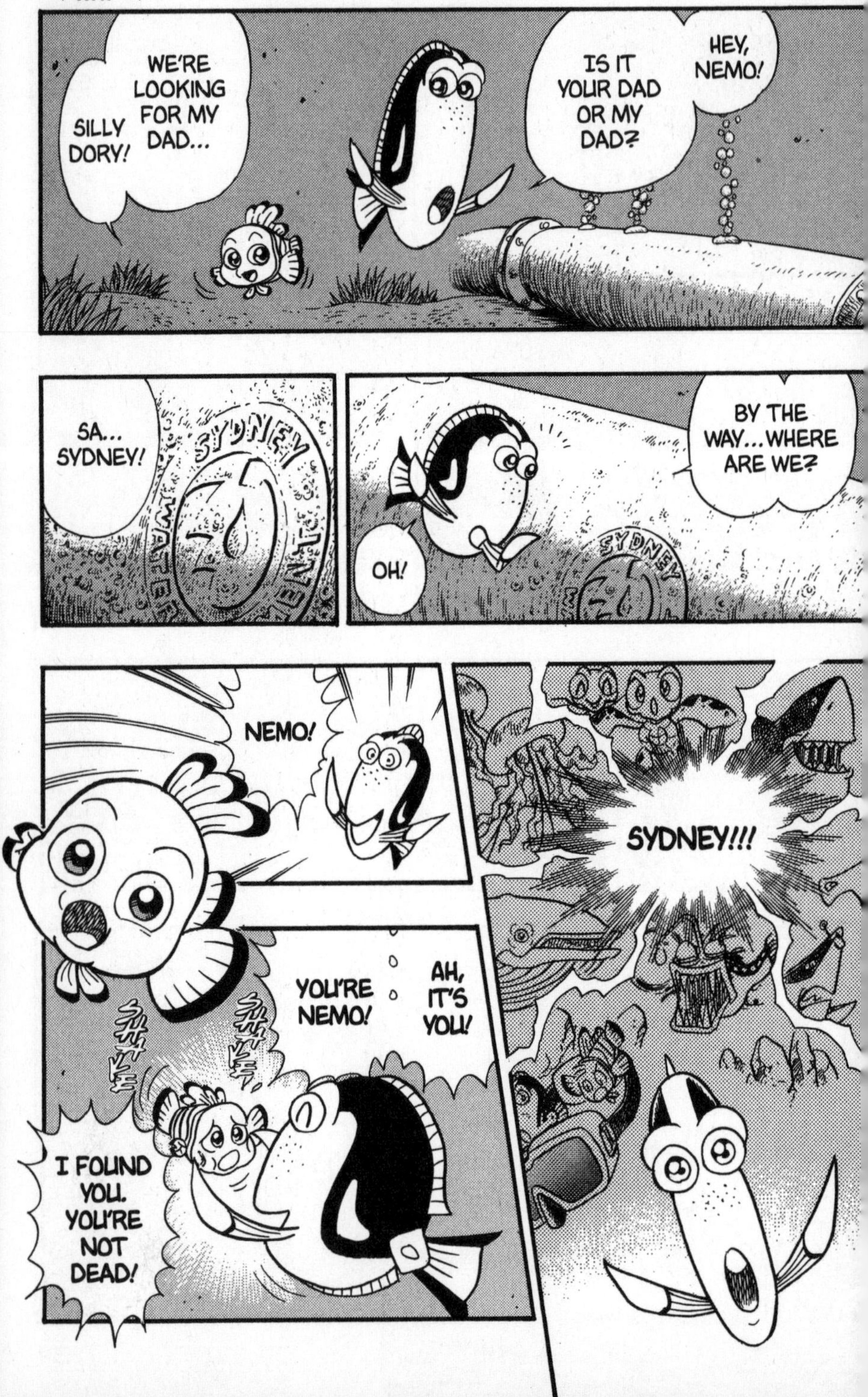
HEY, NEMO!
IS IT YOUR DAD OR MY DAD?
WE'RE LOOKING FOR MY DAD...
SILLY DORY!
BY THE WAY...WHERE ARE WE?
OH!
SYDNEY
SA... SYDNEY!
SYDNEY!!!
NEMO!
AH, IT'S YOU!
YOU'RE NEMO!
I FOUND YOU. YOU'RE NOT DEAD!

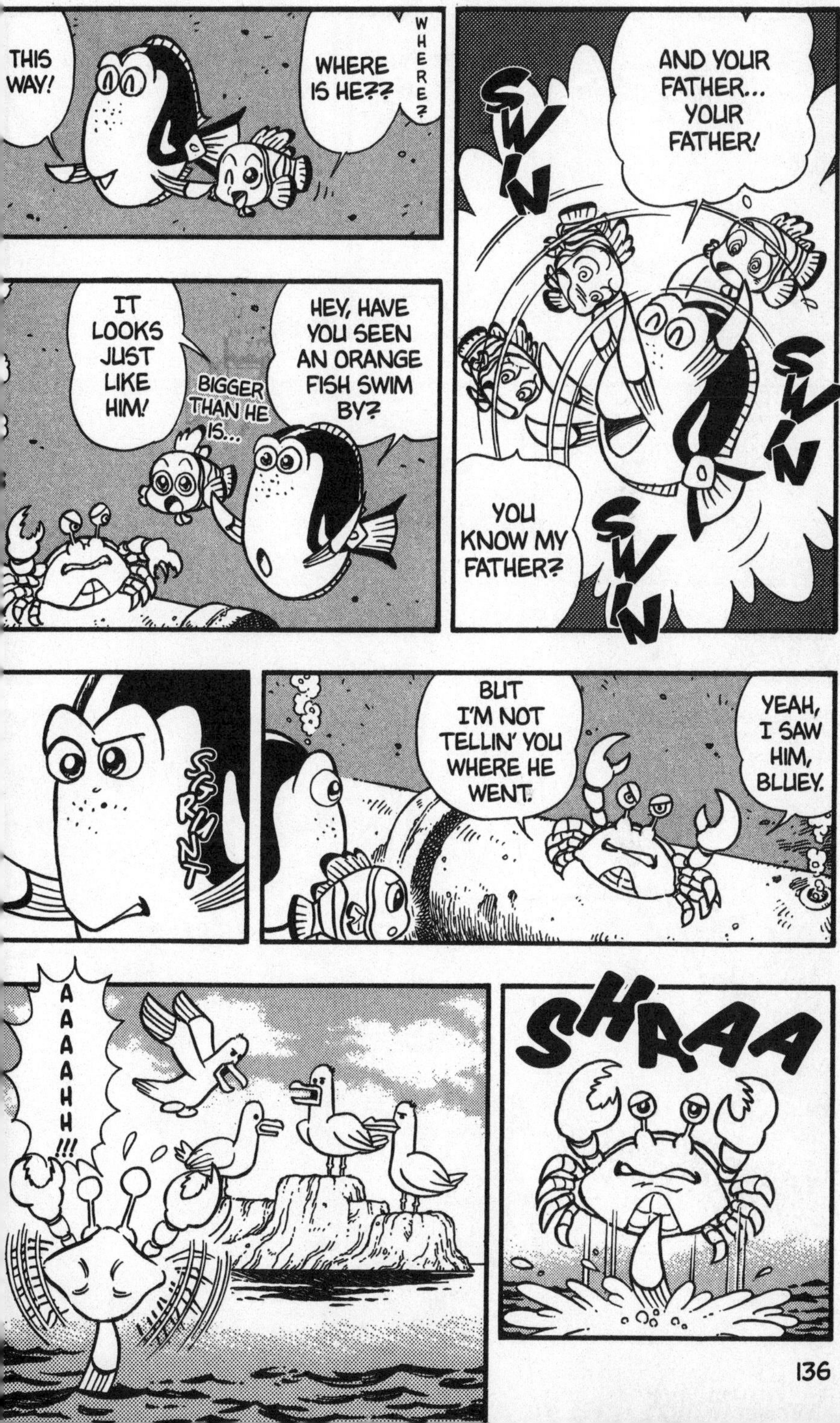
AND YOUR FATHER... YOUR FATHER!
SWIN
SWIN
YOU KNOW MY FATHER?
SWIN
WHERE IS HE??
WHERE?
THIS WAY!
HEY, HAVE YOU SEEN AN ORANGE FISH SWIM BY?
IT LOOKS JUST LIKE HIM!
BIGGER THAN HE IS...
YEAH, I SAW HIM, BLUEY.
BUT I'M NOT TELLIN' YOU WHERE HE WENT.
SGRUNT
SHRAAA
AAAAAHH!!!

READ THIS WAY

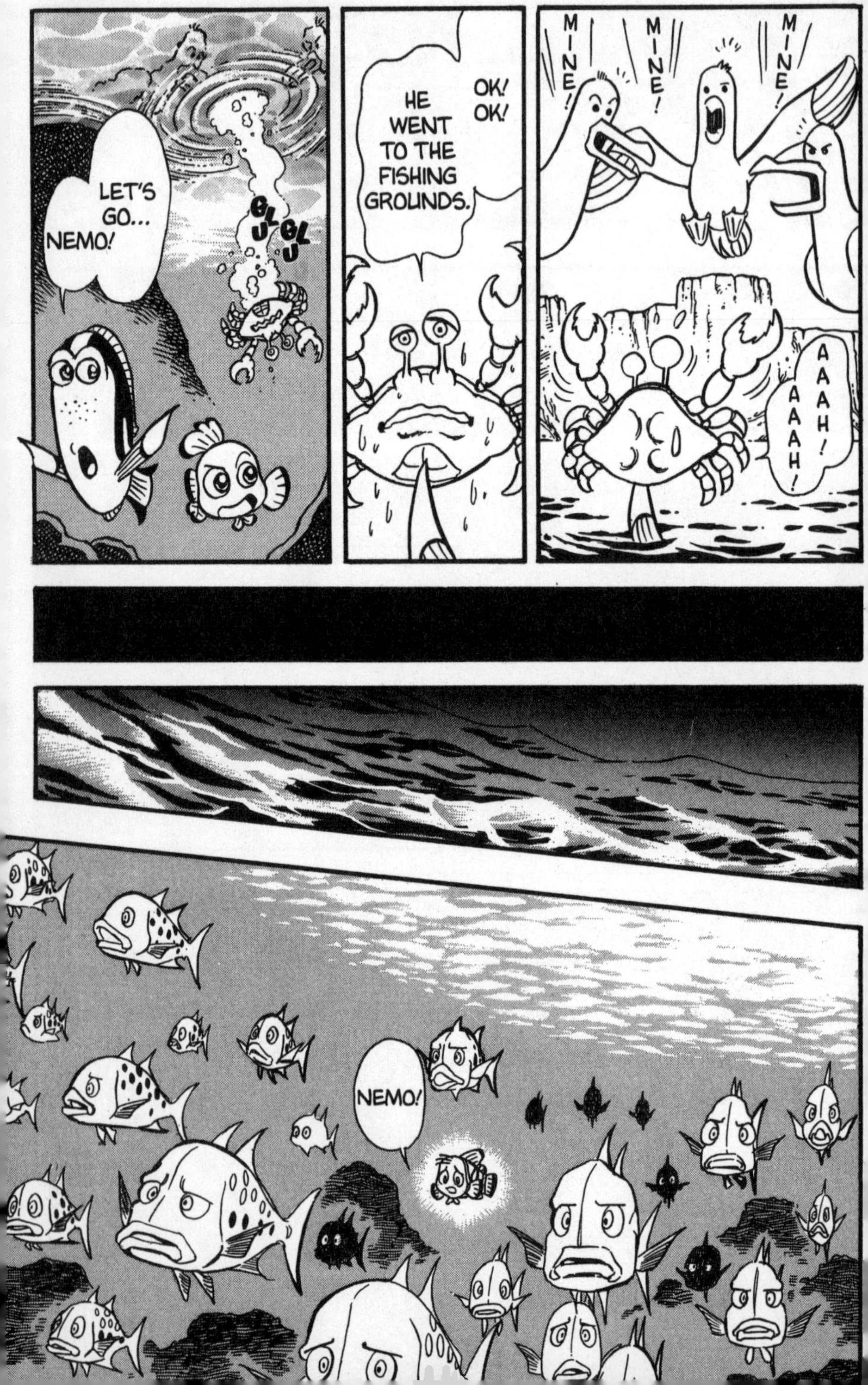

MINE!
MINE!
MINE!
AAAH! AAAH!
OK! OK!
HE WENT TO THE FISHING GROUNDS.
LET'S GO... NEMO!
GLU GLU
NEMO!

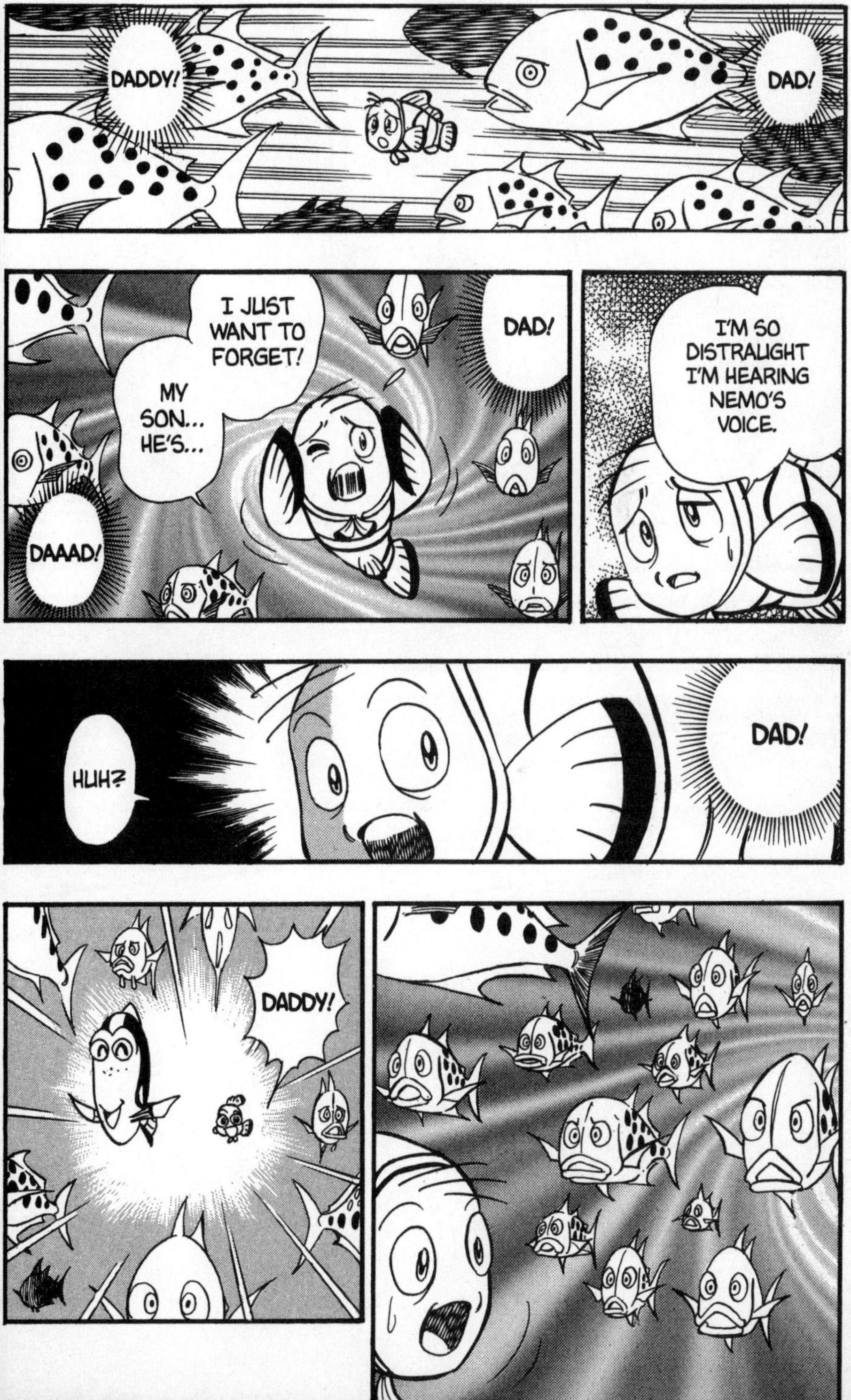
DAD!
DADDY!
I'M SO DISTRAUGHT I'M HEARING NEMO'S VOICE.
DAD!
I JUST WANT TO FORGET!
MY SON... HE'S...
DAAAD!
DAD!
HUH?
DADDY!

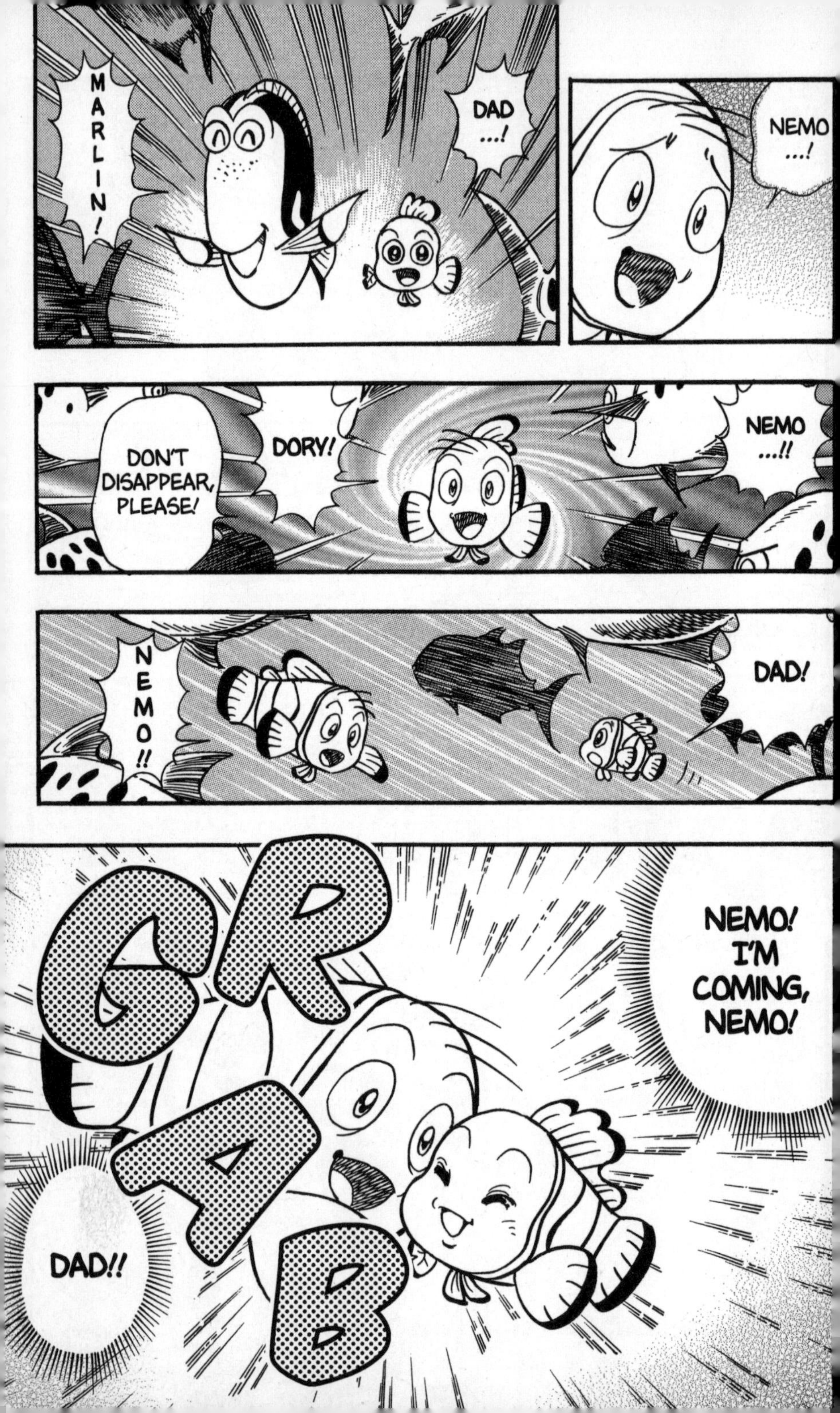
NEMO ...!
DAD ...!
MARLIN!
NEMO ...!!
DORY!
DON'T DISAPPEAR, PLEASE!
DAD!
NEMO!!
NEMO! I'M COMING, NEMO!
GRAB
DAD!!

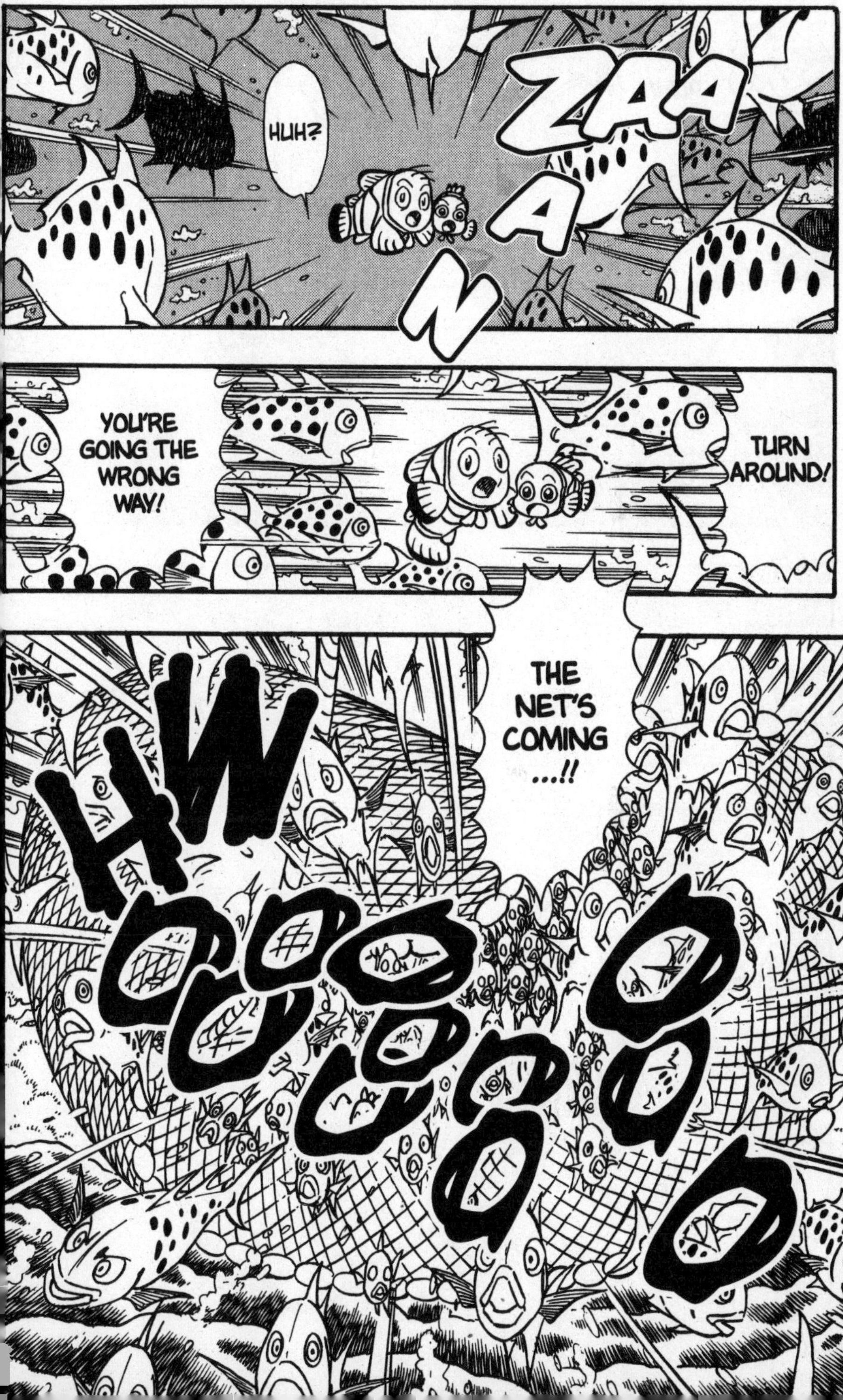
ZAAAN
HUH?
TURN AROUND!
YOU'RE GOING THE WRONG WAY!
THE NET'S COMING ...!!

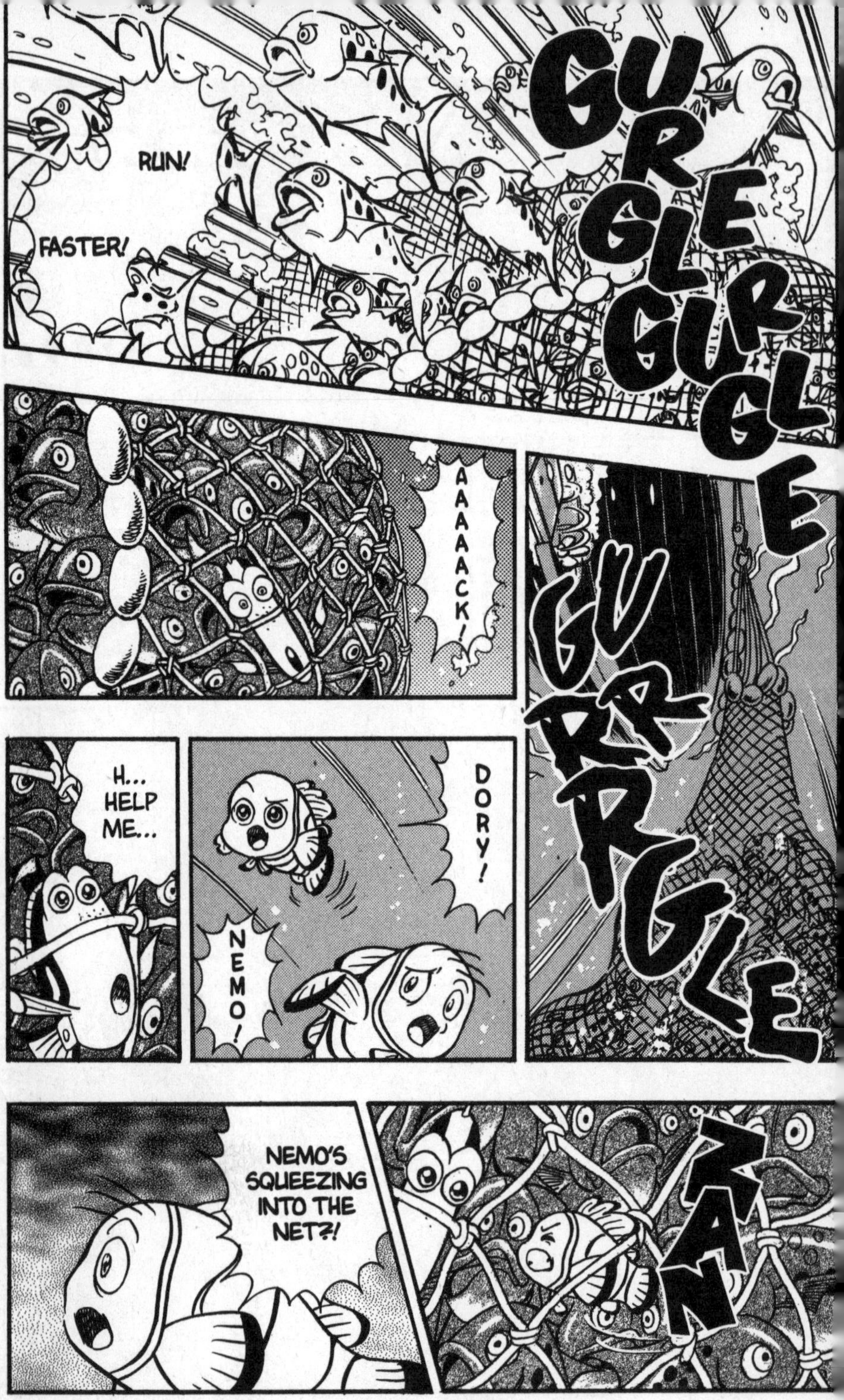
RUN!
FASTER!
GURGLE GURGLE
AAAAACK!
GURGLE
GARRRGLE
H... HELP ME...
DORY!
NEMO!
NEMO'S SQUEEZING INTO THE NET?!
ZAN

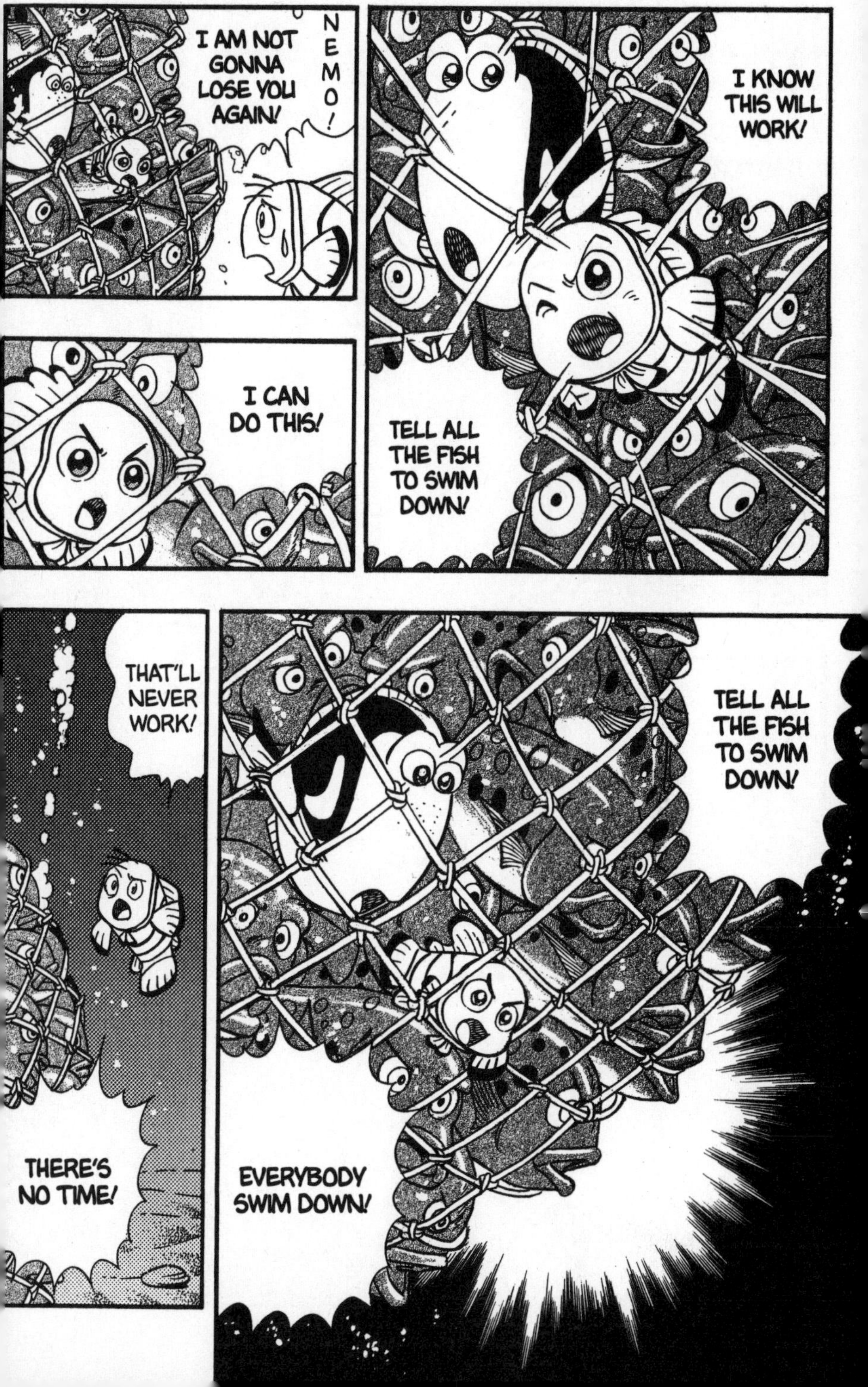
I KNOW THIS WILL WORK!
TELL ALL THE FISH TO SWIM DOWN!
NEMO!
I AM NOT GONNA LOSE YOU AGAIN!
I CAN DO THIS!
TELL ALL THE FISH TO SWIM DOWN!
EVERYBODY SWIM DOWN!
THAT'LL NEVER WORK!
THERE'S NO TIME!

READ THIS WAY

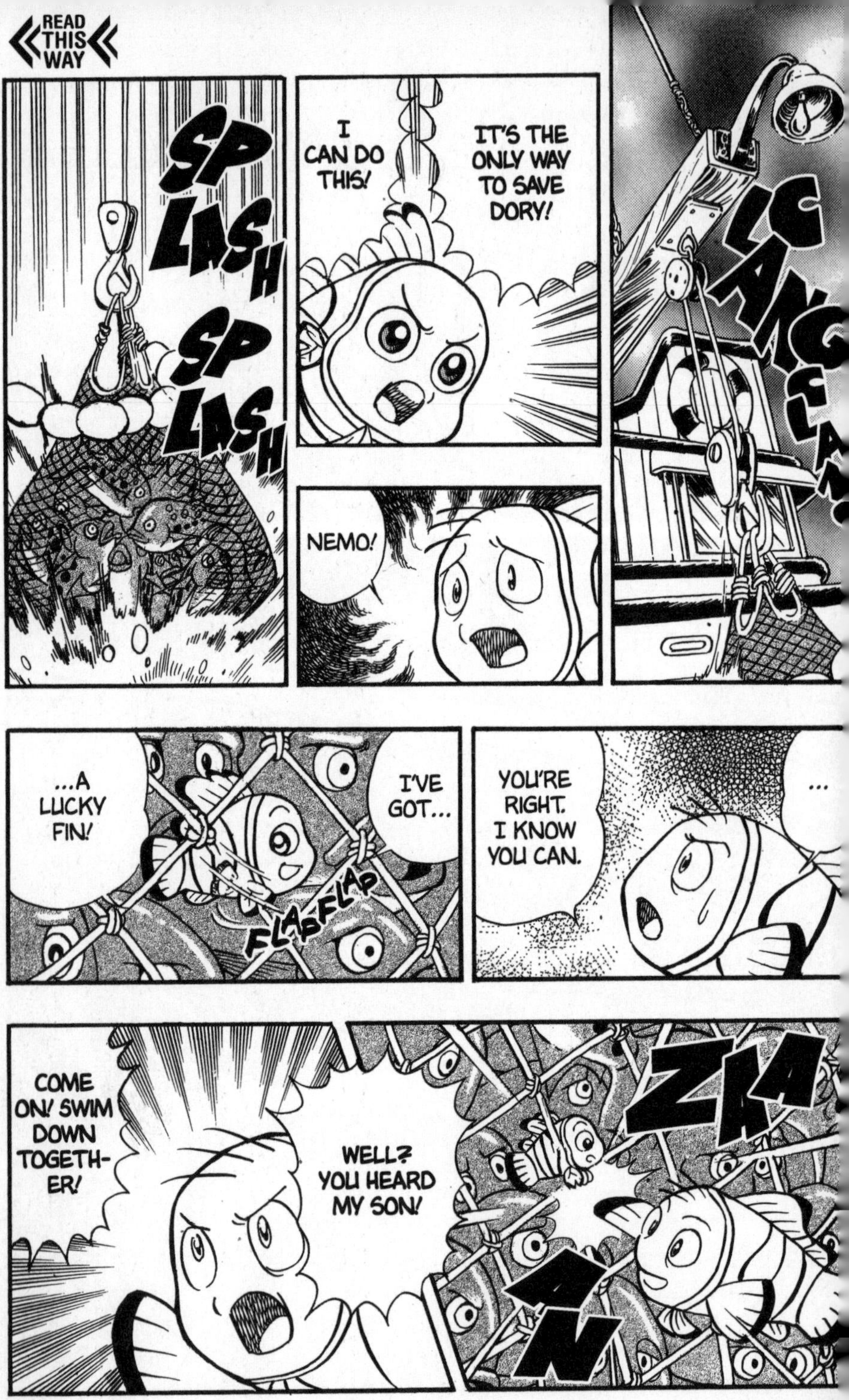
CLANG CLAN
IT'S THE ONLY WAY TO SAVE DORY!
I CAN DO THIS!
NEMO!
SPLASH
SPLASH
...
YOU'RE RIGHT. I KNOW YOU CAN.
I'VE GOT...
...A LUCKY FIN!
FLAP FLAP
ZAAN
WELL? YOU HEARD MY SON!
COME ON! SWIM DOWN TOGETHER!

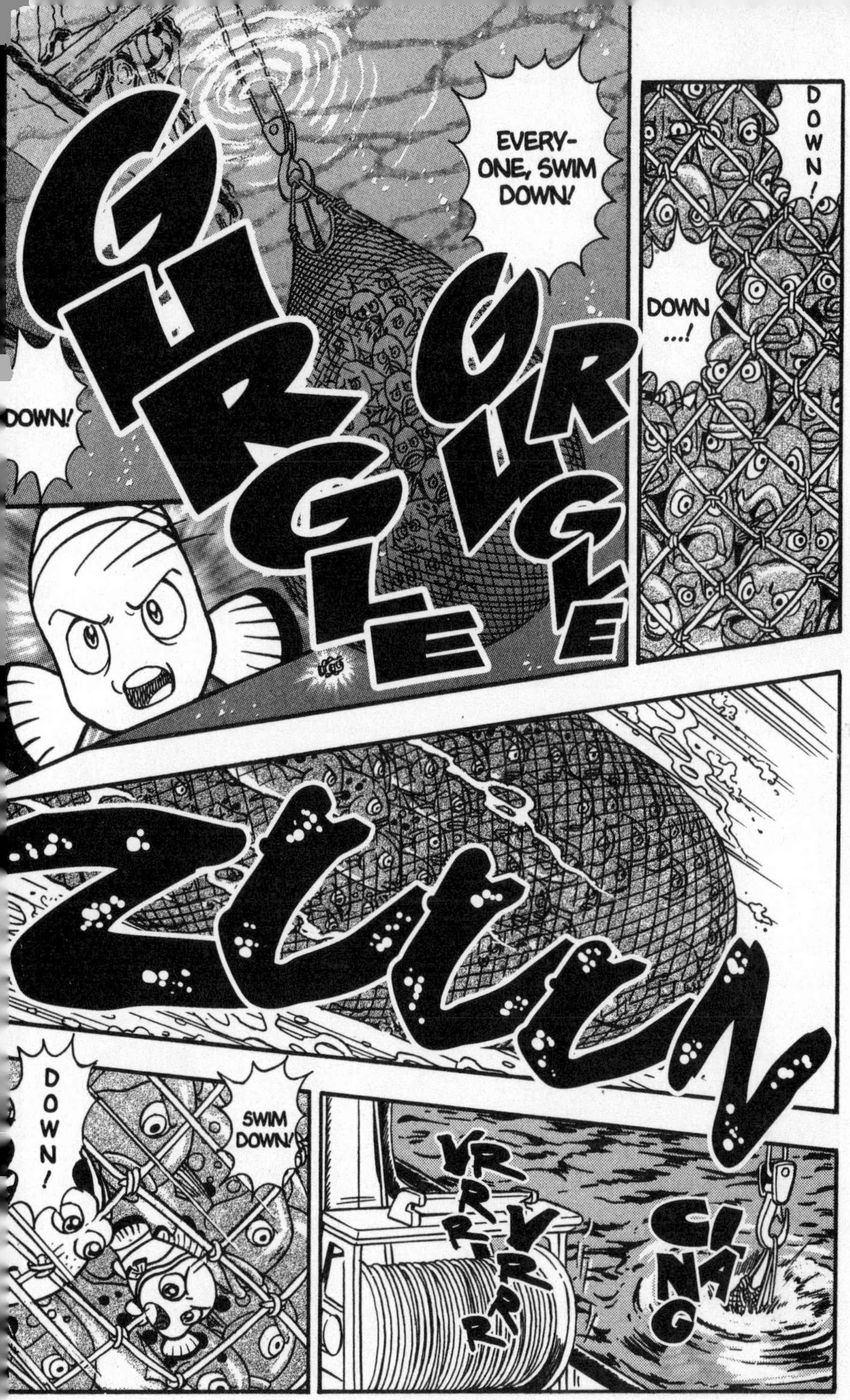

DOWN!
DOWN ...!
EVERY-ONE, SWIM DOWN!
DOWN!
GURGLE
GURGLE
ZUUUN
CLANG
VRRRR
VRRRR
SWIM DOWN!
DOWN!

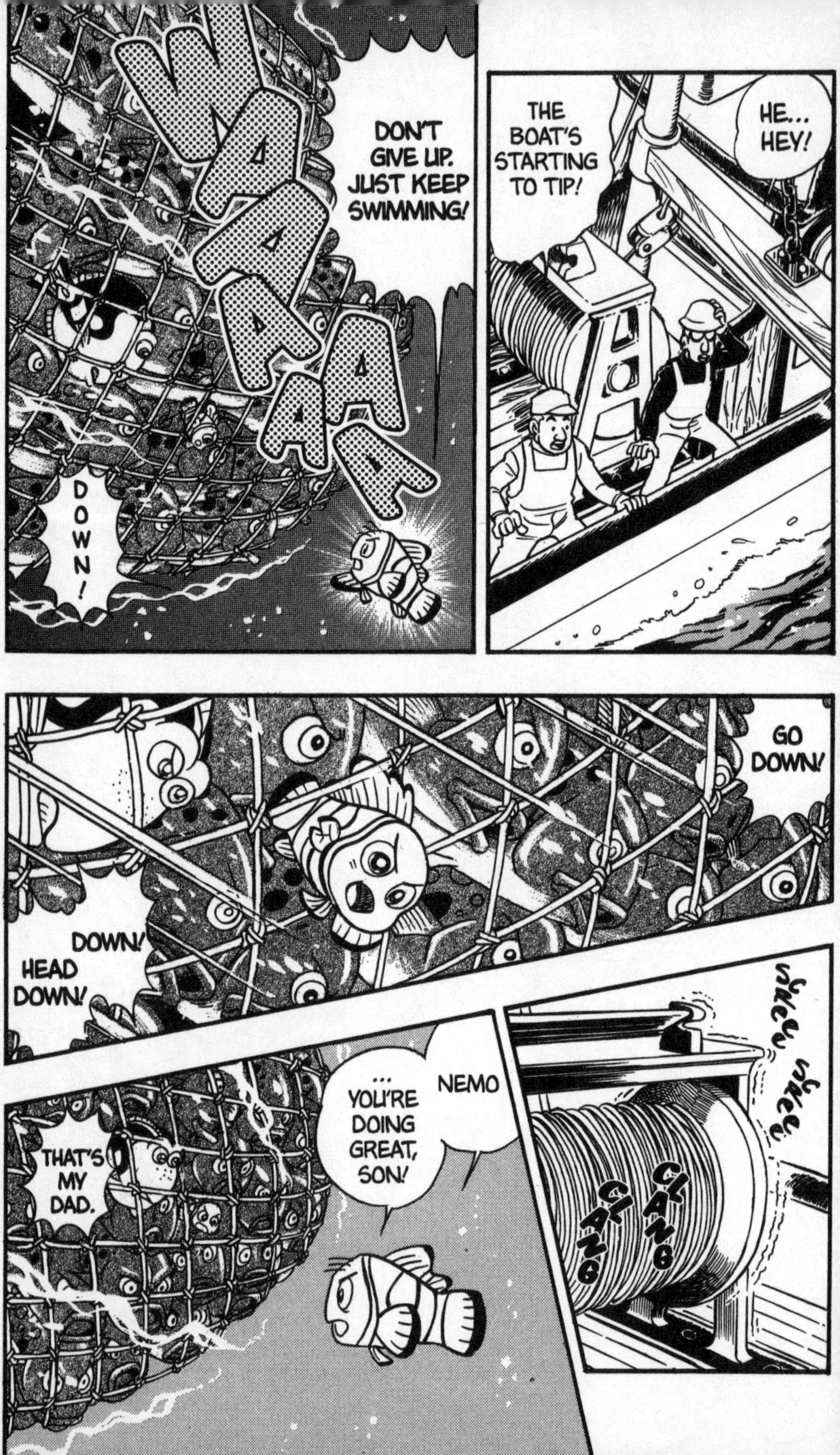
HE... HEY!
THE BOAT'S STARTING TO TIP!
DON'T GIVE UP. JUST KEEP SWIMMING!
DOWN!
GO DOWN!
DOWN!
HEAD DOWN!
SKREE
SKREE
CLANG
CLANG
NEMO
... YOU'RE DOING GREAT, SON!
THAT'S MY DAD.

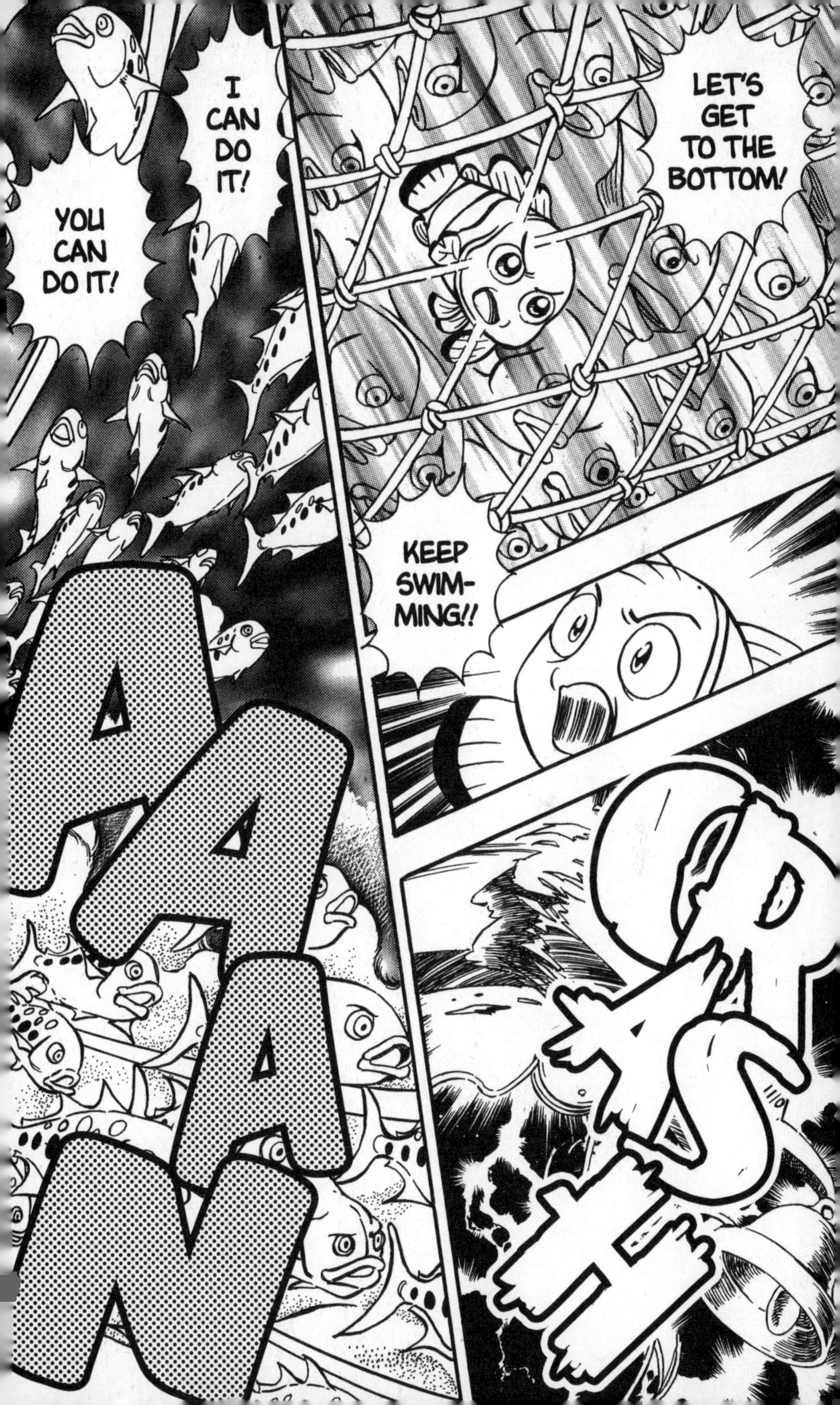
LET'S GET TO THE BOTTOM!
KEEP SWIMMING!!
I CAN DO IT!
YOU CAN DO IT!

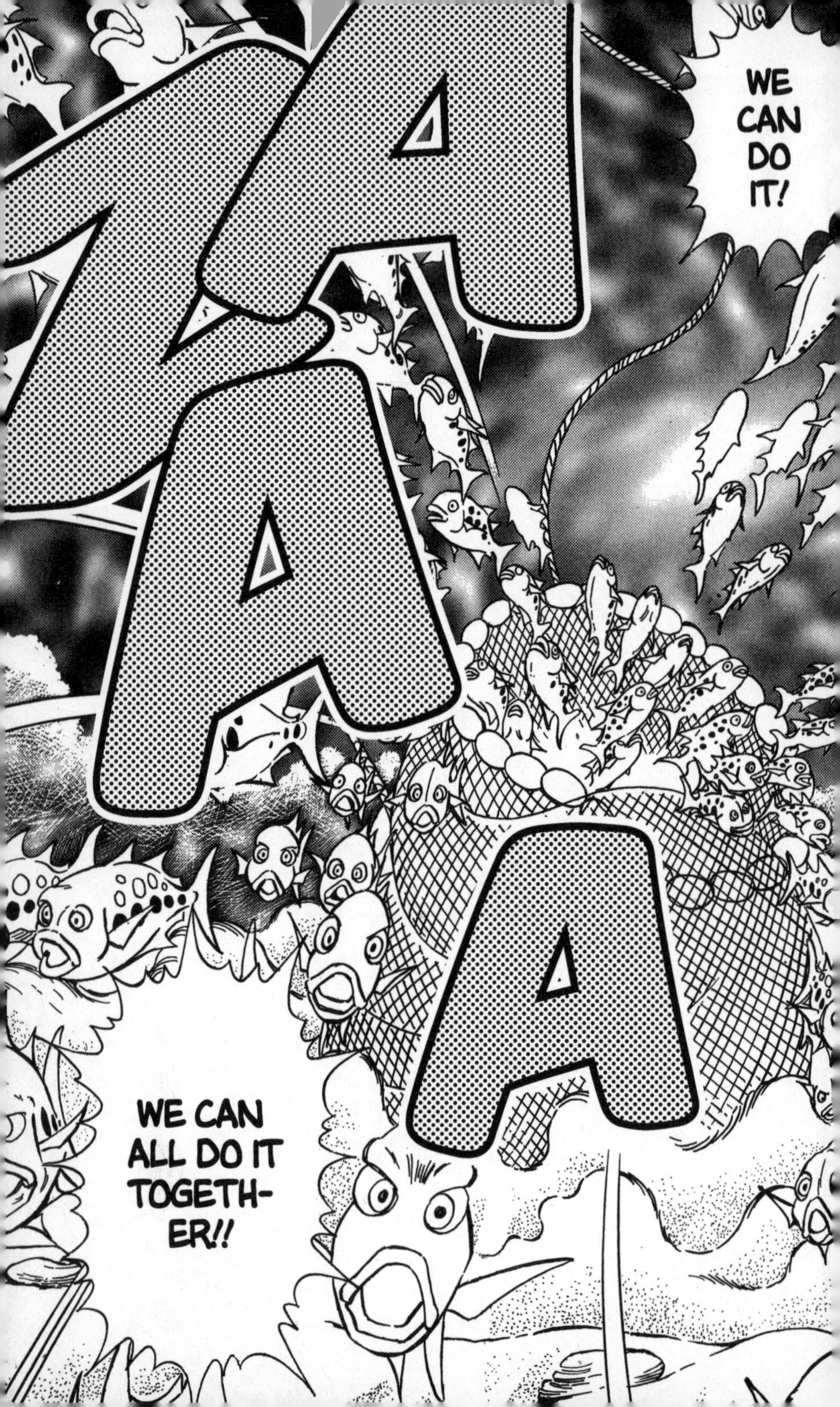
WE CAN DO IT!
AAA
WE CAN ALL DO IT TOGETH-ER!!

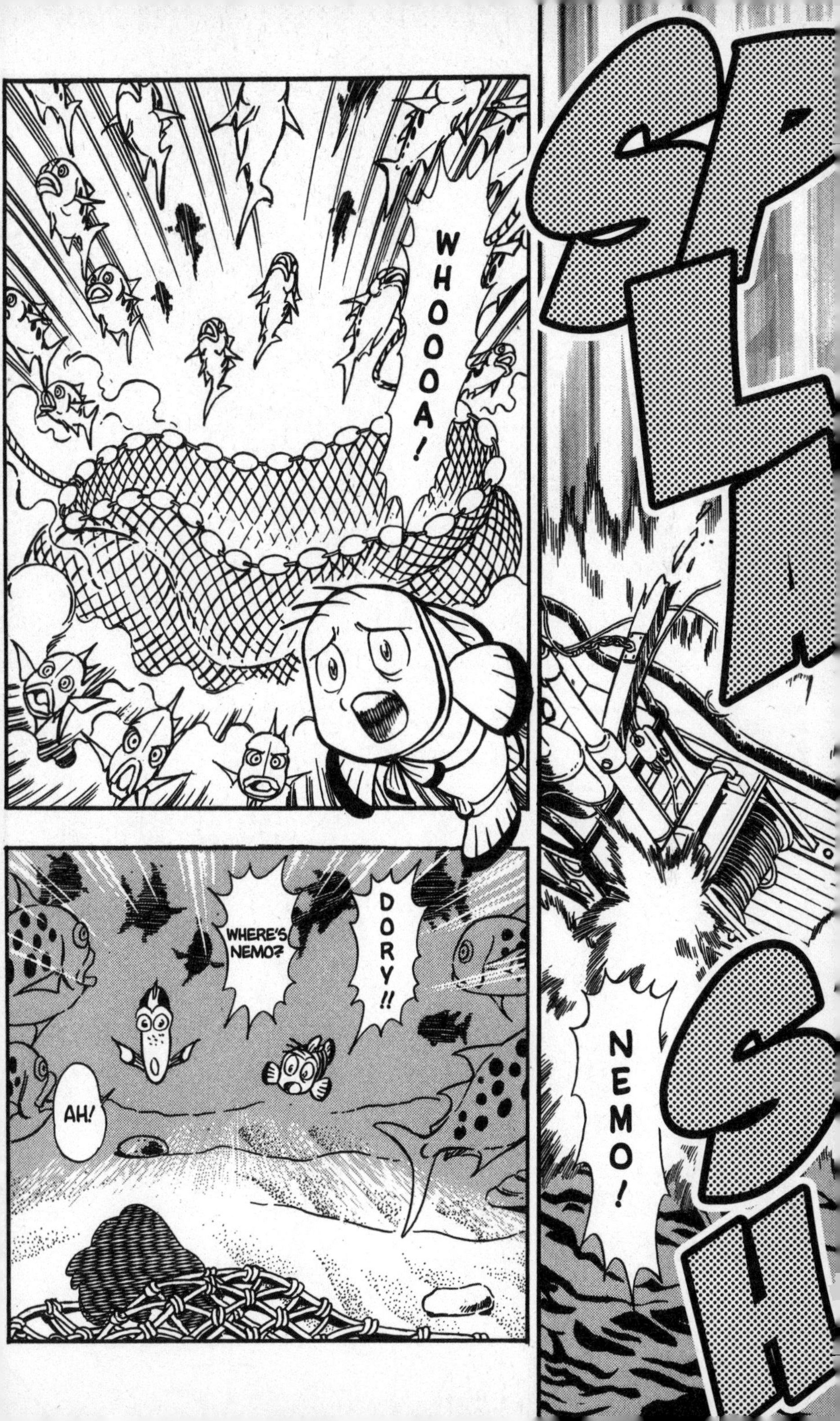
SPLASH
NEMO!
WHOOOOA!
DORY!!
WHERE'S NEMO?
AH!

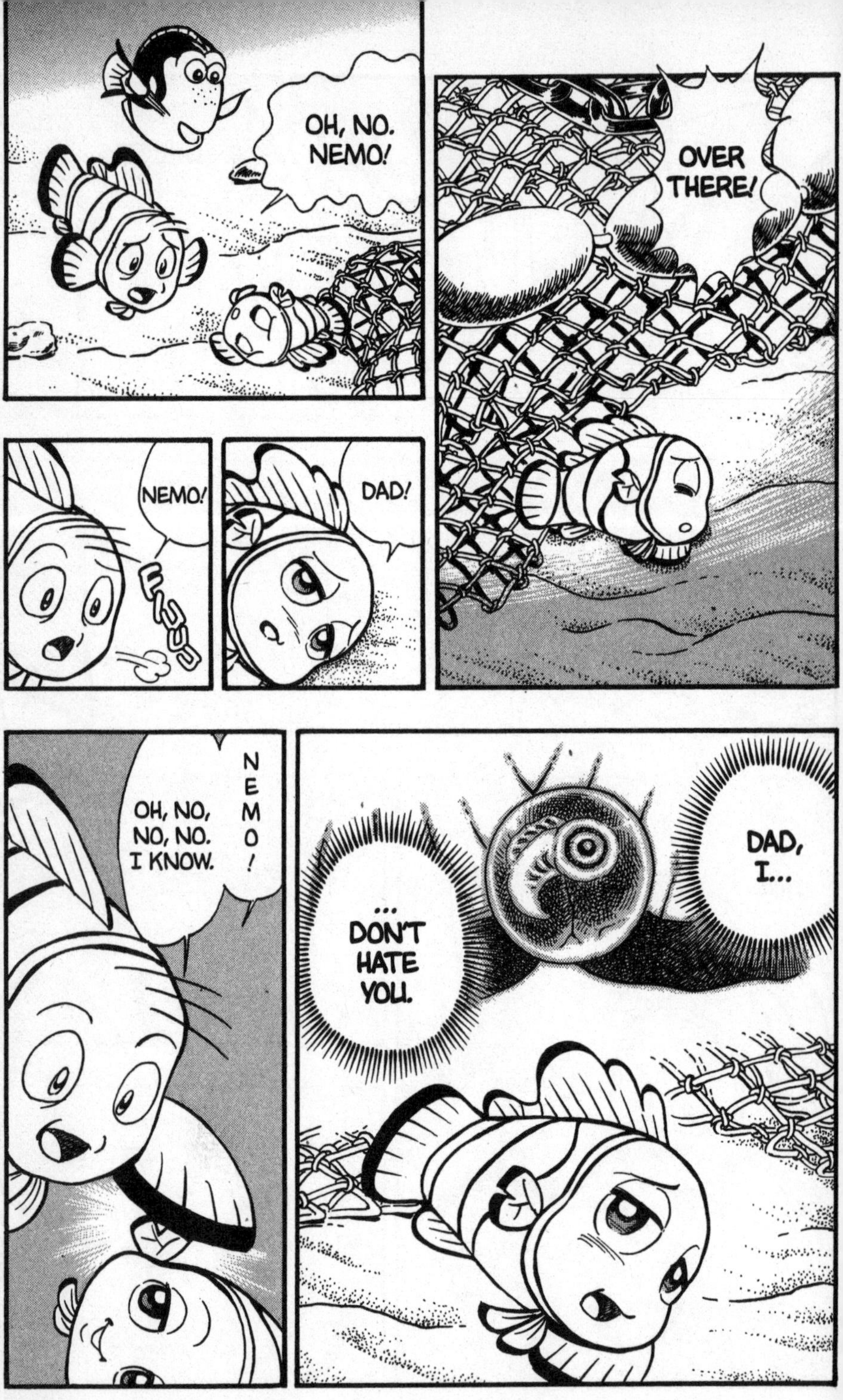
OVER THERE!
OH, NO. NEMO!
DAD!
NEMO!
FLUUU
DAD, I...
... DON'T HATE YOU.
NEMO!
OH, NO, NO, NO. I KNOW.

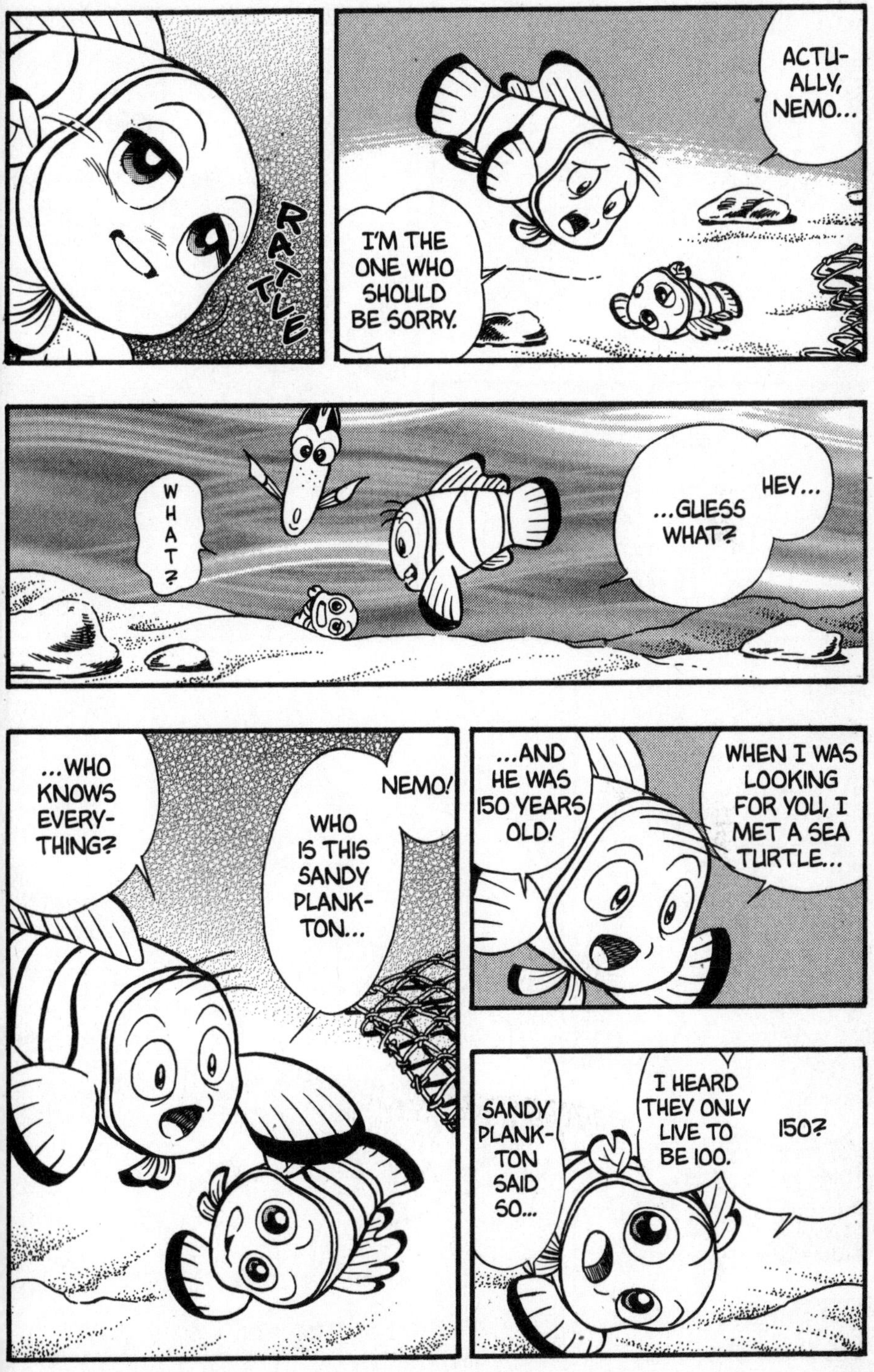
ACTU-ALLY, NEMO...
I'M THE ONE WHO SHOULD BE SORRY.
RATTLE
HEY...
...GUESS WHAT?
WHAT?
WHEN I WAS LOOKING FOR YOU, I MET A SEA TURTLE...
...AND HE WAS 150 YEARS OLD!
150?
I HEARD THEY ONLY LIVE TO BE 100.
SANDY PLANK-TON SAID SO...
NEMO!
WHO IS THIS SANDY PLANK-TON...
...WHO KNOWS EVERY-THING?

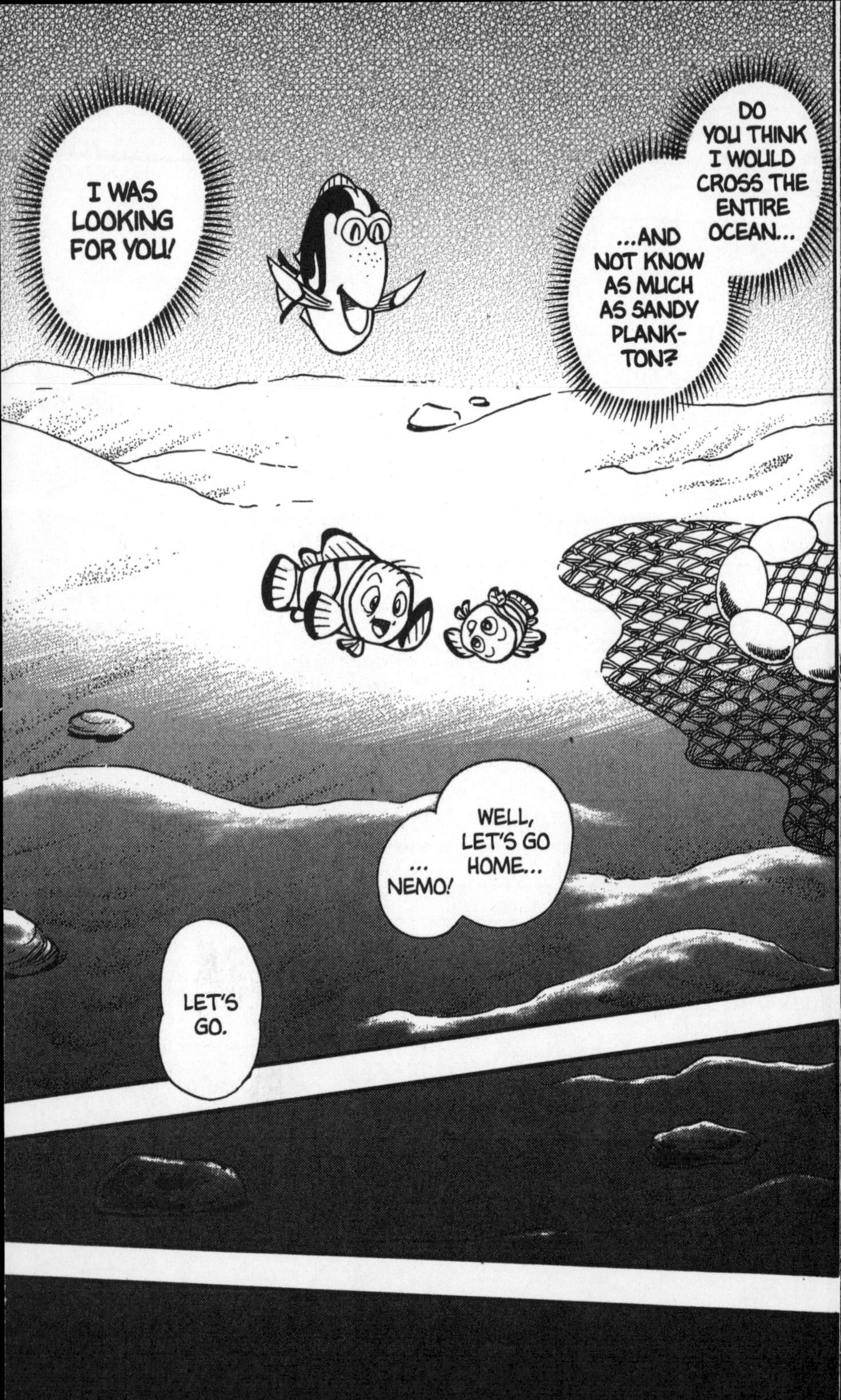
DO YOU THINK I WOULD CROSS THE ENTIRE OCEAN...
...AND NOT KNOW AS MUCH AS SANDY PLANK-TON?
I WAS LOOKING FOR YOU!
WELL, LET'S GO HOME...
... NEMO!
LET'S GO.

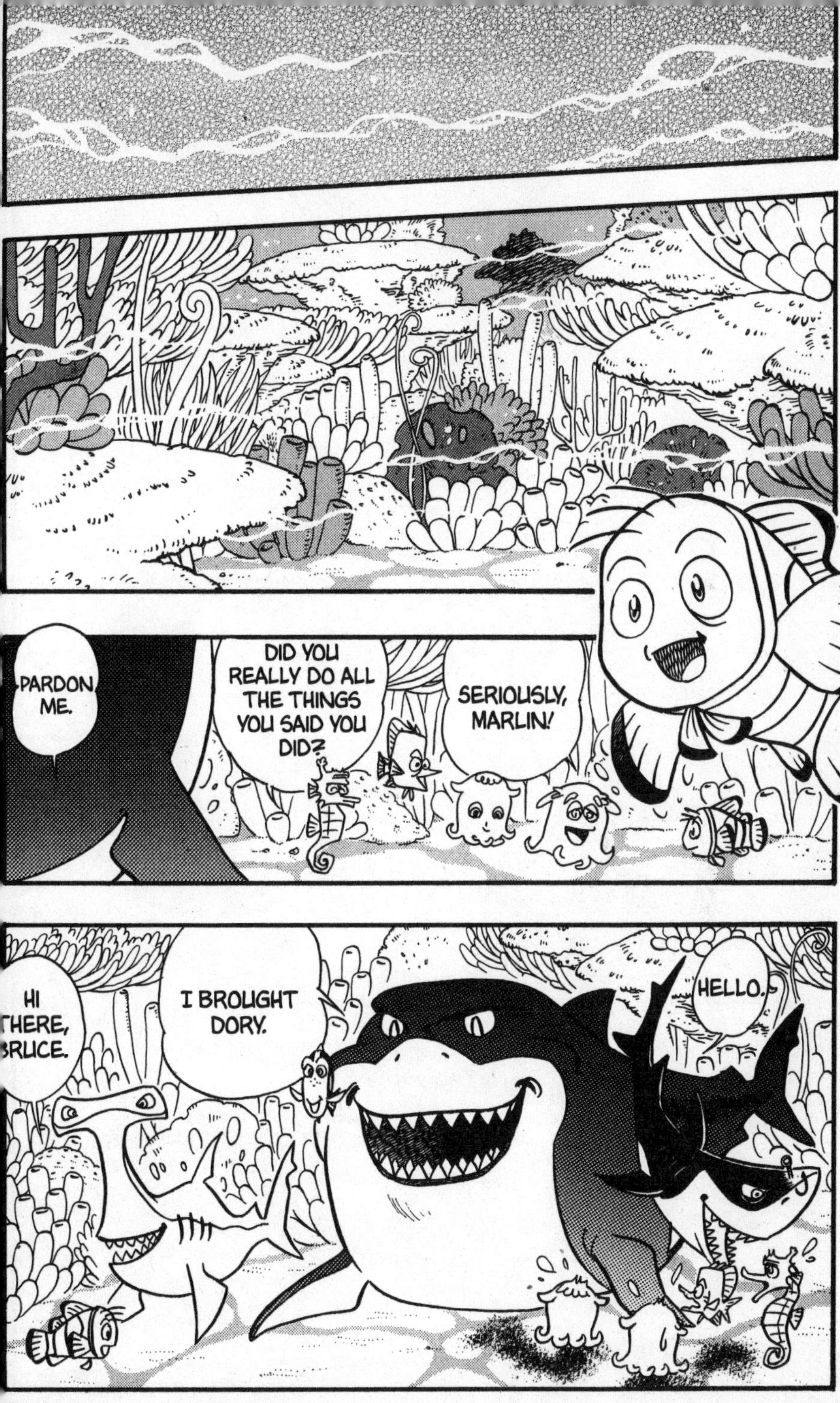
SERIOUSLY, MARLIN!
DID YOU REALLY DO ALL THE THINGS YOU SAID YOU DID?
PARDON ME.
HELLO.
I BROUGHT DORY.
HI THERE, BRUCE.

READ THIS WAY

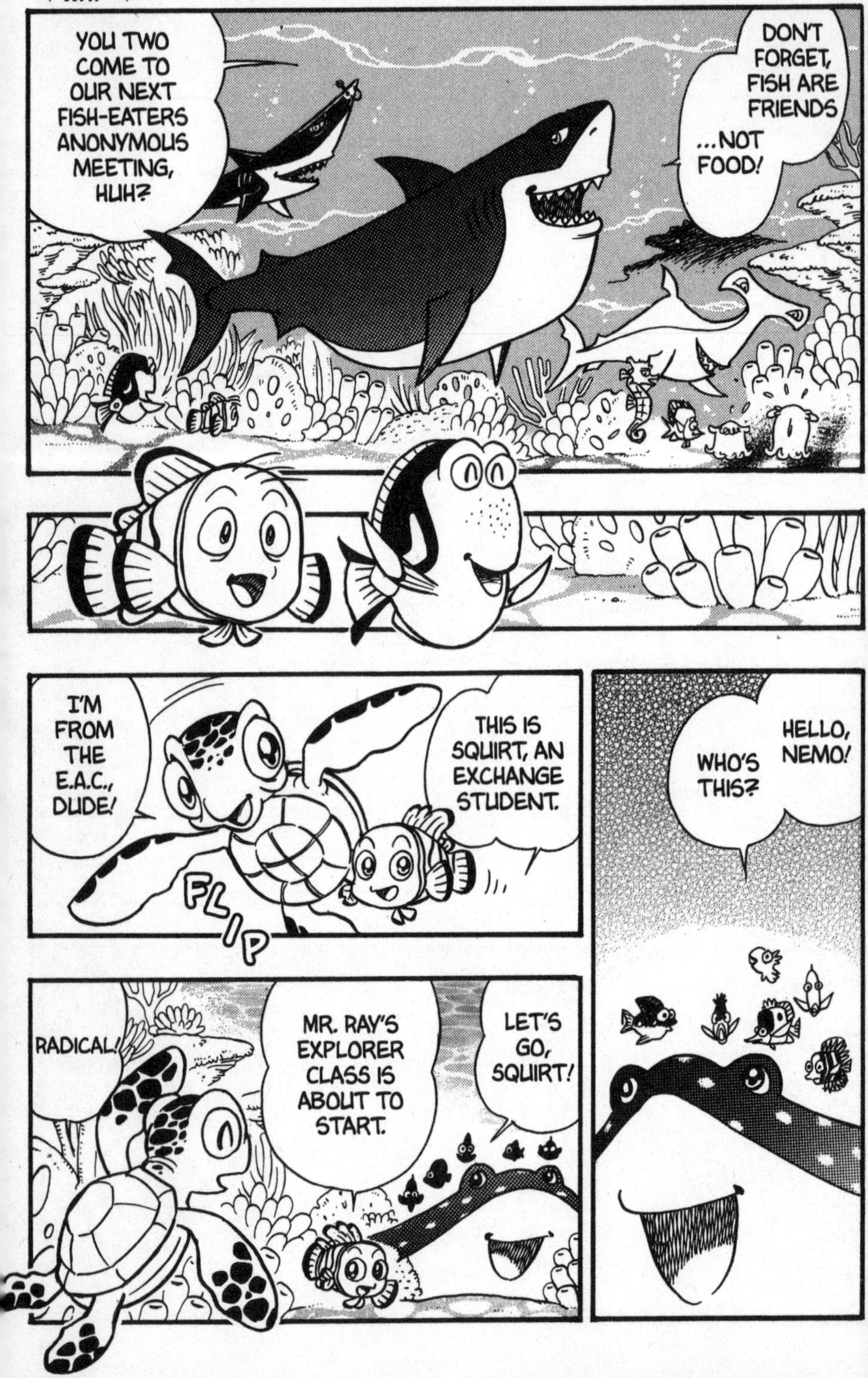
DON'T FORGET, FISH ARE FRIENDS
...NOT FOOD!
YOU TWO COME TO OUR NEXT FISH-EATERS ANONYMOUS MEETING, HUH?
HELLO, NEMO!
WHO'S THIS?
THIS IS SQUIRT, AN EXCHANGE STUDENT.
I'M FROM THE E.A.C., DUDE!
FLIP
LET'S GO, SQUIRT!
MR. RAY'S EXPLORER CLASS IS ABOUT TO START.
RADICAL!

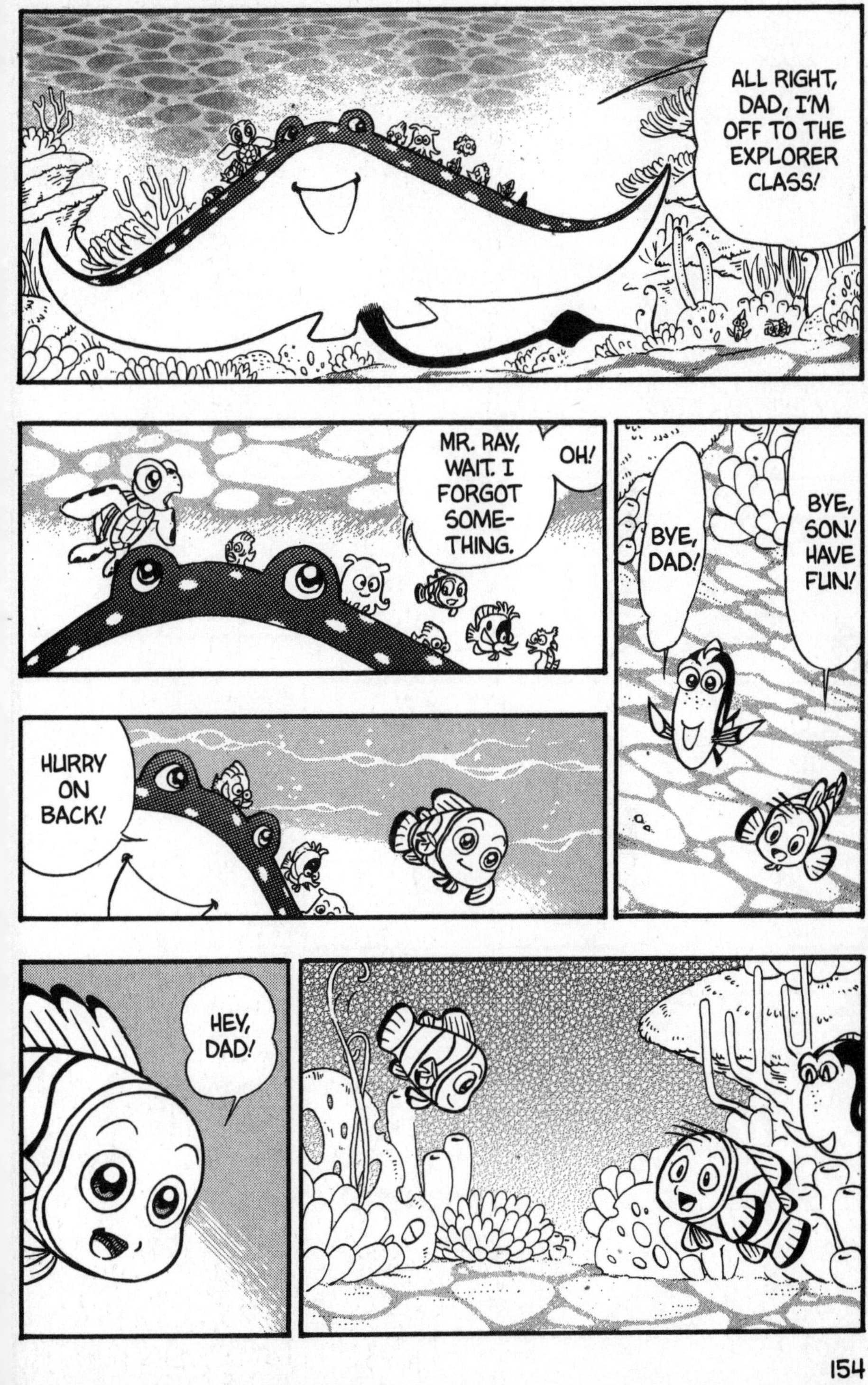
ALL RIGHT, DAD, I'M OFF TO THE EXPLORER CLASS!
BYE, SON! HAVE FUN!
BYE, DAD!
OH!
MR. RAY, WAIT. I FORGOT SOME-THING.
HURRY ON BACK!
HEY, DAD!

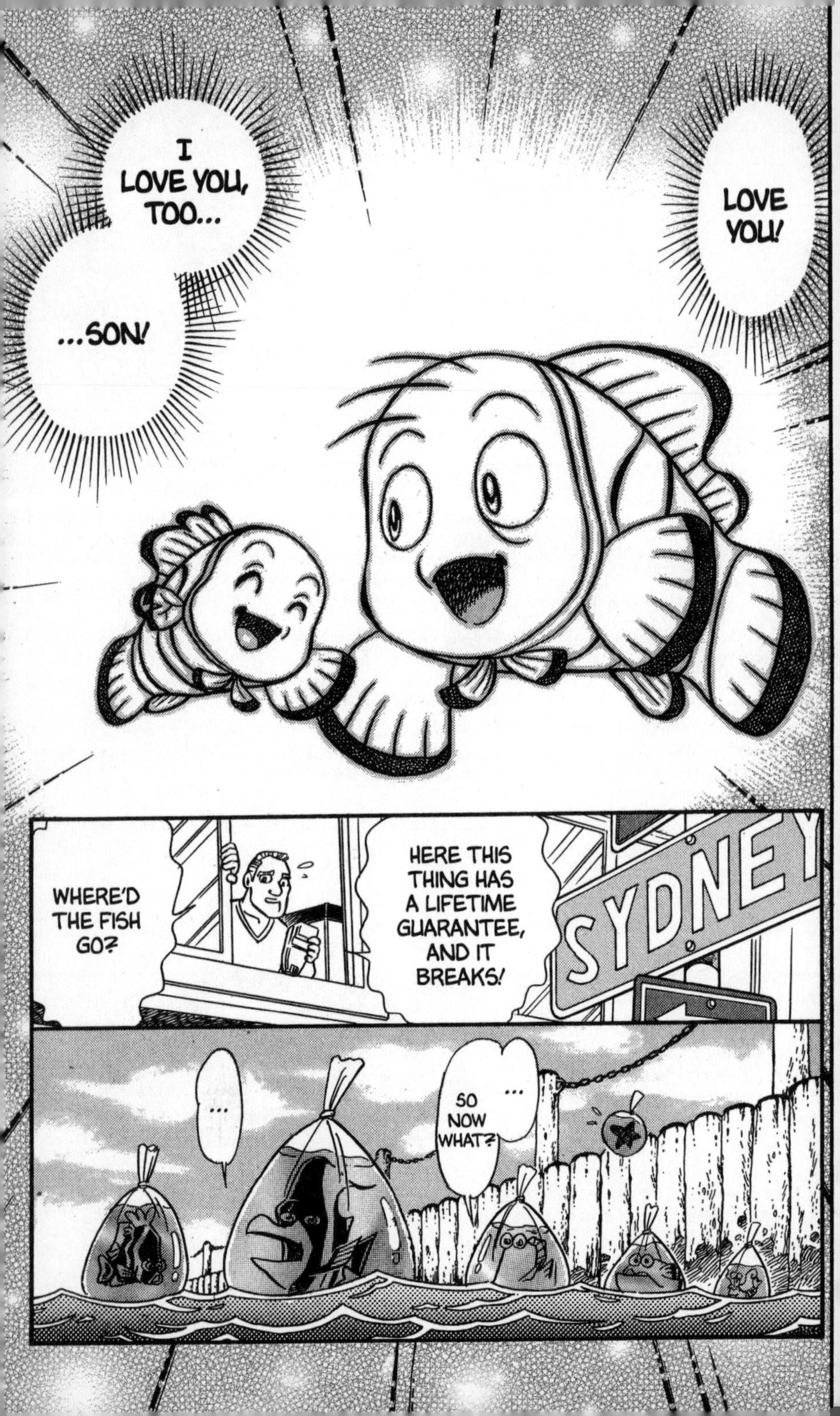
LOVE YOU!
I LOVE YOU, TOO...
...SON!
SYDNEY
HERE THIS THING HAS A LIFETIME GUARANTEE, AND IT BREAKS!
WHERE'D THE FISH GO?
...
SO NOW WHAT?
...

Interview with **FINDING NEMO** cover artists

UrumaDelvi

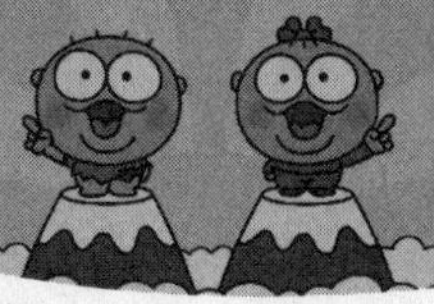

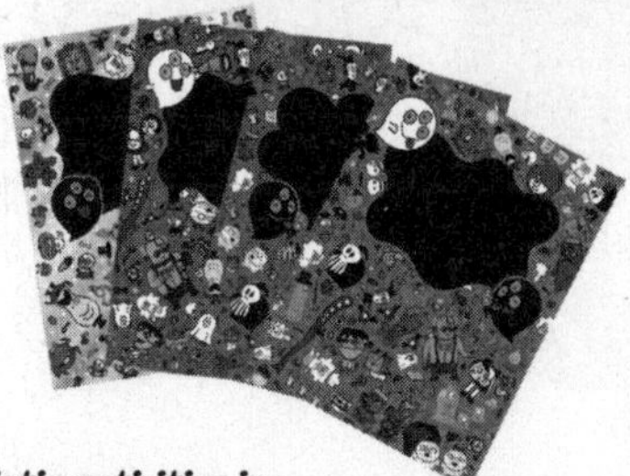

The cover artist for the **FINDING NEMO** manga in Japan are a husband-and-wife team of artists who go by UrumaDelvi. Here, they open up about their creative process, their love for *Finding Nemo*, and what's next.

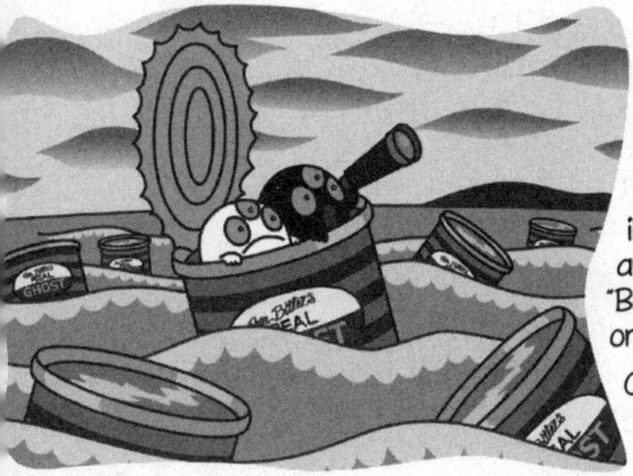

Q: Your artistic activities in Japan are quite broad, ranging from music to illustrations. What are some of the projects you've enjoyed the most?

A: Through our careers, we've created animation, illustrations, character designs, picture books, and music. Our series of musical animation shorts "Bottom-Biting Bug" (Oshiri-kajiri Mushi) became an online hit in Japan.

Our animated short "Shikato" was part of the classic Fuji TV children's animation series "Ugo Ugo Ruga." We're currently working on a book series entitled "Shiro- Obaké Kuro- Obaké No Mitsukete Ehon." We've even been involved in animation tool development, such as an animation-creation app "PICMO," a graffiti app "Rakugaki Art," and an interactive digital installation "Wonder Disc" that creates animation from still images by spinning them.

Q: Most of your illustrations are originals. Is *Finding Nemo* the first time you illustrated an existing character?

A: Actually. it probably is! We have tremendous respect for Walt Disney and adore the Disney films, so this was a unique situation.

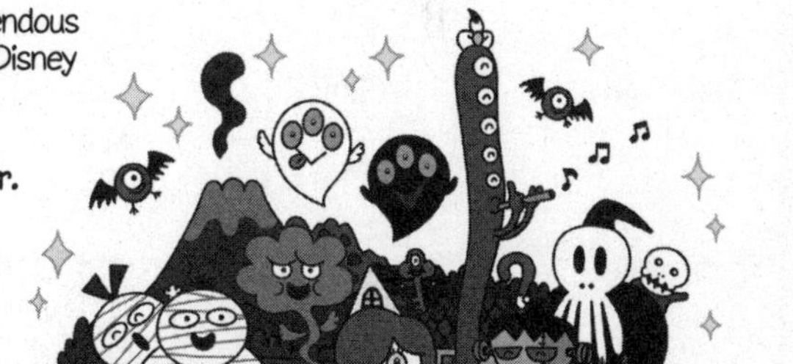

Q: Nemo has become a classic character. What inspired you to illustrate the cover for this *Finding Nemo* manga?

A: Because we love Nemo! We're a married couple and have a little boy who grew up watching *Finding Nemo* every day. So Nemo is part of our family tradition.

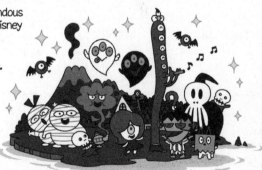

Q: There are various creatures of the sea in *Finding Nemo*. Were any of them particularly challenging to draw?

A: Actually, for us, an ocean theme is very natural, perhaps because Japan is a small island surrounded by the sea. So, we never get bored drawing sea creatures!

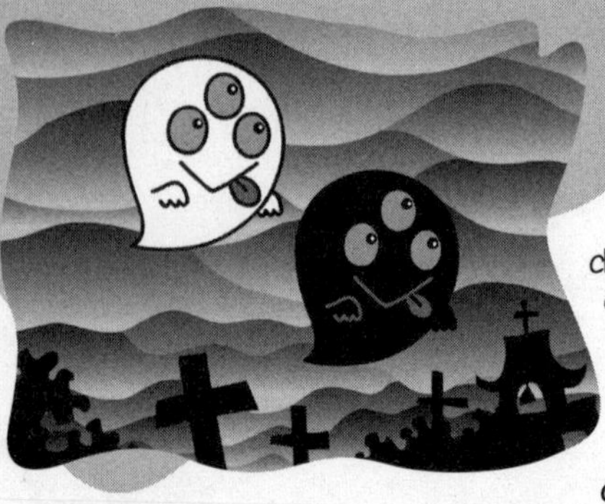

Q: Any final words from UrumaDelvi to manga and Disney fans worldwide?

A: We were raised loving Disney films such as *Fantasia* and *Alice in Wonderland* as well as the recent CGI films from Pixar and Disney. *Finding Nemo* is precious to our family, from the adorable characters to the wonderful story that gives us hope and courage. Our dream one day is to bring such a beloved character to the world - and to embark on an amazing oceanic adventure with all of you!

Q: Regarding your original art, how would you characterize your style?

A: Over our career, we've developed a style that combines unique characters, wonderful colors, and strange music expressed in an offbeat rhythm. "Bottom-Biting Bug" is probably the best example of this style - and we're particularly proud that the series resonated with a wide audience, not only children. We even received a letter from a 60-year-old woman who told us that by watching "Bottom-Biting Bug," she found happiness!

Q: What's up next for UrumaDelvi?

A: We'd love to adapt our picture book series "Shiro-Obake Kuro-Obake No Mitsukete Ehon" for TV or film, as well as continue to create music ... hopefully, a hit song eventually! Because most of our work has been done as a duo, perhaps the next stage for us is collaboration with other artists, ideally internationally. To this point, we've started our own YouTube Channel called UDTV.

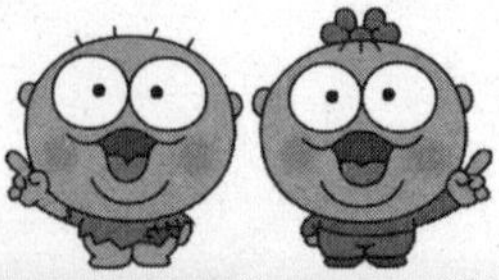

URUMADELVI™

YouTube UrumaDelvi Channel "UDTV"
https://www.youtube.com/user/urumadelvi

UrumaDelvi main website http://urumadelvi.com

UrumaDelvi resume and portfolio
http://www.urumadelvi.info

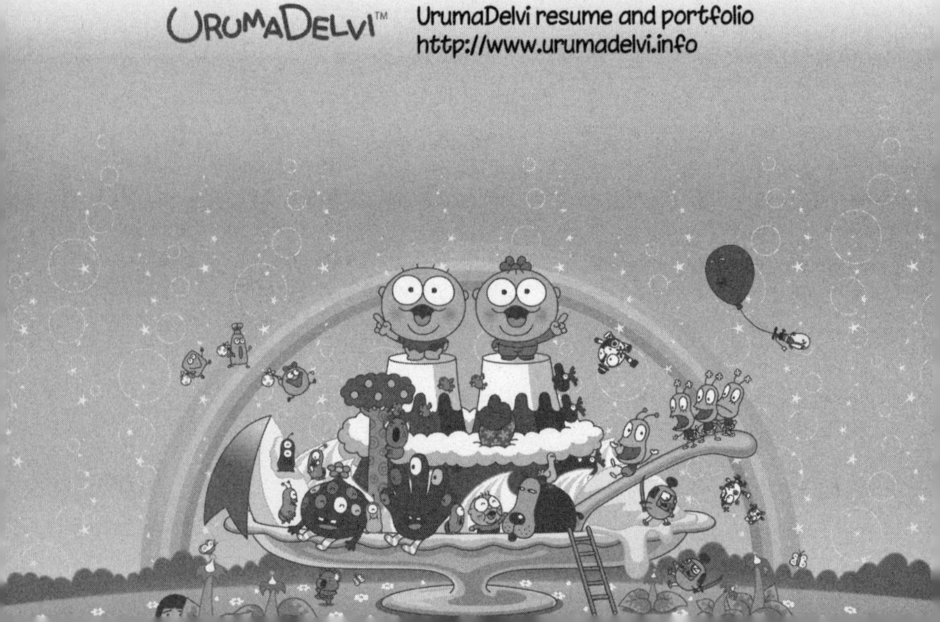

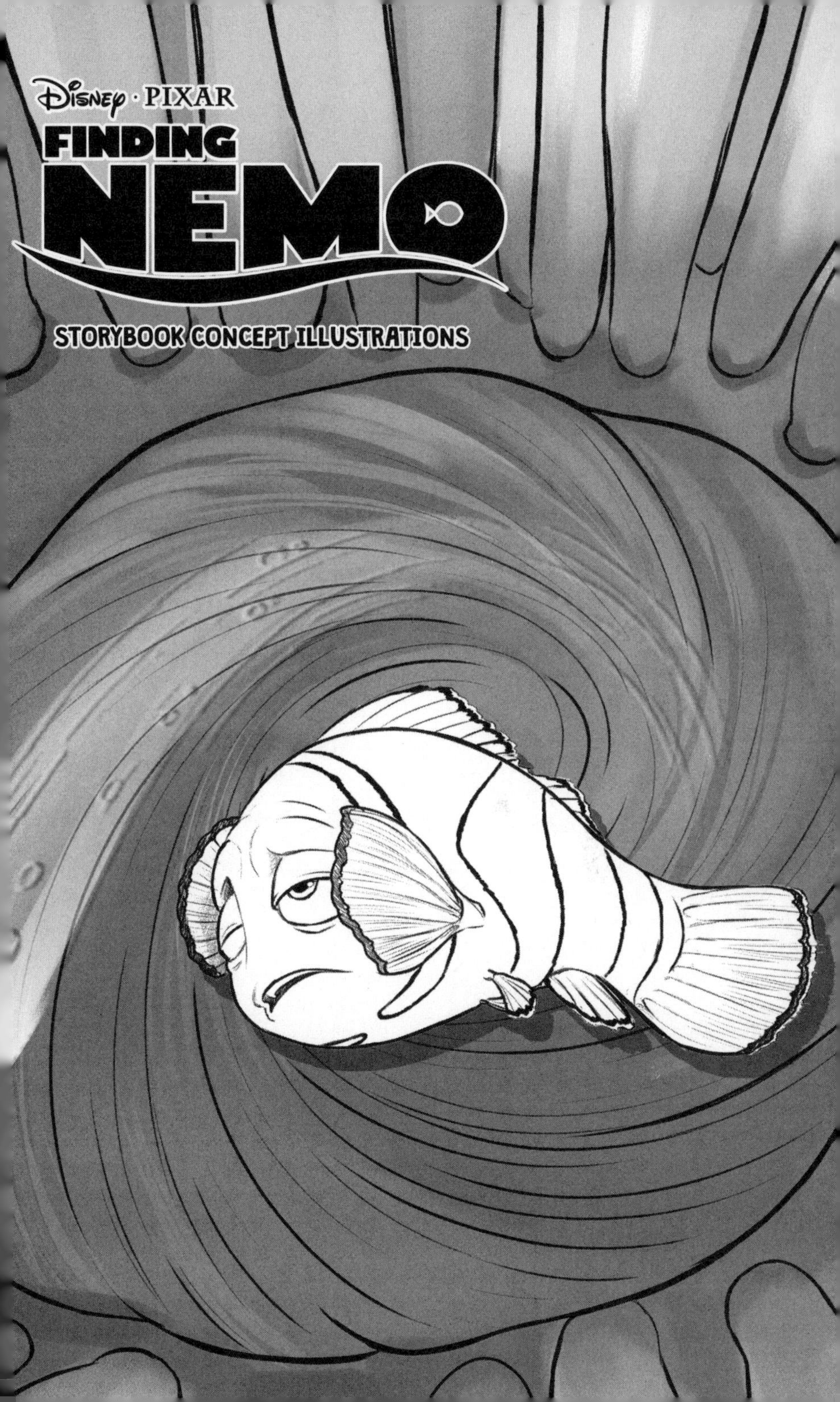
Disney · PIXAR
FINDING NEMO
STORYBOOK CONCEPT ILLUSTRATIONS

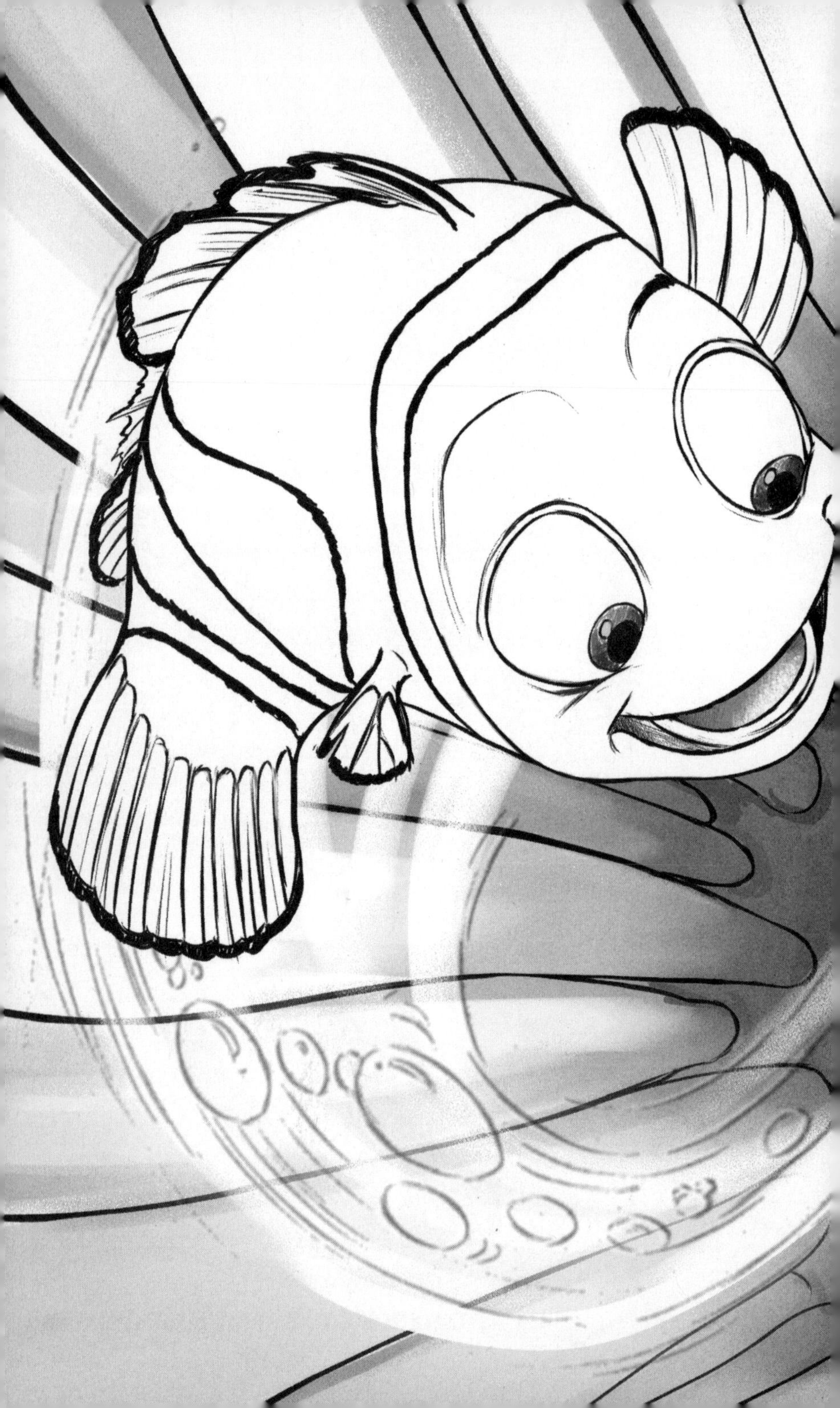

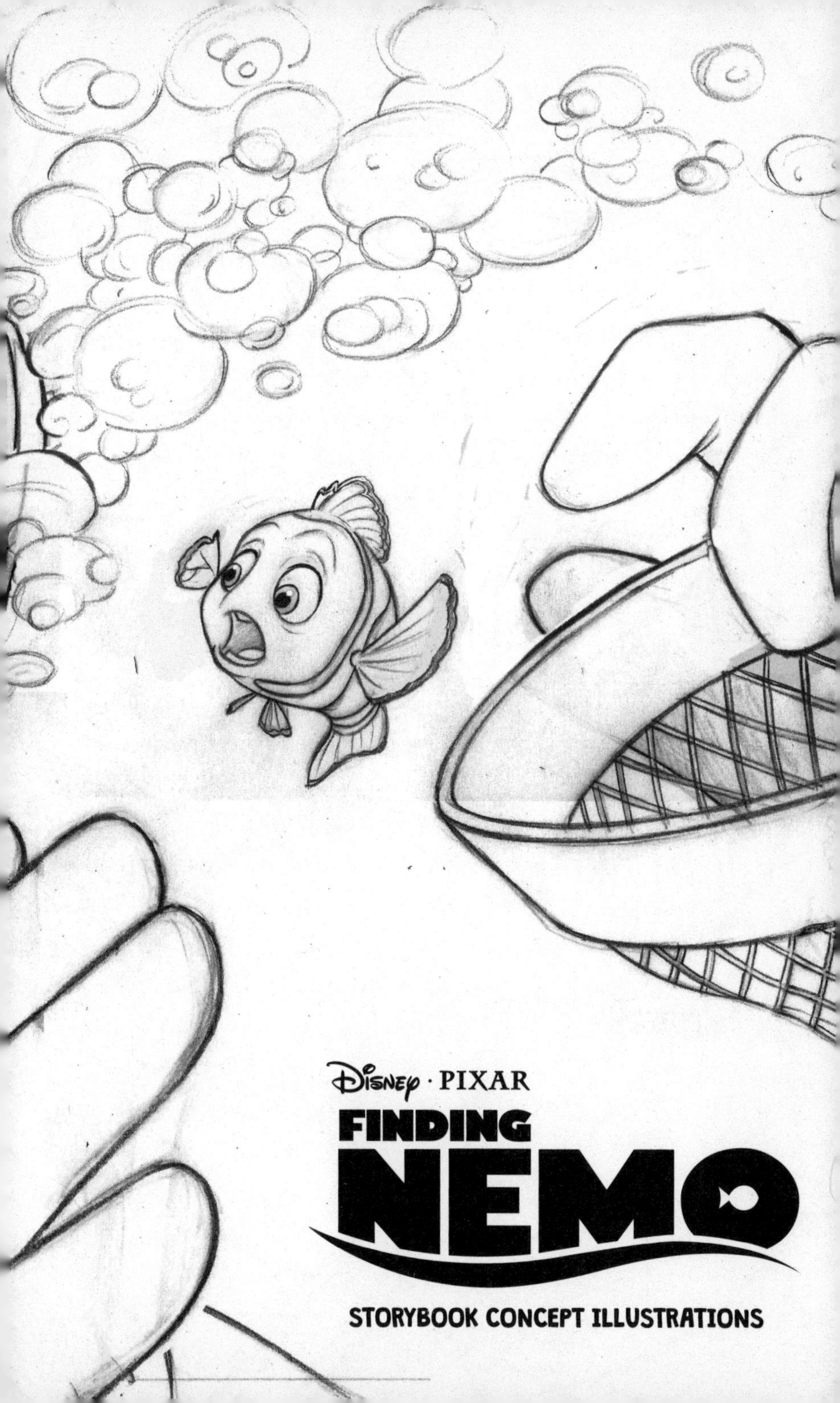

Disney · PIXAR

FINDING NEMO

STORYBOOK CONCEPT ILLUSTRATIONS

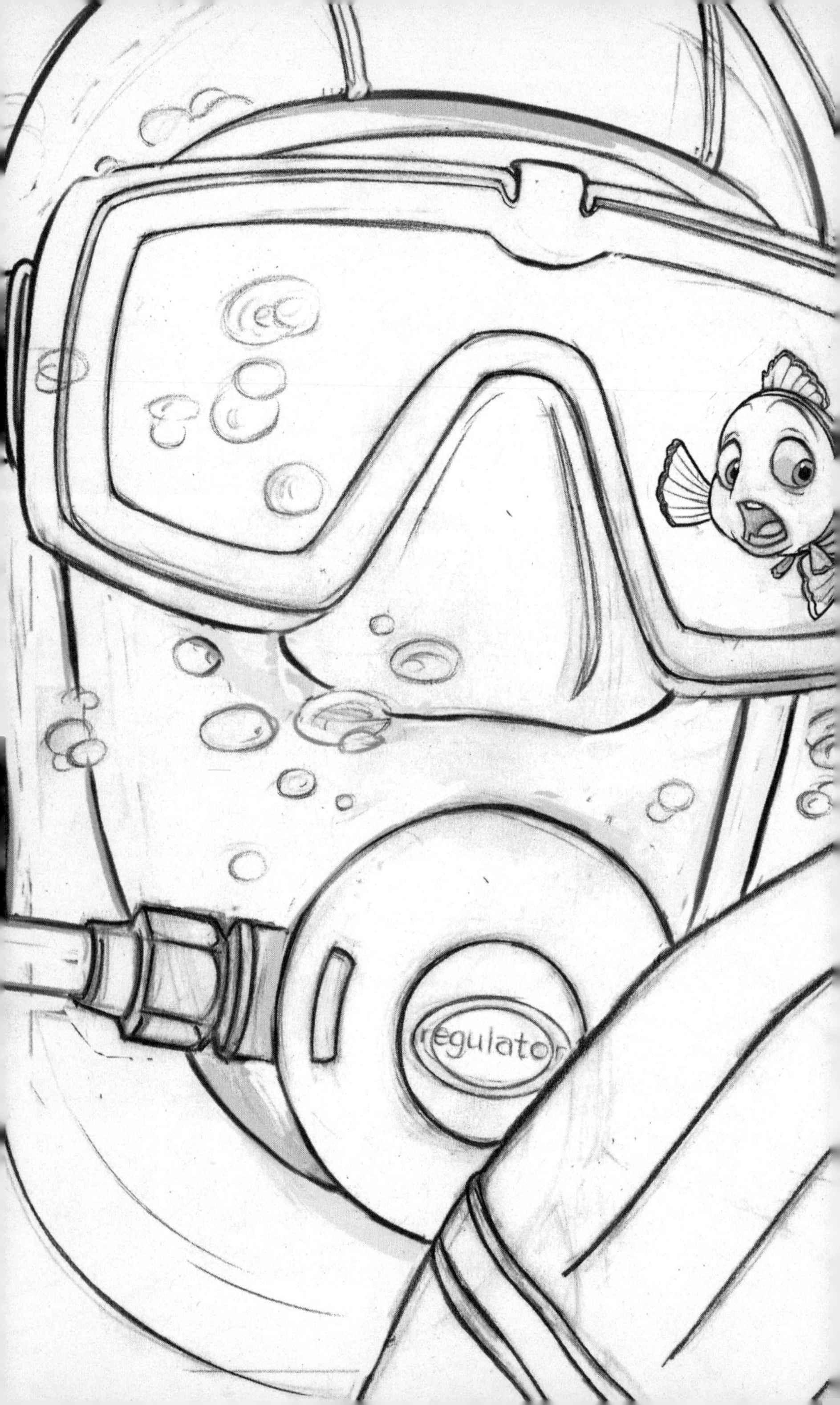
regulator

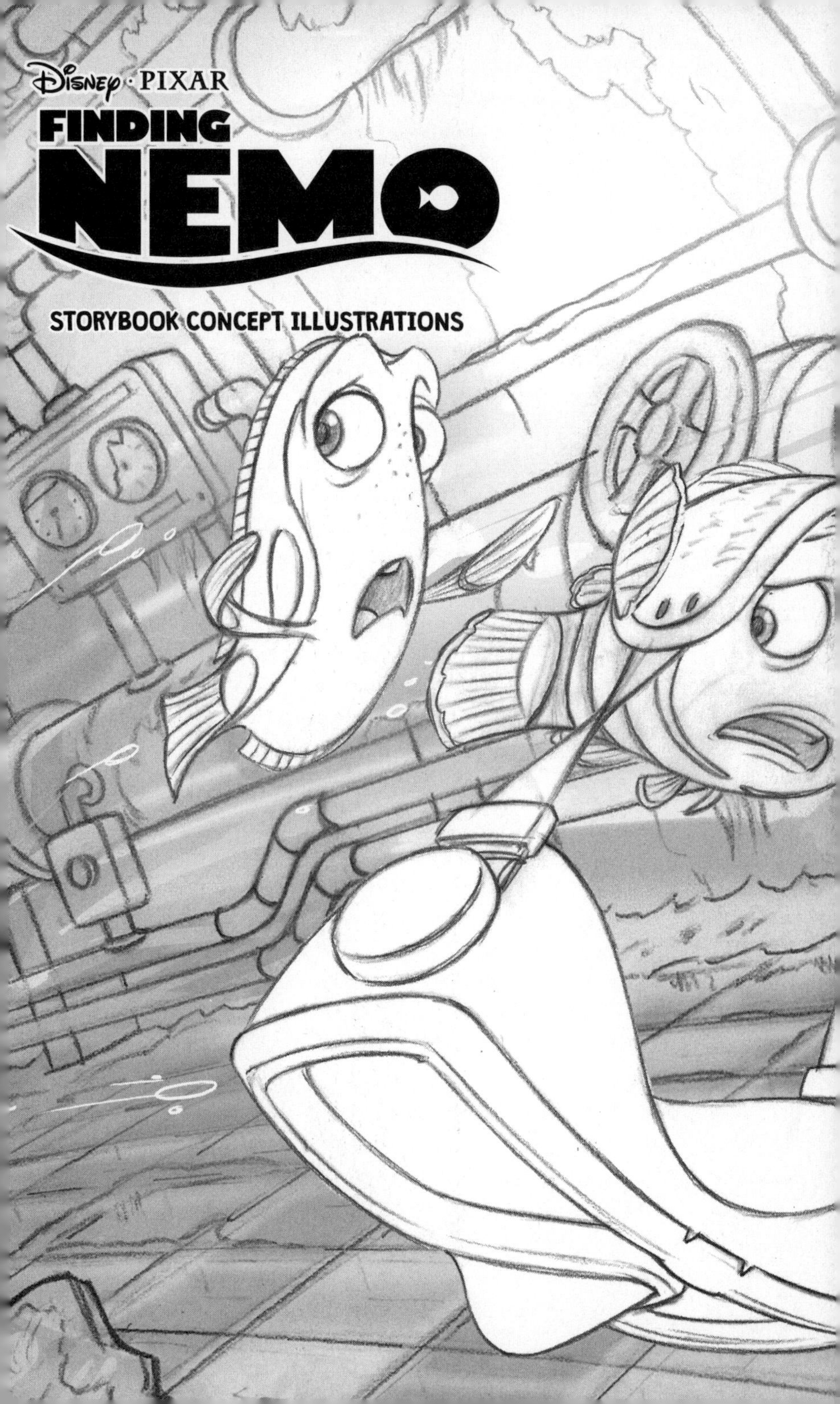
Disney · PIXAR
FINDING NEMO
STORYBOOK CONCEPT ILLUSTRATIONS

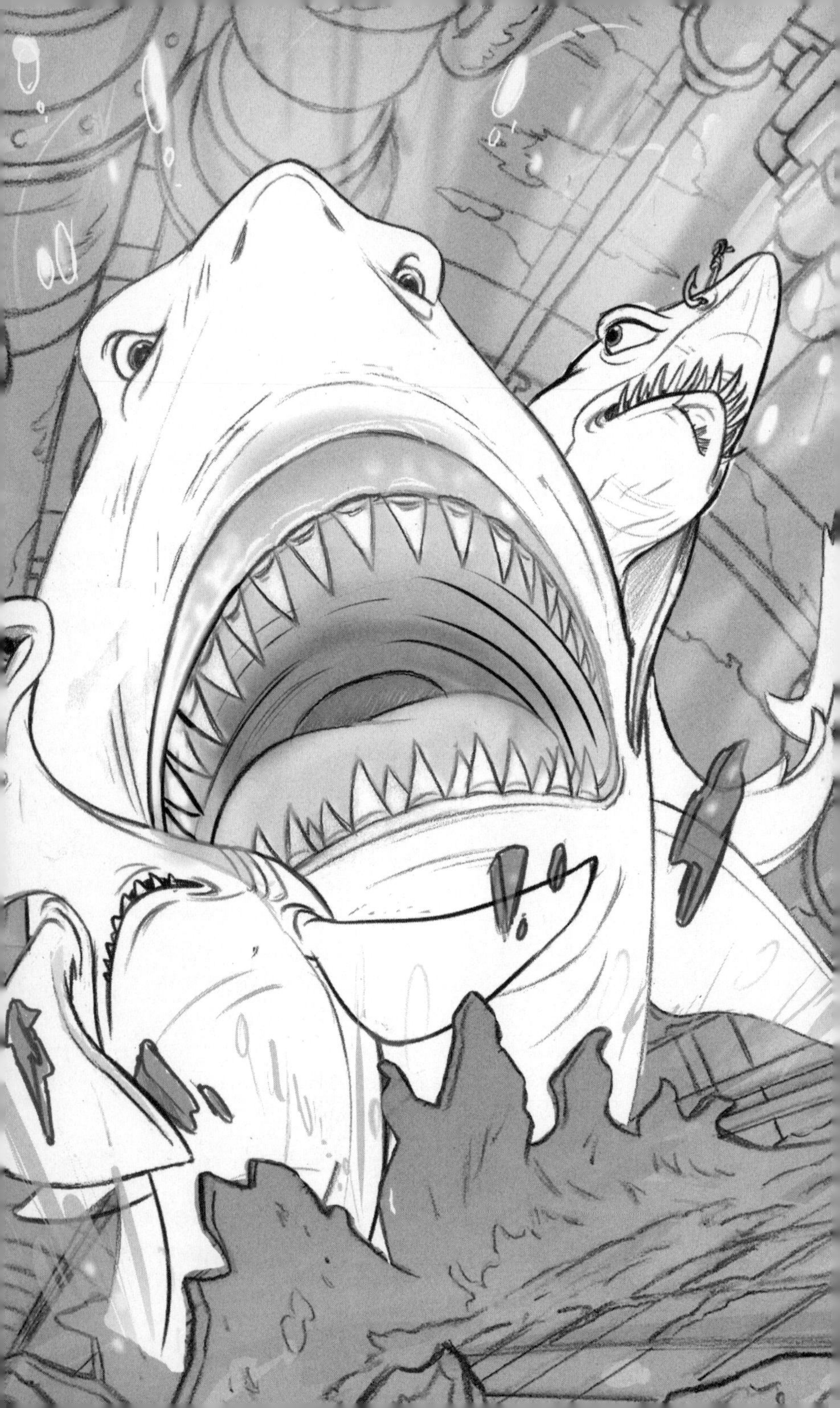

DISNEP · PIXAR
FINDING
NEMO

STORYBOOK CONCEPT ILLUSTRATIONS

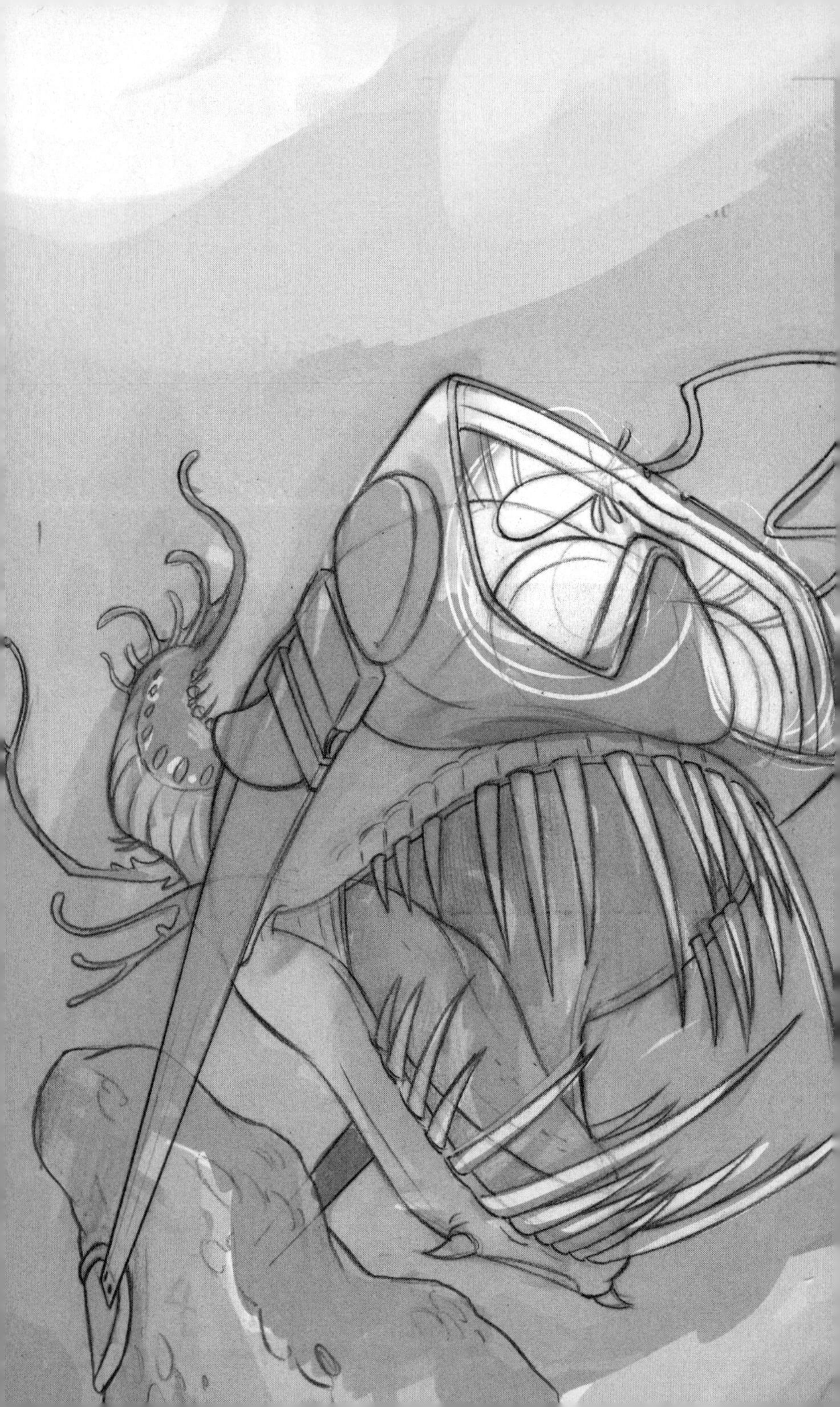

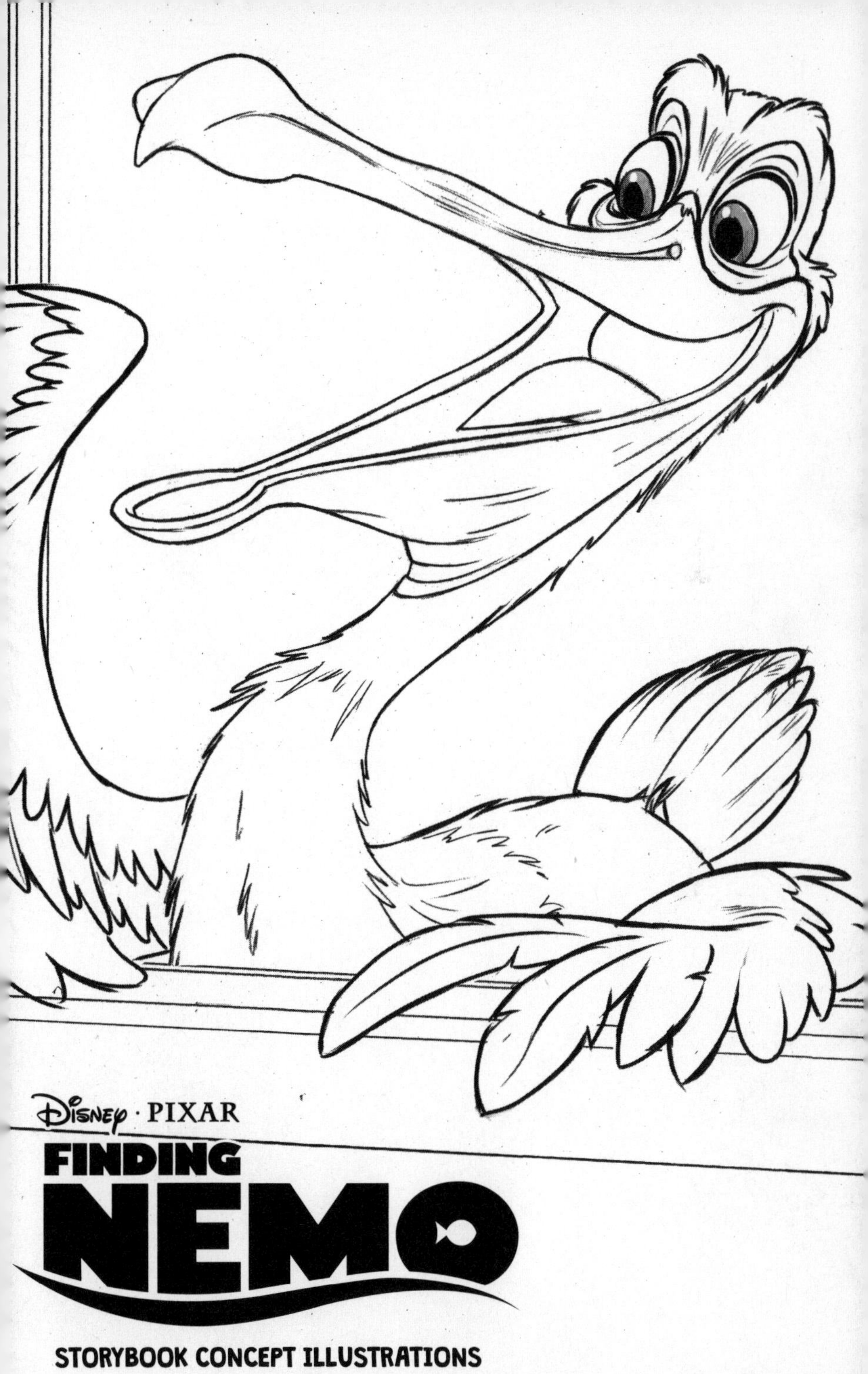

Disney · PIXAR

FINDING NEMO

STORYBOOK CONCEPT ILLUSTRATIONS

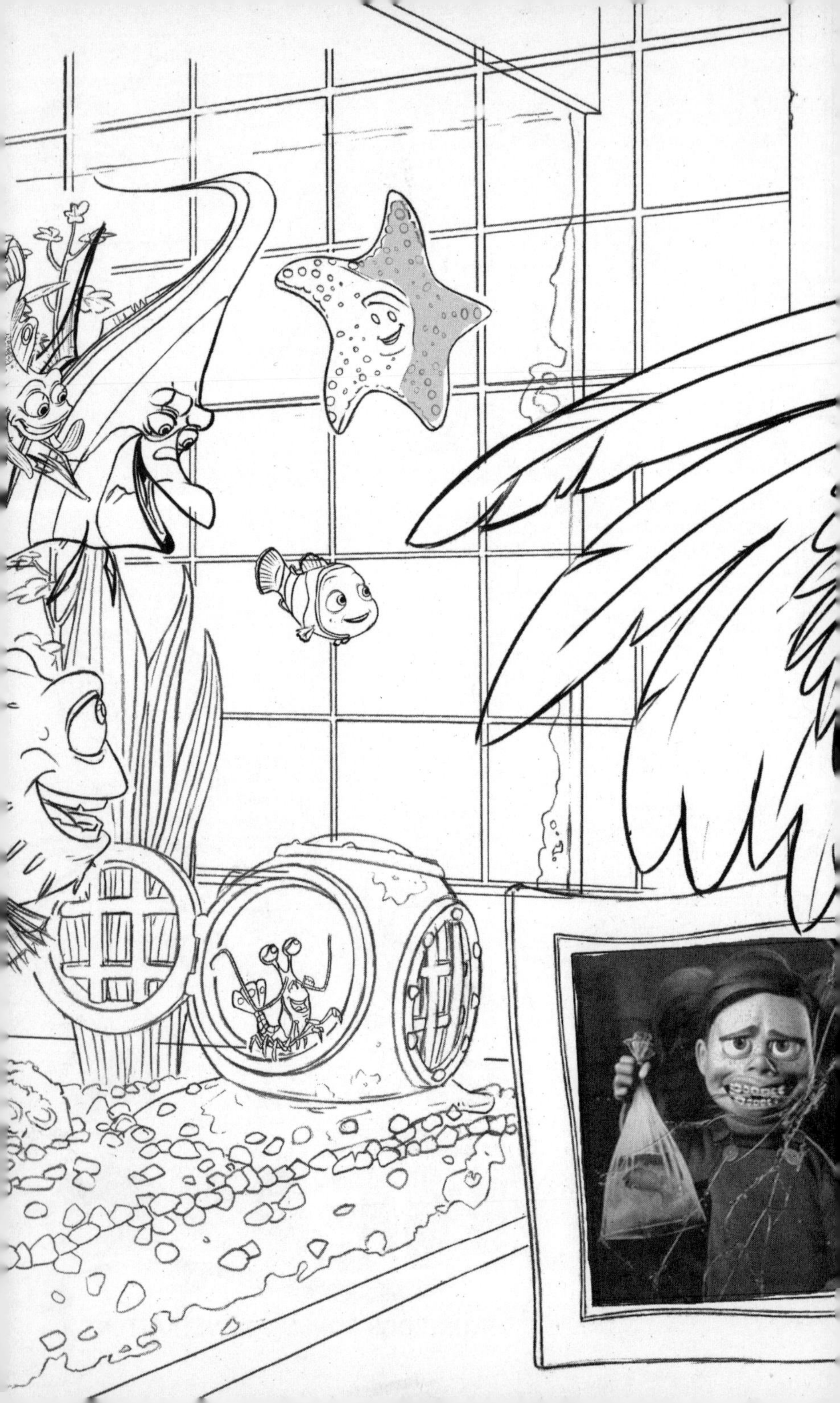

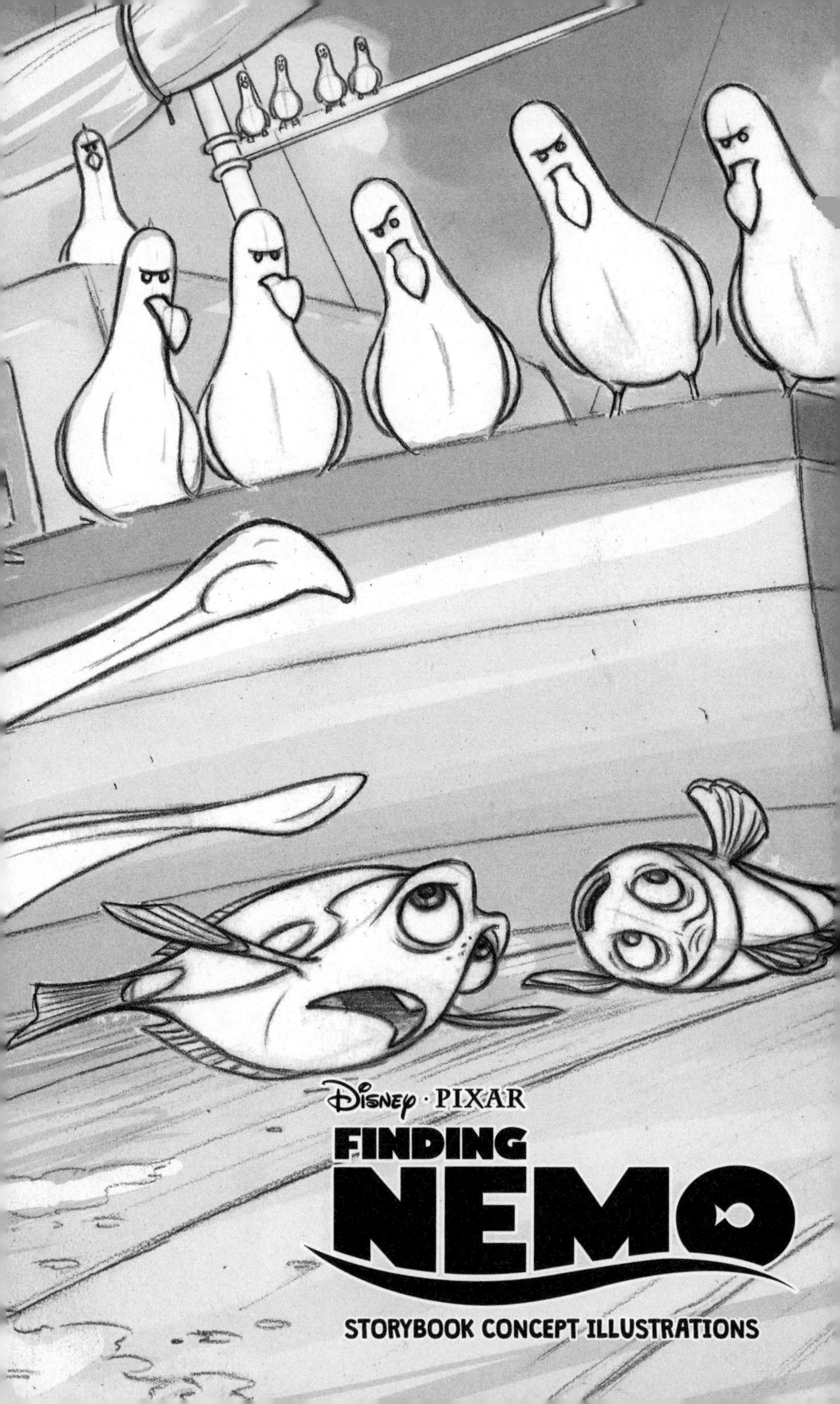

Disney · PIXAR

FINDING NEMO

STORYBOOK CONCEPT ILLUSTRATIONS

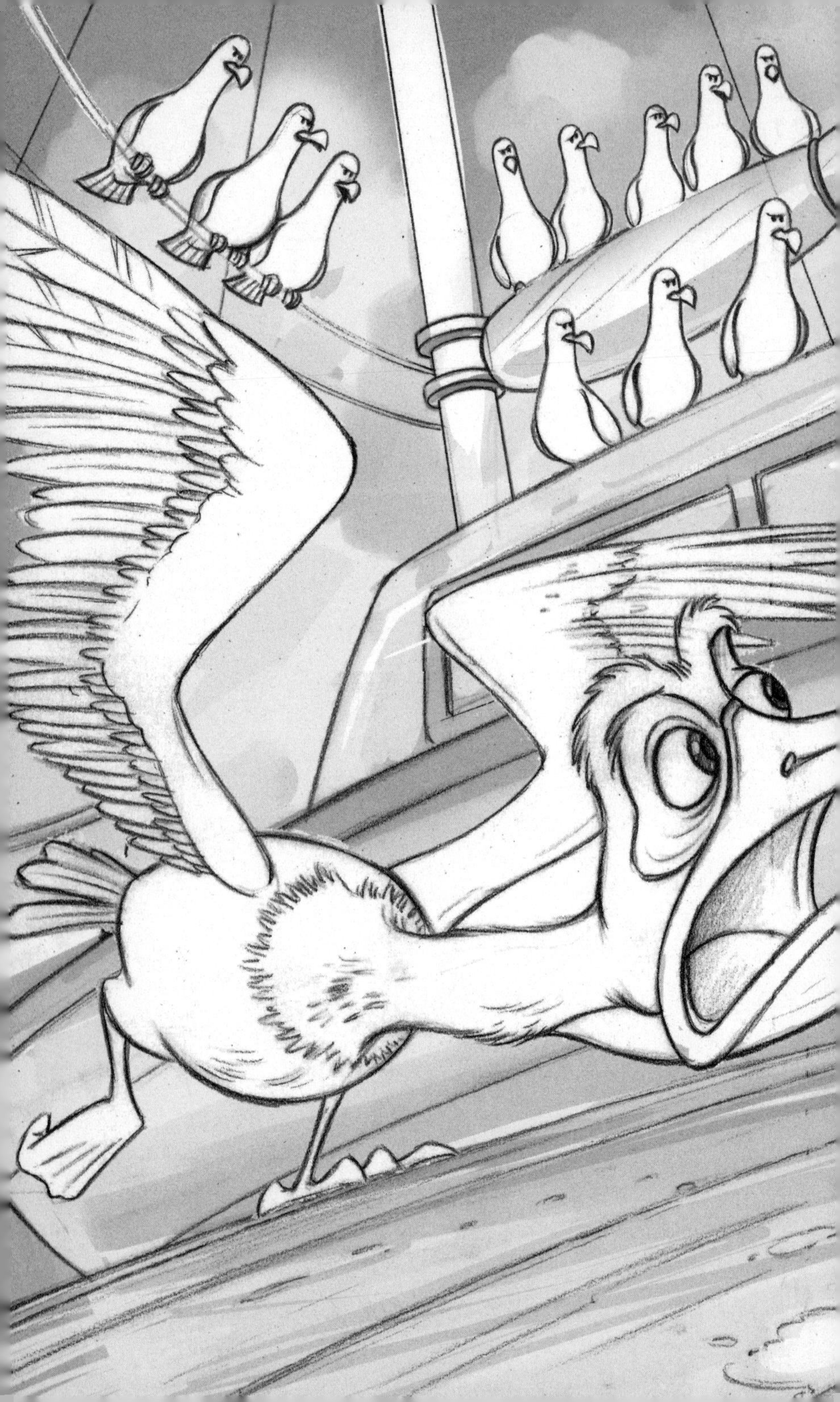

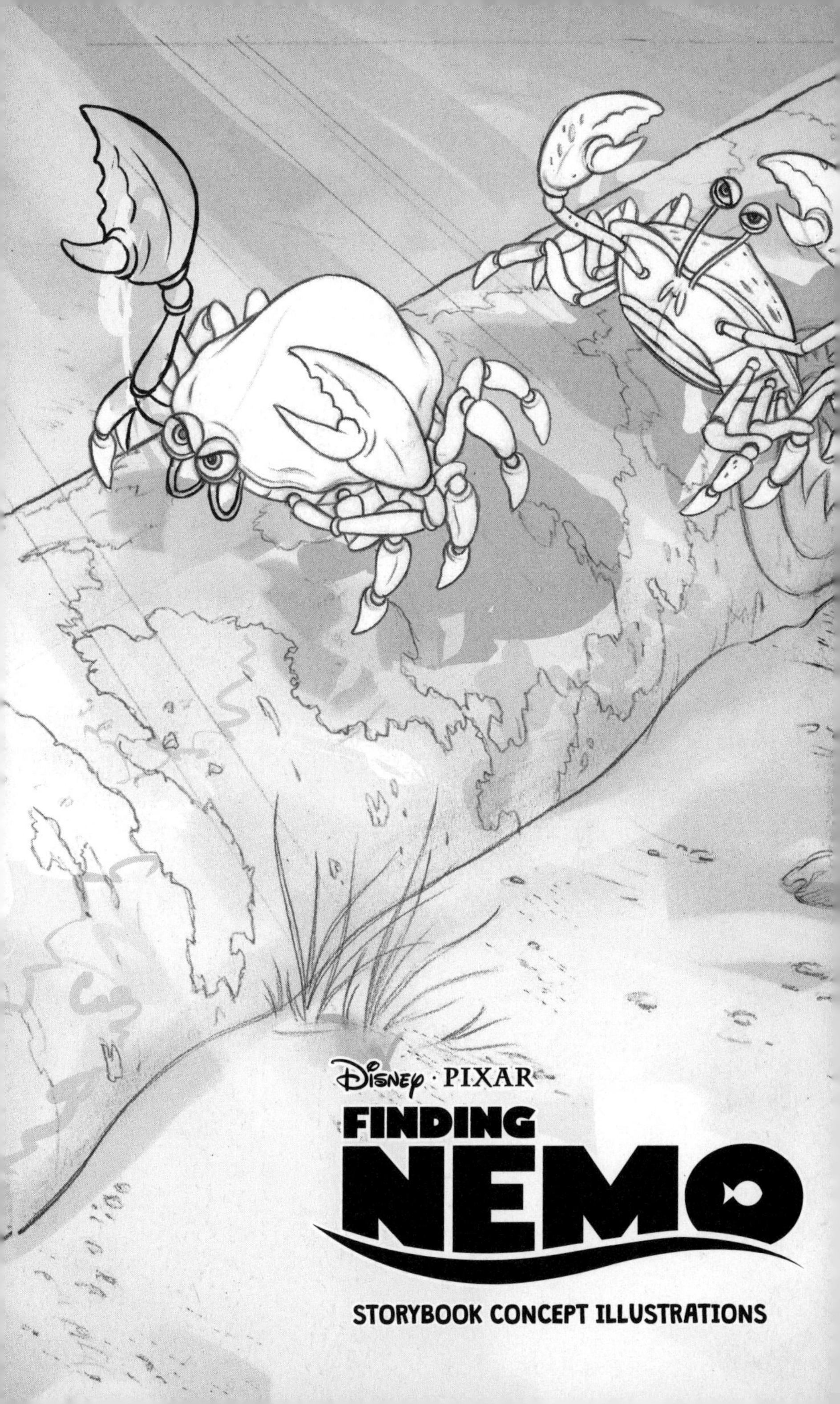

Disney · PIXAR

FINDING NEMO

STORYBOOK CONCEPT ILLUSTRATIONS

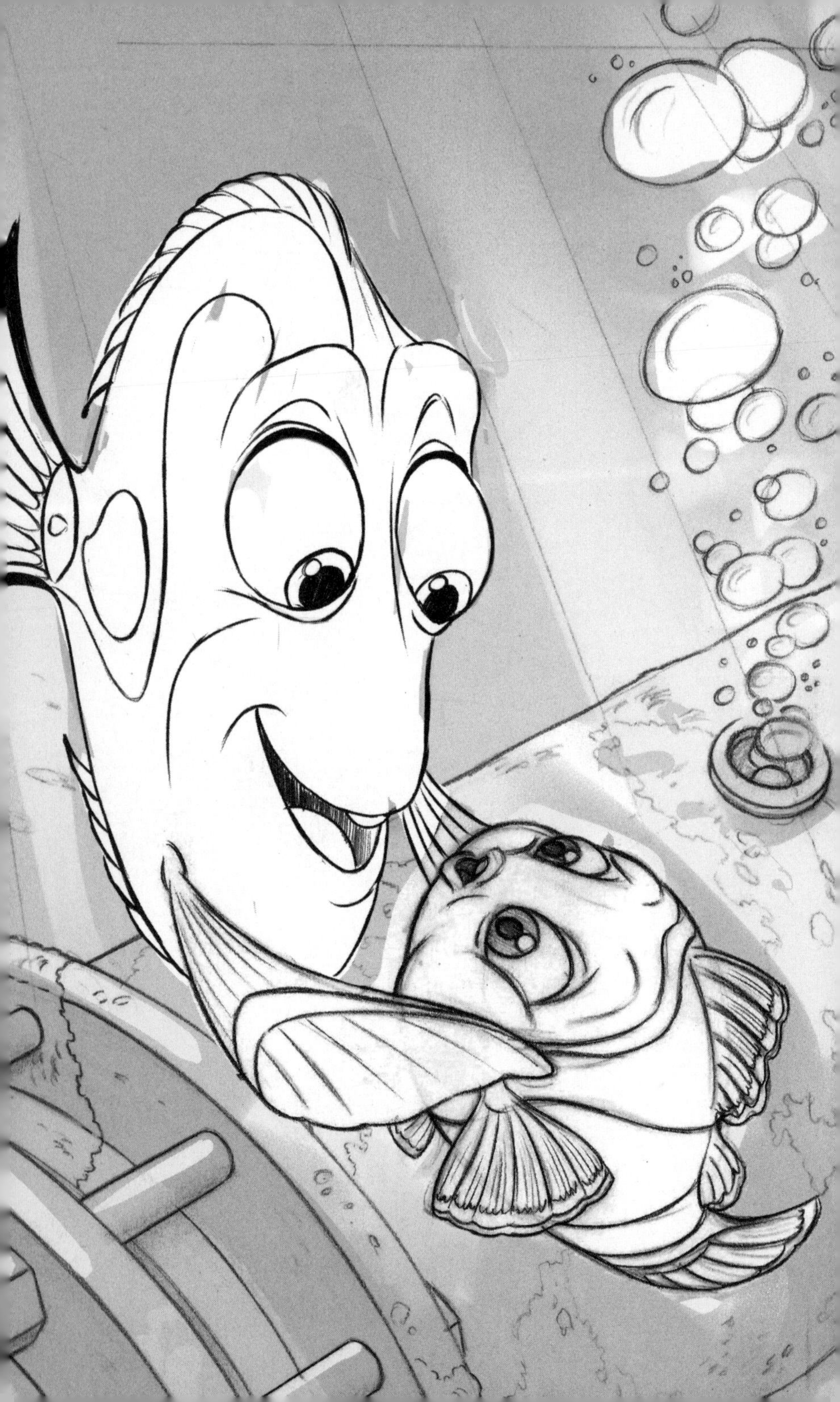

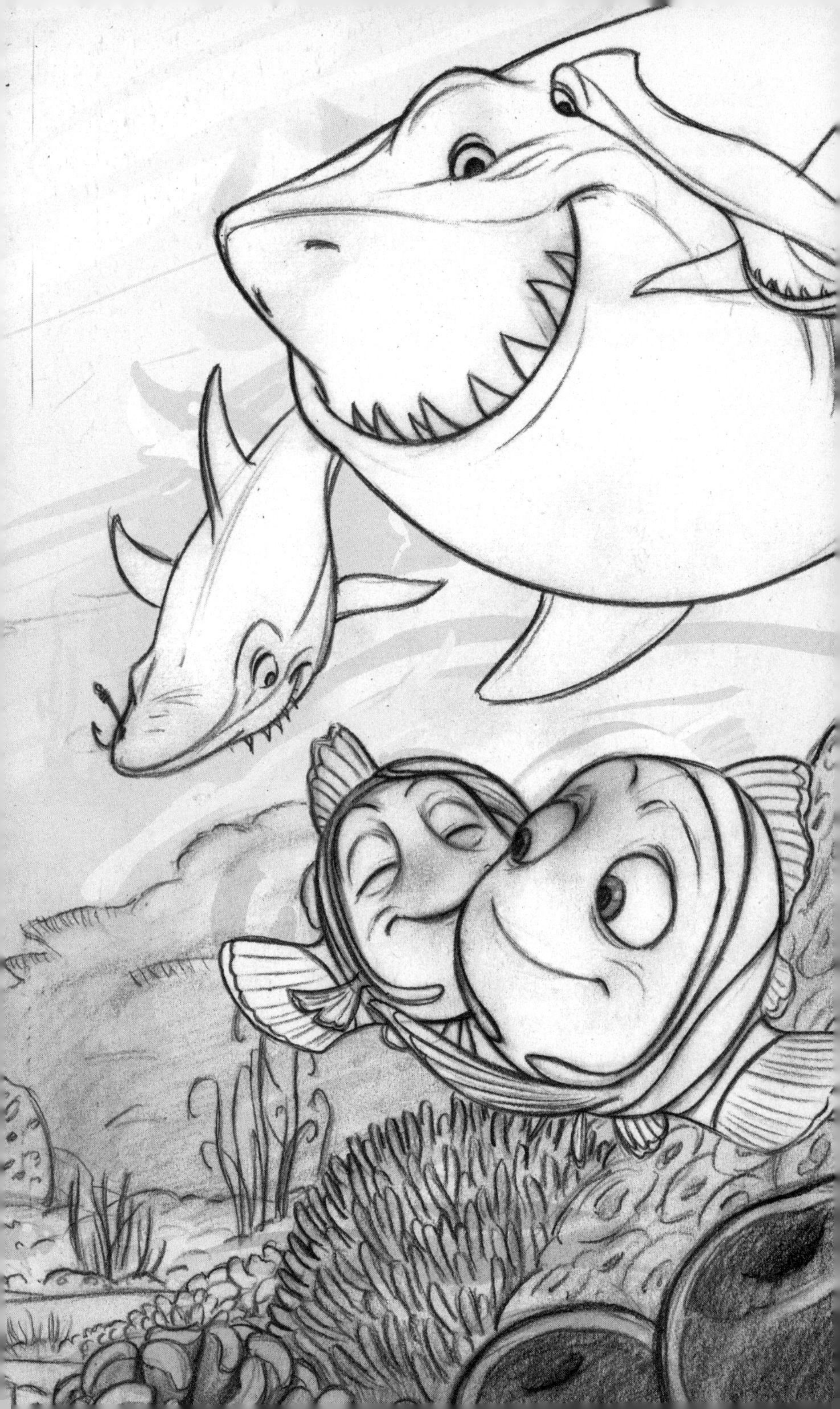

Disney · PIXAR

FINDING NEMO

STORYBOOK CONCEPT ILLUSTRATIONS

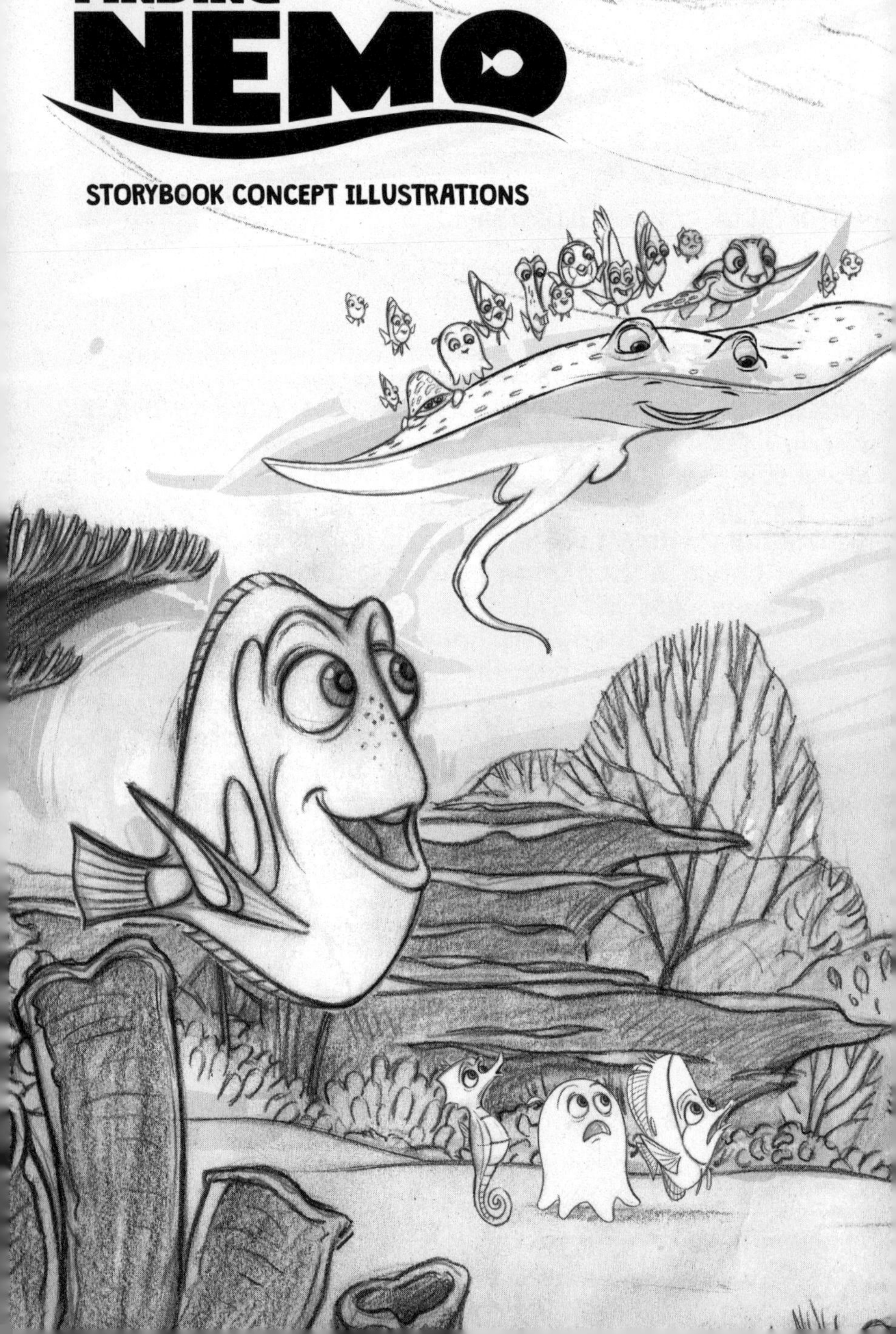

DISNEY·PIXAR

FINDING NEMO

STORYBOOK CONCEPT ILLUSTRATIONS

We hope you enjoyed these special 16 pages of two-page concept illustrations! This artwork was hand-drawn by Disney · Pixar illustrators when creating the *Finding Nemo* storybook. We think it's particularly fascinating to compare the pencil sketches and background shadings in this traditional children's book approach, and then compare that aesthetic style to the manga interpretation. While the manga backgrounds use tones, motion lines, cross-hatching and other traditional manga techniques, the character designs are actually quite similar in both versions. One subtly noticeable difference is in the mouth positions—the American illustrations tend to feature wider, upward-facing mouths, while the Japanese manga tends to be more circular. The position of the eyes is slightly different as well. Both styles are fascinating, so we are lucky to have a rare look at these Disney · Pixar concept illustrations to compare!

--Team TOKYOPOP®

Disney•Pixar Finding Nemo: Special Collector's Manga
By Ryuichi Hoshino

Retouch and Lettering	- Vibrraant Publishing Studio
Copy Editor	- Julie Taylor
Graphic Designer	- Vibrraant Publishing Studio
Translator	- Jason Muell
Social Media	- Michelle Klein-Hass
Marketing	- Kristen Olson
Editor	- Julie Taylor
Editor-in-Chief & Publisher	- Stu Levy

A  Manga

TOKYOPOP and 👁 are trademarks or registered trademarks of TOKYOPOP Inc.

TOKYOPOP Inc.
9420 Reseda Blvd Suite 555
Northridge, CA 91324

E-mail: info@TOKYOPOP.com
Come visit us online at www.TOKYOPOP.com

f www.facebook.com/TOKYOPOP
🐦 www.twitter.com/TOKYOPOP
▶ www.youtube.com/TOKYOPOPTV
📌 www.pinterest.com/TOKYOPOP
📷 www.instagram.com/TOKYOPOP
t. TOKYOPOP.tumblr.com

ISBN: 978-1-4278-5658-6

First TOKYOPOP printing: June 2016
10 9 8 7 6 5 4 3 2 1
Printed in the USA

STOP!

**This is the last page of the book!
You don't want to spoil the fun
and start with the end, do you?**

In Japan, *manga* is created in accordance with the native
language, which reads right-to-left when vertical. So, in
order to stay true to the original, pretend you're in Japan
-- just flip this book over and you're good to go!

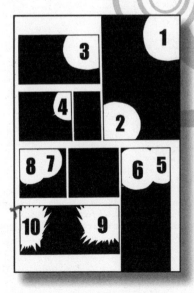

Here's how:

If you're new to *manga*, don't
worry, it's easy! Just start at
the top right panel and read
down and to the left, like in
the picture here. Have fun and
enjoy authentic *manga* from
TOKYOPOP®!!